COURAGEOUS BOOKS

CHILDREN OF WENT

Book four of the Planet Walkers series

A. V. Shackleton

Published by Courageous Books 1081 Wallaces Gap Rd

Ballalaba NSW

Australia 2622

A.V. Shackleton

ISBN 978-0-6455289-0-9

Thank you to Simon, my knight in metal armor, for your tireless support; and also my family, friends and fellow Planet Walkers

GLOSSARY

(Go to **www.avshackleton.com** for more detailed information)

Annangi: the dimorphic race of angels and archangels.

Djan'rū: the point at which a planet can be joined by a navigator's song.

El: Deity. Annangi believe that the Breath of El blows through all. **Asheru** is El's consort.

Great House: There are ten Great Houses, each with a home planet and a leader accepted by El.

Haze: easily visible aspects of an individual's aura.

Mark: the soul mark granted by El to those who become proficient in a particular psychic gift. The Mark appears as a symbol shining through the skin.

Qalān:

- **Personal Qalān** is a sub-dimensional space that surrounds every individual. Annangi access this space for storage of personal items.
- **Planetary Qalān** surrounds every planetary body in a web of interconnected wormholes. Skilled Annangi

can create portals in this Qalān for instantaneous travel between locations on a given planet.

- **Galactic Qalān** connects the stars and planets of the galaxy. It merges with **planetary Qalān** at specific points known as Djan'rū. **Navigators** travel between Djan'rū.

Sajhar: both Mark and title of one who has mastered all powers entailed with the working of metal.

Screen: internally, a psychic construction that hides private information; or externally, a shield that hides one's presence.

Shamkar: the Mark of one who is a master of the power of voice.

Shamkarun: the title of one who bears the Shamkar. **Tiamät:** the Imperial House; the God-Emperor and Empress are of House Tiamät. The three clans of Tiamät are Gok, Enna and Ashik.

Tsemkar: the Mark of a master of mind power. This ability is often strong in those of clan Ashik.

Tsemkarun: the title of one who bears the Tsemkar. Although the current God-Emperor is a Tsemkarun, not all God-Emperors are Marked.

Veil: a psychic construction that hides thoughts and feelings from the perception of others.

Ziquarra: the Mark of one who can leave their body at will and send their soul to far distant locations. A Ziquarran is practitioner of this skill.

Ziquarudjan: the title of one who bears the Ziquarra

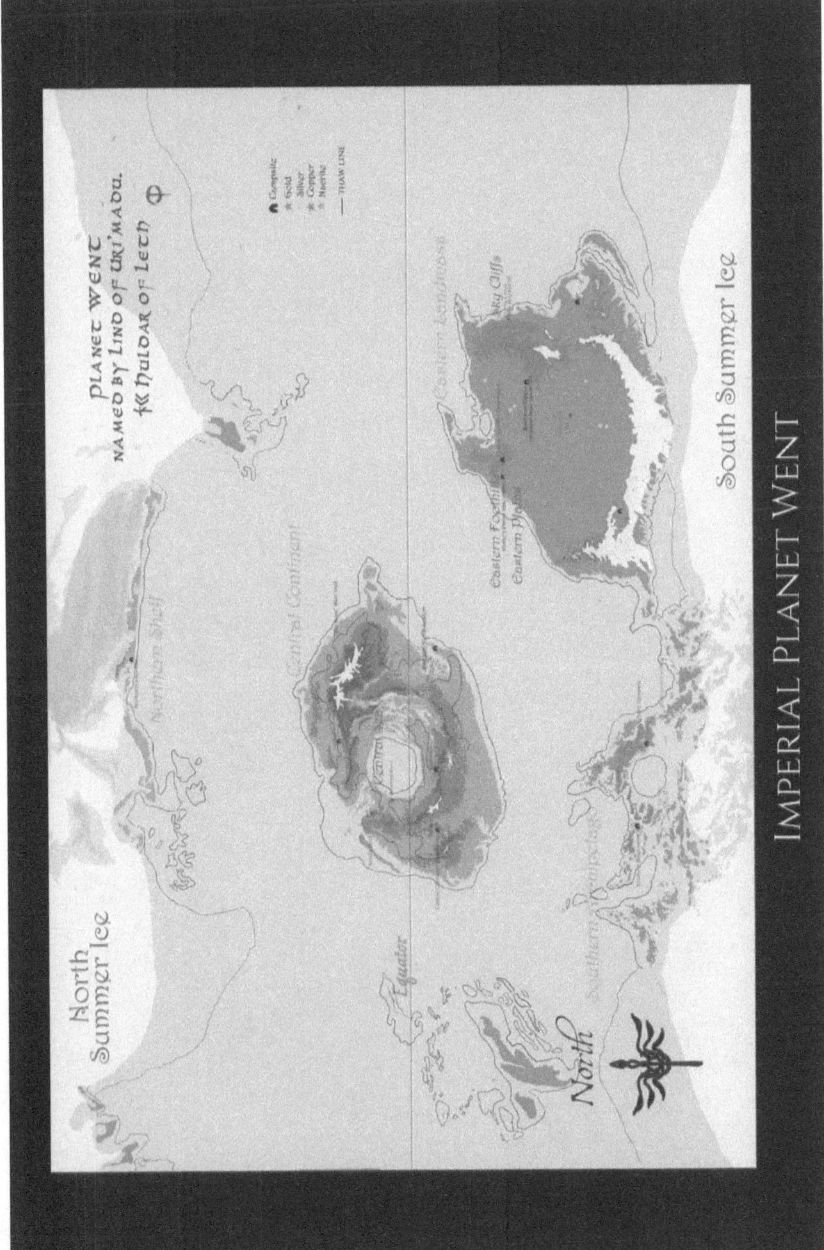
Planet Went
Named by Lind of Uri'madu.
Huldar of Leth
North Summer Ice
South Summer Ice
Northern Shelf
Central Continent
Eastern Landmass
Sky Cliffs
Eastern Foothills
Eastern Plains
Equator
North
IMPERIAL PLANET WENT

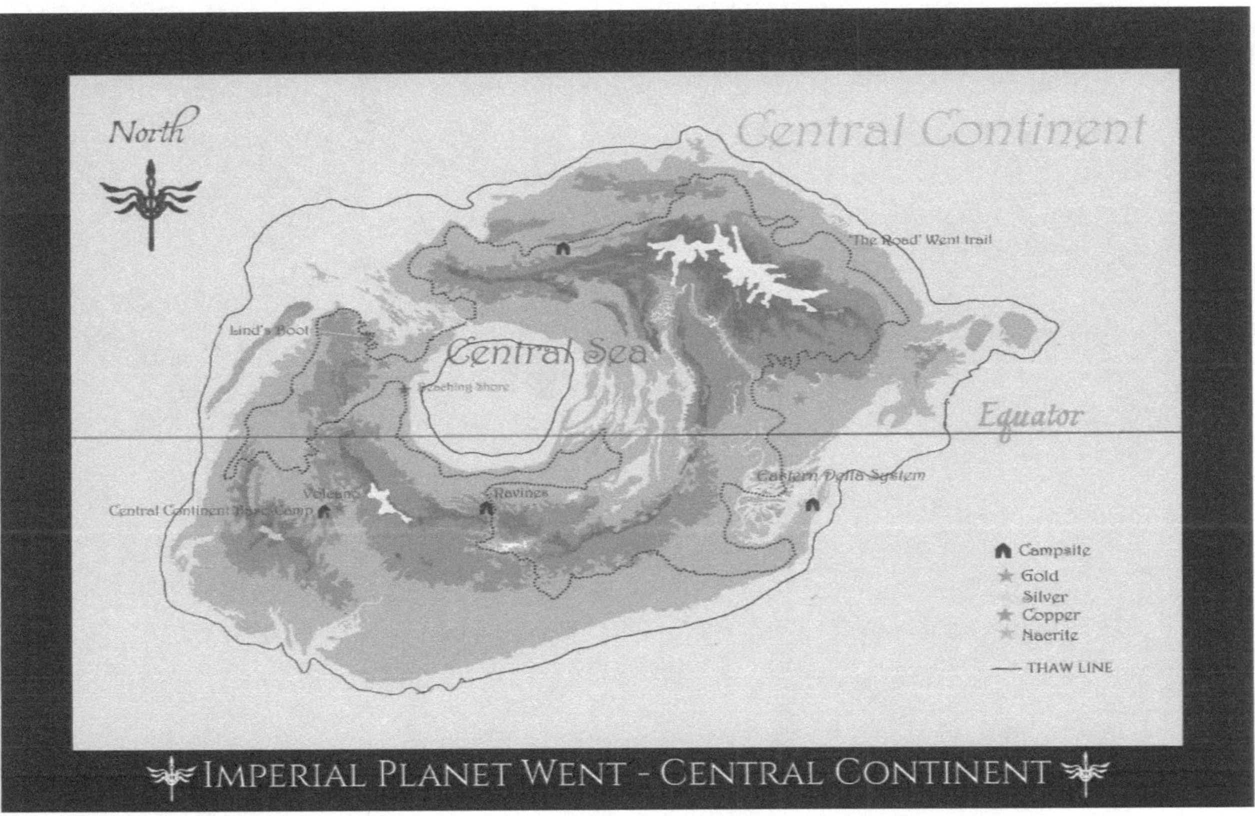

North
Central Continent
The 'Road' Went trail
Lind's Boot
Central Sea
Equator
Eastern Delta System
Volcano
Ravines
Central Continent Base Camp
Campsite
Gold
Silver
Copper
Nacrite
THAW LINE
IMPERIAL PLANET WENT - CENTRAL CONTINENT

TRUTH

Had a scryer had been able to peer through Went's mysteriously impervious shroud and view the planet's eastern land mass, the Uri'madu's lonely camp-ground, set in the foothills of a crumpled range of towering mountains. would likely remain hidden. A few sturdy leather tents, much the same hue as their scrubby surroundings, lay scattered around a camp fire reduced to the glow of a few stubborn embers.

On this night, one half of the midnight sky was bright with stars, while to the north, a ghostly purple nebula clouded the edge of The Great Wheel; the constellation now high in the firmament and close, at last, to its midsummer liberation from the horizon.

Instead, the hypothetical viewer's attention would more likely be drawn to the Central Continent, half a world away. Kami'co, some had begun to call it – the Bed of the Eye, in reference to the great circular sea at its heart.

There, on the coastal plains of the eastern seaboard, the sprawled the Host's main encampment. The humid, mid-morning air was busy with song as shipments of ores and substrates arrived through stone-paved portals to be ferried down rain-slick tracks and set in appropriate stock-piles. Between ordered rows of tents, workers tramped to and fro on muddy, tropical streets.

At a crossroad beside the main thoroughfare, an imposing Faythan, Olatu of Faytha, stood with five Ashik in a semi-circle at his back. He was faced by Huldar of Leth and Casco, the Uri'madu's logistician.

Olatu's chin jutted belligerently. "He has been seen with a sword in hand. No half breed is permitted a weapon. He must face the consequences!"

"Rubbish!" Huldar replied. "As I have already said, it was merely a long knife designed to clear recalcitrant vegetation. We all have one. It's part of our essential kit."

"Then show me yours."

As if anticipating conflict, the Ashik commander stepped forward, steel in her eyes.

Huldar returned her look calmly and made no move to comply with Olatu's demand. Beside him, Casco seemed equally unintimidated, but Huldar could sense the anger beneath his friend's veils.

Please don't say I told you so! Casco whispered.

Huldar recalled day he had discovered Casco training with the Rukh, the pain he felt when he'd had to ask his friend to stop - and the hurt of Casco's embittered reaction.

Casco sighed - a slightly louder passage of breath through his nose.

"I give you my word this is the case," Huldar said, "and that will be the end of the matter." He cocked his head as if waiting for a reply.

The Faythan was still on probation, pending the navigator's return. Doubt momentarily sullied his veil. He gave the Djan-rū a quick glance then motioned the Ashik back.

The edge of Huldar's lip curled upward, ever so slightly. "Now, to the true reason for my visit," he continued. "The South Arm mine's encroachment onto Went habitat is intolerable and must cease immediately. As you well remember, I made a polite request to this effect some days ago. I drew your attention to the issue, yet nothing has changed. Consider this a less-than-polite request. According to the Imperial Articles of Exploration, the Went, as potential citizens, must be allowed to live their lives completely un-influenced by annangi presence. Instruct your miners to take heed, or we will take matters into our own hands."

"Into your own hands?" the Faythan sneered. "What, with the bush-knives you may or may not have in your kit?" He tilted his head to his Ashik escort. "Have a care, Huldar. Dead explorers tell no tales."

Casco's anger hardened.

"Neither do dead Overlords," Huldar replied coolly. He held the Controller's gaze. Poorly concealed shadows flitted behind Olatu's eyes.

After a tense moment the Faythan's gaze slid aside. "What alternative can you suggest? The ore spreads that way."

"Tsemkarun Andel has located a second seam leading in the opposite direction. It's deeper, but only slightly."

Olatu snorted. "She found time for an explorational jaunt? I thought you said she was busy."

"My wife's schedule is none of your concern," Huldar said, "I suggest you explore this new seam she has discovered and leave the other alone. It will still be there on the next rotation, and by then we may have found a way to communicate with its owners."

"Owners!" The Controller sniggered.

"They are citizens," he stressed, "or soon will be. You'd best keep that in mind."

"If you would excuse me, then," Olatu said snidely. "There's a click-bug I need to confer with!" He tipped his head in a minimal salute and brushed by Huldar's chest. The Ashik hurried to follow. One bumped Casco with his shoulder, then made a show of dusting it off.

Steady, Huldar murmured. He watched until they entered the refectory. "Keep an eye on the situation at South Arm for me, please."

"Barto's a bad one. Might get nasty."

"Not if you take Malena with you."

"Shouldn't have to."

"I know, my friend, I know." Huldar clapped Casco's shoulder. "But that's how it is, and the Went must be protected."

On the opposite side of the globe the Uri'madu campsite lay wrapped in the sounds of night. Half asleep on her bed, lulled by a cool draft, Andel of Trianog listened to the rattle of leaves and wondered if they spoke a language she might one day understand. What would they say, she wondered? What would be important to them? She doubted the fleeting presence of annangi would shake their world.

Tent leathers snapped and billowed in a sudden gust, and she groaned. How had the guy-ropes come loose again? Reflexively, her mind reached out to let Huldar know, but the intensity of his concentration stopped her … a new altercation with Olatu. There was a moment when his exhaustion bled through, but the leak was covered so quickly she realized he'd felt her touch and didn't want her to know. These situations had become more common, and however well-meant, they saddened her.

She returned her attention to the tent's surroundings but the wind had stopped. The ropes would hold until morning.

The ache in her back made it hard to find a comfortable position. She stroked her swollen belly, warm hands against taut skin. Why was her baby growing so rapidly? Only six months into her pregnancy, and she looked mid-term or more.

"What are you doing in there?" she whispered to her child. "Why are you in such a hurry?"

In every other way her child was normal. Through Ubaid's senses, she'd seen it for herself. Two arms, two legs … closed eyes, delicate as seashells. But despite the healers' assurances, it was difficult not to feel afraid.. He believed her daughter would be ready for birth in another three or four months.

She smoothed her belly again. Even four months seemed no time at all.

But lately she'd fancied she could sense her daughter's presence – a flickering of personality, although however exciting, it was too early to try to connect. The healers had been most definite about it. Any attempt to hasten or lead that phase of development could be detrimental, but she cradled the smooth skin of her belly and listened closely, just in case.

… There was nothing but the beating of their hearts, and with that magic in her soul, she began to relax. *Whatever happens,* she murmured inwardly, *you are my blessing, and I love you – I will always love you.*

Her gaze settled on the central tent pole. The knots and whirls in its grain were old friends to her now. Slowly, her eyes began to close. Sleep was almost within reach when Sari whispered, *You awake?*.

Andel couldn't help a small sigh. *You know I am.*

Sari's thought withdrew.

Andel chased it with an apology of her own. *What is it? Are you alright?*

Her friend's veil gave a little glow. *He moved,* she said excitedly. *He kicked me, and I said shh and gave him a sort of soothing rub-thing … and I felt him. He's awake!*

You felt him?

Her friend grew silent, as if struggling for control, then … *He loves me. I felt it.*

Oh Sari! She sensed the huge swell of emotion behind her friend's thought, and her own eyes prickled with tears. Only a few weeks ago her baby's development had paused and they'd been afraid he wouldn't survive. *You should tell Ubaid.*

I will, Sari said, *but I wanted to share with you first. You are my friend. The best friend anyone could have.*

Andel blinked back more tears. There was silence for a time. She wondered how it would be when her daughter awoke. Surely it would happen soon. But for Sari, one question was now imperative. She had no 'trusted other' to assist with the birth, and if her son was awake, it was time to familiarize him with that person's vibration.

Are you going to ask him? she said tentatively. The impression of a familiar face passed between them.

Sari's glow dampened. *I will. It's just …*

You and he have been friends, good friends, forever, Andel reassured her. *Of course he'll say yes.*

But – what of Daric?

Daric loves you too. If anything, and if I know Daric – which I'm sure nobody really does, she admitted, *but by what little I do know of him, you may well have not one, but two strong, loving souls to help you and your little one through the birth.*

Despite herself, Sari giggled.

You'll see, Andel said. *Just ask him.*

Sari withdrew.

Andel started to drift off again. "Will you wake soon?" she whispered softly. Would her daughter's soul be one day drawn to find her soul-mate's? Was Huldar her own true soul-mate? They certainly loved each other as completely as she imagined was possible, but she'd heard that with soul-mates, it might be something more, and she wondered, how could that be?

It seemed only moments later when she roused to find her husband standing by the bed.

A soft smile lit his eyes and her lips curved in response.

She reached for his hand. *I'm afraid the guy-ropes are loose again.*

Listen … he answered.

She cocked her head, then sighed. There was no sound but the rustle of fronds and the occasional clack of a bug. *You've done it already.*

His mind projected an image of her flailing after disorderly tent-ropes in a futile effort for control. *Nothing's changed,* he added cheekily.

She laughed and tried to swat him with a pillow.

He dodged and with a whispered charm made the strings in the neck of her night-shirt writhe in imitation of the team's practical joke – an initiation prank on her first day on Went.

Andel closed her hand over the ties and with a scathing eye-roll they were stilled. *You're never going to let that go, are you?*

Probably not, he grinned.

You weren't even there!

But with so many eye-witness accounts to choose from … his lips shrugged.

There's no escape then?

He cast himself onto the bed beside her. *None!*

His eyes laughed into hers, but there was no disguising his deep fatigue.

She wrinkled her nose at the musty smell of his shirt, then reached beneath to caress his firm torso. Love spread like a warm glow wherever her hands passed, and their marriage bond pulsed with emotion.

What would I do without you? they whispered, and smiled at their perfect synchronicity.

He kissed her forehead, then her lips, and time stood still.

What's made you so tired? she asked. *Is there anything I can do?*

Through his eyes she saw the Went lumbering along their endless road. Hair swished. Noses snuffled. Decisions were made. Each evening the gentle creatures would gather in a single massive circular formation and drone in chorus, a deep and eerie sound. When they were done, they would gather around the elders, each clan-group a separate series of knots.

What does it mean? she asked.

He shook his head. *They communicate freely with each other, share knowledge – that much is obvious. But …* He raised one shoulder. *I have no idea how.*

If only we could touch them, she suggested. *Maybe they use psychic emissions as we do?*

He shrugged again. *I have sensed something of the kind, but faint and unstructured.* He smiled. *Look at this … a special relationship between an elder and a particular young one …*

She saw a juvenile, small and marked with several dark stripes, almost like slashes. all other Went had featureless coats. He drew her attention to its head. The corona of orbs so prominent on its shaggy brethren was absent.

Tears welled as she shared her suspicions.

Duvät? he replied. Sadness filled them both. Had this poor creature survived one of their former Overlord's sickening attacks? Somehow, it had continued to develop, but without its eyes.

He showed her a scene he had witnessed, the Elder of the purple-bellied clan patiently showing the blind one how to break a hard-shelled nut and eat the meat inside.

Then this … He showed her a long, steep-sided gorge, and a stretch of their road leading through it. *The path seemed firm to look at, but there was quicksand and no visual cues to tell where it lay – well none I could see. The elders lead the way, but the young ones – especially those who travelled too close together, were sometimes trapped. Twenty or thirty died,* he continued. *I lost count. I wanted to help them so much,* he said, *but this is their life, their culture. Interference is forbidden.*

She shared the tears in his soul. *So sad,* she murmured. *It was so hard for you. I don't think I could do it – just watch.*

He nodded slowly in agreement. *But then …*

Through their bond, she saw his memory of the purple-bellied elder waiting on safe ground at the end of the sand-traps. Another Elder from the greenish clan waited with it for some time, but eventually left.

You could see the first was torn, Huldar said. *Resolve waning, but it stayed.*

As he shared the rest of the story, Andel's eyes stung with more tears. Alone, the small blind Went worked its way between the last areas of quicksand. When the waiting elder saw it, it stood on its hind legs and trumpeted, almost dancing its encouragement.

So joyous! Andel exclaimed through her tears.

Huldar handed her a small cloth to wipe her nose, and sniffed back tears of his own. *But it's blind,* he said. *How did it find its way through when so many failed?*

He showed her how the two Elder Went kept their bodies in constant contact with the exhausted little one as they shepherded it back to the greater herd.

Andel tilted her head to touch his hand as he stroked her shoulder. *If she hadn't seen the story through her husband's eyes, she would hardly have believed it.*

And why am I so tired? He gave a weary grimace. *There are very few gates along the trail. I follow on foot and stay hidden … although I'm sure they know I'm there. Most times I follow for as long as I can, then have to retrace my steps. I was so lucky to witness the episode in the gorge.* He sighed. *South Arm Mine is about to encroach on the buffer zone around their road.*

She frowned indignantly. *But I found another seam just as rich. Won't they follow that one instead? Is that what you were discussing with Olatu? You seemed very tense.*

Among other things. He shared a precis of what had gone on with Casco, how someone had spied him in training and reported him.

Singing against the wind, she said quietly.

Huldar gave her a look.

Such nastiness will come back on its instigator, she explained. *You'll see.*

She nestled into his arms. Skin to skin, their senses tingled, but still there was an elusive something, a blemish on his deepest veils. Her hand moved against his chest. *Would it help to share?*

After a brief but intense inner struggle, he admitted, *There's something I haven't told you.*

She smiled lightly. *There's lots you haven't told me.*

He turned to study her eyes.

She sensed his need for forgiveness, and her heart slowed

I couldn't tell you before, he said. *Ubaid and I agreed – we didn't know whether it would be significant to those blessed or not, didn't want to cause unnecessary worry when there was already a situation to cope with …*

His face twisted in a miserable grimace.

Just say it, she said.

He ran his hand over her belly. *The berries we ate – the ones by the lake, they weren't plant-matter. It was only later, when we went back, that we discovered … they were eggs. The eggs of the Went.*

Her mind froze. *And you kept this from me? From us?*

He nodded. *But now, with the way the pregnancies are progressing …*

She took a deep breath and fought to contain her turmoil. *Our child is half Went?* Thank goodness she had already seen her – two arms, two eyes, two legs. Was that why the babies grew so rapidly? Were they 'pupating' like the Went in the cocoons? She had worried so much, the whole thing – such a puzzle. How had he been able to keep such vital information to himself? Sari had been worried because while some raced ahead more smoothly, her baby grew in pronounced fits and starts. Now it seemed it was back to normal, but what was normal for this situation?

I know our little one is going through a rapid growth spurt, she said, *and I'm hungry all the time! But Ubaid said not to worry because she seems – at least outwardly – perfectly normal.* She snorted. *I thought the babies' erratic development was something to do with the planet's vibration, with being on Went.*

Yes, he said, *and it is, in a way.*

But despite her attempt to remain calm, his tension grew.

Should we be worried? she asked. *Even more-so? Is there something else?*

The Went, he blurted, *don't give birth like annangi do. They split open. Eggs spill directly from the wound – and then they die.*

The image he hinted at was shocking, and she could see why he'd wanted to shield her, but, surprisingly, she felt her spirit firm. … *We are not Went, Huldar. The babies are developing in the manner of annangi. I've seen our daughter, just yesterday.* She shared the image with him again, as a reminder. *She is beyond beautiful, to me at least – and Ubaid assures me she is perfectly normal in appearance for her relative stage of development.*

But …

She kissed his shoulder. *This has worried you deeply, hasn't it? But I think we accepted right from the start that these were not ordinary pregnancies. To know our babies are connected to the Went … such mystical, gentle creatures – citizens, no less – well, to be honest, I don't rightly know how that makes me feel, but it's not bad, Huldar.*

It's not?

She kissed him again. *It is as it is. Even a song in the making, once voiced, cannot be unsung. And we know our daughter will survive because Mother saw her in her foretelling. I told you, remember? And it's in her future to marry someone quite special. A day of days, she said. Think of that. Our child – born here. The first things she'll see will be the beauty of this wilderness … happy and beloved and perhaps one day to be blessed in her turn.*

A slow smile relaxed his face. *It's a good thought.* He sent an image of a wild little annangi walking among the Went. She had bits of stick in unkempt hair, the same russet color as that of his favorite Wentish elder.

With great solemnity, Andel examined the thought, then returned it with the addition of a wedding shawl decorated with the colorful paddles of clicker-bugs.

He laughed aloud, but shreds of worry still dimmed their joy.

No one knows the length of their span, she said gently. *We are mere threads in the greater tapestry Breath has already blown – threads weave as they will. Let it be enough to trust our daughter will live to enjoy the outer Realm.*

The old philosophical you. He kissed her forehead. *I like it.*

So tell me, she said. *What else?*

He took a deep breath. *Daric believes the God-Emperor will try to kill us.*

The God-Emperor? Shock hollowed her anew. *Why?*

Daric came to me about it some months ago, but again, I didn't want to worry you, and the threat is not immediate – but we have to be ready, just in case. We can assume it took Kandät Enna at least eight weeks to travel home. Sometime after that, the Imperial couple would have received the so-called berries. The Empress may already be pregnant … the God-Emperor will celebrate a second Blessing. El's favor at last. He turned to her. *He'll want no one to know he has cheated.*

It was hard to imagine the God-Emperor even knew the Uri'madu existed, but everyone knew of his embarrassment.

If the Empress has been blessed in the same way we have been, he'll kill us because we make him look bad? That's what Daric thinks?

Huldar placed his hand against her cheek. *In a twisted way, it does make sense. We cannot communicate with the Realm, and can only be reached at all by a skilled navigator. No one beyond Went knows of our pregnancies – Kandät Enna is the exception, and I doubt he knows much. Although Malena is a Navigator, she can't save us – navigators can't navigate while pregnant, or for some years after the birth.* He gave a bitter shrug. *An unfortunate accident occurs … Kandät Enna fails to reach us in time and we're left stranded as the planet freezes over? So simple,* he said sarcastically. *How tragic.*

But the half-term communication window, she reasoned. *Some of us are going home. We can call for help then.*

He gave a grim snort. *My guess – and Daric's – is that we won't be allowed anywhere near the northern ice, or the Navigator, when he comes.*

But they can't stop us! she argued. *They have no right!*

Ashik.

Her spirits fell. The Ashik contingent had stayed largely out of the way so far, but she had no doubt of their capability for violence. A new thought came to her … *But if none of us contacts the Guild there'll be questions asked, surely?*

I imagine there may be, Huldar countered tiredly, and she realized he'd been over every aspect many times. *But the window is short and the planet volatile,* he continued. *We don't know enough about her yet. They may simply accept the opportunity was not as predictable as we thought, or bad weather kept us away, or any number of natural causes prevented us from reaching it, especially if we're reported to be alive and well at the supply run.*

And that will be before the window?

He nodded. *By one or two weeks.*

Her hands clasped around the swell of her unborn child. *What are we going to do?*

Hide, he said. "Retreat underground - somewhere to survive when the planet freezes over."

"When the planet freezes over? Seven years underground?" *Under the ice? With small babies?*

"I know it won't be easy," he replied, *but what choice is there? Work has already begun -*

"That's why you've been late home so often."

He drew her closer and kissed her. "It's a relief to finally tell you."

No wonder he'd seemed so remote, she thought. She snuggled into his embrace. As she listened to his slow beating heart, old, inner knots eased, but new concerns were there to fill any breach.

He pulled her gently closer. "Not all need know about this - not yet," he said. *Are there any among the blessed you think we might not be able to trust?*

Images of the Uri'madu passed quickly through her head, Sari foremost, then Malena, Van and Rosheen ... *And the spinners are all so loyal to Malena, and she is one of us ...*

He nodded, *My thoughts also.* He shared the features of the four pregnant members of the Host, Tashel, Clip, Gael and Tish ... *What about them? I hardly know them.*

Andel furnished the images with those of their partners. *Tam is with Tashel. She's a little temperamental, tends toward drama, but if Tam trusts her ...*

He nodded, then cocked his head in thought. *And Shen is supporting Gael. I trust Shen, although what he's doing – it's a great risk …* He sorted through the remaining images … *what of these two?*

She considered, … *Tish and Farrel – both Cantori, both specialist miners. They've worked together before but that's all I really know. As for Farrel, it seems Tish is forever tip-toeing around his moods.* She backed up her assessment with her memory of a scene she'd witnessed at the tin mine.

I see what you mean, Huldar said. *And these two … Clip and Warri?*

Her thought narrowed onto a pair of no-nonsense angels. *They seem happy enough and easy-going, but I don't know them well.*

"Perhaps we could start with Malena?"

We can't just tell one. What of Sari? And Rosheen and Van?

"Calen…" He hesitated. *This must be difficult for her.*

"Because of the termination?" Andel nodded, remembering the deep sadness Calen had experienced. "And now she's partnered Van. She claims she has more to offer support-wise than she would've, but I think another part of her feels a need to atone."

Perceptive …

Being Blessed is forcing me to grow up, Andel said sagely. *It's our turn to be adult.*

"So, with that in mind, what do you think we should do?"

She thought for a moment, and her imagination invented a wealth of probable situations. It certainly was tempting to tell only Malena at first, but that would be unfair. A saying came to mind … *Breath, quiet as a secret, tumbles secrets in its wake.*

Huldar nodded slowly. *In time, truth is always revealed.* He seemed happy to have understood so quickly. *Your father's?*

I can't remember. She imaged her father's face but banished it again as sadness swept her. She missed him so much. She'd sent a letter telling him he was to become a grandfather, but if Olatu of Faytha had censored their mail … and Daric said they should assume that was the case, he would not know - and he would be wondering, worrying, about her silence.

Huldar held her quietly.

"We should call a meeting," she said at last. "Maybe disguise it as a party of some kind? Something for Uri'madu only. Tell us first, then we should make a collective decision about the trustworthiness of outsiders."

"Tam …"

"And Tashel. Yes." She pictured the stocky miner. She could always find something to complain about, but did that mean she couldn't be trusted? "Tell him something sensitive is to be discussed. Let him make a decision regarding Tashel. He knows her better than we do."

"Good plan." He smiled. "What shall we celebrate?"

"Do we really need a reason?"

He shook his head and gave her a smile. "Just a remote location and tight screens."

"How about the southern tip?" She imaged a deeply fissured coastline, a favorite place of hers. "Or we could explore that huge rift valley?"

"You decide."

"You're not the only one with a work-load!" she said sharply.

"Alright," he said good-naturedly. "The rift valley seems good to me. It's warmer there."

"But the fjords are so pretty."

He rolled his eyes. "Fjords it is."

"Good choice," she said. "We could go out to one of the islands, perhaps?"

"If the ice has cleared, and if Daric or I have time to make a portal, yes, we could, but lately Qalān has been reluctant. Sometimes neither of us can forge an agreement."

She frowned and nestled closer within the circle of his arms. He would find a way. He always did, but as her mind slowed with impending sleep, another of her father's sayings came to her. *Who's anger matches that of the duped? … No one's,* he seemed to whisper, and a chill rand down her spine.

TRUSTED

Sari sat on a handy log and swished a shrubby branch at her face. A red and turquoise cloud of tiny flying lizards fluttered around any area of exposed skin, intent on stealing moisture. If one managed to land, sweat would be wicked through a clever capillary system embedded in the minuscule scales of their little flat toe-pads. The process caused no pain or injury, but having her face masked by a rabble of squabbling creatures was not an experience Sari found enjoyable.

She wondered about the picnic Lady Andel had told her about. Uri'madu only, secret location - so secret she wouldn't even tell her, her closest friend. Something serious was up. Secretly, she hoped the site of the meeting - because meeting it would be - had been chosen for its lack of lizards, but given the fauna of Went, it was perhaps too much to expect.

Tenderly, she stroked her belly. The last such picnic had consequences no one could have possibly foreseen and she smiled to think of the delightful impossibility of it all.

Casco's feet crunched lightly through dried plant-matter, and as he drew closer, she stifled a pang of anxiety.

Finished? she asked him.

The broad brim of his straw hat shaded his answering smile. *There's one on your neck. Here. Let me ...*

Her heart raced as he plucked the small thief away. Faint nausea plagued her. She knew he was not interested in her as a lover, but did he ever think back to that afternoon by the lake? Her hand went to her belly again and she was rewarded by a tickle of awareness.

Ready for the next one? Casco said.

The next one? Then she nodded. *Calcite camp isn't it?*

She stumbled as she got to her feet - already the extra weight made her clumsy. Casco feigned disinterest. Perhaps he felt an offer of assistance would embarrass her - or be misinterpreted as romantic intrest. It felt odd to be awkward with one of her closest friends. He was the father of her baby, but such responsibility would have been very far from his expectations during their accidental drug-induced encounter. How could one possibly know how to behave under such circumstances?

Lizards swarmed excitedly as she moved. A scuttling group weighed down the brim of her hat. One managed to land on her cheek. With a sigh, she picked it off. The body felt tough, like gravelly string. Each foot detached with a tiny pop.

"What did they eat before they could get annangi?" Casco said wryly.

"Annangi?" She waved her hands again. "Well, whatever it was, I wish they'd go back to it."

"A pity the zilla charm doesn't work," he said, swatting at a cloud of his own. "They weren't this bad last time."

"Last time, there weren't thirty miners camped near the marsh."

He grunted in agreement. She followed along a red-dirt trail through black-stemmed drifts of orange button flowers. There was no wind, and the smell of dust was sharp in the air.

He glanced at her from the corner of his eye. "Something bothering you?"

"Bothering?" Despite the sudden catch in her pulse, she shrugged. "Of course not."

"Oh." He nodded slowly. "Are you sure?"

Her heart fluttered harder. The baby kicked.

He paused to look at her. "Out with it!"

"Out with it?" she muttered to herself. After a few slow steps, she also stopped, still looking at the trail ahead. Finally, some words came out, "… I want to ask you something."

"Oh?"

"I know it's … well … if you say no … It's just that …"

He raised his eyebrows encouragingly

"Everyone else has one - except Malena, of course, and we all know why that is. If she'd only just swallow her pride and ask him … oh." She lowered her head.

"Ask him what?" Casco said.

"Ask him? Yes." She continued. Regardless of her wavering confidence, she was determined now to finish what she'd begun. "No, I want to ask you." She turned and looked into his eyes. Color flooded her cheeks. "Casco, will you be my trusted other?"

His brow wrinkled. "With the baby?"

"With *our* baby. It's alright if you say no," she hurried to say. "I'll understand. It's not something you'd normally have to think about, and what with you and Daric and you're all so much busier now that we blessed ones, are well, so useless … or getting that way … I know how busy you are," her voice trailed off.

"It's not that." He shrugged. "I … I don't know how. My own parents were dead before I was of age … I don't have any siblings. I never thought …"

"Never thought … yes." Her heart plummeted. " - So it's no, then?"

"No!" He turned sharply back to the path. "I just need some time to think. This is a big thing, Sari."

She stood as if rooted to the ground. He kept walking, but she could not bring herself to move. "A big thing? Yes, it is, to me!" She fought back tears and watched him take more steps away. "Maybe it's Daric? Maybe he wouldn't like you to take more time away … to attend Ubaid's classes and all."

"What's Daric got to do with it?" he snapped. "He's very fond of you."

"Fond, yes. Who else could I ask? You are the father. There's been no one else, no other male - ever."

He stopped. *Ever?*

She shook her head.

He glanced back at her. "And Daric didn't …?"

She shook her head again.

Hesitantly, she took a step. He waited until she came to his side. They continued down the trail - each wrapped in their own silence, each too afraid to touch the other with voice or mind. Even the lizards left them alone. Her heartbeat was a leaden gong in her tightly constricted chest. Tears prickled from her eyes. She willed them to stop. Of course, he would say no. It was very demanding to support someone through a birth, a huge responsibility. It wasn't as if they were married. He hadn't asked her to carry his child - it had just happened. She wiped beneath her eyes with her thumbs, first one, then the other. At least there were no lizards to covet the moisture.

When they reached the portal, he turned to her.

"Do you want to go home?" he said gently. "I'll take you. We can finish the rounds tomorrow."

She nodded, not trusting herself to speak, and let him sing them through.

Casco sat cross-legged on the floor of the island home he shared with Daric. Outwardly, the Uri'madu made a show of business as usual. Fortunately, no one from the Host knew what 'normal' was for them. If they chose to disband to isolated locations, it would not seem suspicious, and no one was sufficiently gifted in far-sight or Ziquarra to spy on them unnoticed, especially through Daric's heavy-duty screens.

The site they'd chosen had a spectacular view of the ocean and the benefit of cool evening breezes to temper the soaring daytime heat, but all that beauty and planning was lost on him now as he worried about Sari and the child they had made together. How should he react? In his heart, he knew what was right, but that step … was a big one, a far-reaching one. What kind of father would he be? Why had he ignored the situation, forcing her, that gentlest of souls, to have to ask?

He looked up as soft 'pop' on his mind told him Daric had crossed the first of their protective boundaries. He rubbed both hands down his face, and tried to push thoughts of Sari - and their encounter, away. One by one the stacked screens adjusted as his lover came in from the night. In ten-minutes he would be here. He snorted at the memory of Daric trying to convince him the alarms were set to give them time if anyone 'unwelcome' should try to sneak up. Daric had sung their portal himself and Huldar was the only other who could access it.

He set two glasses on the bench and pulled a container of golden liquid from Qalān. Beads of dew from the cool of morning reflected the rich yellow hue.

When the tent door parted, Casco turned to Daric with a drink in either hand.

His partner's smile reached inside with wordless appreciation.

Casco felt the sides of his mouth crease in answer. *It's just fruit juice.*

Daric winked. *Just for being here.* He pictured Casco's sword and with a grin, overlaid it with the image of a kitchen knife. *Huldar did well.*

That he did. He put his drink aside and brushed the fine layer of dust from Daric's hair and shoulders. *Been working on the new cave system?* He began to unbutton his partner's shirt.

I think it's our best option, Daric replied. An impression of the cavernous space swam into view.

Casco pictured the giant brown bugs they'd been attacked by when they'd first ventured inside it. The oversized insects had been difficult to discourage, and chittered their outrage the entire time the annangi encroached on their territory.

Only attack if they perceive a threat, Daric assured him. *I've found if I move quietly enough, they don't even see me.*

But babies will move as they will, Casco pointed out, *and make noise. How will they cope with babies?*

They'll make things more difficult, I expect. But just today, with the way they accepted me, I saw a new side to them. I think perhaps we could condition them to behave as guards. Turn their suspicious natures to our favor.

Change their behavior?

More of a cultural adjustment, and we'll have to have something to exchange – the benefit must be mutual. If I can convince them, they'll warn us of unfamiliar visitors, yes, and provide good, natural cover – hide our tracks and so-forth. But to them, all annangi must look the same. I'd have to think of a way for them to identify us.

Daric swapped his drink from hand to hand as Casco slipped the shirt from his shoulders. The smell of him was intoxicating. *Would it help to grow long, striped antennae?* He imaged Daric with a dull brown carapace and waving antennae, one above each eye.

And big clashing mandibles! Daric suspended his glass in mid-air so he could wave his fingers in front of his mouth.

Casco grinned and tapped the side of his head. *Starry nong, ja? Bin too long in de sun.*

Loosin de pram, sho la! Daric's grin was wicked. He crouched low and projected the image of himself as a giant bug, then scuttled forward in a sudden lunge.

Casco jumped aside and collided with the hanging drink. Juice spattered his torso.

You did that on purpose! he spluttered.

Daric-the-bug came in to attack. *Leggyuns be lovin juice, ja …*

Casco put one hand on Daric's head to hold him back, but he was laughing too hard and Daric's deft footwork sent them both tumbling.

… But presented this way? Daric's tawny gaze looked deeply into his. *Tinkin I-nangi be yummin it more!*

His lover's tongue slipped over his chest, following the sticky trail of golden-wheel juice. Casco tried to pull him up for a kiss, but Daric pushed him aside and continued downward.

"Piss-weak Leth," he growled. "Tink un be keppin starriest juice unsel, ja? Na na! No chance!"

The touch of Daric's mouth as it closed around his penis made him arch his back with pleasure. He opened his defenses and Daric's mind arrowed through his body.

Playfully, the inner touch paused. *Ist rule – only if invited.*

I invite you!

Stealthy, psychic probes felt their way through him. Feather-light, they circled his anus while Daric's tongue worked intricate magic on his most sensitive organ.

Orgasm rushed toward him.

Not yet! Daric let go. *2nd rule – reciprocation.*

Is that the second rule? Really?

Sort of. Daric lay back on the bed, arms and legs thrown wide. *Do your worst!*

Casco took a moment to bring his own surging body under control, then turned to face his lover.

The first taste of Daric's sweat-sheened skin filled him with hunger for more. He trailed his tongue over a landscape of wiry muscles, then slowly up the elegant neck, back and forth, allowing the twin sensations of taste and smell to fill his senses. He reached those perfect, slightly parted lips, and covered them with his own. While his tongue plumbed the depths of his lover's mouth, his free hand gently clasped Daric's scrotum and just as Daric had taught him, his mind found and filled those erogenous spaces, but with a tingling touch that was all his own.

He felt a moment's triumph when Daric gasped. Strong arms clasped his back, pulling him down on heated slickness. A strong mind resumed its play. Every movement stroked through them both.

Now! Daric whispered, and their senses joined, each sharing the other's ultimate joy.

Orgasm faded.

Gentle fingers smoothed a lock of hair from his forehead.

"It's never been this way for me before," Daric said quietly. "Laughing, playing … loving …" His steady gaze gravitated to Casco's lips. "Telling it in words … makes it more real - for me anyway." One fine finger traced a line around them.

Casco shut his eyes.

The finger came to rest on the centre of his mouth and wiggled as if seeking entrance.

Casco kissed it.

"What we have," Daric said, "it's more precious to me than you can imagine."

Casco smiled. "I bet you say that to all the juiciest bugs!" He rolled away. His body still tingled. What would have happened if he'd pursued his attraction for Saphella of Hermes? He thought of her delicate smile and wondered. Was his love for Daric fated, or did the threads of the great design change to accommodate their choices. Breath blows, the saying went, and everything tumbles in its path. He stroked Daric's smoothly muscled chest. "Why did you plant that sigil in my head all that time ago? I've often wondered."

Daric took his hand and kissed it. His gaze flickered over Casco's face again, loving yet somehow wistful. "There was something … special."

Casco gave a light shrug. "Just another half-breed it seems to me."

"Kareski on the make?" Daric gave a crooked grin. "Maybe it's because you can cook." He pushed him toward the edge of their bed. "An guessin mun beun's turn."

Casco gave a short laugh. "Must be!" With one last kiss, he left Daric on the bed and went to conjure a cook-fire.

"Me and Sari did the western quarter today," he said conversationally. He reached for a handful of locally foraged tubers. "She asked me to be her partner in the birth." He hesitated as the enormity of her request occurred to him. "Her trusted other."

Daric's face lit up. "At last!" he sighed. "You said yes, of course?"

In the silence that followed, he felt Daric's gaze bore deeper.

A rush of indignation followed.

You refused?

"I didn't –"

"How could you say no?" Daric said angrily. "She must be devastated."

"I didn't know what to say," Casco snapped back. "And I didn't say no. I said I needed time to think!"

"Then think about what it meant for her to ask you." Daric glowered at him. "Think of the trust and regard she has for you. A child? Your own son – as if you were married and Blessed – and you said no?"

"A half-breed child?" he countered with his greatest fear. "You know what kind of life it will have. It's why I swore I would never ... why I broke off with Saphella!"

Daric shook his head. "The Hermes? Another who trusted you. She gave you her name! And now one more beautiful soul demonstrates her belief in you and again, you throw it away? I thought better of you."

Casco's scowl deepened. "You thought better of me?" He had no idea why his anger welled so strongly, only that it had to be set free. "And you?" he barked. "The picture of perfection? I think not! What about those 'accidents'? All those dead miners? Malena nearly died. I know it was you!"

Daric paled, and in that moment, Casco had all the answers he needed. "And *you* lecture *me* about trust!" He reached for his trousers.

"It was for you," Daric pleaded. "They hated you! Dishonored you."

"So you killed them? That was your answer? The best response you could come up with?" He looked at his lover as if seeing him for the first time. "I can't believe I'm hearing this. What about Radätel? We blamed Olatu!"

"It *was* Olatu!"

Casco fastened his pants and cast about for his shirt. It must be somewhere!

Daric sat on the edge of the bed. "You've killed too!"

"Only when attacked! ... and I regret it every day."

He went to look at the foot of the bed. Daric reached out as he passed but Casco danced aside.

"Malena was a day early," Daric cried. "She shouldn't have even been there. If those people hadn't been so hateful to you ... And Radätel *was* killed by Olatu. It wasn't me; I swear it!"

Casco rounded on him. "Then why the guilt? I see it in you every time I use his globes, every time we pass the place where his tent used to be."

Daric turned away. Casco glimpsed tears in his eyes. The sight shocked him, but his anger would not abate.

"I was at the encampment, the Host's encampment." Daric said brokenly "– I must have been there when it happened and yet I knew nothing. Didn't even notice him arrive."

"Then how do you know he even *was* there?" Casco retorted.

"Olatu killed him," Daric insisted.

Beneath their bedding Casco saw a snatch of pale blue fabric – his shirt at last. But to retrieve it meant going closer to Daric. He pulled a fresh one from Qalān.

"The touch on his neck was conclusive," Daric insisted. "If you weren't so bent on anger … Anyone who could read a body would know that. Ubaid could tell … Where are you going?"

Casco shoved his arm into his shirt and stalked from their tent with it half on. "To tell Sari I'll do it," he snapped. "From now on you can cook for yourself."

ROUGH NIGHT

Casco shivered. Midnight was well past. The pale glow from Eastern base-camp was not bright enough to cast a shadow. Here in the foothills the night had turned frosty, but he had little energy to take a blanket from Qalān.

On the one hand, he was bathed in a river of joy and gratitude from Sari. To tell her to stop would be inconceivably rude. On the other, Daric's pain. He couldn't seem to shut out either. All on its own, his mind was doing the job of keeping the disparate streams separate. Sari had no idea he wasn't equally excited by his decision, and, largely thanks to training received, Daric had no idea Casco could feel him.

Finally he mustered the strength to tackle Sari, and allowed a slip of his genuine tiredness show. *We can talk more fully in the morning,* he said. *I'll meet you at the south gate, if you like?*

I'll have hot tea and breakfast ready, she said. Her joy wisped into something more tenuous, then settled, only slightly less than before.

You are brave and strong, Casco, she said quietly. *I know you never asked for it, but no Blessing could hope for a better father. I am glad you decided to be with us in this.*

Tears came to his eyes. His head hurt almost as much as his heart. He took a rough breath and leaned back to look at the sky. Through blurred vision, the purple nebula looked rather like a huge eye staring back at him through indigo darkness. Did he have a history of failure, he asked himself? Of hurting those who loved him?

The Great Wheel took one and a half Giahni years to free itself from the horizon and now was almost clear. Only a few more months and the Bel Nishani would beach themselves. The navigator would arrive. And the births be upon them. The communication window at mid-cycle may be their only chance to contact the Realm and ask for assistance - if Daric was correct. After that, they were on their own. How could he defend his little one through that? Thoughts of what might be, terrified him.

A light, rhythmic crunch carried in the stillness, and he sensed it was Huldar who walked towards him - perhaps the last person he wanted to see. But when a warm mug appeared at face-height, he took it.

"Do you mind?" Huldar gestured at the space beside him.

He shrugged.

His old friend settled into place, pulled a blanket from Qalān, draped it over both their shoulders and wrapped the tail around to cover their knees. It was an action he'd carried out so many times before, it was almost automatic.

Casco raised his cup in muted thanks, but the first mouthful almost scalded his tongue. He blew gently on the liquid before trying again.

The night resumed its silence.

"I've agreed to be Sari's trusted other," he said at last. His voice seemed small against the vastness of the desert below.

Huldar nodded. "Congratulations. It's an honor to assist in bringing new life to the world. I'm sure you'll do well."

He shrugged disconsolately. "Sari's happy."

Huldar sipped his tea and stared into the dark. "I hear the hideout system is progressing well," he said at last, and tipped his head toward the camp. "As lovely as this is, the ploy of remote individual campsites is a good one. We're harder to find, free to work on our projects, and besides, it's not too different from what we would normally do - just a bit more extreme." Huldar glanced at him. "Thanks to Daric Enna, we'll be at least somewhat prepared if the worst should actually happen."

Casco nodded. He was afraid that if he vocalized, pain would get the better of him. He'd been so happy only hours ago - and now? What was he supposed to do? How could he stay with Daric, accept his love, if he knew - actually knew - he'd killed … as retaliation for what? Insult? There'd be far fewer annangi in the Known if that was to continue.

Imagery of decaying vegetation quietly filled the space between them. He saw it steaming in the early light, and felt again the chill, and his irritation with Huldar for sleep interrupted.

Huldar sipped again. "Remember that night?"

He nodded. "It was cold. Lind was still missing."

Huldar nodded with him. "I dragged you out of bed and took you there, to the swamp. I was so confused about my feelings for Andel … We saw a shooting star - remember?

Casco looked up as if it was still there, flashing across the sky. "Seems a long time ago."

"It does, doesn't it? You told me to let her in. That I'd behaved like a fool."

" A fool?"

"You always did have a knack for seeing to the heart of things."

Casco shook his head. If only that were true ...

"I don't know what you and Daric have argued about," Huldar said gently, "but I could never think you'd behaved foolishly. Your life has been too hard for that. Daric is impulsive, and working as a team is a new concept for him - as it once was for you. But one he's doing his best. I know he is. You have been the making of him, my friend, and whatever the issue is, I'm sure you'll work it out."

Casco kept his knowledge of Daric's transgressions locked tightly. The idea of him having a positive influence over someone of such power seemed laughable. Daric did what he did - and had done what he'd done. "I don't know that we can," he said miserably. How could he have given his heart to one with such beauty and danger in equal measure?

Huldar sighed. "Daric is an enigma, it's true, and in many ways, so are you. You are what you are - two separate people. Sometimes, when you let someone in, you discover things that surprise you, even disgust you. It's hard to step back and remember the whole. That the one you love is the sum of all their parts, good and bad. Each tempers the other. It makes the victory of love so much more that it may seem on the surface - or so I believe."

Casco felt tears slide from his eyes. He blew on the surface of his tea and took a sip. There was something to what Huldar said … They were not the same person, not at all. The question was, could he accept the truth he'd discovered? Daric had killed to defend him – it had seemed to him the right thing to do. Was it his way of proving his love? In a perverse way, maybe it was. The tears in Daric's eyes had shocked him – the depth of his hurt … What led him to become an assassin? How much pain had he already endured? … Those were questions he'd never asked. He shook his head. And would any answer make Daric's actions forgivable?

He glanced upward. "Has Lady Andel been teaching you her Trianogi philosophy?"

Huldar chuckled softly. "Maybe." He bumped Casco's shoulder with his own. "I'm off to bed." He extricated himself from the blanket across their shoulders. Tam will be in early to cook breakfast. I'm sure he'll be pleased to see you – if you're still here."

TROUBLE WITH ASHIK

The rhythmic clack of a million bugs shivered the air around central basecamp. Sun beat sharply on Ariben's head as he waited for Banga to join him. His regrown arm ached, but there were no storms imminent.

Banga emerged from the second gate and nodded a greeting.

The plan stays the same, Ariben said. *I'll scan to make sure the place is deserted. We'll head in from the left, get to the back of the tents as quick as we can. then make for block three.*

Banga nodded again. *And if we're caught?*

Let me do the talking.

Banga gave a wry smile. *Whatever you say, Shamkarun Ariben.*

Don't start, Ariben warned. He looked doubtfully at the portal. It seemed settled enough, but one never knew these days. *I wish Daric was with us.*

Never thought I'd hear you say that, Banga scoffed. *Too damn clever, that's what I think. And something about him … haze too shiny … Don't know what Casco sees in the toffy bastard anyway. You and Malena, on the other hand – that's obvious.*

Leave her out of this, Ariben snapped. She couldn't have the baby on her own ... could she?

Don't ever play Ashut, Banga said. *Not with me, anyway.*

Why not?

Your mouth twists when you're doubtful and pretending not to be.

Thanks. I'll remember that.

Banga grunted. It might have been a laugh.

There was a moment as they stepped through the east gate, as if Qalān had rippled, then they were through. Neither mentioned the anomaly. They cast the new screens they'd learned from Daric and made their way across the clearing toward a series of long tents on the outskirts of the Host's encampment.

Once among the tents they moved stealthily toward the third in line, yellowish and made of tight-woven plant fiber rather than animal hide.

A drop of sweat rolled down Ariben's back. Daric's screens took effort to maintain, but the thrill of their impending raid made the strain well worth it.

He waved his finger for Banga to follow, then slipped through the door-flap into the amber gloom.

In the mid-morning warmth, the sticky smell of dried fish rose above a hundred others. A quick glance up and down the rows showed there was no shortage of staple grains, but there were plenty of empty spaces too. If Kandät Enna didn't make it through on schedule, the diet of the Host might become lean indeed.

Our need is greater, Banga whispered. He pictured Malena, and Sari's wise eyes.

Ariben gave a slow nod and brought to mind the list he'd memorized.

Taking separate sides, they worked their way down the rows. He felt a moment of satisfaction as he rifled among a pile of sacks to find two large bags of little-attar. It was not everyone's favorite, but retained its nutrient value over time. If they could put aside enough, at least they'd stand a fighting chance if the God-Emperor marooned them here, and their blessings would not starve.

He frowned sharply as Banga bumped a box with his foot.

Be more careful, Ariben snapped, then glanced over as Banga shared the image of a bag of dar-leaf tea wedged between two crates.

Perfect, he said sourly. *More tea. Can never have too much tea.*

Banga snorted. *Sari will thank you.* He tucked his find into Qalān. *Did you get that grain?*

Ariben's wary screens vibrated. *Shh!* He held up his hand.

The spinner tilted his head as if listening. *What?*

Small sounds gelled into rhythmic footsteps. *Ashik, I think – coming this way.*

Banga nodded. He was good, but an archangels' senses were always more acute.

They held motionless as two soldiers stationed themselves by the door.

Banga flicked his glance toward a clear stretch of canvas and on the narrowest of psychic bands, imaged a knife.

Ariben kept his mind still and shook his head.

"... Raise security on stores," one Ashik murmured sarcastically. Her pompous tones were a clear imitation of Olatu's.

"At least it's something to do," the other replied. "I'm bored witless. What are we here for anyway?"

There was a swift mental exchange and both chuckled.

"You seen em?"

Her companion grunted.

"Hulking lumps," she continued. "I guess if we run out of food ..."

"One of those'd do us a day or two." He grunted again. "Probably taste like shit though, and you'd have to fight the Leth for every one."

"All they've got are those knives, or so they say - clearing vegetation my arse!" There was a thoughtful pause, then, "Might not be such a bad idea? Bit of practice?"

Banga gave an exaggerated eye-roll.

"Well, we'll have more to occupy us when that poncy navigator gets here," the female one continued.

"That's if he doesn't get lost," the other said.

"Enna!" she retorted. "Useless knobs. Soft as saroo. All that intellectualizing ... Couldn't hold a weapon if it were charmed in place."

Abruptly, their conversation ceased. Ariben sensed Shen's approach and winced in annoyance. First the guards - then the cook? This was supposed to be a time when the stores were traffic-free.

Shen stopped. "Excuse me?" he said firmly.

The sentries stepped aside. He pushed through the door flap and looked right at the two intruders despite their careful screens.

Ariben held his finger to his lips and shook his head.

Shen sighed. "Are you two going to take all day?" he snapped. "I need that box of dried fish now, not next week!"

"Sorry," Banga's eyebrows shot skyward. "Having trouble locating ..."

"Over there by the weipa." Shen said imperiously. He pointed at a box, then beckoned for them to leave with him. "Do I have to do everything myself?"

They retrieved the dried fish and hurried to the door.

A burly arm barred their exit.

"What's this?" The Ashik glared at the Uri'madu. "Where'd you come from?"

Her companion looked them up and down. "What's going on?"

Shen frowned. "What do you mean? I need these stores."

"And you sent two of the Uri'madu?"

Ariben stepped between Shen and the Ashik, drew himself up to his full height and looked the commander in the eye. With a small whisper, he made his Mark glow – just a little. "Who I choose to do favors for is up to me," he said sharply. "Stand aside."

After a fractional wait, The Ashik bowed.

"Your pardon."

"Your pardon ... lord Shamkarun Ariben of Leth!" Ariben corrected.

"Of course, sir. My apologies, lord Shamkarun."

Ariben gave an arrogant snort, but as he and Banga followed Shen toward the kitchens it took effort for him not to look back.

Thanks, he said to Shen. *I don't like Ashik.*

They don't get in the way too much, Shen said, *not yet at least, but Olatu's a bit suspicious about the stores - don't ask me why, but he thinks there should be more there than there is.*

Banga rolled his eyes. *Faythans. I'll bet he knows how much each grain of Talemgal's worth. Every Breathless tea-leaf.*

As they neared the kitchens, Shen beckoned them aside. He put his hand in his pocket, pulled out a rounded green stone, murmured at it then put it back into hiding. Ariben felt a tight screen snap into place.

"It's alright to speak now," Shen said quietly, "but keep it down. What have you got and why? It's not just Faythans who notice such things."

Ariben sighed. "Two bags of little attar, one talemgal, some kanth, some dar, a box of dried kreth, and one of dried fish … two now."

"Stocking up for when the Blessings come," said Banga. "It'll damn near double our contingent."

"Why not just ask?"

"Olatu told us to fuck-off - not in those exact words of course," Banga replied.

Shen shook his head. "Even I could've told you the answer there. What I meant was, why not ask me?"

Ariben winced a little. "Huldar - wouldn't want to compromise you."

"Mothers with babies need food," Banga added quickly. "And strangely, Casco didn't account for that in his original estimates."

Shen gave an exasperated huff and pictured Tashel for them - "I'm just as invested as you are."

"He wouldn't want you to take the blame …"

"… The obvious suspect, an all," Banga added.

"So, this wasn't Huldar's idea?"

"Of course, it was," Ariben retorted. "He's not stupid - just nice."

"We're just - covering for him. If you need anything returned …" Banga added doubtfully.

Shen shook his head. "Keep the extra fish." With a whisper, the screen dissolved. They followed him into a tent abustle with preparations for the lunch menu. "Lucky you were passing," Shen said for benefit of the staff. He went to a shelf in the spice-larder, removed a tall jar of galano twigs, and with a short bow, presented it to Ariben. "This is for Tam. Lady Andel's favorite. He'll be pleased I remembered."

"Of course," Ariben said. "I'll be sure to give it to him."

They turned to take their leave, but as they headed up the bank towards the portal, Ariben's neck began to prickle. He glanced Banga's way.

The spinner shrugged, but his eyes were wary.

"Good of Shen to share this galano with us," Ariben said casually.

"Song shared ..."

Ariben nodded. "Shamkarun Huldar will be pleased."

"Casco, you mean."

"Huldar will be pleased because Casco is pleased because Sari is!" Ariben retorted.

"And Ubaid." Banga nodded. "Galano is good for pregnancy, or so I heard."

"No wonder we'd run out then."

They paused by the portal.

"Central base-camp?" said Banga.

Ariben inclined his head.

Although the unknown viewer's surveillance was broken as they stepped through, the feeling of being watched soon resumed. Ariben waved his hand as if chasing flies away. "Nuisance," he muttered.

Banga produced a sheaf of papers tied with a brown ribbon - Calen's signature color. "Better not forget to leave these for Lady Calen. She said she was almost out." His tone was very deliberate.

Ariben nodded and replied in a clear voice, "Leave them in the box by the door. Clickers will get them otherwise."

Banga waved the parcel slowly in the air before stowing it in the box outside Calen's tent.

Ariben stifled a grin.

Abruptly, the prickle at the back of their necks stopped.

"An Ashik feel to that little episode," Banga suggested. "Clumsy."

"Well it certainly wasn't Daric," Ariben replied. "If it was him, we'd never have known."

Where to first?

Pick up the rest of the stuff and take it to Casco at Eastern. He'll sort it from there.

Banga grinned. *Just in time for dinner!*

SMALL MEETINGS

Andel stood on the beach of a lonely island and stared at the seemingly endless expanse of the Southern Ocean. A bleak southerly slid unimpeded over the icy shore. Foam shredded from ranks of angry waves. She hugged her heavy coat around her and peered at the blue/green divide of the horizon, trying to decipher where the sea ended and the skies began, but the wind and cold soon became too much. Behind the nearby headland, she settled in a sheltered hollow and waited.

She considered the portal she'd arrived through, one made by Daric Enna as part of his own secret network. Only the vaguest of shimmers gave its presence away. Not even Huldar knew where she was. The thought made her somewhat nervous. Then her baby kicked again and she smiled.

Lively one! she said gently.

As taught by Ubaid, she opened a delicate line of communication and shared the sensation of being in the chill cove and the booming reverberation of the huge, grey waves.

Her baby lay quiescent while her evolving senses absorbed the outer world as filtered through her mother's mind. Whether she could make sense of it didn't seem to matter, only the feeling of inclusion and affirmation of love.

Had her own mother had communicated with her in the same way. Of the other Blessed, only Malena had said so, but what she shared seemed more esoteric - the vibration of things - a musical sense of place. Andel had to admit she struggled to understand. Maybe it was the natural navigator's most basic understanding of the world around them. Whatever it was, the process seemed to help Malena accept her impending motherhood, and even enjoy it.

Finally, Daric let her know he'd arrived.

She lifted her head and squinted briefly into the gale. Farsight seemed a better option. Despite several layers of clothing, Daric negotiated the stony rubble with usual confidence, although the set of his shoulders was low. His haze was as unreadable as ever, but she didn't need to see his eyes to know the sadness in him.

Malena will be here soon, he said.

Malena's coming? she replied. She made room as he rounded the corner. All hint of melancholy was gone, except that she knew it remained. How deep it went was anyone's guess. She gave him an encouraging smile. The issue was between himself and Casco, and all she could do was love them both for who they were - whoever they were.

What's this all about? she asked.

Sorry for the secrecy – I know you think it's just second nature to me, and it is, but in this case ...

Whisper secrets to the breeze, she said, *and the grasses sway in time.*

He raised his brows in salute. ... *Best be careful, then. There's no shortage of breeze here.*

From the Works of Kaskarudjan Imahtara, she said. *Huldar gave me her book – seems so long ago now.*

He returned her smile, but it only seemed to accentuate the sadness in him. *The only way to keep something to yourself is to forget that you know,* he said. *A knack I've developed over the years.*

He looked out to sea. "Don't feel sorry for me, lady Andel. I've done terrible things."

"Daric –" she paused to consider her words. "What you say is most likely true, but we, the Uri'madu – you're one of us now."

He nodded unconvincingly.

"I ... well I don't know if you know," she started, "or even if you're interested, but I've done things too." An image of her mother flitted close to the surface. As always, it was accompanied by a stab of intense grief.

He turned, and his expression invited her to continue.

"For a long time, I couldn't cope." She raised her shoulders. "The person who had captured us, held my mother to ransom, he shouldn't have done it, but I didn't think Huldar could ever forgive me, or even look at me without thinking of the terrible thing I'd done. The screams – they still echo in my mind. I didn't know how I'd done it and I was so afraid that somehow, I would do it to him too. For a while, I couldn't even bring myself to touch him … but, of course, I was wrong."

I knew him, Daric whispered.

She looked into his eyes and he opened to her, just a little. The enormity of guilt and grief contained in his slight and elegant body - even just that glimpse, was terrifying.

He saw her flinch and his veils snapped shut. His face attempted a more formal neutrality, but his hands clenched with the effort.

"You knew him?"

"We were rivals - of a sort. When he vanished, I was already reconsidering my future."

"Rivals?"

"He was not a good person, Lady Andel. Neither was/*am* I."

She took deep breaths and counted their release as Ubaid had showed her. When the nausea subsided, she pushed on. "What I was going to say, and I'm sorry if … anyway - things had to change - I knew that - but it was not him I had to forgive, nor did I have to rationalize events that led up to what I did. I had to forgive myself."

He shook his head. "I doubt that's possible, for me, at least - or even desirable."

"Casco knew who you were," she said. "I'm sure he wouldn't be so …"

"Callous? Insensitive?" One corner of his mouth lifted. "He's not. He's the best person I know." He turned to look out to sea again. "I've never been in love before … I don't know how I'm supposed to behave, or even what it means." When he returned to her, there were tears in his eyes. "It's this planet - the isolation. It's changed me." He gave a crooked smile. "Forced to spend time with myself." He stared into the distance. "And that - "

"Can be hard," she finished for him. "Don't give up. I know he loves you. You'll find …" she stopped as he turned sharply toward the portal. When he looked back, he was his normal self, the mask complete; poised and urbane.

Malena strode across the dry reef. "Thank you Daric," she said, "Sorry about the location, but you'll understand when I show you what I've found." She beckoned with her hand and set off across the island, agile as if her belly hadn't swelled at all.

After a mile or so, she paused to give Andel time to catch up. "It's the training," she said. "One or two hours every day. You're welcome to join us."

"Martial arts?" Andel almost laughed. "I wouldn't know where to start!"

Malena glanced Daric's way. "Haven't seen you in action the last few weeks."

"Busy making bolt-holes for you lot." He waved his hand forward. "Care to show us why we're here?"

The navigator turned her head like a bird searching for prey, then set off again, a little slower this time.

Moving with care over rocks and gravel, Andel tried to keep her labored breathing quiet. Eventually they came to a weather-worn natural platform, crisscrossed with pink quartz seams. She wondered what other minerals were nearby.

Malena stood center stage, opened her arms and turned on the spot. "Can you feel it?"

Daric looked around. "I can feel … something."

"Open your mind, little Enna … it's a Djan'rū, the largest on the planet."

With knowledge came perception, and suddenly Andel could see the powerful distortion in the planet's energies.

"Brilliant!" Daric jumped up beside Malena and peered slowly skyward. "And the Host don't know?"

"I only found it by accident," Malena assured him. "And as you might guess, for much of Went's cycle, it's either covered with ice or underwater - which is why it's been hidden 'til now."

"It's beautiful," said Andel.

Malena's buoyancy faded. She stroked her swollen belly. "Of course, sea-level may have risen by the time we can get someone to use it, although we might still be able to wade … But the whole thing's useless with no one to tune it - or operate it."

"Do you really think it will come to that?"

"I do," Daric said, "and so does Huldar."

Malena nodded. "I've met Ishät Ashik, and his Chosen." She shuddered. "Ruthless, the pair of them. If he decides he doesn't want anyone to know about us - and I'm sure he will." She turned to look Andel in the eye. "No one will leave here alive."

Andel's mind skipped for alternatives. "But the navigator, Shamkarun Kandät Enna - he's the Empress' uncle, and he'll know."

"Know what? That we're all dead? What of it? New planet, incomplete studies, anything could have happened." She shook her head. "Daric's right. We have to be prepared to survive on our own, and the fewer who know where we are and what we're doing, the more likely we'll be to see the Realm again."

"But the freeze ..."

"That's why we've asked you here," said Daric. "To brainstorm while we're beyond the range of prying minds."

"Can you find us a cave?" Malena said hopefully. "Ideally a deep one with geo-thermal heating. Somewhere along this ancient portal-line we're on now. Somewhere we might stay alive for the next seven years or so. It's a shame Radätel is no longer with us. As a lightsinger, he would've known how to make it bright enough to grow food. As it is, we'll have to improvise as best we can."

"Casco knows something of the lightsinger's craft," Daric said. "Radätel was teaching him."

Andel looked around. "A thermal cave ... with soil?"

"Preferably."

"There's no hope of rescue?"

"If we can get a message to someone during the communications window, there's a chance. But we have to plan ahead. It'll be too late once the worst has happened, especially with a herd of little ones to care for."

She peered at the unforgiving landscape. They'd had more than enough taste of what the planet, even partially frozen, would be like. Then a memory came of herself and Casco, the very first time they'd linked minds. "I know of one place," she said. "But it's nowhere near here. It's on the Central continent."

Malena seemed disappointed. "Anywhere else?"

Daric smiled. "No, it's a good start. They'll never suspect we'd be so close by, especially if we lead them to search elsewhere, and if there's scope for a portal to this place - with one, or two steps at most ..."

Andel showed them what she and Casco had seen on the volcano's flank, the first time she'd scryed in that way. It seemed so long ago. She'd linked with Casco's strength, and something of his essence came through with the memory.

Daric's pang of loss was masterfully contained.

"Leave it with me," he said. "I'll let you know when we're ready to explore."

Another cave, she thought, another lava tube, just like the one where she'd lost her brother. Was this coincidence? Was it truly their only chance at survival? "What about the Djan'rū at Central base-camp?" she suggested. "Couldn't someone rescue us from there?"

"Unlikely," said Malena. "As far as they know, it's the only other option, and they don't have to look far to see it. Imagine getting the Uri'madu and their Blessings organized and loaded without anyone noticing?"

She looked around. Her spirit fell.

"If we could tune it, if we could somehow keep it hidden," Malena said. "... If, if, if! The structure wouldn't even have to be finalized, just poised and ready to tie in - I'm sure it could be done. But I'm useless now." She looked down at her belly. "I can't sing a coherent note."

"I'll sing it," Daric said quietly. "Join with me. Show me. Use my voice the same as Alis did when she healed you."

Malena studied him. "Join?" She gave a short laugh. "I should trust you?"

"We sang the domed windows together," he said reasonably.

"Granted - but that was only surface interaction. If you want this Djan'rū sung …"

"Why can't Huldar do it?" Andel said. "He developed the one at Central."

"And did a good job," Malena said, "- for a non-navigator. But this is different, Andel," she said kindly. "The energies involved are too great. And Huldar is too precious to us. Without him we'd be lost. Daric and I, on the other hand …"

"How can you say that?!";

"So, you'll do it?" Daric said.

Malena shook her head. "Against my better judgement."

"We would be lost without you, too, Daric. Without either of you," Andel insisted. "You've been Blessed, Malena. It's not a death sentence."

"It might be if we can't keep this work away from prying eyes," Daric reminded her.

Her stomach fluttered. "I have an idea about that," she said slowly. "The structure of calcite contains filaments. I was wondering if they could be refined and woven …"

Daric tilted his head. "An invisible fabric?"

Andel nodded. "Yes, and if the strands could be combined with nacrite, I believe such a material could also be impervious to psychic emanation."

"Nacrite?"

"Huldar and I believe it to be the reason we can't communicate with the outer Realm."

Malena's face twisted as if she struggled to understand. "Nacrite? It's awesome in swords, but ..."

"Every time some escapes it floats into the upper atmosphere." Andel raised her hand and rubbed thumb against fingers before opening it to the sky. "What if it breaks up into smaller and smaller pieces - becomes a dust?"

"Ah!" said Daric. "I see where this is going - a most intriguing hypothesis. And ... Ariben!"

"Ariben?" Malena showed fresh, slightly guarded, puzzlement.

"Substrate specialist. Absolute genius. You knew that didn't you?" He returned to Andel. "If we could make your idea work," he said excitedly, "think of the applications, especially when the babies come." He looked at their bellies. "We have to get onto this right away."

"What about my Djan'rū?" Malena said. "Surely my idea is more important?"

"That too," he said.

"A secret blanket?" she said scathingly. "A charm - a feat that may or may not be accomplished? This," she waved her hands at the bubble of energies, "we know can be done. This could be our means of escape. There'll be no need for invisibility, no matter how cleverly achieved!"

"I beg to differ." Daric started back toward the beach without waiting for them to follow. Malena soon caught up, but as before, Andel picked her way carefully. Her companions' presence receded, and her buoyancy too.

Alone again, she thought sadly to herself. *I'm the one who found the nacrite. I'm the reason the miners rushed in. It's me they could do without. This whole thing is my fault.*

As if they'd heard, Daric and Malena stopped.

Daric hurried back. "I'm sorry, Lady Andel. Enthusiasm - new ideas - my head is spinning. Again! It's this planet. I don't think I've ever learned so much in so short a time."

Malena smiled and held out her hand. "And now I've agreed to let him help me, I don't want the slippery kalla getting away."

They started for the portal again.

"We should begin work on the calcite cloak immediately," Daric said. "If it can be done, and we can be reliably hidden, singing the Djan'rū and hiding its location will be much, much easier."

Agreed, said Malena reluctantly. "I suppose it won't take more than a few days to get this site ready for action." She looked at Daric. "Maybe you could turn into a navigator as well? Get us off this Breathless rock before anyone gets a chance to kill us."

"Not much chance of that, I'm afraid. My sister's the one. I have no calling."

"Perhaps, although Kandät Enna has a theory that navigation, at least in its most basic form, can be learned by rote. If that's the case, anyone powerful enough could make short journeys; say between Giahn and Parsay, or Mecca even, then to New Belhadi and the Faythan group. Faythans like that idea of course! They could undercut us at last," she snorted. "Dissolve the Maatu monopoly and replace it with their own. Needless to say, the Guild has discouraged Kandät's research quite vigorously."

"As far as the research here and the new Djan'rū, what do you want me to do?" said Andel.

"When the time comes, we'll need you to keep watch while we work. In the meantime, tell no one what we have planned," said Daric. "Not even Huldar."

"I'll try," she said, but the thought of keeping things from him was a difficult one.

Those who don't know can't be forced to tell, Daric said to her. *He and I talked about this. Our safety – his family's safety – is what matters most.*

After they'd stepped back to the Eastern Continent and gone their separate ways, Daric's plight and the darkness she'd glimpsed inside him wouldn't leave her. Who was he – really? Could anyone ever know? But then another saying came to mind … *Enlightenment comes when darkness is realized and becomes a conscious choice …*

ARIEN LETH

The navigator's last chord chimed and the envelope dissolved to reveal the bays at Giahn's Imperial City. Arien Leth's stomach churned - his usual response to the end of an interplanetary journey, but this time the nausea didn't fade with the sound.

Rumours of the God-Emperor's increasingly uncertain temper didn't help - every story seemed more troubling than the last.

He waited for his head to stop spinning.

The Mark on his back itched.

In a neighbouring bay, another chord chimed.

At last he felt able to take a dignified first step, and gave the navigator a nod.

The tall Maatu bowed politely in return. "Welcome to Giahn, Lord Leth," he said, his voice still full of the sound of the stars. "Breath smile on your endeavours."

Arien nodded again and with a brusque turn, headed for a beautifully worked door, the private entrance to the inner sanctum of the Bays. He knew it to be fashioned from a single seed-pod, the fruit of the giant Kahlian momoa tree. It had been the gift of House Leth to the navigator's guild during the last major renovations … it must be five thousand years ago now – during the time of his father.

It was a short walk to the entrance, but with every step he could feel the navigator's measured gaze against his back.

His palm pressed the cool metal of the key-plate, worn from how many similar pressings? It tingled to his touch and the door hissed open. To him, he grand dimensions of the corridor beyond had always seemed a tad pretentious, but the decorative carvings, images of fauna and flora so dear to Leth, were certainly beautiful.

He slowed as a familiar mind made contact.

Arien?

Pieru, my friend, he replied. *Any news?*

Since yesterday? The Guild Lord gave a sour laugh. *How could there be?*

Arien continued down the lofty hallway. *So Breathlessly convenient,* he returned sourly.

A mix of sarcasm, worry and friendship flowed back to him. *Take care with Ishät, Arien. His moods are unpredictable.*

So I've heard, he replied. *My mother was Ashik. I'm prepared for the worst.* He gave a sour grunt. *In a way, we're kin.* But when Pieru's image of Tiamät incarnate came to him, his steps slowed to a halt. The tentacles' slick skin glimmered. Eyes like polished stone beads glowed with malice.

His complex expletive punched through their communication.

And this is first hand, Pieru assured him. *He does not want to discuss Went at all.*

Arien walked on again, each step an exercise in self-discipline, until he arrived at the courtyard door. *Well, he's going to have to talk about it,* he said firmly. Anxiety churned his guts, but he pushed it open with a decisive shove. Ishät Ashik must be faced. The issue of his people's safety must be addressed and resolved, Huldar's in particular, or what did it mean to be 'Sacred to Leth'?

In the centre of the courtyard, the ten golden tentacles that draped God-Emperor's personal portal seemed more like fanciful vines than lethal weapons. The song was a closely guarded secret, known only by Chosen House Leaders and direct members of the Imperial family. He straightened his coat and stepped through into an irregular octagonal antechamber. Each slightly skewed angle harboured an identical marble door. One had to know which exit led where. A mistake could prove embarrassing - or worse.

Four flat-eyed Ashik guards snapped to attention.

Since when was this room guarded? he thought to himself.

A fine, silvery vein in the rock oriented him. He chose the second to the left. Behind it, a featureless corridor led to a pair of tall grey doors with a pearly sheen. He gave them a determined glare, then began the long walk down to the God-Emperor's room of state.

The doors opened as he neared them and Tsemkarun Delemät Ashik strode toward him.

Arien caught a momentary glimpse of Ishät Ashik's burly form illuminated by a ray of golden sunlight and fought the temptation to sneer. Ishät had chosen his own brother to fill the military position traditionally held by House Maatu, though none dared mention their family ties - least of all, the thug himself.

Delemät gave a perfunctory nod as he strode past. The smell of him lingered, an aggressive mix of sweat and arrogance.

Arien caught the door on the back-swing and held it still for a few seconds before he stepped through. On the central dais, Ishät stood with his back turned, face and arms tilted toward a shaft of light from the domed roof high above. Golden walls gave the room a look of warmth, but the regal presence chilled.

He walked forward and made his most correct bow.

At length, the God-Emperor turned. His gaze held palpable antipathy. "My days are busy," he said flatly.

The taut rein on Arien's emotions stretched even thinner. "My lord, there has been no contact from my people on planet Went," he said evenly. "I have been in contact with the Explorer's Guild again upon my arrival here this morning. No reports have been received. None."

The emperor gave a miniscule frown.

"My lord," Arien pushed on, "You demanded Went's exploitation against my strongest opposition, its *immediate* exploitation. Millennia of protocol ignored. There was a reason for those restrictions. How can we know the dangers - the risks - without proper assessment?"

Ishät left the dais, strolled to one of the narrow windows that encircled the room and gazed beyond it, his demeanour unreadable.

Arien eyed his back, wary of the monster within.

The muscular shoulders shrugged. "Risk?" He turned. "I risk injury when I practice the sword." He assumed a fighter's stance, lips stretched into a faint sneer. Arien stepped back as he crabbed forward. His arms flailed in wild imaginary thrusts. With the most skilful of whispers, an ancient blade appeared in his hand. He tilted his head and peered coldly down its glinting edge, straight into Arien's eyes. "My sparring partner risks death, yet it happens." The sword vanished again into Qalān. The God-Emperor clapped his hands into the empty space with a flourish. "Worry about something that may never happen? As any *great* leader would know, sometimes gain outweighs all."

A bead of sweat prickled Arien's upper lip. What did this odd display mean? Was it a threat? It seemed like one - but so childish. Did the God-Emperor truly hold himself beyond the tenets of El?

As if sensing his disdain, Ishät's eyes turned flinty. The air at his back distorted.

Arien returned his cold gaze as calmly as he could.

"I have reason to believe your people are still alive," Ishät said at last. He tilted his head pointedly to the doors.

Arien held his ground. "Huldar, leader of my team, is titled Sacred to Leth. I have a right to know what's going on."

"A right?" Ishät's gaze narrowed. Tentacles shimmered into being.

"How do you know they live?" Arien said stubbornly. "The Guild's concern is genuine. No reports, no messages, no personal letters - yet you refuse to speak with them."

"You will address me as 'Your Imperial Highness'", Ishät snapped. The slow tilt of his head reminded Arien of a water-bird aiming at fish. As his tentacles gained substance, his already substantial figure seemed to grow with them.

Arien gazed stonily at the face framed by the writhing array and steeled himself for death. “Is that it your Imperial Highness? Threats? Your father … always treated us with utmost respect.”

“My father?” Ishät snarled. The Tsemkar on his forehead bloomed. Arien felt the iron spike of a thrust against his shields. The sign of Leth burned on his back, enacting his strongest protections.

Ishät narrowed his gaze. Perhaps he’d forgotten that Arien was himself half Ashik and well-schooled in defence.

The icy pressure receded. Arien’s heart beat loud in his chest.

“I have granted you this private audience,” Ishät said coldly, “yet you have given me nothing in return. If your insubordination continues, I will consider it treasonous. Measures will be taken against yourself and the House you embody.”

“Measures?” Arien shook his head. “These are the measures I respectfully request, your Imperial Highness. Please, send another navigator to Went immediately to ascertain the health and wellbeing of my personnel.”

Ishät minced closer. Tentacles writhed in a halo about him. “This is your last chance.”

“Measures?” Arien said hotly. “Leth provides Giahn with eighty-seven percent of its food, your Imperial Highness. Try that for measures.”

For a split second, Arien knew he had gone too far. His cry was at the ready. He would join his wife, safe in the Breath at last …

The God-Emperor fixed him in a life-shredding glare. Every tentacle froze, every head aimed at him. Ishät's mouth twitched, his mark flared. But the attack faltered. Instead, he stalked back to his preferred window and held onto the sill as if to steady himself. His shoulders shrugged beneath their seething load as if the movement might shed them. Slowly, the tentacles faded, seeming to slide spine-ward as they did so.

When at last he turned, the fire in his yellow eyes was raw.

"Leth would hold me to ransom?" he hissed. "Threaten me? I am El's Chosen!"

"No, Imperial Highness, of course not," Arien said. "I merely state the fact that Leth cares very greatly for Giahn and its people."

"But not for me?"

"Our personal differences are meaningless, your highness. Governance of House Leth is my concern. My greatest duty." Arien took a breath and savoured its cool pressure beneath his ribs. He continued in his most reasonable tones, "Please, your Imperial Highness, all I ask is that you send a second navigator to Went. Then I will get my reports and know that my people are well. That is all I ask."

Arien kept his eyes fixed straight ahead as the God-Emperor left the sill. He held his breath as he circled behind him. The royal footsteps slowed. Arien's Mark burned. Ishät's attention crawled over him like a thousand rustling snakes. If Arien wished to live, he knew his psychic emissions must be kept utterly devoid of fear or weakness.

At last the steps continued. The sensation of snakes receded.

The Royal personage came back into view, paused again, and glanced up to where the sun would be in the sky as if to remind himself of the time. "Arien Leth, I hear your concerns," he said formally. "I will inform you in due course of my decision."

He flicked his fingers toward the doors.

Arien bowed, but despite this apparent change in his demenour, it was hard for him to turn his back on the God-Emperor to take his leave.

Ishät held The Leth in his mind's eye until he stepped through the state portal and was gone.

His thoughts seethed … but his wife's rosy glow rested in his mind like a tonic. She didn't care if they'd cheated, only that her longed-for second blessing had occurred.

Gradually, his emotions calmed. The jangle of Tiamat receded. Had they cheated? Of course not, he answered himself. El would not have blessed if it were.

He thought again of Arien and smiled to himself. As it turned out, he already had plans to send someone back to Went, but not for the reasons Leth demanded. Starve them all, would he? Everyone had a breaking point. Swift action now would negate the Lethian issue nicely.

Delemät! he called, and with the contact sent a detailed list of instructions.

He smiled again to think of his glorious future. Leth would be brought under control, the Went issue silenced forever, and Maatu - Breath-forsaken Maatu, would be destroyed. He almost laughed aloud.

However Manu Maatu, that wily diplomat, had couched it; when House Maatu had withdrawn its services, it had seemed the ultimate insult. Millennia of protocol ignored! What was Arien thinking? HE was the only protocol, him and only him. He'd sworn vengeance, and vengeance he would have. Now his own Clan Ashik were his military advisors and Delemät, his brother, was hungry for his approval.

He imagined Manu Maatu moralising at him in the same way he'd moralised at the last God-Emperor and fingers flapped his fingers against his thumbs in imitation of empty talk. Truly, the Maatu defection had been Breath's gift.

He imagined the fanfare and fuss when he paraded his new daughter, the Second of Tiamät, the new Ashik princess. And when the pregnancy was announced he could bask in the empire's belief of El's approval - so long as he took steps now to ensure their secret was safe. And who knew? If El still existed, if he or Asheru even had time to look, maybe they *had* planned it this way.

TROUBLE WITH QALĀN

Deep beneath the equatorial desert of Went's Eastern Continent, lines of energy streamed as they had since time immemorial. Older paths lay buried and forgotten, while, in accordance with their own slow ecological dance, younger currents formed and flowed. Always, the surface was fed. Eons of change, the rise and fall of ice and oceans, the gradual shift of the crust itself meant little to them. Even the Great Cataclysm had barely ruffled their ways.

Occasionally, circumstance gave older streams access to the sunlight again, and gradually, the dim currents brightened. But despite being deprived of the sun's energy for eons, their power had grown, and when an upstart entity sought to use them as it had their, younger, weaker scions, they resisted. Trust had been broken; the mother of all unsettled. Nothing the visitors had yet offered was enough - except perhaps another taste of their own unique and novel life-force. 1 … 2 … 3 … 4 … It had tried calling them. The beings heard, but foolishly, none listened …

On the desert's surface, first light touched Huldar's broad-brimmed hat. Within his crouched and motionless body, a delicate battle raged. As fast as he extricated himself from one ravenous barrage, another coil of energy would trap him. Should he call to the planet for help? ... but that held dangers of its own. Finally, he found it, the last slim tendril of contact with his body, and the race was over. At last, he breathed a conscious lungful of air. Its searing dryness burnt his nostrils - but he'd rather that - infinitely so - than the eternal white fog of Qalān.

He lifted his hands from the ground and stretched to ease cramped muscles. Did patterns in the imprint of gravel on his palms have esoteric meaning?

This branch of the ancient system had no links to any younger ones already in use - perfect for the hideout project. He and Daric had engineered two gates into the elder streams; The first to the mine for the rescue of Malena, and one since, to a cavern on an island in the Southern Archipelago. The first had been tricky, the second even more-so. He'd been a fool to think he could do this on his own, but at least now he better understood the dangers.

On their first trip to Went he'd discovered a decayed portal leading to the beach of the Bel Nishani. It had initially been forced, and at the time his thoughts had been scathing. But now? Perhaps its maker had encountered similar opposition and used brute power as an only option.

The thought saddened him. The planet had hinted Qalān had life of its own, of sorts. He believed the 'counting' to be evidence of the planet's unease. Since the mine collapse there had been no further incidents, but perhaps the difficulty they were experiencing with portal travel in general was a new level of protest. If so, these older currents may prove unusable.

He reached out to Daric. *How busy are you?*

Daric's retort barely missed a beat. *You gave me this schedule yourself.*

The schedule's changed.

He received a brief sense of frustration, but predictably, the Enna's curiosity won. Huldar gave a lop-sided grin. The wiliest of assassins so easily lured by a new puzzle? Was this a symptom of their growing trust, or had be found Daric's weakness at last? Perhaps both.

The long shadows of day-break shortened. He took off his hat and sweat soaked hair cooled with exposure to the breeze. Around him, the table-flat landscape was punctuated by occasional low mesas. Coarse red gravel extended to the horizon on all sides. The only vegetation was the occasional stick-like plant with small, tough leaves, and some tussocks he knew were alive but appeared as if long dead. By midday, the baking heat would be unbearable and by night, the cold was so stiff you could hear the stones cracking.

Daric stepped into view, a small dark shape in the distance, and started his way. *Lovely day for it.*

Thanks, for coming, Huldar said. *I could use your help.*

I missed morning tea for this. It'd better be good!

"Take a look here," Huldar said as he got closer. "What do you think?"

Daric tilted his head and studied the energies. "Another primeval system?"

"Two potential exits interest me greatly," Huldar replied. "One leads to another underground cavern - perfect for secret storage, or as an emergency base."

"Natural light?"

"No, but I glimpsed an underground lake. The cave is deep enough. Impossible to find from ground-level unless you knew its location. And as for annangi occupation - if Casco could manage the lighting, there's enough water to grow things and keep us going ... but let's hope it doesn't come to that."

"And the other exit?"

"Leads to the northern ice."

Daric's eyes narrowed - a slight reaction but telling.

"It would be irresponsible not to be prepared," Huldar said.

"And why do you need me?"

The strange knot of energy before them shimmered faintly. "I tried to negotiate a portal, but I couldn't control it." He shared a sense of the storm that had almost trapped him. "It was only that I've had some experience - "

Lind?

Yes. I made a range of anchor-points - he showed Daric the innovation that had no-doubt saved his life.

"You were fortunate to get out," Daric replied.

"An understatement." Huldar waved his hand at the innocuous-seeming knot. "You've a gift for understanding these ancient ways. I thought if we tried together - unless you want to have a go on your own?"

Daric gave a modest bow. "Your anchor-point system certainly evens the odds." Gravel crunched as he circled the site. He reached out as if to touch it, but of course, his hand passed right through. "I'll give it a try then - get a feel for what we're up against."

"Very well," Huldar said, "But with extreme caution, understand?"

Daric gave a scathing snort.

Huldar bottled a flash of irritation. Since his split with Casco, Daric's temper had been uncertain, but to mention it only made things worse.

With little aplomb, the slight Enna seated himself cross-legged and placed his hands in contact with the ground. At first, after he'd closed his eyes. there was no external sign of strain, but gradually, his breath-rate increased. His body began to shudder. His teeth bared in an slow grimace.

Daric! Huldar pushed through the light bond they'd maintained and found his collaborator caught in a maelstrom of conflicting forces, but from this perspective, he could see what was happening far more clearly.

Push here, he said, *then release … that's it …*

In the next breath, Daric blinked up at Huldar, eyes wild. "Not quite what I expected." Sweat dripped from his face. He glanced northward. "But you're right. We need that link."

Huldar hesitated before saying, "I know you and Casco are having difficulties, but I think we need him here as well. He is the only other with experience in dealing with extreme Qalān … except Andel, of course. But I can't subject her to such trauma - not now."

"Of course." Daric dabbed at his face with a fine white cloth, "… And thank you for your sensitivity."

Huldar nodded. "I don't doubt your professionalism - or Casco's." Perspiration trickled down his own back. "I'll tell him what's going on. Let's regroup here this evening. It's too hot to concentrate now and only getting worse. Six after midday?"

Daric bowed. "At dusk, then. I look forward to the challenge."

Their feet crunched steadily as they retraced their steps toward the existing portal.

"There is something else we need to do," Huldar said. "Andel has asked for a portal to the southern fjords, but as you know, Qalān is moody these days. Come with me while I work?"

"Huh!" his companion retorted. "Rather be with you than that calcite crew any day."

"Oh?" Huldar glanced his way.

"Somehow, I offended their supervisor."

Daric's image of the Cantori miner jogged Huldar's memory. She was the one Daric had terrified in the mess-hall.

Daric snorted. "Hates me."

"Probably still has nightmares," Huldar said. "One thing you learn with life in a closed community - sins always come back to bite you."

At six after midday, Huldar and Casco stepped onto the southern desert to find Daric already waiting.

Casco's haze shivered - his only sign of unease.

Rough stones crunched as they walked.

Casco kept his gaze on the desert floor. *It's like walking on a cooker!* he said at last.

Huldar closed his eyes to enjoy the cool as a southerly air-stream washed their backs. Conditions were more bearable than they might have been.

"How was your first session with Sari and Ubaid?" he asked.

"Glad we were on our own," Casco said at last. "That style of linkage … it's very deep. Some things …" He turned to Huldar. "Sari has suffered in her past. I had no idea how much. I feel … ashamed for not going to her - that she had to ask for my support." He glanced ahead to his estranged lover. "Daric was right - and you." *None of us are perfect.*

Huldar sighed in agreement. "That's why trust is so important."

"Except Olatu, of course."

"Olatu?"

"He's perfection personified - isn't he?"

Huldar grinned. "Of course!"

Balls of spindly grass rolled ahead, pushed by the breeze. Casco watched them pass, wrapped again in silence.

"Will you be alright?" Huldar asked.

A grimace was his only reply.

Daric stood, carefully casual, veil smoothed to perfection. "Casco," he nodded.

"Daric." Casco nodded in return. Almost, their eyes met.

Daric turned to Huldar. "What is it you want me to do?"

"I was explaining our idea to Casco on the way here," Huldar said. "Daric, if you and I join forces to wrestle this old monster, while Casco manages the anchors and watches our backs? We'll try the portal to the north first." He looked at them both. "Any questions?"

"Just one," Daric said.

"Share it," Huldar offered a hand to each of them. "We'll have to be linked for the process anyway."

Casco nodded brusquely.

Hesitantly, he and Daric closed the circle.

Huldar took a long, slow breath and felt the others do the same. Daric's presence swirled through his mind with a series of arcane images. *I was thinking, if you tie this – and this here, Casco's link will retain its strength, but be more tenacious.*

Casco?

I heard.

Wouldn't want to lose you Daric said. … *Either of you,* he added softly.

Casco's reaction was minimal, but Huldar knew him well. Tensions flared then eased. Daric's adjustments were made. Then, with a tacit nod, battle was joined.

The ancient network tore at them as if it had been waiting for the chance. *ONE,* it shrieked. *TWO, THREE* … Memories of Lind flooded in, distorted and cruel. The shock was overwhelming. Like rapacious roots of a giant tree, rogue energy tore at their psyches. It took their combined power to still their minds against it and together, they waited out the initial attack. Then with Casco firm at their backs, Huldar led Daric deeper.

A history of tectonic violence shook them.

We are not that, Huldar explained.

Melodious sound wove through their senses and Huldar recognized the song of the Bel Nishani. It ended sharply, and a sense of outrage replaced it. The lines of force firmed their grip.

We did not do that, Huldar projected his own horror at what Duvät Gok had done. *Not all of my species are bad.*

A terrible hunger lurked like a shadowy predator ready to pounce at the slightest chance. Again, images of Lind were forced on them; she known what Duvät had done, she'd seen the eyes, those precious souls, and approved of their taking.

It is our intent to rectify, Daric put forward, strong yet humble. *But we need your help …*

Primal forces swirled as if confused. Cautiously, the annangi showed what they wanted and why.

In silence, they waited. Without warning, resistance crumbled. They were shown two shiny new gates already completed and ready for use, but for their use only.

Huldar directed Daric to learn the key to the northern one while he tackled the one in the underground cavern. When each note had been fixed to memory with correct timbre and cadence, he reached back to Casco's firm handgrip, and his eyes blinked open.

The last rays of sunset seemed over-bright.

Daric returned soon after, tired but elated. *As simple as that! It knew what we wanted. How can that be?*

Memories of Lind? Huldar looked at the ground beneath them. Just how much knowledge did the old flows contain?

Casco seemed shaken. *I didn't expect that.*

Huldar's sadness was tempered by fascination. Did all planets remember their past in such a way? Could such histories be accessed? His thoughts were broken when Daric gave a mischievous grin and envisaged the north gate.

The north's still frozen! The gate may well be under ice.

Better not be if we're going to use it in a few weeks. You saw it. It's perfectly safe, Daric pleaded.

Huldar shook his head. *I've been caught out there before. If we get trapped there's no rescue. But what do you think, Casco? The cavern?*

And who's going to rescue us from there? Casco retorted. *No one will know where we are. That's the whole idea.*

They looked at each other.

"Good point," Daric admitted.

Casco rolled his eyes. With a simple movement, he hefted a globe from Qalān and breathed a whisper onto its surface. Long shadows coalesced around them. "Are we explorers or not?" he said. *Lead on!*

Huldar sang, ready to bounce them straight back if the step didn't work as expected. The last note echoed through vaulted walls. Casco wafted his globe higher to reveal an enormous space. Deep silence pressed on their ears. There was only the sound of their breathing and the slow plink, plink of dripping water. Then, high above, glowing pin-points began to bloom.

Dim the globe, Huldar whispered excitedly.

They watched entranced as the first few bright dots multiplied into a galaxy. Amorphous blobs oozed across fields of stars like faint green clouds. Yellow filaments fanned, flower-like, from the walls, while among them, small creatures became visible as a moving array of flashing colors. There was no sign of wings, they seemed to float without effort.

Sensing a surge of emotion, Huldar turned to Daric and was surprised to see tears on the assassin's face.

It's so beautiful, he wept. *And I – am unworthy.*

Unworthy?

The lithe archangel stepped away and stared upward, pillar-like. He seemed unable to completely mask his feelings.

Unworthy? Casco repeated hotly.

You of all people know I am, Daric cried hopelessly.

Huldar hurried to give the two space, but couldn't easily extricate himself from their psychic link.

I can never escape, Daric continued. *I am myself. Nothing I've done can be changed.*

No, it can't. Not ever! Casco turned on him, fists clenched. *But you can reflect and learn. You are amazing. More intelligent than anyone has a right to be, and caring and perceptive and funny, and with all that locked inside you, weighed down under all that darkness, no wonder you struggle!*

I am evil. How can you even look at me.

The globe stationed itself above them.

Look at you? Casco shook his head. "Look at you?"

Flashing creatures startled at the sound of his anger. Waving tendrils sucked themselves in.

Casco gave a look of exasperation and turned away. *How could you do those things? Why?!*

I love you …

You say you did it for me, Casco said, *but I never asked you to, how could you think I would want that?*

I didn't. I … didn't, not really. Please don't cry. … I won't bother you any more …

Casco rounded on him. *Bother me?* he yelled. *What the fuck? Do you love me or not?!*

Of course I do, I just thought, Daric shrugged hopelessly … *maybe you didn't. Not anymore.*

I said you could cook for yourself. I didn't say I wasn't coming back.

Huldar wandered to the edge of the light and tried not to listen. Beyond the distant edge of glowing creatures – the edge of the lover's anguish – lay darkness so complete even archangel eyes could not penetrate. He wished Andel was here, then they could find their way to the underground lake. Her powers of divination were so well developed she didn't need light to see a path. But as Casco and Daric's anger was spent, slowly the bioluminescent creatures reignited and the cave's features were illuminated in a soft blue glow.

The globe gave a lurch towards him.

"Lake?" Casco said. "Good idea."

Shadows moved and tilted as they wound their way along the cavern floor. Daric followed meekly. His haze was contained and neat as always, but the confusion in his eyes could not be masked.

"Love is the one true beacon," Huldar said softly.

Daric looked at him.

Something the planet said to me, he explained. "You are not unworthy to see wonders, Daric. El's Breath blows through all, and it has blown you here to be an integral part of the Uri'madu. I depend on you. We all do. The past is gone, a myth, and each day is new."

"Lady Andel again," Casco said.

Huldar nodded. "Maybe, or perhaps just her training. She has lit up my life in ways I couldn't imagine."

They dodged boulders and clambered over the slick surface of fallen stalactites until Huldar saw a faint, horizontal glimmer. "There it is!"

As they neared the dark shores, the water's surface rippled. High above, more cave-stars bloomed.

"Worlds within worlds." Casco mused.

"Maybe it's a metaphor," Daric said quietly. He turned to Casco. "Will you come back?"

"We'll see," Casco said.

Daric merely nodded, but Huldar noted his haze brighten.

"Take a sample of the water," he said to Casco. "Alis will soon tell us if it's safe to drink."

Casco got out his kit and selected a sample jar while Huldar scanned the lake for predators.

"All seems pretty clear, although I noticed a few larger presences out where the water deepens."

"I'll be quick," Casco assured him. He stepped into the shallows, swooped a vial through the water and held it to the light. "Looks nice and clear."

"Protozoans?"

Casco narrowed his eyes. "Some. Alis will know."

"If that was Olatu of Faytha's piss we'd be able to use it to light our way home," Daric said.

Casco's bark of laughter was cut short as a deep cough reverberated through the cave. Something splashed further out in the lake. He moved quickly from the shallows and stepped back from the edge.

Huldar sharpened his awareness and soon found the same large beast he'd sensed before, but now it seemed agitated. Several others cruised the waters behind it.

"Territorial, I think," he said. "That's the dominant one."

"Then there must be more," Casco said. "Best take our jar of piss and go home."

Huldar let Casco and Daric lead the way. He watched them share another laugh and was glad. Would the darkness in Daric be vanquished, he mused? It was impossible to know, but what soul had no potential for evil? There could be no light without dark. *We are what we are,* he said to himself. *Uri'madu.*

COME TO THE PARTY

Gento stepped from the new portal onto a rough slope and nodded to himself. The clearing was just as Huldar had described - a neat plateau about twenty paces across, sheltered from the prevailing westerlies - and the view! Beside him, Rosheen gazed through a lace-work of spindly branches to where the restless blue-grey ocean met the cloudless sky. Veils of white spume trailed on the wind as violent breakers curled and crashed against the headland. Debris lay in spaced tide marks up the exposed cliff-side. To the east, the sea curved around an ice-worn headland and transformed into the glassy stillness of a deep green fjord.

You going to light this or shall I?

He'd barely noticed Rosheen had left him, and turned to where she waited by the pyre of driftwood Cobar had already gathered. Her burgeoning stomach protruded from her fur-lined coat.

How beautiful you are, he said to her.

More cold than beautiful right now, she retorted, but she smiled and he was happy.

With his minds-eye he could see Cobar laboring up-slope with another load of wood and dry weed scavenged from the shingle far below. They had always been good friends, but since Rosheen's Blessing they had become as close as true brothers. Which of them was the father was impossible to tell, and ultimately unimportant. Both loved her. Both had sworn to stand by her and their Bless, whatever the outcome, for as long as need be, and a Rukh's word, once given, was unassailable.

Gento knelt by the shallow fire-pit and conjured a flame. With a little encouragement it tickled the material he'd given it, but when he added the dry sea-weed Cobar had collected from the shore, the whole pile exploded with a whoof. He leapt backward, putting himself between Rosheen and the flame.

What was that? Cobar asked.

Rosheen coughed and waved her hands to clear the smoke.

Accident with the fire! Gento replied. He turned to Rosheen. *Are you alright?*

He relaxed when she broke into a wide grin.

Seconds later, Cobar came over the rise. His eyes widened. "Lucky I'm the handsome one," he laughed.

Gento cringed as Rosheen reflected his image back to him. Ice-blue eyes stared from a dark mask of soot.

"It was that dark stuff," Gento pointed to a matted clump in the flotsam Cobar carried. "Better throw it away."

He cleaned the soot from his face and set about preparing Tam's kitchen. A short time later, they had a pit of coals glowing at just the right intensity, several rocks heated and a broad trestle erected nearby.

Cobar shared the idea of hiding a handful of the explosive weed in the kitchen fire.

Rosheen snorted. *Don't expect him to cook for you for a while.*

Be here any time now, said Gento. *Apparently, it's of a stretch to look after young Tashel. Tucker singin a sad second song.*

Tell me about it. Cobar poked the fire. *That stew last week?*

Not one of his best, Gento agreed. *What was that stuff?*

Black mushy bits? Your guess –

Leave him alone, said Rosheen indignantly. *He's trying so hard. Tashel's a handful at best. And he doesn't have a crew of assistants like Shen, just you lot of lay-abouts.*

The two males looked at each other. *Lay-abouts?*

Shh! He's here.

Gento and Cobar stood in greeting as Tam came down the slope.

"Is there anything else we can do to help?" they asked.

He gave them a suspicious look and paused to survey their efforts. "Fire looks good," he said, then turned to the south with a worried frown. "But the wind's swinging. Is there anything we can do about that?"

They looked up as the gate chimed softly.

"Daric." Gento said with a nod. "He'll fix it."

Cobar nodded. "He can fix just about anything"

"With one, notable exception ..."

"Well, if Casco was here, he would have thought about the wind-change before all of us and fixed it already," Tam said. "Here, make yourselves useful, since you're suddenly so keen to help, and set these pots on the fire. Gento, we need water please before Arko gets here."

He gave Rosheen a wink. She smiled in return and accepted his offer of a mug of galano tea

---

When Andel stepped out onto the wind-blown peak she couldn't help but rotate on the spot, transfixed by the promontory's wild beauty.

"You said you wanted scenery," Huldar said. The smile on her face made the dangers they'd faced in cajoling another portal from Qalān, worthwhile.

He opened his coat and she burrowed beneath it. Her arms wrapped around him.

It's wonderful! She turned within the circle of his embrace and pointed to vague blue bumps on the horizon. *Look, you can see all the way to the Southern Archipelago.*

"The view's not *that* good," he laughed. *But that island chain carries on from here almost to the Southern Isles. Hundreds of miles. Drowned mountain tops – I haven't been there yet, or given them a name.*

"Then let's call them the Blessed isles," she said. "Maybe we'll take our little one to visit them some day."

"Maybe we will," he replied, *but the way Qalān is at the moment …* He pointed downslope to where Tam and Arko had begun preparations for the feast. "Let's see what they're up to, before you get too cold."

"I'm fine," she said. "Are there lizards here?"

"Nothing to worry about. Woolly things, about this big." He pictured the six-legged scavengers for her and moved his hands apart to indicate the size. "I expect they'll be thrilled by the opportunity to clean up after us."

"Our food won't hurt them?"

He grimaced. "Tam's cooking isn't that bad."

"I'll tell him you said that!" Her grin was impish. Strands of hair glinted copper as they blew across her face. He bent to kiss her, but quickly straightened as the portal flickered and Ariben stepped through. The archangel pulled his coat more firmly around him, and with a quick grunt of greeting, continued down the hill.

Andel's eyes twinkled.

Huldar snorted. *At least he's here.*

Worse for him than even Casco and Daric. She treats him like some sort of annoying toy.

He stayed close while they picked their way down a faint trail to the plateau.

Andel frowned when his hand went to her elbow. *Thanks, but I can do this myself, you know.*

I know, he replied, but his mind's eye followed protectively just the same.

In the small clearing, a newly constructed rustic bench was draped with a luxurious rug. Before it, piles of cushions strewn over damp-proof matting gave the setting a delightful air of decadence. Empty crates had been transformed into comfy seats with the aid of yet more cushions. In the centre of the accumulation a cheerful fire was protected from by a window-wall which joined ground to cliff face in a transparent, wind-proof triangle.

Sari sat beside Casco, close to the fire. Their conversation seemed animated, and from Sari's gestures Huldar guessed it had something to do with Ubaid's child-birth classes. By contrast, Daric's expression was drawn and remote. He wished the three could close the gap.

Cobar and Gento sat on cushions with Rosheen between them. A generous shawl, richly colored in a simple chevron design, covered her shoulders. Huldar wondered where it had come from - it had no resemblance to the somber garments she usually favored. He suspected she only wore it to keep her two attendants happy - a small concession to her condition.

Ariben stood with his back to the flames. "Could've picked somewhere warmer," he complained to no one in particular.

"What, this?" Gento scoffed. "Bracing, is all."

"He's forgotten already," Cobar murmured to Rosheen.

Gento nodded sagely. "As one ages ..."

"Don't push it," Ariben muttered. He turned and held his palms toward the heat. "A good few thousand left in me yet."

"Maybe," Tam laughed from his impromptu kitchen, "... if you weren't such a whinger."

Banga and Kira were next to arrive, soon followed by the rest of the spinners, including Bush and Topper. Malena clambered down the last few steps and sauntered into the clearing, graceful as if her enlarged abdomen weighed nothing.

"Who's complaining?" she said.

Ariben kept his gaze firmly on the flames.

"Laughin lad there." Banga tipped his chin toward Ariben. "Pining away to a shadow, and all for the love of you." He glanced at Daric. "Good mate for our other love-lorn comedian."

Daric chose not to respond.

"Shut up, spinner!" Ariben snarled, and continued his scrutiny of the flames.

"Hit a sore point there, mate?" said Bush.

Topper elbowed his brother. "Praps his point's not sore enough!"

Ariben winced. "Grow up!"

"Here, have one of these," Tam held up a tray.

Ariben scowled at Tam, then the honey-cakes, then rolled his eyes and took one.

"See, that wasn't so hard," Topper said.

For a moment it seemed Ariben would throw the cake at him, but he turned to the flames and took a bite from it instead. "Why waste a perfectly good cake?" he muttered sourly.

Next to make their way from the portal were Calen and Van, with Ubaid and Alis not far behind. Ubaid paused to help his wife negotiate the final few steps. Daric started forward, ready to assist, but the healers smiled him away.

Arko busied himself plating food on the trestle by the cook-fire while Tam applied finishing touches.

"Where's Ronnin and Nachiel?" Huldar asked.

"Just nicked back to Central for some cilfra dressing."

"Cilfra?" said Calen appreciatively. "Where'd you have that stashed?"

Tam's left eyebrow flickered. "You know the best way to keep a secret?"

"If all who know it are dead," Ariben said bitterly.

Daric gave a dry laugh. "Couldn't have said it better myself." He glanced toward the hilltop portal. "Here's the cilfra now. Ready to do the honors?"

Ariben tilted his head.

"Secrets must be kept," Daric said, "or they're no longer secret, are they?"

"Always got to go one better," Ariben sniggered.

Daric lifted his chin as Ronin and Nachiel as they neared the gathering. "You two don't know how lucky you are!" He flashed Ariben a cynical glance.

Nachiel shrugged. "I'm always lucky." With a deft flick of mind he ferried the dressing to Tam, who placed beside a multi-colored concoction of salad leaves peppered with slices of golden-wheel fruit and crusty squares of toasted nut-bread. A steaming tureen of broth sat beside the bread, then a large ceramic dish filled to the brim with hot, wild-caught seafood.

"Come and eat!" Tam said.

The Uri'madu surged forward, eager to oblige.

Huldar ate a bowl of stew and tried not to appear nervous. Eventually, when feasting slowed and the company relaxed with their drinks of choice, Huldar held up his bottle of ale. "If I could have everyone's attention?"

"You got it," Topper replied jauntily.

People shuffled closer. He waited for them to settle. "There are a number of issues we need to discuss as a team, which is why this gathering was limited to Uri'madu."

"And spinners!" Banga called out.

"Spinners *are* Uri'madu," said Tam.

"He wouldn't cook for you otherwise," said Casco.

Huldar raised his bottle again. "Issue one - and this is not necessarily in order of importance - There will be no more new portals. Daric and I have agreed." He nodded Daric's way. "Qalān has become increasingly intractable. We must work with what we have. If there is a need so urgent that a new portal must be attempted, well, we'll cross that bridge when we come to it … but we all know the dangers."

"That we do," said Nachiel softly.

"Make sure have your song well in order before you step, and don't attempt it if you are too tired or emotionally unstable. Which brings me to the next, and maybe the most important point." He paused. "I'm afraid there is no easy way to say this." He looked at Andel and drew strength from her discreet nod. "I have come to believe the Imperium may try to prevent our return to the Realm - that they will attempt to strand us here … or worse."

Their silence hummed in his ears. Waves crashed loudly on the rocks below.

"Or worse?" Tam murmured at last. "What does that mean?"

"But they can't," said Rosheen.

"Why would they do that?" Gento added.

Cobar rubbed his chin and looked into the flames.

"What of the miners going back with the half-time run?" Kira said.

"I would love to go home," said Rosheen. She looked from Gento to Cobar. "But only if I could take you two with me."

"And run the risk of birthing in transit? These pregnancies are unpredictable enough as it is. I'm going nowhere," said Kira.

Minna looked at her sister, Tala as if for support. Tala's gaze found Bush's, then looked away.

"You'd stay? For him?" said Minna indignantly.

"He's a spinner too," Tala replied.

"As if that makes it alright!"

"I'm not going without him," her sister said firmly. "And who'll help you with the birthing if Topper doesn't?"

Huldar held up his hands. "You are all aware by now that the berries you ate were actually the eggs of the Went?" he asked.

The spinners nodded.

"... And that the majority of those eggs were stolen, then recovered by Casco?"

There were more nods.

"It is my firm belief that two of those eggs were given as a gift to the God-Emperor."

"The God-Emperor? So that they will be Blessed?" said Sari. "But that's cheating ... isn't it?" She looked around guiltily. "I'm not saying *we've* done anything wrong."

"Of course not, Sari," Andel said quickly. "The difference is, that we didn't know."

"And that's the point Huldar's trying to make," said Malena. "If it is the case that the Empress Ishiquel has become pregnant as a result of eating a Went egg, we will know she has cheated."

"What if her pregnancy is accelerated, like ours?" said Kira.

"All the more reason to quell any rumors," said Daric. "She'll say it's a late announcement, that she didn't want to give the Realm false hope. Who would be brave enough to say it's a lie?"

"But that's ridiculous. The whole court will know."

"Will they? I heard that Ishiquel rarely socializes these days. They say she's embarrassed by El's displeasure."

Malena snorted. "If anyone should fear El's displeasure it's him - and yes, I've heard much the same."

Daric inclined his head as if corroborating her point.

Banga swirled his drink. "What are we going to do?" he said at last. "We can't just ..."

"Just what? Wait to be killed? How can we know all this has actually happened?" said Ariben. "Maybe no eggs have been eaten. Nothing to worry about."

Malena shook her head. "Breath! Everyone knows how Ishät longs for a second child. It's as if El spurns him - as well he should."

"Malena!" Banga said.

"What?" she retorted. "We're not in the Realm. No one can hear us. No witnesses. Huldar is right to be afraid."

"We should be ready to fight," said Gento. "The lives of our children are at stake."

"Fight? How can we fight?" Van raised her arms in a hopeless shrug. "Three hundred of the Host plus their pet Ashik? And if you're right, I'm betting there'll be another troop of pumped up meat-cakes in the next supply run."

"You're assuming that the Host *will* be allowed to return," Daric said darkly.

Calen frowned and said slowly, "They know too, don't they?"

"What, he'd kill us all?" Van cried. "I don't believe it!"

Daric shrugged. "A small price to pay for Imperial harmony - or what he thinks of as Imperial harmony."

Casco looked at him. "Maybe they'd work with us - if they knew?"

"I've called us here because we need to make plans," Huldar said. "Let's get the discussion back on track. How many of you would be prepared to fight if need be? Gento, Cobar, Daric, and Casco - and Ariben? I know you all have training and ability. I must admit, I have no idea at all."

"What of Rosheen and I?" said Malena indignantly.

Daric gave her belly a glance. "You'll be indisposed. All the Blessed will be."

"I'm a Maatu," Banga said proudly. "We take our training seriously. And the rest of us spinners," he indicated three males seated together at the back. "Daram there's a Maatu …"

"Is it my eyes that give me away?" Daram quipped.

"... and you two, Blik and Scar, you've had experience as mercenaries - is that true?"

The two Cantori looked at each other and nodded.

Topper held his hand up.

"We can learn," said Bush.

"I'm sure you can," Huldar said, "but there are other things we can do - are already doing." He picked up a stick of driftwood and scratched a map of Went on the ground before the fire. "Casco, Daric and I have been working on a series of hideouts - here, here and here." He made vague crosses on the map, and was careful not to reveal the full extent of the network. He looked up into a ring of expectant faces. "The best plan I can come up with, and I admit it most likely needs work, is that we be ready to run at a moment's notice. As Van has pointed out, more Ashik may come with Kandät Enna's next arrival. If they do, I think we should waste no time - just go. Be safe. It could be that the births will be imminent. We will be at our most vulnerable when they begin, and not just our blessed, but those of us who support them. We may need to fight, but it must be a last resort."

"Defence rather than attack," said Gento.

"Exactly."

"What of Tashel and the blessed among the Host?" Tam asked.

Huldar had been expecting this question. Ties between expectant mothers were close. "This may seem harsh, but can we trust them? I think it best to say nothing until the last minute. Just one slip, and we may all die."

"He's right," Andel said. "I know they are Blessed too, and I am as fond of them as any of you, but do we know them?"

"Then why tell us at all?" asked Calen.

"We are Uri'madu," Andel replied. "We are family."

"How can I not tell her?" Tam said. "I won't – I can't let her down."

Ubaid spoke up. "The necessary link you will need for the birth is very close, as you know, but if you concentrate more on the physical …" He gave Daric a look.

"I may be able to help with that," Daric said reluctantly. "There are ways. I am happy to teach anyone who wants to learn."

"Ways?" Ariben scoffed. "Is this another la-de-dah Enna thing?"

Gento snorted at him. "You have no idea, do you?"

"No idea about what?"

"What he is," Cobar rumbled.

Ariben's head tilted.

Daric stiffened.

"No secrets, Daric," Alis said quietly. "The time for that has passed."

"He's an assassin," said Gento flatly.

Huldar stood up. "He *was*," he stressed.

Calen jumped to her feet. "And we're the last to know?"

Suddenly everyone was speaking at once.

Daric stood quietly and studied the scene.

What should we do? Andel asked.

Nothing just yet, Huldar replied. He'd dreaded this moment since they'd left the Realm, but if they were to have any chance at all, they must trust each other. If such a secret were to be revealed at a critical moment, the shock could jeopardize everything they'd worked for. At least this way, there was still time - and Daric's exemplary history as a member of their team.

At length, Daric broke his silence. "It's true."

There was a further outcry.

Alis' eyes met his.

"Let him speak!" Huldar commanded.

"I came here looking for a new life," Daric said in even tones, "and I've found it. I do have certain abilities … but I am no longer the person I was." he shrugged apologetically.

"Abilities …" Sari said thoughtfully. "Like the singing thing? You showed us how to make our voices work even when we're too stressed?"

"Yes. First I taught Huldar, then I remembered Lind and realized how helpful it might be."

"We've known all along," said Gento, glancing at his Rukh clan-mates. "We may not like it, but we trust him."

Daric's veil remained steadfast and smooth, but there was a wildness in his gaze as he faced them. "I thought you'd hate me."

Cobar glanced up from beneath his eyebrows. "Tempting, but no."

"I knew too," said Malena. "His sister's a navigator."

Casco studied the flames. "Daric is ..." he hesitated then looked the assassin in the eye "... I'd trust him with my life."

Daric's gaze widened. Huldar saw his veil waver.

"Life, yes," said Sari stoically. "He saved us - all of us - when we first arrived, with the dome windows, and when the mine collapsed, he was amazing."

Huldar motioned for Daric and everyone else to sit. "Startling as this news is to some of you, let me remind you, as Sari already has, that Daric Enna is one of us now, a valued member of the Uri'madu. The real issue here is our future."

Malena looked him up and down. "And let's be thankful he's on our side, not theirs."

Ariben gave Daric a measuring glance. "Our secret weapon?"

"Alis and I also have deep regard for Daric Enna," Ubaid said. "But as Huldar says, we have other things to consider, especially regarding the blessed. Even though we are Healers, for obvious reasons we may be unavailable when your times come. We cannot stress enough how important it is for all support partners to be well versed in what must be done."

"I'll help if I can," said Kira. "I never thought I'd be blessed for a third time, but I've been through it before. And perhaps a class about how to keep our babies quiet?" She glanced at Alis. "Not their voices so much as their minds. If secrecy is vital, it'll be more important than ever."

"I know a little about that," said Alis, "but not as much as you, Kira. We're lucky to have you."

"What about Lathan, the Host's Naghari? Will he be there for us?"

Ubaid turned to answer Van's question. "Lathan of Naghar knows of our situation, of course, but has agreed not to be involved unless there is an absolute emergency."

"And there's no way we can escape the planet without another navigator, is there?"

"Sorry, Calen," said Malena. "Shamkarun Kandät Enna is the Empress' uncle. He's not going to stand against the Imperium."

"Can we call for help?" asked Van. "What about the communications window?"

"Maybe," said Huldar, "but I envisage difficulties there too. I have plans, but we'll discuss them at a later time." He turned toward Tam as the savory smell of hot easenberry tartlets wafted from the kitchen. "I think I've given you enough to think about. Let's take a break."

Chatter rose and fell. He saw Cobar give Daric a slap on the shoulder, and the Enna respond with a pantomime of being knocked sideways. Casco watched him covertly, then laid another stick on the fire and watched it catch alight.

Andel shivered. "It's getting cold, Daric," she called. "Do you think you could extend the window?"

"Certainly!"

Huldar sent his wife a grateful smile. If Daric's response was more enthusiastic than usual, it was certainly understandable, but on the whole, the admission of the assassin's shady past had been less problematic than he'd feared. *The Rukh knew all along?* He shook his head.

Full of surprises, Andel replied.

Where Daric is concerned, nothing is ever quite as it seems, he replied. *Not even us!*

I think his love for Casco is genuine though, and if Alis and Ubaid vouch for him …

I have no concerns for the safety of the Uri'madu at his hands, he assured her. *Otherwise I would never have included him among us, no matter what Shamkarun Pieru said. We're a long way from home.*

And help.

Folk scattered as the transparent window wavered and buckled, but once it reached Daric's anchor-points and enclosed the plateau, it set firm. The wind died instantly. The delicious fragrance of warm easenberry grew stronger.

"Much better," said Rosheen. "Now, how about that fire, Gento? Could you liven it up a bit?"

"Anything for you, my little bunch of platsy!"

Cobar snorted a laugh.

"That's enough of that," Rosheen retorted. "Just fix the fire."

"Platsy?" Sari echoed.

Daric's lips crinkled in a gentle smile. "Pink flowers, Haas natives," he said quietly. "Quite dainty."

"They smell pretty," Casco added. He looked at Daric as if there were memories they might share.

Sari stifled a smile.

Arko clanged a wooden ladle against the side of a huge cook-pot, and the Uri'madu needed no second summons.

Seated beside his wife with a steaming fruit pie on his platter, Huldar clasped his moment of relief and let it roll around his soul.

Andel leaned against him. *You're happy.*

His eyebrows lifted. Surprisingly, he was.

We'll find a way, she said. *You are our strength, and we are the Uri'madu, and if we have to endure years of hardship before rescue comes, we'll do it with grace and fortitude. You'll see.*

As the sun dipped below the horizon, a last blaze of orange warmed their complexions. Stars came out, one by one. The Great Wheel was incomplete so far south, but the purple nebula spread a frothy veil high above. The Eye of El, some were calling it.

Andel's mind bumped his and he realized he'd closed her out.

If El could see us, he asked, *if he noticed our small comings and goings ... what would he think?*

She stared with him at the horizon as the last glow slowly dissipated. *I hope he would see that we, at least, are doing our best to protect his creation.*

Would he punish the Faythans, do you think? Would he stop them ... return the God-Emperor's eggs ... set things right?

I doubt it, she replied. *That's our job. The same Breath blows through all, remember? What we see as a disaster may just be the start of the next chapter unfolding. All we can do is listen to the song around us as best we can and act as we believe we should.*

Spoken like a true Trianogi - philosophical yet practical. He hugged her close. *Have I told you recently how much I love you?*

No need, she said softly, *I know it every moment of every day.*

MOTHER'S LOVE

Ariben rubbed his arm. The weather was changing … again. He leaned back on soft cushions and looked up at an indigo sky. Clouds of stars peeped from the cover of the nebula. High above, the constellation of the Great Wheel was bisected by a trail of moons. Tough shrubs, pruned flat by the perpetual winds, clung to the headland as if they relished the challenge. Surf boomed against the cliffs, but here beneath the dome, all was warm and at peace … except for the pain that gnawed at his heart.

She looked at him, a fleeting glance. Vibrant green eyes brushed him like a fresh breeze then moved on. He knew she was beyond him - might as well pine for the stars above, but for a short time she'd been his. That she'd moved on was not surprising. How could a barely-Marked Lethian with nothing but a re-grown arm and an interest in substrates ever hope to hold the likes of her - a great Shamkarun, a navigator, and niece to The Maatu himself? But she was yet to choose someone to trust for the birth, and his stupid heart still dreamed.

Kira came to sit beside him. He shuffled sideways to let her in. Her look was knowing.

"She'll come round," she said. "She likes you."

"How can you tell?" he murmured sourly.

"Worked with her since she was apprentice. Banga has too. She likes you. You give her space."

"Space?" He snorted dispiritedly, but despite his skepticism, a smile moved his lips. He sighed and took the cake she offered. His jaw moved up and down mechanically. He watched Malena hold court with a group in animated discussion.

"Light-spirits?" she said mockingly. "I've never seen one."

"I saw one once," Calen said carefully. "His hair - all matted. No clothes. He scared me."

"They scare me too!" said Nachiel.

"I met a Shamkarun who specialized in releasing them," Andel said.

"That'd be a Trianogi gig for sure," Banga laughed.

"As a matter of fact, it was," Andel replied. "She said you had to convince them to either find a blood-relative of some sort to take their cry, or, as a last resort, she had a way of taking the cry herself."

"Breath!"

"A difficult job," said Casco.

"Difficult, yes. And very sad, I expect," Sari added.

Ariben felt his heart begin to beat faster. "I know a story about light-spirits," he murmured to Kira.

She nudged him and glanced Malena's way. "Then tell it."

"But it might be …"

Kira waved her drink in the air. "Ariben has a story he'd like to share!"

"What story?" Malena asked.

Kira winked at him.

Huldar seemed a little surprised, but Ariben thought he saw interest there as well. He beckoned to Tam. "The shawl, please? For Ariben."

Ariben's felt his cheeks flame. "It's nothing much, really Huldar," he rubbed his aching arm. "And I'm not good at storytelling. That's your thing."

"You just need practice!" Nachiel laughed. "Come on, let's hear it."

"Is it about a light-spirit?" Andel asked.

"It is," Kira said. She took the shawl and draped it over his shoulders. "No escape now," she murmured wickedly.

"But it might not be right," he said quietly. "I didn't think. It's about mothers and a child."

"Sad then?" said Nachiel.

"Just tell it," Huldar said. "We won't know until you do."

"Here!" Tam shoved a freshly opened bottle into his hand. "For courage."

Ariben took a deep breath, then a long, cold mouthful of besh. The shawl warmed his shoulders. Everyone was looking at him.

"Alright," he said gruffly, "but don't say I didn't warn you."

Tam shuffled closer. Malena's eyes twinkled in an encouraging smile.

"A Mother's Love," he began, and took another swig to calm his nerves. "This story is about a mother's love, and may El blow favor on us with the knowledge it imparts.

"El blow favor," the group intoned.

Ariben nodded, and before his resolve could waver, he began. "Long ago, but not so long ago that no one remembers, a couple were married and Blessed so soon after, all thought it a sign of El's great favor. They lived on Cantor, he a Cantori and she a Leth. Both were poor and their lives had been hard. Neither had family to fall back on, but they had each other, and at the start, at least, that was enough. But as the pregnancy progressed and the birth grew near, it occurred to them that three would be harder to feed than two, and with her unable to work while the infant was young, their resources would be stretched indeed."

"I think we can all relate to that," said Bush.

"My oath," said Topper. The brothers grinned at each other over the heads of the spinner sisters they'd paired with.

Ariben nodded again. "So, the young husband went in search of more lucrative employment, and eventually found a position with a travelling trader based on Giahn. The new job would involve a fair bit of back and forth between the two planets. It might have been easier for them to move to Giahn, but his wife was unwilling to leave Cantor since it was the only city she knew." He shrugged. "This might have been a problem, but the young husband was a good worker, so the merchant assured him he could take leave for the birth so long as he returned to work soon after.

"In due course, they gave birth to a beautiful baby girl. When the husband had to return to Giahn, the mother didn't especially mind. Her beautiful daughter filled her heart with joy, and any sacrifice to ensure her health and happiness seemed worthwhile.

"Picture this," Ariben looked around as if he saw the scene he was about to describe. "Fine summers day on the outskirts of a largeish town, sun shining, birds singing ... Sweet young mother, husband due home and she decides to go down town to buy him something special for dinner. Baby in her arms, she heads to the more expensive stores - they have more coin now and she wants to be sure he'll get something he'll really appreciate. Then - disaster." He shook his head sadly. "There's been an accident in the chime. When her husband's death-cry hits her, she collapses. When she regains consciousness, her baby is gone."

He paused, again unsure if this story wasn't too close to home.

"Gone?" said Malena.

"How can that happen?" Andel asked.

Ariben shook his head. "It was terrible. That poor young thing," he continued. "The pain was crippling. She could sense her baby calling, feel her distress. She searched and searched but the child was too young to form coherent images - eyes still blurred by infancy, and mind too young for words.

"Then the link was cut. On top of the trauma of her husband's death the agony of loss was almost too much to bear, but no second death-cry came so she knew her baby had been taken into Qalān and off-world.

Two days later, their link was renewed, but much fainter.

Then it was lost again.

"Over several such instances the link between them faded to almost nothing. The young mother was alone and lost, as was her child."

"This is terrible!" Kira said.

"I'm sorry. I can stop if you want," Ariben offered.

"No!" said Malena. "I need to know what happened. Did she find her baby in the end? Don't tell me the baby was a light-spirit ..."

Ariben glanced at Huldar. Their leader gave a small nod of encouragement, so he took a mouthful of Besh and continued.

"Years passed. The young mother worked and saved, visiting planet after planet but the trail was cold and each time, the work seemed harder. Her life and the search became one. Night after night she cried herself to sleep. Sometimes, the pain ... she just wanted it to stop, but she would remember the joy in her little-one's smile, the warmth of their heart's embrace - until one night, a dark night indeed, some one hundred and sixty summers since, she realized her little baby was no more. Her daughter, wherever she was, would be singing her first charms and old enough to have found her own Qalān. She would know nothing of her, or of her search. It was then that it came to her - the best chance of finding her daughter would be in her own death."

The company's faces closed in shock. Ariben could feel it, but no one asked him to stop. He threw a stick on the fire and watched the sparks fly into the night.

Malena frowned. "So what happened?

"Well," Ariben said. "Far away on Giahn, as it happened, in the city of Clouds, in a beautiful house in the expensive end of town, lived a couple Blessed with a single girl-child, or so it would seem. But the child was always sad, and the relationship between mother and daughter was troubled. Neither seemed to understand the other, they argued often, and she didn't have the look of a Tiamäti - like her parents.

The arguments grew more bitter - shouting and crying. At such times, the father would step in and try to soothe his daughter's tears, but it would not be long before raised voices and ill will flowed from their stylish premises again.

"Neighbors felt sorry for the situation, but there was nothing they could do. They gave the girl treats when she came to them for refuge and assured her that her mother loved her, really, as all mothers loved their children. But when they said this to her, the little girl would start to cry again, and in the end, they just gave her treats and said nothing.

"Then one day there came the wonderful announcement that this couple had been Blessed again. "A second child," the mother said. "Blessed at last." She was very happy. But the very next day, mother and daughter had a truly terrible row. The mother slapped her so hard she knocked her to the ground, and the daughter ran from the house, clutching her bruised cheek, vowing never to come back.

"Good riddance!" the mother cried.

"Neighbors tut-tutted and hoped the girl would come home, or at least find happiness, and the father would sometimes stare wistfully down the street, but true to her promise, she didn't return.

"There were rumors of sightings in the markets district, and he was sure she was not far away. He wanted to look for her to bring her home, but his wife would not relent."

Kira scowled. "Hard Kalla. Why steal a child if not to love it and care for it?"

"Why steal a child?" Malena held her belly protectively. "A horrible thing to do."

"It was indeed," Ariben agreed.

"Clouds can be a chilly place," Daric said.

Ariben grimaced in agreement. "Anyway, the girl lived on the street for a while, but she had a talent for charm-singing, and found a special affinity for fire. The Isatudjan's Guild took her in," he continued, "and under their tutelage and care, she began to settle and make her way …"

"Until what?" Malena asked.

"There she was," he said. "Just bought herself soup and sweet-cakes after fixing someone's kitchen fire, and bang! It hit her – her mother, her *true* mother's death cry."

"No!" Sari gasped.

Ariben nodded sadly. "All those years, she had felt something was wrong, and now she knew what had been done and who her true mother had been. Grief became anger. She was too young to control it. Anger became rage and rage became an all-consuming hatred in her heart. She marched back to confront her false parents, and on the way, a fire charm of elemental force was born.

"In the conflagration that followed, all three were killed. The father's cry went out, but although the remains of all three were found in the rubble, from the other two, no death cry had come."

Sari's eyes filled with tears.

"They became light-spirits?" asked Casco.

"Yes, they did – after a fashion."

"What do you mean, 'after a fashion'?" asked Malena.

Ariben lifted the bottle of Besh again and took a long drink. His lips twitched with the hint of a wry grin when something rustled in the bushes and Malena glanced quickly over her shoulder. She snorted as a wooly lizard skuttled by, the crust of a tartlet held high in one paw.

"Finish the story, for Breaths sake!" she said crossly.

"Please, yes," said Tam.

All eyes followed as he took another swig then put the bottle down, then stared into the coals as if he could see the lost ones there. "Many times, over many years, people tried to rebuild the house in Clouds, but charms went awry and building blocks tumbled despite the skill of any Zaīkhanun employed."

He looked out into the night, imagining what it must have been like. "Apparitions were seen … a weeping child and a ghostly mother-to-be. Voices were heard, screaming and crying. People stayed away.

"Eventually, a Shamkarun was called," he tipped his head toward Andel, "an expert in such matters. Feeling the intense negativity spilling from the ruins, he set careful screens for himself before reaching out to lead the lingering spirits to make their cry and begone to the care of El and Asheru. But it was not so simple. Locked in the timeless world of between were two souls so welded together in hatred and grief that neither seemed to know or care that their bodies were no more. The child had become the pain she felt, and the false mother, so full of self-hatred for what she had done, could not escape the endless punishment the child inflicted on her.

"The Shamkarun tried his utmost to separate them, but to no avail. Eventually, when his efforts were completely spent, the eerie voice of the little girl came to him …"

Ariben paused again. Sparks crackled into the waiting silence. Slowly, his lips tightened. "… When Giahn crumbles and the winds blow through naught but ruins … when the planet itself lies empty of all, then she will see that *this* is what I have become."

Wind moaned outside their transparent dome. Coals in the fire-pit creaked. Farther afield, waves crashed against the unforgiving rocks of the headland below.

"So the spot where the house was is still bare?" Huldar asked.

He nodded. "It's a park now, trees, flowers and the like - but no one goes there after dark."

"How sad!" said Nachiel.

Banga left Kira with a wink and sneaked closer to Malena. "Ha!" he cried as his stealthy hands grabbed her shoulders.

She jumped. "Don't be silly!" she scolded. "It's a new planet. There couldn't possibly be a malignant spirit trapped here."

Gento snorted. "New planet or no, I'll be sleeping with one eye open tonight."

"Yes, I think it's time we called it a night," said Huldar. He nodded to Ariben. "Excellent story."

"Just something I heard," Ariben said. He bowed and handed the shawl back to Tam.

No one seemed in a hurry to move. Andel peered doubtfully into the dark. "Let's sleep here," she suggested. "We have the dome to protect us, and I have spare blankets."

“Good thinking,” Nachiel said quickly. “We wouldn’t want to lose our way.”

GANG OF FIVE

On Went's eastern continent, it was mid-morning. Following lines of glacial rubble, banks of snowy white blossoms arced between masses of red and orange, thick with life. From a sunny spot on the edge of camp, Andel looked out over the flower-strewn plains and smiled. It really was as beautiful as she remembered.

Soon the rains would stop. The colorful carpet would give way to low stubble, the creatures would die or move on, and for a time, the desert would rule. But for now, she could feast her eyes on one of the glories of Went.

She turned as the portal gave a faint chime. Ariben stepped through and stalked towards her. It was as if he'd never broken stride.

"So what's this about a … ?"

He stalled at her warning glance. She pointed vaguely upward and gave her finger a small whirl.

Sorry, he said. *All this secrecy. Not thinking straight.*

"Thanks for offering to help, Ariben," she said brightly. "I think I've left it on the southern plains."

"Err … no problem," he said. "Lead the way."

She stepped him through to the western corner of the continent. Rain slapped them with an instant dowsing.

"This is fun," he yelled through the wind.

With a grimace to his sarcasm, she signaled him to follow. After a ten minutes scramble through piles of round-edged boulders laid in a honey-comb of glacial tide-rows, they stepped through a second portal into the southern desert. From sodden cold, they were struck by a wall of heat.

Where are we going? he said.

You'll see. She paused to rest her back. *Sorry to be so mysterious. We could have taken an easier route, but this way, the second step is Daric's. That's why it was harder to see.*

He grunted sourly. *Might have known.*

At least our damp clothing is keeping the heat at bay.

They set off over red grit. The unbroken horizon seemed endless. Hot wind seared her nostrils with the smell of burnt stone. She squinted into the heat-haze, and tried to remember Daric's directions. The last step was nearly invisible, a mere distortion of energies, and by the time she'd found it her clothes were dry.

When she stopped, Ariben gave her prominent belly a meaningful glance. *Are you alright? Not a good spot to take a break.* He wiped perspiration from his face and peered at the stark expanse of their surroundings. *It's so … empty.*

She moved her hand back and forth through the gate. *You can't see it?*

See what?

This result was even better than they'd hoped. Ariben was a powerful archangel. If he couldn't see or sense this portal, chances were no one else would - unless like her, they knew it was there.

There's a portal here, she said, and motioned him to stand closer. *But don't try to use it until you've had some time to practice the toning.*

She sounded the deceptively simple pattern of the ancient track-way, and stepped them into the deep cavern Huldar had found.

It was as if they'd been swallowed by darkness. The air was still and dank.

Ahh, she said with more confidence than she felt. *We're the first to arrive. Hold still!* With a whisper, she activated the globe Casco had left there. Slow, soft light gave their eyes time to adjust.

Ariben's mouth opened as the size of the space was revealed. Like an excited child, he turned on the spot, then suddenly he darted off to pick up a small rock. As he examined its shining yellow facets his habitual heaviness of expression evaporated, and a genuine smile transformed him into someone surprisingly handsome.

She joined him, and he held his find for her to see. At first, the shiny layers seemed like common mica, then she saw the difference. *Chasite?*

Yes, it is! he said, thrilled by her recognition of the rare mineral. *I've heard about it, but … Do you know what I can do with this?*

She grinned. *By the tone of your mind, I'm guessing it's quite special.*

It's the facets, see? They continue right through the structure.

She probed with her mind. *The vibration is quite unique.*

"You want secrecy?" His voice echoed slightly in the cavern. "This single pebble is priceless! I can make a screen so dense, so powerful," he went on, "that even Daric Enna might not be able to crack it. It's the facets, see? Each one will hold a different vibration, and once embedded, the charms will act both independently and as a whole, and you'd think that the complexity of it would make it stand out like a … but no. It blends. Very hard to spot."

He looked at her, eyes shining. "This is what House-leaders use - when they can get it. What the God-Emperor himself would use!"

She took the stone and studied its complexities in wonder, while Ariben bent to look for more. They had come to talk of a secret project, and here was the perfect cover, but the thought of activating the pattern he described was daunting.

He shook his head. "No, it's quite simple, once it's set up. That's another of its unique properties. The downside is the charm's lifespan. Once activated, it only lasts a day or so, then the whole thing crumbles."

"Still, a lot can be accomplished in a day."

She sensed a jangle and turned as Daric and Casco stepped in.

"You," Ariben said coldly.

Daric shrugged.

"What's this?" said Casco indignantly.

"Stay away from me," Ariben said.

Daric's expression flattened. It was as if now they were hidden from the judgement of others, he had freedom to inhabit his old self – the one they had never seen. Fluid as a hunting bento, he moved behind Ariben and whispered silkily into his ear. "Don't be silly. If I wanted you dead, it would have happened long since."

Casco flashed him a warning.

"Daric! What are you doing?" Andel said sternly.

"Just playing –" Daric's small grin didn't reach his eyes, then he noticed the stone in Ariben's hand and leaned over his shoulder. "Is that chasite?"

Ariben gave a wary nod and spun to where he could keep his eyes on him.

"What's chasite?" Casco asked, but before Ariben could gather his wits to answer, Malena entered.

"Ah," she said. "Good to see you two making friends." She looked around. "Is it my imagination, or is it a bit chilly in here?"

Ariben's scowl deepened. "Now I'm more confused than ever."

"Why are we here?" Malena asked Andel. "If anyone but you had asked me, I'd have told them I'm too busy."

"We may need your help."

"I can't sing, you know."

Andel gave her a rueful smile. "I have this idea," she explained, "but it's important it goes no further than we five."

"Huldar?"

"Doesn't know."

"And it has to do with Nacrite and calcite?" Ariben gave a light snort. "I remember you hinting as much when you conned me into coming with you."

"Yes, it does. Daric thinks he may be able to spin blue calcite into fibers that could be woven into fabric, and if we could alloy the fibers with nacrite ..."

Ariben winced. "That's a good idea?"

"It's the nacrite," she explained. "Huldar believes it's the reason this planet is impervious to external communication. I wondered if it was possible to alloy nacrite to the calcite fibers to make a fabric that's super lightweight, invisible, and impervious to psychic observation.

Ariben frowned. "I ... don't know." He studied the cavern wall where flashing creatures floated through strange vegetation - if vegetation it was. "That'd be quite some cloak." He said at last, and looked around. "Is there anywhere to sit?"

Daric raised his eyebrows.

"I've brought a rug," Andel said quickly. Casco took it from her and spread it over a level sandy spot further inside the cave. With another whisper, she produced a cushion for each of them. A far-away splash and gurgle made her look deep into the impenetrable shadows. She remembered Huldar's description of the creatures in the lake.

Malena arranged herself over several cushions. "Prepared for a longish session? Lucky I brought food." She looked up at the glittering ceiling. "And the scenery's beautiful."

"Yes, it is rather astonishing, just as Huldar described." said Andel. "Even the lake monsters."

"You wouldn't want to meet them face to face, I don't think," Casco said.

"No indeed!" Andel replied. "Your hamper looks enticing, Malena. I'm always hungry these days!"

"Me too," Malena said, and pulled an extra bowl of fruit from Qalān. "Just to keep our energies up."

"So. Can you do it?" Daric said to Ariben. "Can it be done?"

Ariben selected a golden wheel fruit from one bowl, then another from the smaller one, and placed them carefully on the rug. With a decisive mental tug, he slid the larger vessel sideways to align it with a small dish of salt. His scowl deepened. "If I used Baylät's charm with a tensile twist …" He adjusted the salt. "It's a possibility."

"Yalden's arc?" Daric suggested.

He shook his head. "Too forceful. Calcite's brittle …" He thought for a moment. "But if I modified the arc with a string of Hayman's and applied a little heat." He cocked his head. "It's a place to start."

"Yalden's arc?" Malena peered at Ariben, bemused. "Baylät's charm? What are you talking about?"

"You may not realize," Daric said wryly. "But beneath that surly and somewhat modest exterior lurks one of the foremost substrate specialists in the Realm."

Ariben frowned. "I wouldn't say foremost."

Daric nodded. "He is."

Ariben snorted with sudden humor. "So that's why you haven't killed me?"

"Not before I get a chance to pick your brains," Daric said with a grin. He held out his hand. "If you would allow me? I think we could work much more efficiently this way."

Ariben gave Andel a quick look.

She nodded encouragingly, but his arms remained woodenly at his sides.

"I'm not touching that," he said. "Who knows what he'll do to me!" But Malena flashed him a glance, and slowly he opened his palm.

Daric gave a sardonic sigh. "If I was going to kill you … remember?"

Ariben hung his head and gave a rueful grimace. "I feel … stupid," he admitted. "The things I said at the picnic on the bluff …"

"La-di-dah Enna?" Daric tilted his head. "Actually, I've encouraged you to think of me that way," Daric admitted. "So if we're trading apologies …"

"I guess you wouldn't want anyone to see you as dangerous, would you - not in your line of work."

"Ex line of work - but yes, a dangerous appearance does rather get in the way." He offered his hand again. "I won't hurt you. I promise."

Ariben shrugged his lips and closed his palm against Daric's.

The two bowed their heads.

Andel sighed.

"Might as well tuck in," Malena said to her. She grabbed a slice of pie from the spread between them and bit into it hungrily. "You did bring some nacrite with you ...?"

"And we've got calcite," Casco said. "Hope it's enough. Their camp is on my weekly checklist."

Savory talemgal smeared Malena's chin. She gestured from the food to Andel. "Go on, or there'll be nothing left of you when the baby's born."

Ariben held out his hand, head still bowed. "Calcite, please."

The lump of white mineral Casco gave him levitated from his fingers and began to glow. His Mark brightened, and they saw that although it was not as extensive as some, the whorls within it were tight and intricate. When his lips whispered, the calcite hummed as if in reply. It was soft at first, but the sound sharpened and soon became piercing. Creatures faded or fled. Andel covered her ears. Then, just as she felt she could take no more, it gave a burst of light and crumbled.

Falling dust sparkled in the light of the globe.

Daric dabbed at a cut on his chin.

Ariben's eyes were squeezed shut. He covered his face with his hands. "Think I've got a splinter."

"Perhaps we should've included a healer on the team," said Andel worriedly.

"Let me look," said Casco. He prised Ariben's hands from his face. A residue of white soot stuck to them. "Which is it?"

"This one." Ariben shook his head to the left.

Casco covered that eye with his palm. After a moment of intense concentration, he lifted his fingers away and massaged between the knuckles.

Ariben opened his eyelids carefully and squinted at the light. "That's better," he said.

Casco showed him the sliver of stone he'd extracted. "Picked up a thing or two over the years. There's a mark on the cornea and it will be a bit bloodshot for a while, but otherwise it's fine. Are you up for trying again?"

"Of course! We know now that Yalden's Arc is the wrong amplifier. What do you think, Daric?"

"Gibberish to me," said Malena.

"Not sure," Daric replied. "Maybe if we'd gone *this* way with the modifications - followed your first instinct?"

Ariben cocked his head as he examined Daric's proposal.

"But this time," Daric continued, "I think we should shield the stone to contain the blast, if it should go that way again."

"Can you do that?" Malena asked. "Is that a thing?"

"You'd be surprised what he can do," muttered Casco.

"More calcite, please."

This time there was no hesitation. The two joined hands as if it was the most natural thing in the world. Soon, the calcite glowed again, but now, the hum was muted. The sound continued, but the stone remained unchanged.

Daric and Ariben looked at each other then turned to Malena. "We need more power."

She put her half-eaten tart down with great aplomb and dusted off her hands. "Let's do this. Just don't expect me to sing."

"Of course not," Daric assured her politely. He turned to Casco. "And perhaps it would be wise for you to join us too - as an anchor - just in case?"

"And as an over-view?" Malena raised her eyebrows and offered him her hand. "You have a bit of a gift for that, you know."

"A gift?"

"Yes. You see where things fit, and what needs to be done. It's why you're so good at your job."

Daric glanced at Casco then quickly away.

Andel gave him a gentle smile. "It is a talent you have, Casco, among many others - must be if even Malena's noticed it."

The navigator rolled her eyes and shook her hand impatiently.

Casco gave Andel a nod, then took it, and after a moment's hesitation joined hands with Daric.

The quiet smile on the assassin's face gave Andel a pang of grief. Would they ever make up? Seeing them so, she realized how much she missed the versions of themselves they'd been when together.

Ariben stared at Malena's other hand.

"What's this?" she demanded. "Are you going to take it or not?"

The circle of reluctant ex-lovers was closed.

In the centre between them, the calcite slowly levitated and began to glow. The hum it gave this time was gentle and pervasive. Andel lay back on the cushions and tried not to doze. It had been left to her to watch for danger. But apart from an occasional splash and moan from the lake, there seemed little to worry about. The light crystal dimmed as Casco's attention waned, but there was till enough to glimpse small, wingless creatures flitting across the distant ceiling in that mysterious way they had.

Then the hum changed.

She sat up.

While the others remained physically linked, Ariben's fingers wove around the glowing calcite in a purposeful dance. She had never seen him so graceful. His eyes glowed. The Mark on his face pulsed with light. Malena watched as if she'd never seen him before.

Slowly the stone began to spin. Casco turned to Andel and said quietly, "Nacrite, please."

A small bag popped from Qalān. It was already secured to a lead weight. When it settled, she reached up inside and took its contents in a firm grasp. The empty cloth fell to the ground.

Casco nodded toward the centre of the circle. "Close to the calcite but not touching."

Ariben's fingers stilled. His hands clasped the space around the glowing stone as if holding it together. She pushed the nodule of nacrite toward it, but the closer it got to the calcite, the more resistance she felt. She glanced at Casco nervously.

"Let go now," he said.

She blinked in surprise when the rough grey nodule stayed in place. "Thought it would escape to the ceiling!"

Casco answered with a small smile, then bowed his head as the work resumed. At his gesture, the nacrite nodule touched the glowing calcite. Through a spray of sparks, Andel glimpsed the stones shapes becoming elongated and more fluid. All four of the participant's faces were blank with effort. Sweat beaded on Ariben's forehead. His whispered song grew louder. Blue flames bloomed around the objects. Both shone white with heat. Daric's voice wove with Ariben's in eerie dissonance, but as the stones began to merge, harmony was approached. Malena seemed strained, but as the rocks finally melded, Casco's expression settled into one of satisfaction.

"Hold it there," he said softly, "just a moment longer ..."

At last, his fingers lifted and their creation sank slowly to the ground.

The cavern was bathed in complete silence.

Andel closed her eyes to banish the after-burn on her retinas. An acrid smell lingered in the air. Her baby turned uncomfortably.

Daric shook his head. "It worked!"

Casco shrugged. "Just seemed to be the right approach."

"What's this?" Andel asked. "Don't forget, I wasn't with you."

The others turned to Casco. Malena bobbed her head in respect.

"Our friend, here, masterminded the whole thing," said Daric.

"A trick I learned in a blacksmith shop. You and Ariben did the work," Casco waved his hand to include each of them, "and without Malena's power ..."

"All would've come to nothing," said Ariben abruptly. He turned to Andel and surveyed the severely depleted picnic. "D'you leave us any? I'm starving."

She smiled, said, "As it happens …" and whisked a second hamper from Qalān.

While they were eating, the rock on the ground cooled to a bluish color, although heat still shimmered from its surface.

"Take a look," Ariben suggested proudly. "You'll never see another like it."

The stone had the signature of neither of its native materials and resisted her probing with promising vigor, but she kept pushing and eventually the inner structure was revealed - smooth, but fluid and restless.

"Metal and mineral and something else besides," she mused. "Both and neither." She glanced at Ariben. "What's the next step?"

"Spin it into fiber," he said around a mouthful of savory pie. "Hardest part's done." He looked at the others. "Anyone know a weaving charm?"

"I do," said Andel. "My mother taught me. She liked to weave sometimes. Said it helped her to organize her thoughts."

"What about the baby?" Daric asked. "You won't be able to sing."

"True," she said. "But I can teach someone – I think. The knowledge is there, it just can't be executed."

Daric shrugged. "Teach me. I'll learn to be a weaver – might come in handy someday. Breath blows," he said philosophically, "and we but tumble in its wake."

Andel turned back to the stone they had worked so hard to create, and gasped as it faded from view. Not even a shimmer betrayed its presence, just the slight depression it made on the sandy floor.

"Yes!" Ariben crowed.

Andel stared. Her eyes narrowed. "I can't even see it with my mind!"

"If it can't be seen, or detected …" Casco said slowly.

"We'll have to heat it again." Ariben said. He turned to Andel. "Will that be a problem weaving it?"

"Can be seen when it's hot enough," Daric mused, "but will cool quickly as a fiber."

"Weave above a flame?" said Malena. "I don't know the first thing about it, but that would seem … difficult."

"Need a row of several - a steady, even heat will be the trick."

"But when it cools? How will we find it?" Casco asked

"Marker threads," Andel suggested. "Weave the two together then remove the marker when you're done. Simple."

Ariben raised his eyebrows doubtfully. "So long as the marker thread doesn't burn."

"Who knows a fire resistance charm?" she asked.

Ariben snorted softly. "Me," said. His mouth opened in a wide yawn.

Andel and Malena soon followed suit. "Maybe we should be done for this session," Andel said. "If the next part is ruined because we're too tired and loose concentration …"

Casco looked at the others and seemed to come to a decision. "Let's go then. Leave it for now. We can hide the alloy here and come back in a few days with a fire-proof cloth or cloak." He tipped his head toward Daric. "If he has time - since he's the one who's volunteered to learn the charm."

"When would be a good time for that?" Andel asked Daric.

"How about now? Too much on tomorrow." He frowned at the depression in the sand. "We've lost a full half day on this - more!"

"It's an important project," Ariben said.

"Yes, I know," Casco said impatiently. "But we still have to catch up, and quickly. No one is supposed to notice our absence, remember?"

"And with Huldar so engrossed with the Went …" Malena said.

"He has to," Andel said sharply, "or else how will we prove their citizenship to the imperium?"

"I know," Daric said. "It's just that - forget it."

Casco seemed about to make another sharp remark, then stopped. "I have to get back to Sari."

Malena stretched and yawned. "I'm tired, Ariben. Will you take me home - please?"

Ariben frowned as if waiting for the catch.

Her eyebrows lifted.

"Ahh - certainly," he said. "Just as soon as we've hidden the stone."

"Good. There's something I need to talk to you about.

Daric raised his eyebrows in parody of Malena's. "And I can take you home, Casco, if you'd like?"

Casco grunted. "I need to see the Lady Andel home safely."

"We could all go home together," Andel suggested.

He tipped his chin toward Daric. "He knows his way."

WHAT'S MIRASHAEL DOING?

"But my love, my lovely one," Mirashael argued. "It is there we will be safe. I have family - we have family."

"What family?" Leahät said stubbornly. "I haven't met any family."

"I did not want to overwhelm you, my shining light. But now is the time."

"For me to be overwhelmed?"

He gave a rueful grin. "Yes. Exactly. This is correct. It is too dangerous for you to stay."

"For me, but not for you?" she said archly.

He winced. "Dangerous for me too, yes? But I have obligations - duties to fulfill. People have paid and I must deliver."

"But we are a team. We do things together. I can help you."

"Yes, my love, yes. But not with this, you understand? You can help me best in this instance by doing as I most humbly request."

Leahät frowned. He took that as a good sign. She always frowned when she was coming to a big decision.

"And I can accomplish ... necessities more quickly," he insisted, "the sooner to join you on Cantor, yes?"

Her arms folded.

He sent her a wordless plea. "If any harm should come to you, dear lady, if any should even threaten ..." he stifled a welling of panic. If he should lose her – it did not bear thinking about. "My work requires precision, focus. I cannot afford distraction, yes?"

And you are certain? The Empress is definitely Blessed?

He nodded. *Most certain. Quite definite.*

"And this is why I must leave?" she asked doubtfully.

That is the root – the core of it, yes.

"But the announcement should be months off, not till the end of the first trimester." She counted on her fingers. "So if she ate the berry then –" she looked up. He nodded again. He knew exactly when that Breath blown meal had taken place. "– and only three months have passed," she counted three fingers, then the same three again, "that won't be till part-way through Lassen'so, at least another three months from now. There's plenty of time. And the baby won't be born for another twelve months after that."

"Yes, my dearest one. Normally, this is what would happen, how things would progress."

Her frown twisted. "Normally?"

The Empress Ishiquel will announce her Blessing tomorrow and claim she has hidden her condition from the adoring public so as to be absolutely certain.

Leahät cocked her head. "But it's only three months."

Yes, but no one else knows that – no one! He glanced over his shoulder as if checking for sly listeners. She took the hint. Their house screens were the very best, but extreme caution should be taken. *It seems the fruit of the berry is in a hurry to see the world it has come to.*

She frowned.

It … the Blessing … it may not be fully annangi, he whispered. *Or at least, I don't believe so.*

What?! She raised her hands in disbelief. *How can you know that?*

This is why you must leave – we must leave, but you much sooner.

He sensed her growing fear, and gave a tight smile. *The palace is already in turmoil. One healer has been killed.*

A healer? Killed by whom? Who would do that? Not the God-Emperor?

Indeed. He killed all but one of his brothers – you know that don't you?

She shook her head.

One he killed himself in 'training'.

I do remember that, she mused. *It happened not long after Maatu left. The whole of Giahn in mourning. Didn't the other die in an accident?*

Yes, a most unfortunate accident. He gave the thought a sarcastic twist. None of his operatives had anything to do with it, or at least so he believed, but Daric's early mentor was a maverick and the work had been extremely tight, not unlike Daric's style, although before his time, of course. *Only Delemät Ashik remains,* he continued, *and I think he has forgotten he is the Chosen's sibling – for his own continued safety. It will be interesting to see how long he survives in Maatu's place.*

"Duvät Gok believed the Maatu were traitorous," Leahät said. "That they should not have left the God-Emperor's side."

Mirashael gave a derisive snort, but at least she was confident to talk about her former husband now. "Many more now see the wisdom in what they did, although sadly, our own Ishät Ashik is not one of them." *And as for our healer at rest in the Breath, he was another with something to say that our glorious God-Emperor did not want to hear. Thankfully it was not old Shamkarun Rohnia of Naghar who was killed. She was called away to attend an important Faythan birth –*

Healers come go as they are called, even within the imperial household. Even I know that.

He gave a doubtful shrug. So many traditions seemed under threat right now. *She alone may be able to soothe her highness, when she arrives back. She has birthed royal babies before as Naghar's assistant, and was present at the birth of Aqumät, our God-Emperor's illustrious First; but perhaps fortuitously in this instance, Rohnia has delayed her return.*

How did Naghar respond? What does one do when a healer has been murdered – by Him!

Daniel Naghar is, apparently, quite upset.

"Upset?"

An understatement. However, he has already assigned another, more 'combat experienced' healer to her Highness for now. He imaged the work-a-day face of the new healer. He certainly had a capable, competent appearance. *We must hope this one's … skills, are enough to preserve his life.*

Leahät was quiet for a time, but he sensed her thoughts churning, as had his own when he'd heard of the healer's death, and even more so when he'd discovered what the unfortunate one's cry had been.

"There will be huge celebrations, of course," she said at last.

"Pageantry galore," he answered. *No one knows what we know, dear lady. These secrets are of the highest order, and now it is even more imperative you should leave.*

I can screen well, as you have taught me!

Yes, you are an apt student, but I could not bear if those skills were to be put to such a test. While the party continues, that will be the time to slip away, like a little silver fish into a navigator's expert care. Once on Cantor, none will harm you.

But I don't know anyone on Cantor. I have never left Giahn.

Mirashael smiled and showed her the house they would share there, or one of them.

Her eyes widened. "It's very grand," she said cautiously.

And the markets there, you'll love them. So much color, so much noise! And far less regulated – or more, depending on my cousin's mood, I expect. But less policed, yes. It's a game to be played on a day-to-day basis.

Your cousin?

Yes, I may not have mentioned that. He could see no way to soften the blow. He had deliberately omitted to tell her he was cousin to the leader of House Cantori.

"Your cousin is The Cantori?" she said flatly.

He nodded shamefacedly.

"And you have never told me? Why have you never told me?"

His hands came up as he attempted to explain, then balled into fists and came down again. He had let her down, hurt her by not telling her, but he'd never lied. She just hadn't asked.

He looked up in surprise as she laughed.

"Oh my dear," she said warmly, "you never fail to astonish. This will be more of an adventure than I thought. Will I be considered a lady?" She struck a pose. "Make small-talk? Follow the latest fashions?"

A fierce sense of love and pride washed through him. "You *are* a lady, always. Never forget it, my dearest one. Yes, yes, a lady through and through!"

She gazed through the window at the rolling surf beyond. He knew how much she loved this house, and their more modest abode above the restaurant also, yet in all honesty, they would most likely never return. The café was already working under management and doing nicely. The warehouses could be leased out, and they could still supply the guild, but with less space needed here since their primary storage would now be off-world. It could be done - it would take effort to set up … he showed her his thoughts.

She nodded, turning the ideas over and added embellishments of her own. *And with extra concessions, no doubt, because of your connections. Yes, I can see this working out well.*

He smiled brightly. *I always thought it best to build my businesses without family assistance, but perhaps it's time to leave such limitations behind. Yes, yes, dear lady! A new start for us indeed. I will book passage as soon as we have an official date for the celebrations.*

SNAPPING ROCKS

To get to the research site near South-Arm mine, Huldar had to pick his way through a trackless region of heavy vegetation and rough, lichen covered stones. Tall, green trunks sported rafts of lacy grey-green foliage. In the richly patterned light and shade, it wasn't until Banga waved that he could be seen.

"Where's Ariben today?" Huldar asked. "I thought … is he with you?"

"Van's here instead. Laughing boy's off with Daric somewhere, working on some new idea of his."

"Daric's?"

Banga gave a derisive huff. "Who else? Poncy Enna thinks he owns the place."

"Hmm. Any problems?"

The spinner shrugged. "All good."

"Is Malena with them?"

"Huh! Those two? Floating about in their own private song. Can't separate em."

"I think it's rather lovely," Huldar said with a smile. "Romantic."

Van started toward them ."It is very sweet," she said. "They've acknowledged their feelings for each other at last."

"Yeah," said Banga sourly. "And only took a completely unnatural pregnancy to do it."

"I beg your pardon!" Van said indignantly.

"Banga!"

"Sorry boss." The spinner's green eyes glinted mischievously. "You haven't known her as long as I have."

Huldar studied the two of them for a moment. Van's pregnancy was at the same stage as all the other Blessed – awkwardly large, but not debilitating. "Well, if I can't have Ariben or Daric, can I borrow you two for an hour or two? But there might be some difficult terrain involved."

"What sort of difficult?" Van asked dubiously.

"A mountain side," he said. "A bit steep, but not epic. And some carnivorous plants."

Banga looked around the rocky habitat the two were sampling. "Van?"

"Don't see why not."

"Are you sure you're up to it?" Huldar glanced at Van's ample midriff. "No problem if you're not."

"If I say no, you'll just get someone else to join you on one of your fabulous adventures!" She shook her head. "This is the first time you've asked. You boys will keep me safe. I'll just let Calen know what I'm doing."

"Fabulous adventures?

Banga rolled his eyes.

"Kira?" Huldar asked him.

"She knows where I am."

Van gave a firm nod. "Ready."

"Then come with me," Huldar said.

"Gotta be better than rocks and lichens," said Banga.

"And don't forget the sting-tails," Van added dourly.

"Unpleasant little critters," Huldar agreed.

"Unpleasant? Banga wiggled his fingers like a bunch of legs. "All guarding their little hoards, tails primed and ready for action. Reminds me of Olatu on a bad day."

Huldar sent them an image of a red-faced Olatu with his back-side morphed into a stubby, sting-tipped tail, held high while he circled a nest of quota-sheets.

Banga barked a laugh. "How do you do that?"

"Really?" Van gasped. "However you do it you shouldn't." She cradled her rounded belly. "Wouldn't want to go off prematurely!"

When they reached the portal, Huldar turned. "We're off up north," he said. "Still daylight, but significantly colder, so rug up now before we step through."

"What's the problem?" asked Banga.

"I'm evaluating a new area for later exploration. The vegetation is - quite unusual." He glanced at Van. "Some seem to be carnivorous, but I'm not sure what they eat."

"So long as it's not annangi!"

Huldar closed his eyes as a wave of terrible scenes came back to him. How could he have forgotten Joumelät Enna's dreadful death?

"Boss?"

"It's nothing." He took a breath to steady himself. "Just be very, very careful. They're not that big, but as I said, I'm not sure about them yet. They have poisonous blooms, about this size." He held out his hands as if cupping a dinner plate. "At least I think the might be blooms. You'll see when we get there."

"Using us to test their dietary preferences, are you?"

"Tempting," he joked, but laughter came hard while his guts still churned.

Banga's wise eyes flicked over his haze.

"It's nothing," Huldar said. "Well, not really. We lost someone - one of the Uri'madu. A while back now."

"Lind? So tragic," said Van.

"Yes, Lind," he said. "But this incident was before that. Joumelät Enna … our diviner at the time. She got careless, too close to a carnivorous … plant, for want of a better description. Cunning things used to stalk us." He shuddered, remembering her screams, and his desperate, but ultimately fruitless dash to save her. "As I said, it was a while ago on a planet quite different to this one."

"Must have been hard," Banga said.

Huldar nodded. "Let's go," he said, and held out his hands. "Remember, don't let go while we make the step. It's not safe anymore." He readied himself to accept their touch; contact, but not too deep - then stepped them through to a wild, open plain. From there it was a short, wind-battered walk to the next portal.

"You may have to duck your heads for this one," he explained, voice loud against the onslaught. "There are blooms hanging right above."

Banga and Van gave each other a doubtful look. He sang them on again to a basin sunk deep in a towering mountain range. A spectacular show of blood red flowers cloaked the slopes beneath the snow-line. As promised, one drooped directly over the portal gate. He quickly pulled them aside.

"Thought they didn't eat annangi?" Banga said.

"They don't, well not these ones, anyway. It's the pollen. Quite toxic to smaller creatures. Those, on the other hand …" He indicated a bare bush covered in crimson flowers, each with a sharp, black thorn at its heart. "Don't get too close to that one! The thorns are projectiles, each held at the end of some quite tough tendrils coiled inside the cup of the bloom. Triggered by proximity."

He picked up a fallen branch and waved it within range. The bush shook as it let loose a cloud of needle-sharp thorns, one from every flower, and there was an explosion of sweet scent into the air. Some thorns had fired solidly into the wood of the branch.

"Shit!" said Banga.

Huldar let the stick fall. It scraped unevenly over the ground as the tendrils contracted. Empty needles slithered back to their beds without a sound.

"Watch this," he said. Moments later, the stick stopped moving. The tendrils fell free of their small harpoons and quickly retracted into the flowers, leaving a piece of wood that seemed to have sprouted stiff black hairs along one side.

"How do they know?" he asked his companions. "It's quite extraordinary. They never pull anything inanimate back to their lair."

On closer inspections they could see rotting lizard bones piled beneath the naked branchlets.

"The thorns grow back overnight," he explained. "Make sure your defensive shields are up and you'll be fine. There is venom, but harmless to us."

"All the same," said Van, "I wouldn't want to end up like that stick!"

"Get us out of here," Banga said.

Huldar led them downward, himself and Banga on either side of Van as they slipped and slid through dense vegetation. The heavy smell of damp moss thickened the air. More than once, a bush shook with sprays of thorns and perfume. The force of the projectiles was absorbed by their defensive screens, but the attacks put them on edge.

"Where is this site?" Banga asked.

Huldar winced at the irritable tone in his voice. "Not far now," he told them, and envisaged a small clearing strewn with evenly spaced stones.

Van was sweating despite the chill.

"Do you need to rest?" Huldar asked her.

She gave a grateful nod. "I think you should've sent Olatu to investigate," she wheezed.

"Or that kalla, Barto!" Banga said.

Daric hates her – she added.

Huldar smiled inside. As if he didn't know!

– *And she hates him,* Van continued. *By all accounts he made her look pretty stupid in that refectory escapade.*

That's our Daric. Banga gave a snide huff. *Overachiever.*

Given what we know now, she should be thankful to have survived! said Van.

Banga nodded slowly. *And that's the truth!*

Ready to go on? Huldar asked.

Just a minute more, Van said apologetically. *Sorry.*

Don't be sorry, Huldar replied. *We needed a breather too.*

She laughed – a silvery sound amid the slow swoosh of forest and flowers. The turned when a thorn-bush rattled close by. There was a small scream and the air clotted with over-strong perfume.

That's it! Van said. *I'm ready now.*

They continued downslope. When Huldar sensed the marker he'd left, they turned to make their way along the mountainside. Gravel and rocks replaced brush, then the slope levelled and they emerged onto the stony clearing he'd shown them.

Banga went to walk past, but Huldar put out his arm with a peremptory, *Wait!*

Van studied the ground ahead more closely. *Those aren't rocks,* she whispered.

No, they're not, Huldar said. He picked up a palm-sized pebble – *Watch this …* and tossed it onto the clearing. Before it had time to land, four of the 'stones' split open. Fleshy, red-brown maws shot skyward on ropey stalks. The mouths closed with a resounding chorus of clacks. A snapping chain reaction rippled across the field, then, just as with the black thorns, the heads were drawn back into place. The one with the captured rock burped it up and continued its retraction.

They stood silently for some time after the clatter subsided.

How did you survive? Van asked quietly.

Huldar compressed his lips, and composed an impression for them. *If you listen in this way, there is a faint murmur – out of place even here.*

The other two closed their eyes, trying to understand the information he transferred.

Here – this one. He attempted to isolate the actual sound from the background song.

Van shook her head, but Banga's eyes opened into a narrow squint – *I hear it. Like the sound of an asteroid field that needs to be avoided. Adjustment in the song.*

Exactly!

Van shook her head again.

Never mind, Huldar said to her. *You'll get it in time.*

If you hadn't shown me, I might not have had more time! Her eyes closed as she tried again.

Casco would've picked that up easy as you, wouldn't he? Banga said.

Huldar nodded.

Then why didn't you bring him?

Catch-up class with Ubaid. And besides, no harm in learning new skills, is there?

Banga released a tendril of amusement. *Never thought that would be true at my age, but no, not at all.*

I hear it! Van said at last. *A strange one that. I've studied quite a few planets over the years, but … a stream of potential song, rather than an actual one?*

Huldar congratulated her with a warm smile. *A good way of putting it. I think it's part of their disguise.*

"Do they react when we speak aloud?" Banga said.

His comment was drowned out by a rich chorus of snaps, but no mouth propelled upward.

Need movement for the strike to happen, Huldar explained.

We can't just go around them?

He shook his head. *The silver deposit starts at the outer edge of this clearing and continues on. If you look further, there's fields of these things as far as the eye can see. I think the ore is what keeps other plants from colonizing, leaving the ground open for these charming little fellows.*

Screens? asked Van

The attack is too slow to be repelled, and while a single one can be avoided, several at one time cannot. We have to work out how to relocate them, or, ideally, a way to become uninteresting or invisible to them.

Banga tilted his head. *Venomous?*

Not enough to kill an annangi, but without prompt attention they could make you pretty sick. Any ideas?

One of Daric's window thingies might work, said Van.

Yes, if it could be worn as a shield. Or I thought Ariben might be able to come up with a repellent – something we could wear as a talisman, perhaps.

Banga grimaced. *I'm betting the zilla charm doesn't work.*

Sadly, no. It hasn't worked on any of the creatures of Went.

Van studied the field for a moment more. *There's this planet – Grava, mid-belt, class three? There were serpent-like creatures – sort of like scaley sausages, about as thick as your arm. Highly mobile, hard to see and quite deadly. We found a sound that repelled them. Someone had to be in charge of making that sound for every moment we worked there. Kept us safe.* She turned to him. *That was your thing, wasn't it? Something to do with sound?*

He shrugged. *I made a charm that used the exact opposite of a rather piercing alarm call to cancel its effects.*

How did that work? asked Banga. *I thought only navigators sang to that capacity – a self-actualizing song?*

He remembered the presentation of his coat from Arien Leth. *It did cause rather a stir at the time.*

Stun-charm? suggested Van. *No? How about something to send them to sleep?*

Banga looked doubtfully at the quiescent rocks. *How could you tell? It's not like they move around.*

No, Huldar laughed. *You would have to test it rather thoroughly, but a sleep charm is definitely worth a try.*

I've been studying them – sleep charms – quite a bit since this pregnancy happened. She smoothed her hand over her rounded belly. *Kira knows so much! Not that I'll be able to use any myself, for a while, but Calen might.*

Huldar looked at her appreciatively. A baby-soothing charm just might be the answer – if it could be adapted to work on whatever these were. He held out his hand. *Can you show me?*

She smiled. *Of course! You may need this knowledge soon yourself.*

Banga settled nearby while Huldar tried to sort through the charms Van presented. All but two were variations of a single theme, and one of those showed promise.

A bit heavy-handed for an infant, surely, he said.

Maybe, Van replied, *but Kira assured me it would get a lot of use. Apparently, most Blessings go through a stage of sleep resistance.*

He snorted. *Applied with the right twist, this could knock out a kadderin.*

He proffered his hand and Banga clasped it firmly.

Hah! That one. The spinner nodded. *Worked a treat on my Second. Toddler stage – they just want to be a part of everything. Feel they're missing out if they go to sleep. Well mine did, anyway.*

Huldar felt his eyebrows lift. He hadn't thought much past the actual birth, but if this was what was needed to pacify a sleep-resistant youngster, maybe that would seem the easy bit.Banga looked at him and laughed. *Ahh, the fun is just beginning. Why do you think I took up work as a spinner?*

THE CLOAK

The atmosphere in the cavern was neither chill nor warm, and with the strong, sure light of a globe above them, Daric felt more at ease than he had for some time. They were safe here, and he was among friends - two more life-conditions quite new to him. He glanced at his companions, Ariben and Malena. With every loving glance they shared, Casco's absence hurt more. But despite the current difficulties between himself and the love of his life, and however that situation might eventually be resolved, more than ever, he was thankful Breath had blown them together, and he'd discovered the Uri'madu.

He shifted slightly to alleviate stiff legs.

Beside him, Ariben held out two perfectly visible hands and examined the ephemeral fabric draped over them. A low, subliminal buzz emanated from it, somewhat reminiscent of a hive of psychic wasps.

"So, that's it then," the substrate specialist said tiredly.

"A bit noisy, isn't it?"

"I did the best I could!" Ariben snapped. "It's the fire-proofing – doesn't sit well with the charm I used to draw fiber from rock."

"I'm not disparaging your work, Ariben," Daric said, and he meant it. What the gruff Lethian had achieved was miraculous. "I'm just saying … Not much use being invisible if you can be sensed psychically, and the jangle would get on my nerves."

"Once those sight-threads are drawn, the noise will be less," Malena said. "And the blood-bug charm comes to mind, if you can remember how to sing it, Daric? But how will we find it at all if we make it completely undetectable?"

Daric gave her a huge grin. "That's it! Malena, you're a genius."

"What's it?" Ariben said.

"This charm Huldar came up with – the blood-bug charm. It's perfect."

"Blood-bug?"

Ariben paused as Daric showed it to him.

"Breath! It's complex. I don't know …"

"Maybe we should leave it again for now," Malena said. "It's getting late. We could come back."

"But this is our chance," Daric insisted. "We should finish it now."

Ariben shook his head doubtfully. "What if there's flash-back? What if you make a mistake?"

Daric shrugged. "You're not the one who's going to sing it. It's stable now," he frowned, "This is our chance. One thing I've learned; you can't count on tomorrow."

"Can't count on tomorrow?" Ariben frowned. "Well, not if you might be dead, I suppose."

Daric opened his mouth as if to retort, but Malena's warning glance stopped him.

"You're sure you're up to it?" she asked.

"Have we decided how we'll find it?"

She shrugged. "How about a carry-bag attached to one corner? If its contents are noiseless and invisible, the bag will seem unremarkable."

"Good idea," he said, and stifled an inner laugh. The most innovative and valuable piece of cloth ever, and it would be stored in a lunch-bag. "Got a something with you?"

Malena's face fell. "Could you make one from the threads?" she asked apologetically.

He rolled his eyes. Why was nothing ever as simple as it should be? "Maybe," he said, "but it will take time. I'm no expert, as you know."

She waved her finger at the cloth in Ariben's hands. "You did alright with this."

Ariben grunted. "Pull the threads to one corner and make them into a rope. You can un-lay the rope later and weave them into a bag when you have time."

He nodded. It was a good solution. "Now give me a minute to work out how this blood-bug charm's going to work."

Ariben and Malena decamped to a rock at the edge of the light.

“It’s too cold for you,” he heard Ariben complain. “Should’ve put a blanket down, or brought some cushions with us.”

“I’ve more than enough heat to keep your neat little bottom warm.” Malena purred. She arched her back suggestively. Her pregnant belly made the sight impossibly erotic. She gave a tinkling laugh. “You’re blushing!”

“Of course I’m blushing!” Ariben growled.

“Don’t mind me,” Daric said. How was he supposed to concentrate with those two playing around in the background.

Malena laughed again. “I’m sorry, but Ariben looks so adorable when he’s embarrassed.” She ran her fingers over the Mark on his face. “And your haze goes all pinky-gold.”

“Leave my haze out of it,” Ariben growled. “You know how I feel about you. Why make a joke out of it?”

“Because she’s afraid of the truth,” Daric murmured.

Malena frowned. “Maybe we should move further away.”

“Sound travels in a cave.” Daric pointed out. “I need to concentrate right now, so if you two …?”

“What truth?” Ariben said.

“That she loves you.”

“Daric!”

The wiry Enna shrugged and turned back to the cloak. His annoyance level rose, but it was his own fault, he admitted. He should have stayed quiet.

"You love me?" Ariben said, and despite his irritation, Daric found the pathos in his voice endearing. An image of Casco stole through his mind. Love …

"You?" Malena said scornfully. She looked casually upward as if to watch the little glowing points on the ceiling. "Love? I wouldn't say that."

"Then what would you say?" Ariben snapped. "I'm tired of all this game-playing, Malena. I want to help you give birth, be there for you when you are at your most vulnerable. You'd trust me with that, but not with this? You know I love you - you know it! But if you can't at least respect me in return, you can birth your own child!"

He stood and stalked toward the portal. His haze seethed like a dark cloud around him.

Malena's brow lifted. Her hand caught his sleeve as he passed.

He stopped, but would not look at her.

"Wait! … Please!" she said. "We need Daric to sing us back. Don't try it alone - you'll get stuck."

"So what!"

"You might die!"

Fuck you! He reefed his arm free and kept walking

"Breath's sake, Malena!" said Daric. "How can I be expected to work in the midst of this? Just tell him and be done with it. There's no shame in it, you know."

She raised her hands in exasperation. "As if you're the one to talk!"

Daric shook his head. "Ariben, she's right. Qalān is difficult these days, and the ancient ways even more-so. So please wait. I, for one, would miss you if you were gone. Not much, mind you, but enough to make me uncomfortable for a day or so."

"Big of you," Ariben snarled. He sat on the ledge near the portal and studied the ground at his feet.

Daric sighed. Why was she so difficult? But at least they were quiet now. Finally, he got to his feet and brushed the dirt from his trousers. "Right, if you two have finished bickering, I could do with your help."

Ariben sighed and got to his feet. "What do you want us to do?" he asked sullenly.

"Come here and link with me again," he said, and immediately felt ashamed of the bark in his voice. "Malena, I need your strength. I'm tired. And Ariben, if you could keep watch over what I do and be ready to pull us out if need be?

He felt a pang when Ariben gave a nod; that role should have been Casco's. But when their hands were joined, he let the song take his full attention.

Energy from Malena flooded him with heat, and through their increased trust, felt her surprise as the song deepened with the adaptations he'd made. He peered deeply at the fabric and saw the alloy fibers shiver as the notes wove and blended. The elegance of his creation filled him with a quiet pride.

As the song concluded, the fabric disappeared. Only the rope of silken threads at one corner remained visible. But just as his companions expected to be released from the song-structure Daric drew them inward.

What are you doing? Malena said sharply.

The assassin made no reply. With iron will and firm intent, he brought the lovers' individual essences together, so close to each other they bumped. This was a skill he'd honed over years of necessity, but this was the first time he'd used it for … good? Or was it temper? He no longer cared.

Ariben, show her how you feel, he commanded.

She already knows!

Show her!

The Lethian was reticent, but his eventual revelation; a tangle of love and hatred, was brave and full.

To his great satisfaction, Malena responded. Like a brief sunburst through dark clouds, he glimpsed her love and her terrible fear of abandonment, then he let his song go.

When he opened his eyes, he found Malena's gaze still locked with Ariben's. She touched his face, tenderly this time, and as he kissed her, their hazes merged in a warm, rosy gold.

"I do love you," she whispered, "but don't let it go to your head."

Tears stung Daric's eyes. What he'd done had been an unthinkable breach of trust, but the result made his transgression worthwhile.

He gave a discreet cough. "If we could get going? … The charm was successful, by the way. But I think we should leave the cloak here for the time being, until I have time to weave the bag. … I'd do it now, but I am so tired … Ariben? Malena? You can thank me later …"

Ariben smiled, his expression bemused. "What if I let you go," he said softly, "and things return to the way they were, as if nothing happened?"

Melena grinned, and whatever private thought she shared, Ariben blushed again.

Once back in the outer world, Daric trailed the pair to the next gate.

"You go on," he said. "There's something I have to do."

Ariben flashed him a strange look before he disappeared through the portal with Malena. Was it gratitude? He shook his head and walked back the way he'd come.

Once alone, Casco's absence gave him physical pain. Seeing those two together, their hazes aglow with love - he'd thought it might help - Breath knew it was better than their endless mincing dance of avoidance, but instead it bought grief so thick he thought he might choke. He was an assassin. A trained killer. A pariah, and once proud of it. … Now? He was nothing. He'd given too much of himself away, and all that was left was emptiness.

He'd seen Casco with Sari, how she followed his every move, watched him even when he didn't know she was doing it. He'd been the same.

With a long breath he forced himself to calm before stepping back to the cavern.

He fancied the cool darkness still alive with the potency of his song, but on the walls and ceiling, busy life continued in its patterns, heedless of his pain. *And why should they notice?* He asked himself. He had no meaning to them, no meaning to himself.

When the small globe was sung to life, he placed it on the floor part way between himself and the portal. Even the light gave him pain - memories of Casco's joy of learning, his anguish at Radätel's death, then, worse still, his suspicion. And who could blame him? How could he ever be forgiven?

"What should I do?!" he screamed into the darkness. A slight echo repeated his words as if the darkness wanted to know too.

"Forgive me!" he cried. "Please ..."

His voice died to a whisper.

Part of him, a very large part, wanted to follow Lind into oblivion, but he remembered Alis soft expression - her moment of trust, and knew he could not.

What have I become? he asked himself hopelessly. He felt as if he had been wearing another's skin for so long, he no longer knew where his own began or ended.

Almost by rote, he settled on the floor and made himself very still. He hid his haze as he'd been taught so many years ago - the familiar ritual gave him comfort of sorts. He closed himself to distraction and waited. Besides Ariben and Malena, only Casco knew where he might be. When he didn't return ... would Casco come? Eventually, he would see.

The sigil would call him if activated, but that was not what he wanted.

Time passed - another distraction he denied himself.

His tears slowed.

The globe dimmed.

Life moved all around as if he wasn't there. A gliding creature worked its way up his torso, barely touching but close enough so that Daric could dully sense its curiosity. For a moment, he thanked Huldar in his heart for waking him to the beauty of life … then cursed Casco for the same. Would he come, or was his commitment to Sari too strong? Would he feel he was betraying her by seeing him, or was it just that he no longer desired … or loved him.

The thought fell like a stone into the pit of his soul.

He covered it deep and the ripples returned to stillness. The stillness of a master assassin.

A disturbance in Qalān plucked at is awareness. He came back to himself, rested as if from sleep, faced the portal he'd constructed with Huldar and held himself poised. But the gate did not move. Instead, a long sigh came to his mind.

What are you doing?

He looked around. *How did you find me?*

Like this.

Slowly, Casco's image shimmered into being. His look was unreadable.

Ziquarra? He'd thought himself undetectable. *Since when are you Ziquarra?*

It seems emotional turmoil freed the talent in me. Ask Alis when you see her next.

How did you find me, though … through all this rock? If you could do it …

I doubt anyone else could, and it wasn't easy. What is it Huldar says? Love is the one true beacon.

Love?

Casco paused. *It's hard to lie when you're in this state,* he said tiredly.

You still love me? I thought – now you're with Sari, … after all I've done …

That's what I hoped for, Casco said bluntly, *but it hasn't happened. Now, if you've finished with this particularly obtuse game, can you come home, please?* Casco flashed him a precis; A sleep charm gone wrong, Banga bitten by a flying rock, saved by Alis after being rescued.

Rescued by who?

By me, Casco said irritably. *Home. Please.*

Why not Huldar?

Because Huldar couldn't leave Banga and was using all his strength to keep the rocks around them from striking.

Daric steadied his pulse and looked the apparition in the eye. There was so much he wanted to say, but he had no idea where to start.

Not now, Casco said. *Just come home.*

He swallowed his words, gave a nod of affirmation, and the sending winked out.

GLASS HOUSES

After his contact with Daric, Casco came back to his body with a rush - one of the strangest sensations he'd had in his life - and peered up into the eyes of Alis.

She smiled. "You found him? Well done."

He sat up and moved closer beside her. His head felt like it had been hit with a particularly determined rock. "How did you know?" he asked.

"Just a guess," she replied, and reached for his forehead. "It goes hand in hand with your particular talent."

"Talent? He held his head still, and the headache slipped away like surf from sand. "Alis, I have no talent. You've known me long enough to realize that."

She gave a mysterious smile. "Isn't it odd when people see so clearly all that's around them, but filter that reality from themselves?"

"I don't," he insisted. "I can do a bit of Tsemkar, some handy Shamkar, and now, as it seems, I can learn a little Ziquarra, of all things."

"Yes, it's a rare and special gift"

"But I'm not especially gifted at any of them."

"Getting stronger every day though, or had you not noticed that either? And you never thought it strange?"

He shrugged self-consciously. "What, that I'm not special?"

"No. As you know, if Kareski *are* gifted, their ability is most usually quite strong and specific."

"And mine's not?"

"But it is, Casco, just more complex." She looked at him thoughtfully. "You are Archerran."

He laughed. "You're just making this up."

She smiled again.

"I've never heard of an … Archerran," he said.

"Not surprising," she agreed. "I have only met one other. And what do Archerrani do, I hear you ask?"

He shrugged again. She seemed determined to continue even though he doubted.

"Like Sajhar, they have many talents focused on one outcome. For Sajhar, it is the working of metal. For Archerranni, it is the working of people - or their skills to be more precise. Your ability to see all at once - to oversee complex charm-working, co-ordinate and guide it - did that not seem special to you? Do you know someone else that does that?"

"I don't know many people."

"Rubbish," she said fondly. "It is your gift, and working here in this highly pressurized environment is forcing your development at last."

He watched her for a moment. She did not seem surprised. "How long have you thought this?"

"I have known, or suspected, all along, but the ease with which you mastered Daric's window song while guiding Huldar's charm and holding off the snapping rocks ... all I needed to see was your Ziquarra just now, and my suspicions are confirmed."

"But Daric can do all that. He's been teaching me. Is he one too?"

"He is extraordinarily gifted, it's true, and you could have no better mentor, but he has no Ziquarra, and he hasn't your knack of overseeing, has he?"

"No, but maybe he could learn. He can learn most things."

"There is no one more intellectually capable, I'm sure - but Casco, one can't learn a talent if it isn't there."

Her knowing eyes studied his. He felt as if he'd fallen into deep water and could no longer tell which way was up. He was a half-breed, a Kareski, a nobody. He had no particular talent. Such things, if they were present at all in such as he, showed at an early age, and he was no longer young.

"Do not feel shame, Casco. Feel pride. You are gifted, and strongly. When your Mark manifests, your life will change forever. Be ready."

"Mark?"

"I can feel it, even closer than Daric's, perhaps because of your purity of soul. El favors you, Casco."

She placed her hand over his. Warmth spread through the contact. "When we return to the Realm, I can find you the mentor you need - when you are ready, of course. She lives on Haas."

"I was on Haas," he said, "with Daric, learning the sword."

"Yes, and you did extremely well. Maybe Breath will lead you back there whether you will or no. Maybe you will meet without my intervention. We will see." She looked toward the portal. "Daric comes. Maybe it is time you two talked. He is extraordinary, Casco, but also extraordinarily tortured. I know it is difficult, but he needs you - your purity, to give him hope - to draw him to the light."

"I could never tell him that."

"No need." She smiled again, a gentle farewell.

Casco stood up and took her hand again to help her to her feet. More so because of her advanced pregnancy, she felt small and delicate. He wondered how such a slight body could house such a big soul.

She touched her belly reverently. "She is a wonder - a marvel. Who would have thought such a thing was possible?" She looked up at him. "But here, it seems many things are possible. This place is of special significance to Breath's Design, or so Ubaid and I believe. And don't worry about Banga, he will be fine in a day or so, just a headache is all, and Kira enjoys having him in her care."

The portal chimed and Daric stepped through, disheveled and dark of spirit. He saw Casco and stopped. His haze rippled with confusion.

Casco sighed. Alis was right, there would never be a 'good time' to talk. Might as well get the conversation started. There was too much at stake to leave things unresolved, he told himself, and Daric was central to their efforts.

"Ziquarra?" Daric said. His head tilted slightly.

"Seems so," Casco replied.

Daric took a step closer. "I miss you."

Pain shot through him. He turned his head to disguise his expression. "I miss you too," he said evenly. "Do you have time to talk, or are you too tired?"

Daric's haze brightened. "I have time. I'm not too tired. Are you?"

It was clear he was exhausted, physically and emotionally, and Casco gave a soft snort. Their hazes sagged with equal intensity. They a Breath-blown match for sure.. "Come to mine, then. I'll make us some tea."

Daric stayed put. "Is Sari there?"

"No. Why?" His voice was sharper than intended. "I can get her to come over if you like, but she's been working on this side and it's late."

"No, it's just that …"

"That what?"

"I thought you and Sari might be …"

Daric's words slowed.

"I don't know whether to be angered by your assumption," Casco snapped, "or impressed that you didn't look," he said. "I am Sari's trusted other, not her lover. You could also assist with the birth, if you can get your head around a selfless act."

"I'd like that," he said quietly.

"Then come on, for Breaths sake. You'll be asleep standing up. Lucky the weather is fine. A stiff breeze would blow you over – so long as you weren't side-on." He beckoned him to motion. "You wanted to talk. Let's do it."

Still, Daric hesitated. "I'm afraid," he said at last.

"Me too," he answered, and it was the simple truth.

Suddenly, the wait was too much. Either Daric wanted to talk, or he didn't. At this very moment, whichever way was fine. He started for his tent without looking back, resigned to his frustration. There was so much else to think about; Archerra? Purity of soul? How did thoughts of his maverick assassin fit with that? Hopefully the whole mess would cancel itself out and he'd get to sleep.

But by the time his first few steps had crunched across the ground, he sensed Daric following. The sigh he kept to himself was visceral, as was the guarded surge of excitement.

GIAHN'S JOY

At home on Naghar, in the private parlor of the rambling Naghari Palace, Kariiel Enna's vibrant amber eyes snapped with irritation.

Daniel Naghar studied them gently and wondered again how he had been so fortunate as to win the love of such a one. Shining Marks covered her face in a mask that reached down her neck right to her chest, and even curled up over her head as if one slight body could not easily contain such a wealth of talent. Her sculpted features were framed by wispy locks of palest gold. But despite being Kaskarudjan and niece to the Empress herself, or perhaps because of it, she had cut off her hair - as if she were a Kareski impostor. If asked, she said it suited her, but any who were involved in the Kareski troubles knew what statement she made. If possible, her brave and typically outspoken gesture made him love her all the more.

His own hair was an unusual deep brown color and worn in a simple traditional queue. He was sure it seemed drab by comparison. He hadn't cut it in support of her; she'd asked him not to. One outspoken rebel was enough in any family, she'd said. But somewhere inside, he felt guilt.

A slight lift of her eyebrows brought him back to the present, and the argument at hand. "Of course, we must be there," he said reasonably.

She broke gaze with him. "But it's all a bit odd, don't you think?"

"Yes," he agreed. "But it is still our duty to attend. You of all people should understand that."

"A duty?" she said. Her veil laced with scorn. "I have 'duty' to no-one."

"It's a moot point, Kariiel. And the way he's been lately …"

"Yes! And what about poor Alel. Killed! And Ishät makes no apology. Nothing! Just a request for a 'more suitable' replacement."

"Varael was quick to volunteer. Let's hope his defensive skills are up to the test."

"And his death cry?" she continued. *She's not quite annangi?* "What does that mean?"

He snorted lightly. "You're the Kaskarudjan. I'm just a lowly healer. When I've examined the health of her Highness, maybe we'll work it out."

She looked him up and down. Her mien softened. "Daniel Naghar, the lowly healer."

"At our service!" He gave a florid bow, then put his arms out and swung her in a playful circle.

She laughed with delight, and he knew he'd almost won.

"There'll be dancing," he said encouragingly. And Ariiel and Manu will be there."

"Although I'm betting Anu will not." She referenced Manu's graceful and unprecedented withdrawal from Ishät's side, and let her admiration for him shine bright. "Always interesting! Such a clever statesman - no one can dance our God-Emperor like he does ... and it would be lovely to see our daughter." She gave a sigh of resignation. "Just so long as you keep Him away from me."

"I'll do my best - although he *is* El's Chosen."

"El must've been out of his mind," she murmured darkly.

"Kariiel!"

"And we'll holiday for a few weeks afterward? Naghari weeks," she warned, "not standard ones."

"Where ever you like," he assured her. "Breath knows we'll need it. I mean, you'd think a simple dinner at the palace would be enough, and maybe a luncheon the next day, but a whole week of expensive display?"

"It *is* the longed for Second, Daniel. Though what they've done to earn El's Blessing at this juncture is beyond me. Ishät's a monster, and why Aunt Ishiquel simpers after him as she does - it's very hard to watch."

"Yes," he agreed. "I can't imagine you simpering after anyone."

She rolled her eyes and went to the window. Her hand came up to her head and her long fingers smoothed through its fine platinum strands. "Maybe I should cut my hair right off," she said. "Do you think he'd notice then?"

"I think he notices everything about you, all the time." He ruffled her shortened locks. *Leave it as it is,* he smiled. *I like it.*

She bowed. "Yes, your highness, of course, your magnificentness! You are absolutely right."

Her eyes danced with laughter and his heart leapt. No wonder Ishät Ashik lusted after her. "I'm sure your comment has been seen - but understood? It may be a little subtle for him." He gave her a gentle smile. "But I know the Kareski value your support enormously."

"I wish we could do more." She turned to him, feelings unveiled. "They should be able to live in peace wherever they like - on Giahn, on Haas - anywhere! It's ridiculous. Cruel."

"It is, indeed," he agreed. *But there's no reasoning with him.*

She sent a wash of love through their bond. *Breath, and it isn't as if you haven't tried. I should say something. Shame him into … but you're right, of course. He has no shame. And Aunt Ishiquel laughs and accuses me of jealousy.*

He nodded sagely. *An accusation only she could believe. Another mystery.*

"One that does not need solving!" she laughed.

"Ahh!" Daniel tilted his head. His grin was wry. "You *were* his first choice."

She grimaced. "Don't remind me! Can you imagine? Ughh!"

He shrugged. "The royal couple can," he said slyly, "- both of them … in detail."

She laughed, and he felt her flow of warmth light up his soul.

"I'll book the navigator, then," he said. "Two tickets to 'Giahn's Joy'".

"Is that what they're calling it?" she said. "Interesting. Not 'The Joy of the Realm', or the Known. I know something's not right with this Daniel. I can feel it. I don't think we should go."

As open as she was, he could see her genuine misgivings, and that perturbed him. She was seldom, if ever, wrong. When he took her hand and further opened the bond between them, he saw all the usual disturbances – it was as if Ishät understood everything she knew to be right and deliberately set himself against it; but now there was a new edge to it. She could feel a build-up of forces and feared they would be trapped at the forefront.

"I was there," he said, and shared his memories of the Moment of Choice – the blinding flash as the young candidate stood naked atop the glowing rectangular rock that was the Throne of El, the massive sigil's descent into Ishät's convulsing body. *I supported him after the Acceptance. He was proud, arrogant for sure, but not innately evil. If he had been, El would have rejected him. We would have had to sift through his siblings to find a more suitable vessel. It's happened before, and with three more to choose from – I'm sure one would have been accepted.*

Maybe he was the best of a bad lot? she said sourly. *Imagine if they were all like Delemät?*

They weren't. Balät Ashik was very like his father, Chorät was nothing if not ordinary, and even Delemät wasn't so bad. Not then.

Now he's just pathetic. She imaged the general's face. The expression he wore seemed sad and frightened, rather than fierce. *Way out of his depth, and he knows it.*

What's the alternative? Dead, like his brothers? Daniel took her back to the scene of Balät Ashik's death. *There's no healing a beheading. Ishät claimed to have done it accidentally. His comment at the time? … 'I always was too quick for him.' It still disturbs me. Why El Chose Ishät, we'll never know, but in the meantime, we have to be at his side when his wife gives the official announcement of her pregnancy, and I will have to be there for the birth.*

At least I won't be obliged to accompany you for that.

He nodded. Kariiel understood the movements of The Breath more deeply than anyone else on this side of life. The forces she sensed were very real, but as yet, their natures were indistinct. He hoped they would become clearer soon enough so they could forestall or dilute the worst outcomes. It would not be the first time, although Breath forbid Ishät should ever discover the Kaskarudjan's true purpose.

"So, 'Giahn's Joy', here we come," she said solemnly.

"Ready or not," he replied.

WHERE ARE THE BEL NISHANI?

Huldar gazed out over the sparkling sea of the central eye. Pale, blue-green waves shushed over the sandy beach. A slight breeze plucked at his hair and clothing, filling his senses with the scent of salt water and distance. But despite all this natural beauty, his heart beat firm against his chest, spurred by deep unease.

He shaded his eyes and squinted into the horizon, but, as yet, there was no sign of the Bel Nishani.

Further up the long, gently curved beach, figures squatted on dunes. Others strolled bare-legged through the wavelets. One started purposefully towards him but even at a distance, Farushael of Cantori was recognizable by his uncertain haze and determined gait.

The Cantori nodded a bow. "Shamkarun Huldar."

"Farushael," he replied blandly.

"No sign of these … Bel Nishani," Farushael said, and gave him a long look. "Would you tell us if there was?"

"Probably not," Huldar said.

"Don't blame you." Farushael joined him in looking out to sea. "Our orders are to prioritize nacrite production. It may well be that we don't have personnel to waste, waiting for an event that may or may not happen."

Huldar's head tipped fractionally to the side. Was Farushael, whom he'd always thought of as Olatu's toady, offering him support?

"Of course," Farushael continued, "as chief in charge of how our so-called 'surplus' workers are deployed, that would be my decision to make; and Olatu of Faytha," he scuffed the sand with his toe, pushing it into a little pile. "Well … he's quite concerned that we may not meet our extremely important nacrite quotas. Did you know that?"

"I was unaware," Huldar said cautiously.

He nodded. "Yes, that is the case."

"Nacrite - I've heard it may be vital to our God-Emperor's plans," Huldar offered. "He would most likely be quite upset with Olatu if the shipment was underrepresented."

Farushael nodded encouragingly.

"And no one wants to make the Imperium unhappy," Huldar said firmly. "With that in mind, perhaps these good folks could be put to better use in the nacrite mines. I will continue to keep watch here, and if I notice any beaching of Bel Nishani, I will definitely inform someone."

Farushael bowed. "That would be most kind, Shamkarun Huldar."

"Of course, we are not even sure if the behavior is, indeed, an annual event," Huldar told him. "We have not had time to make appropriate assessments and studies. It may be that there will be no beaching of sea-creatures this cycle, and that absence is an entirely natural occurrence."

"Time will tell," Farushael said. "But for now, I am sure Olatu will be relieved to know all available staff are hard at work of fulfilling our all-important nacrite quotas." He bowed again and called to the beach-goers.

Slowly, and somewhat reluctantly, the small party made their way up the dunes to the portal.

When they were gone, Huldar sat on the sands and smiled. Had something just gone his way? He closed his eyes and let the sun shine down on his face. After basking this way for several minutes, he noticed the strange absence in his core and began to listen intently for the planet's voice. He received no feeling of her involvement, no sense of joy at this reprieve. It seemed odd.

The sun went behind a cloud. He opened his eyes, and when it came out again, there, just beyond the breakers, he caught the flash and slide of a long, unbroken fin.

A quick glance up the beach showed him the Host were truly gone.

How could the Bel Nishani's timing be so perfect? He stood up for a clearer view.

Lazy cloud-shadows dimmed the gloss of diminutive breakers in patterns of light and shade. He waited, hardly daring to breath, until yes! There it was again. Superimposed imagery given him by Pieru the Guild-Lord confirmed what he saw was true. The Bel Nishani had come home at last.

What's happened? Andel asked.

Come to the beach, he said, and let his excitement spread through their bond. *But absolutely no one is to know where you are going, or why.*

He sent Casco a similar message, then Daric, then settled down to enjoy the wait.

It seemed only minutes before Daric trudged along the line of dunes towards him.

What is it? he asked curiously. *Has Olatu died? Don't tell me you killed him yourself!*

Huldar laughed. *No such luck. Come and stand with me – ahh! Here's Andel.*

Casco's not far off either, Daric continued. *So what's going on?*

Huldar saw another roil of fins and forgot to answer, or even acknowledge his wife when she stepped onto the dunes.

Daric's brows levelled. *Lucky I'm good at giving excuses. Left Banga to fend for himself for a while, but the copper camp won't police itself.*

Andel sent a wordless enquiry.

He waved her closer without taking his eyes from the bay.

She followed his gaze and gave a small gasp. Mixed excitement and dread flooded him. *It's them, isn't it?* she said. *Bel Nishani. But what will we tell Olatu? We can't let … what happened last time happen again!*

"It would be nice if you'd let me in on whatever it is," Daric said sourly.

"Look!" Andel pointed out to sea.

Daric went still all over. His head tipped slowly to the side. "Breath be sweet!" he breathed. "It's just as he saw them."

Andel gravitated to a comfortable place beneath his arm. The churning agglomeration grew, roiling with energy as more silver fins joined it.

Casco arrived sometime later, but the apology on his mind evaporated as he turned to see what they were looking at. *You can't tell them,* he said. *Really, you can't! Shut down the gate. Blame Qalān.*

"Farushael called the Host off, just this morning," Huldar told them. "Seems the nacrite quotas are behind schedule."

"Farushael?"

Huldar sighed happily. "Maybe there's hope yet."

As if they'd been waiting for Casco to arrive, the Bel Nishani began to sing. Only one at first, so subtle as to be barely detectable - merely an exaggeration of the vibrations of the life all around them. More joined in and the sound seemed to coalesce until it swelled to an eerie, yet joyful chorus, each thread pure and clean.

Casco and Daric clung to each other, their hazes conjoined.

Andel wept into his shirt.

Tears slid down his cheeks.

Then the rush for the shore began.

Bright rainbow flashes pierced the wavelets. It was as if orbs of living water propelled forward and onto the sand, driven by shining silver bodies. The singing became more urgent as they wormed higher and higher, seeking the dunes above.

The air soon reeked of fish. Pectoral fins dug and thrashed. Mouths gaped. Slashed vertically along the creature's sides, rows of indigo gills opened and closed in the hunt for air.

Huldar and his friends were completely ignored as they walked among them and tried to stay out of their way.

The Bel Nishani's song ended when it found a suitable dune. Its head would rear and plunge forward, while the body thrashed and wriggled with all its power, driving it into the sand until it was totally concealed.

No creature attempted to burrow where another lay hidden.

Finally, the last tail was absorbed and the beach was silent but for the fine sound of windblown sand forming and reforming in endless waving patterns, the same across every planet in the known.

"How could he?" Andel said quietly. She looked into his eyes. Inside, her soul wept. "How could he do that? How could anyone harm, deliberately destroy such glorious beings. Their eyes? How could he look into them and see only profit?"

Casco peered out at the sea, now restless and grey. Slowly, he shook his head. "That sound - that glorious sound. Who could even describe it? And that monster!" he turned to Daric. "I looked after him. Showed him what kindness I could. Why did I do that?"

Daric touched his lover's face, tracing the path of his tears. "He's gone, beloved. He's gone."

"I hope you weren't too gentle," Andel said firmly.

Huldar looked at her in surprise.

"Such evil!" she cried. "The Breath was too good for him."

He hugged her close and let her cry. Her body wracked with all the pain she'd held inside her since her mother's death.

Casco raised his eyebrows in tacit concern.

Huldar shook his head and tenderly kissed her hair.

"You go," he said softly. "We'll be along later."

"Are there more?" Casco asked. "Will they come again tomorrow?"

Again, Huldar nodded. Andel's head was wet from his tears.

I will close the gate. We will be the last.

Daric's expression was doubtful, and he knew why. No one closed portals. And in truth, he had no idea how to make that happen, but if there was a way, he would find it.

THE PROGRESS OF THE WENT

Summer sun baked down on the herd's shaggy backs as they meandered upward between patches of sparse forest. Spindly purple vines clawed their way up spongy trunks, pale and twisted by hardship. Clusters of toxic red berries sprouted from ropey tendrils. Above, furtive grey leaves wafted like flakes of solidified cloud and scratched and rattled, as if embarrassed to draw attention to the meagre shade they provided.

Hnarse paused at the top of the rise and surveyed the barren plain ahead. In the direct sun of midday, it was hard to see the shallow pits that pockmarked it.

Went clustered in the dappled light. Their corn-silk hair rippled in conversation as they waited, hungry and anxious, for the right time to make the crossing. A small group bent to report observations to the Heart.

Hnarse listened to their drone, but felt no urge to join in. Its trunk strayed onto Nielli's back. The smoothness of its hair was pleasant but unnerving. Hnarse was sure that if the movements of speech could be mimicked, others could also understand, and urged its companion closer so it could feel its words.

"We are waiting for the right time," Hnarse said as clearly as it could.

Nielli's trunk joined his. *The right time?* it repeated happily.

Hnarse bumped Nielli playfully, *Now your turn,* and stepped back to watch.

Nielli's hair follicles moved with heart-warming determination.

It picked up the young one's trunk and placed it against its side. "Well done!" it said.

Nielli's sense of pride reassured Hnarse the little blind Went had understood.

"Nielli, to survive the crossing, you must avoid areas which smell sweet," it said. 'You must avoid', was said on the back – the easy part for Nielli to read, but the movements pertaining to sweetness and smell were signalled on the face.

Hnarse felt Nielli's trunk move over it like the touch of a leaf in the breeze. It brought the young one's trunk to its face, and rippled its facial hair again. "Avoid areas which have a sweet smell."

Nielli squeaked with delight. *A sweet smell! Avoid areas that smell more sweet!*

Yes! Hnarse's joyous bugle turned a few heads. *Well done! Now, try to repeat the words back to me.*

But it is hard, Hnarse, and I am tired.

You must learn, Hnarse said. *I will not always be here to guide you. When we return home, you will claim a burrow and sleep through the white waste. Afterwards, you will wake and feed and grow strong to find the next new purpose. Already, your unique observations have enriched our communication with the Heart, but it would be even better if they could be related to the herd when I am gone.*

Gone? Nielli gave Hnarse a gentle bump. *You will never be gone.*

I will be, Hnarse assured the young Went. *All revolve through the great circle. It is how we know our names. The part spent here on the trail are vital for the world to be reconstructed correctly after the waste destroys it. Went are creators. Without us, nothing will be as it should.*

But I am not as I should be.

You are exactly as you should be, Hnarse said. *You are here for a purpose – to teach us a new way of observation. To instruct the Heart in a way no other can.*

Really? Nielli stood quietly, as if this concept had surprised. *Other Went don't like me. I feel their thoughts now, whether they want me to or not. Some of them think I am a wrongness. A mistake. A burden.*

You are none of those things!

How am I to know?

Hnarse turned to face the young one. *That we can speak in this way … we are the first Went ever to do this. I know you are special, Nielli, and your presence, your blindness, is no mistake.*

Nielli gave Hnarse a soft head-butt, then shuffled around to press against its side.

Hnarse said no more. The love it felt for Nielli was beyond any emotion it had yet experienced, and was therefore, inexpressible. Suddenly, it could take it no more, and fell to its knees to drone to the Heart. Whatever happened, whatever else was lost on this sad, strange trail of trials, Nielli's beauty must remain.

Later that day, only a short time before the crossing must be attempted, Hnarse watched the alien, strangely graceful on its two thin legs, rock across the hillside. It saw the strange being's gait as a matter of balance and recovery, and stored the insight to be sung to the Heart of the World. Like the others of its herd, it had only two eyes, and these were as blue as the sky above. Perhaps, in the same way as a Went's coat and under markings, the alien's eye colour was an indication of purpose?

As the two-leg approached, Hnarse's breathing quickened. There had been no deliberate contact between the new-commers and the herd during this cycle, but this one watched them nearly every day, and it wondered if it was about to learn why.

Atop the aliens head were strands that might be hair, but these filaments were twisted into a single tight vine which hung to halfway down its narrow back. Perhaps the structure was a sort of tail, and not hair at all - but if so, how could it communicate?

Hnarse moved its own hair follicles in greeting.

The bottom of the vine swung slightly, but there was no discernible pattern and Hnarse could make no sense of it. Perhaps the movement had just been caused by the wind.

Hnarse remembered the design of different coloured skin beneath the alien's eye. On closer inspection, it saw this marking had become more complex since the last cycle. An Elder's markings changed over time in much the same way, so Hnarse reared up and displayed the patterns on its own skin, the indigo of a stargazer marked with yellow and red stripes.

What's happening? Nielli asked. *What is that smell?*

An alien! Hnarse replied. *A two-leg. The watcher has come to visit us.*

To Hnarse's astonishment, the alien mirrored its actions and also opened its arms wide. Hnarse saw no colour. Paler than a young one. The blue-eyed alien lowered its arms but Hnarse remained upright. Maybe this would encourage it to try again.

The Went's patience was rewarded as the alien stepped slowly closer. Its naked face was level with the gap between Hnarse's forearms.

At first it seemed unsure, but then it reached out one appendage.

Hnarse stood very still. It connected with Hnarse's mid-leg foot-pad and tingled … such as might indicate an approaching storm.

Sounds issued from the alien's mouth. Hnarse found them pleasant and soft. There was rhythm and changes in pitch. Maybe such sounds were its way of communicating? Hnarse knew many insects, and even certain types of running creatures used the same technique, but understanding was impossible.

The two-leg paused. Its appendage dropped back to its side. Its head tilted. Was it disappointed?

Again, Hnarse waited.

When Neetha came and stood nearby, the two-leg addressed the Grassmover with the same, or similar series of sounds, and Nielli bumped Hnarse's rear.

It's talking, Nielli said. *It's talking like we do!*

What's it saying?

I don't know … there's ideas … another being it is a part of – if that makes sense? … I think it's a Mother!

A Mother? How extraordinary! Hnarse peered at the alien more closely. It didn't look like a Mother, but Nielli seemed confident.

Yes! Not this one – the other one that's not here, Nielli exclaimed. *And there are other Mothers. This one … worries for them. Is afraid …*

How wondrous! More Mothers!

But all conjecture fled when the two-leg began to sing. Hnarse's aural receptors were bathed in rich, melodious sound, and it was overcome by the possibility that the song may cease before there was a chance to record its beauty, and it would never be heard again.

Neetha watched as if stunned while Hnarse slowly lowered its head to the ground and began to drone. It said nothing itself, but took the marvellous alien's song and presence directly to the Heart.

The alien melody moved through several variations, and was as if the Heart heard and answered. Hnarse felt calm, soothed and cared for. Tears dribbled from its nose. It hoped this alien creature found such peace in their shared sounds as it did. Perhaps it understood Hnarse was preserving their encounter by sending it to the Heart of the world for safekeeping.

Huldar stood tall and opened his arms again, but although his charm-song had faded the Elder's head remained bowed. The long, low sound it made vibrated the ground beneath his feet and seemed to go ever deeper.

The way their vocalisations had melded amazed him … and had he heard the Planet in it?

Reluctantly, he turned for the portal. His head spun with snatches of his profound experience. He decided it had been as if the blind one understood him at some level … especially the concept of 'mothers'. He'd designed charm to augment the possibility of connection, yet that tenuous feeling of understanding between himself and the blind one had faded as it took hold, as if the sound itself had been a distraction.

Maybe annangi charm-songs had no effect on these creatures, but he could not be happier with the result. The blended song he and the Elder had made was rich and full – as if it were a song made merely for its own joy! … And in their combined voices, he'd felt the planet's presence.

He peered back for a last look at the shaggy creatures, the newest citizens of the Realm. Led by the few remaining Elders, they had begun to walk In single file down the stony path into the valley.

What's happened? Andel asked him.

He gave a short laugh. Of course she'd felt his excitement. He recalled the magnificent song of the Bel Nishani at the beaching shores, and the catharsis it unleashed. Since that outburst, he'd noticed a new clarity in her, a lightness of spirit which had been missing since her mother's death.

He remembered her father's wise eyes, their pain made deeper because he could not ease his daughter's burden. *El's favored grow on a scaffold of scars …* he said to himself, and his smile deepened. Maybe her Trianogi ways had rubbed off on him – a little. The Andel he knew was as strong as the minerals she divined, and more beautiful to him than the rarest of gems.

As he stepped toward the campsite, he could feel the thickness in Qalān, and it made him wonder at the relationship between the Planet and the energies that flowed around her. Did she define them, or was it the other way round … She had approved, even aided his closure of the gate to the beaching shores, but since then, traffic for the Host had become more difficult.

When the step was completed, he saw someone waiting and his head came up. "Farushael? What brings you to the Eastern Continent?"

"Greetings, Huldar." The Cantori bowed. "I am sorry to intrude, but I must ask … Olatu tried to send a crew to check for the Bel Nishani," his eyebrows lifted, "but they could not find the portal."

"That is a problem," Huldar agreed.

"You are an expert with portal construction," Farushael said. "Apparently one of the best there is."

Huldar grimaced. Farushael clearly suspected he'd somehow closed it, even though the feat was widely held to be impossible. He sighed. "Farushael, Qalān is tricky right now. Go nowhere without careful preparation. It is possible to be trapped, and as you may know, I have seen the consequences. I would not wish such a fate on anyone."

Farushael bowed again. "So … the portal has vanished … unaided?"

"I know it seems strange, but …"

"What else could have happened." Farushael finished for him. The Cantori gave a neutral nod. "This is a wild planet, after all, and anything could happen, couldn't it?"

"Yes." Huldar smiled. "Anything at all."

DJAN'RŪ

Andel dabbed perspiration from her face and grimaced at the mid-morning sun. Time to get moving. She pushed herself out of her chair in the shade and started for the marquee. At least the nights were cooler here in the foothills, but the days were often unbearable. The flowers had wilted, her legs swelled and her back ached - and the number of times a day she needed the latrine was just silly.

You've got a warm coat with you? Casco said.

Yes. It was an effort to block her irritation. When did he turn into her mother?

I'll be there shortly, he went on. *It's not safe on your own. Huldar would kill me …*

I'll be perfectly alright! she snapped back. Qalān was sometimes difficult these days, resistant to the songs, but she was no beginner to this world. She needed no chaperone. He should know that. Huldar had taught her a thing or two, and so had Daric - and Casco had more important things to do than act as a personal portal attendant.

She sensed his apology and was immediately contrite.

Her baby turned uncomfortably. She rested her hand on her belly and sent soothing thoughts. Despite her rapid gestation, it seemed her daughter was impatient.

It's this heat, she said to Casco. *We'll be glad to be out of it.*

He imaged their destination. *I'll get there as soon as I can. If you get into trouble, just wait. I'll find you.*

I'll be fine!

She waddled toward the cook-tent. Sand slowed her going. Tam pummeled a mound of dough beneath the heels of his palms.

"Up and about so soon?" he said sarcastically.

She shook her head and sighed. With the navigator due in a week, they were all feeling the strain, and the half-way mark - the communications window, was almost upon them. She recalled how excited they'd been on their first stay, when it had been just them, the Uri'madu, tense with anticipation for news from the Realm.

This rotation was different altogether. Fear and uncertainty preyed on their tolerances, especially with the imminence of the births. How could they possibly be ready? How could *she* possibly be ready? Today's work was a crucial step, but what if it went wrong?

Her daughter kicked again, and she took measured breaths. Apprehensiveness was not good for either of them.

She gave Tam a rueful smile, and the air between them cleared. "We'll need extra lunches today," she said. "Four, if that's alright?"

He flicked a glance at her bulging figure, and she gave a tired nod. "Yes, extra-large ones please."

"Off with the Blessed?"

She smiled again.

"Then I'll make sure you have a few galano twigs, and maybe some golden wheel pies?" he said. "I know how you ladies love them."

"Thank you, Tam. We'd be lost without your care."

"Have to look after our Blessed ones, don't we? Young Tashel gets so hungry these days - it's as if she's eating for three, not two - or maybe she's got a whole army in there!"

He smiled, but a shimmer of worry crossed his veil. Had he allowed it to show, or been unable to hide it? She held her expression steady, as if she hadn't seen. She didn't want any discussion about feelings or worries today. It was hard enough to hide her intentions as it was.

He handed her several baskets, and one by one she tucked them into Qalān. Then a smaller, fifth container came up from under the bench.

She looked at him enquiringly.

He winked. "An extra snack-pack won't go astray."

"Where are you getting all this from?" she asked. "I thought we were on rations."

He lifted one eyebrow. "All the study our poor dear Lind did, working with Alis on what local plants were edible - now it's paying off. We didn't have supply runs, or tents full of goodies then, did we?"

"No, we did not."

"So, no need to worry, Lady Andel. Whatever happens, we'll be able to feed ourselves for the duration. You'll see."

"Thank you, Tam."

She stifled an upwelling of emotion and gave him a small, heart-felt bow. From the bottom of her heart, she hoped such a dire situation would not come to pass. A questioning feeling came from her baby, and she sent a calming reply. Her little one could not yet organize her thoughts into firm structure, but felt her mother's emotions and often responded, especially when those sentiments were strong.

She saw Tam's knowing gaze shift between her belly and her face.

"Won't be long now, Lady Andel," he said stoutly, "and our new little Blessings will see the light of day." He imaged the Host's encampment. "Let's hope that day is a good one."

She nodded, but with thoughts of the future and what it might hold, her smile faded and was reluctant to return. As she turned for the portal, her tread seemed over-loud on the sand. Several paces later, the thump and push of Tam's fists against the dough began once more.

Shh, my baby, she whispered. *All will be well.* Negotiating the first few portals would require her firmest concentration. Oddly, the last step, which would take her through ancient Qalān, would be smoothest. Perhaps because of Daric's influence, it recognized her? Once such a concept would have seemed preposterous, but now she was almost convinced it was true.

It took longer than it normally would have to travel to the ends of Went, but when she arrived, the coolness was a great relief. On the stony shore of that nameless Southern isle, morning shadows were long. Waves pounded and sighed. The ever-present wind spat spray in her face and moaned as if in pain. She took shelter in the hollow where she had met Malena and Daric a few months earlier, but although the tide was at its lowest ebb, sea-levels were rising apace and waves lapped at her feet. She had to move on. Their portal would soon be covered and even if the weather calmed, it would be hours before they could leave.

By the time they needed to use this, their ultimate escape route, if indeed they ever got the chance, the Djan'rū would most likely be covered by a foot or so of icy water. Malena assured her it would still work, but they would be forced to take a little of the ocean with them, and obviously, the portal she'd just used would be inaccessible. An alternative would have to be forged. She sighed. Another job for Daric. Huldar was already run off his feet, and besides, he wasn't supposed to know about this - another of Daric's perhaps extreme safety measures.

She surveyed the rock-strewn landscape. Low shrubs with stiff, sparse foliage hid little, and the idea of walking across it made her heart sink. What were they letting themselves in for?

Suddenly her father's face loomed large in her mind, and a rush of tears prickled her eyes. He would've known exactly what to say, what would give her the courage she needed. Huldar didn't even know she was here, and although she understood the necessity, it felt awful to exclude him.

A strong gust, wet with salt spray, buffeted her sideways as if forcing her to action. After a last, lonely look, she pulled her coat tight around her shoulders and began to pick her way over a reef slick with spray.

It still seemed strange to see her belly where she should have seen feet. She gasped and stumbled when she misjudged the height of a rock. Her palms smarted where they had broken her fall. She climbed back upright, breathed deeply and tried to divine her way over the uneven terrain, but her fine-honed senses simply weren't as effective over land, and the journey seemed to take forever.

Personal time is relative to one's desire to be elsewhere, … the clear memory of her mother's lecturing mind-voice came to mind. More tears blurred her vision, and she cursed her mercurial emotions, but when she looked up, the dark-edged rock platform where the Djan'rū would be loomed ahead.

She scanned it on the off chance Casco was already there, but found only an irritating psychic silence and the endless whine of the wind.

Her stomach rumbled.

A glance skyward assured her she wasn't too early.

She perched uncomfortably on the edge of the wave-worn basalt and using the basic anti-inflammatory techniques Ubaid had taught them, rubbed her swollen ankles, then the knee she'd bruised in the fall. With another flow of energy she tried to sooth the ache in her back, but success was limited.

Time passed. The sun crawled higher. The pain in her body calmed. Her baby slept.

She remembered their first trip to this location and laughed at herself. To think she'd worn 'heavy and awkward' as a badge of honor, and had felt quite excited by the prospect of giving birth. Now she felt more like a cast kreth awaiting Breath's touch, and excitement had given way to anxiety. As a distraction, she pressed her palms against the rock and let her mind rove at will through its tight crystals.

A strange anomaly made her pause - traces of nacrite where it should not be, and she honed in on an area on or near the surface.

Andel!

The call brought her back with a jolt. She opened her eyes to see Malena, graceful and self-assured as ever, with Casco not far behind.

Where's Daric? Andel asked. *I thought he'd be here by now – he's usually so punctual.*

And we're not? Malena snapped.

Casco tried to support the navigator's elbow as she started up-slope, but she shook him off.

That's not what I meant, Andel snapped back, then she smiled a little inside. Despite appearances, Malena also felt the strain.

He should've been here already, Casco said. *I saw him leave.*

Andel's smile broadened. *So!*

Casco rolled his eyes. *Yes, if you must know. Things are better than they were.*

Malena's eyebrows flickered. *Better than they were before, or better than before before?*

He frowned, but before he could mask it, his haze brightened with a rosy flush.

Andel looked away, but he reached out with private reassurance. "And no, Lady Maatu," he said to Malena, "it is not 'better' yet, but I firmly believe it will be. Happy now?"

There was a stealthy crunch behind her.

Casco and Malena's eyes opened wide with shock.

Andel turned to see Daric standing on the rock behind her with arms grandiosely outstretched. The grin on his face was pure triumph.

"How did you get here?" Malena demanded. "I might be voiceless but I'm not blind!" she glanced behind at the way they'd come. "You didn't sneak all that way. Even you're not that perverse. You must've made a new gate!"

"Been here the whole time," he assured her gleefully. He shook his hand as if there were something in it, and as he did so, parts of his torso disappeared in crisp section.

Casco barked with laughter. "It works!"

Daric jumped nimbly from the natural platform and kissed him. "It does indeed."

Andel smiled as comprehension dawned. *The cloak?*

Malena shook her head. "Well I'll be Breathless! There's a song and a half."

He held out his arm and they watched, wide eyed, as it vanished.

Where it should have been, Andel's fingertips discovered silken fabric with texture so fine it seemed to melt beneath her touch. When she reached below to weigh it, her own hand disappeared, covered in cool heaviness.

"Weighs more than I expected," Malena said, "which is just as well. Wouldn't want it blowing away. You'd never find it."

Daric's yellow-gold eyes glowed like a child's with excitement. She'd never seen him so open and unafraid.

"With this, we'll be able to hide the Blessings perfectly, even if it's only one by one," she said.

It's completely silent? he asked her.

A tiny hint of nacrite is all, and only because I'm a diviner and I happened to be inside the rock you were on.

Daric gave a happy sigh. He reached for what she assumed to be one corner - half a hand sidled into the air - and she noticed a small bag that swung as if suspended by an invisible thread.

He grabbed the bag and stuffed the cloth into it, finally sealing it with a plainly twisted tie.

"Don't want it to draw attention," he said, and swung the bag back and forth before them. "Hiding something precious?" He winked. "Boring is best!"

"How does it sit in Qalān?" Casco asked.

"Restless," Daric replied. "But bearable." He beamed at them again. "And here we are, ready for fresh adventure!"

Malena shook her head. "Hope you've had the sleep of Bless," she said sharply. "or you'll be no use to us here."

Casco blushed again.

Andel sensed a quick exchange between him and Daric.

"We'll be fine," Daric said aloud. "Nothing like a physical workout to keep the mind sharp." He nodded solemnly at Malena. "As I'm sure you well know."

Malena gave a soft snort. "Let's get started then."

"What's the plan?" Andel asked. "Will this formation resist in the same way Qalān does now?"

Malena and Daric shared a glance.

"Hope not." Daric shrugged "Hard to say."

Casco indicated the other two. "The plan is, Daric and Malena will join minds in a rehearsal to see how tough it's going to be – is that right?"

They nodded.

"Then, when they're ready," Casco continued, "I'll join them and oversee the process."

Andel squinted skyward as the sun emerged from scudding clouds. "Sounds fairly straight-forward," she said.

"It's not," Malena replied bluntly.

As if on cue, the landscape darkened once more.

"The forces we'll be dealing with are immense," she explained. "One mistake and the whole thing will collapse, or worse still, we'll become enmeshed in the construct and unable to extricate ourselves. Without Casco to mitigate, shield, and/or direct, the danger would be ten times greater." She looked away for a moment, studying the energy-field they were about to manipulate. "Make no mistake, Andel, or any of you. Someone could easily be killed." She returned to Andel. "This has never been done before. We are breaking new ground."

"Again ..." Casco murmured.

Daric clasped Casco's shoulder. "Archerran, remember?" he said softly.

Malena gave a quick frown and studied Casco intently, her eyes lingering on elements of his haze. At length, she gave a slow nod. "I don't know why I didn't see it before."

He grimaced doubtfully and shook his head.

Daric's eyebrows lifted. "It's what Alis thinks."

"Why not?" Malena said. "This is the work you're doing, and it's not to be taken lightly."

"Let's just get on with it, shall we?" Casco said shortly. "If you two are ready?"

Malena eyed the rock. Daric jumped up onto it and reached down to help her. Their hands stayed clasped as they centered themselves where the Djan'rū would be. Energy whisked lightly around them. Andel thought she recognized some of the configurations Huldar had set for the Djan'rū at Basecamp so long ago.

She could feel Casco's gaze on her.

"Now that I know some of what it takes to make these things work," he said, "it's still no less miraculous." She noticed his voice seemed more resonant, but the Kareski accent was still strong. "Huldar did well to tune Basecamp as he did," he continued, "and using only what he remembered of Kandät Enna's brief instructions."

He gazed in Huldar's direction, as if he felt his presence on the other side of the world as keenly as she did. "He'll be disappointed not to be involved in the making of this one - when he finds out what we've done."

"Yes, he will," Andel said sadly.

Malena's stern gaze haunted her. She contemplated a world without Casco in it, and knew without doubt it would be untenable.

"And what's this about you being Archerran?" she said lightly.

He shrugged, clearly ill at ease. "It's what Alis thinks, as he said, but...?"

"It does make sense, you know, now it's out there," she assured him. "Although it's very rare. I've only ever met one other - an Enna, and she was, well, amazing. Had an ability to see what was needed for any project, no matter how complex, and make it happen - just like you."

"I'm no genius." Casco tipped his chin Daric's way. "Not like him."

"How do you know?"

He shrugged. "I'm just not, am I? I didn't invent window domes, or an invisible cloak."

"No," she agreed. "But we all had a part in the cloak's manufacture. I was there, remember? It was my idea. And without you, it could not have been made." She remembered the first time she'd really looked into his blue-grey eyes. Then, his gaze had been reserved - now, it burned almost as keenly as Huldar's did when faced with a new puzzle.

"Remember when we linked minds for the first time?" she said.

He nodded.

She returned his soft smile. "We were far-seeing - remember? I was good at it, but not strong. It's still not my best skill," she laughed. "But you? I was surprised by your power, and by your potential. Your abilities have grown and grown. Now, Ziquarra has manifested?"

"How did you ...?"

"Huldar," she replied. "Although he told me to keep it to myself. It's a gift few beyond the Hermes share." She smiled up at him. "I am no longer surprised when you do great things, Casco. And I think that by the time we get back to the

Realm, you and Daric will make a formidable team – outrageously gifted and definitely one of a kind!"

He snorted good-humoredly. "You're teasing."

"No, I'm not," she replied.

A strong gust pushed him a step closer. She turned toward the rock as the crescendo of energies surrounding Daric and Malena reached a high-point then lulled. In the peace that followed, Daric looked down at them and smiled in satisfaction.

Malena shook her head. *If he wasn't Enna, I'd marry him,* she said jokingly.

It's time, Daric said, and held out his hand for Casco. *All warmed up and ready to go.*

I've heard that before, Casco replied.

As he stepped into place, Malena looked at Andel. "I've made quite a few Djan'rū, although never by proxy. Daric is strong and I'm fairly sure we'll survive," she said, "but remember, call Banga if things go wrong. He'll know what to do. … And get further back. Too dangerous."

She took backward steps until Malena nodded.

Casco bowed his head and as the three meshed minds, she saw the surrounding energy coalesce into distinct lines.

Malena's mouth opened, and Daric responded in song as if they were one. Forces swirled as his voice lifted and wove an intricate chord.

Andel moved even further away, alarmed by the field's strength and scope. She'd envisaged the new gate as much the same size as the one at Central basecamp – now she saw how wrong she was. This would be three times the size, bigger even than the Host's.

As the work progressed, she watched Daric and wondered how he could make himself a vessel for another's will. Perhaps his core identity was so strong as to be unassailable? With a little effort she could discern each unique energetic input - although what the differences were, she couldn't put into words, and despite his willing subjugation, Daric's tsemkar was also part of the equation. How could he do both at one time? Casco was right. The Enna was genius.

She barely noticed when the wind died. Warm sunlight, filtered by the violent forces her friends manipulated, wandered the rocks in nebulous refracted blobs. The boom of surf against the shore seemed muffled. A flock of curious, darkly banded lizards studied them for a while before skuttling back into the scrubby, rock-strewn plain.

She looked at the rock again when the song changed timbre. Beads of sweat adorned Daric's forehead. His tone increased in urgency. He tilted his head back as if to open his throat beyond its given capabilities. An eerie chord ensued, then a flash of light encased the thrashing forces, stabilized and condensed into a brilliant transparent hemisphere.

Malena's mouth remained tightly closed. Her eyed were pressed shut. A deep frown furrowed the skin between her brows.

To Andel, it looked like a fully activated Djan'rū. The three figures within it were bathed in a bluish light, blurred and somehow unreal, as if figments of a particularly vivid dream.

She clapped her hands softly together, lost in the marvel of their achievement, but as time passed and the light didn't fade, she began to worry.

The participants seemed frozen. The unchanging chord rang loudly in her ears.

When Malena's Shamkar pulsed faintly, Andel gasped, but the Shamkar's light quickly faded and nothing had changed. It must have been a move of desperation, Andel concluded, and it had failed.

Was it time to call Banga? She paced back and forth unsure of what she should do.

Daric's shirt was dark with perspiration. Signs of strain marred his tone as the chord looped on. She gasped again when he stumbled forward as if to keep his balance. Casco's firm grip held him upright, and a deep reverberation shuddered through the dome as the Archerran began to sing. His strong arms raised slowly skyward, taking Daric's and Malena's hands with him as if they were welded together.

Daric slumped beneath the strain, as if no longer able to stand alone, but Casco pushed his fists higher, almost lifting the assassin from the ground. His voice soared into spaces where Daric's faltered. The smell of ozone filled the air. Then the dome emitted a sharp whip crack and with a last flash of blinding light, was gone.

Casco tore his hands from his companions' grip and clutched his head, then screamed and collapsed to the ground.

Daric stumbled to his side.

Malena stood as if stunned, then fell slowly to her knees.

Andel clambered awkwardly onto the rock. *What should I do!*

Daric looked up at her. Tears streamed down his haggard cheeks. *Get a healer, Alis or Ubaid. Quickly! Now!*

She glanced at Malena, but the navigator seemed frozen in shock.

Alis! She closed her eyes and called again. *Alis, Ubaid! Help us!*

There was no answer. Surely one was in range? Casco writhed in agony. Daric held him firmly as he began to convulse. She turned away, unable to watch, and tried again, calling as loudly as she could. Her baby kicked, and guilt brought fresh tears. She knew such stress could damage her Bless; leave permanent scars, but there was no one else to help. She tried to send love to soothe and cushion the trauma, but as if in answer, a new love washed through her from the inside out, and a thought formed between them.

… Help mama …

Andel, what's wrong!? The healer's response was faint, but clear.

She flashed Alis a visual of the scene on the rock then the trail of steps she would need to follow to get there. *Hurry!* she cried. *Please hurry!*

She blinked as the contact broke off, and turned back to Daric. "Alis is on her way."

Daric nodded miserably. Casco lay unconscious in his arms.

Malena opened and closed her eyes as if coming back from the brink, then, while her hands cradled her unborn baby, folded back down over her stomach. She lowered her head and Andel saw her lips move in an urgent whisper. Even though Daric and Casco were right in front of her, she seemed oblivious.

Huldar's thoughts pushed at her, sick with worry, demanding answers.

Andel stopped herself from wringing her hands. She longed for his presence, his smell, to feel his arms around her, for him to take charge and know exactly what to do - but all she could tell him was not to worry. There'd been an accident and Alis was on her way.

Her baby lay quiescent and unresponsive, but did not seem distressed. Had she really helped? Had she really structured a thought? The idea was incredible, but how could they know what these young ones would be capable of? *Help mama …* did she ask for help, or give it? She suspected it was the latter, but what form that help had taken was undetectable - only that Alis had suddenly reached back and replied even though it had seemed the healers were beyond range.

After an agonizing wait, Daric's head turned with a hunter's intensity toward the portal on the beach.

Andel gave a cry of relief as Huldar reached out with a visual of hip deep surf all around and Alis held above it in his arms.

Tell me! he said.

It's Casco, she cried. *He's collapsed. He's dying. They were making a Djan'rū, a secret one, but it got too big, or too wild and I think Casco saved them but now he's dying!*

Huldar's long legs propelled him at speed over the stones.

Alis clung grimly to his back with her arms around his neck.

He set the healer down on the platform, then turned and held Andel so tightly she could barely breathe. The love between them flowed strong and fierce as a river in flood, and his understanding of her secrecy held a bittersweet pride.

But now you know! She buried her face against his chest. *We should never have tried such a foolish thing!*

They turned as Alis spoke aloud. "Let me near him, Daric … please."

Daric looked dumbly up at her.

"I won't hurt him. You know I won't," she said.

Moments later, Daric bowed his head.

Alis knelt by Casco's side and took his wrist. She placed her hand on his forehead and examined his meridians with practiced care. Finally, she brushed his hair upward, examined his hairline then beckoned Daric closer and invited him to look.

Daric seemed visibly shocked by what he saw.

"It's happened," the healer said.

Daric touched Casco's still face with a gentle hand, rubbed his forehead as if removing a smudge of soot, then gently parted his hair to view his scalp.

"Archerrani," he said softly. Andel saw fresh tears in his eyes as he peered up at Alis, then at Huldar, then herself. "He's not dying, he's Archerran. He's been Marked."

ARCHERRAN

Huldar closed his eyes and held his face toward the phantom sun, barely visible beyond the racing clouds. After a moment spent like this, he took a deep breath and started for the scrubby hinterland.

"What are you doing?" Andel asked.

"Seven hours, more or less, before we can safely leave." He glanced at Alis. "Fire and food are essential."

Andel looked down at Malena's hunched form. Alis crouched, still hard at work, beside the navigator.

Go with him, the healer said. *I'll be here.*

With a last look at Malena, she let Huldar take her hand to help her from the platform's edge. Guilt stained her veil.

Nonsense! Huldar gave her hand a light squeeze. *Alis is there. She has not been left alone.*

Andel gave him a sharp look. *You're angry?*

He glanced back at the sad tableau on the rock. His eyes snapped. *Yes! A dangerous and foolhardy undertaking. They could've died. You should've told me.*

Hurt pinged through her body. *Daric said not to! He said it was a security thing, and that you two had talked and you would understand … and you did – when you got here.*

When I got here, he snarled, *I didn't know what to expect. I was relieved just to see you unharmed!*

You knew I was safe, she said indignantly. *Alis would've told you – didn't she? And you would've known if I was hurt.*

He shook his head. *I knew you were in danger. I could feel your fear. I was trying to work out where you were so I could come to you.* His eyes narrowed. *Daric and his Breathless secrecy …*

She clutched the charmed shell she still wore around her neck. If she had only thought to use it.

He saw her gesture and she bathed in fresh remorse.

Then Alis sent me an urgent summons and a map. That's all! he said. *Nothing else. I had no idea. No clue! I was so afraid!*

Andel reached for his hand. *I am so sorry – but I was scared too. I didn't think Alis had got my message at all. I tried my hardest, but she was out of range. I didn't know what to do. I was too emotional to go back a step to find you … I could've used the shell, I know! But in the heat of the moment, with all that going on, I … didn't think of it.*

His emotional field changed. *She didn't get your call.* He paused. *It was her Bless. She said her baby showed her …*

She bowed her head as her baby's words came back; *Help mama.* She drew him around to face her. *I have something to show you.*

He looked into her eyes as the recollection played, then faded. His hand moved reverently to her stomach. *How is that possible? The babies must be connected in some way.*

I … I think so … in my heart. It seems so incredible, but you said they – the Went – understood the concept of 'mother'.

He frowned into the distance. *Are all the Blessings able to do this?*

I don't know, she replied. *And as for forming words – I expected lucid thought would come sometime after birth, a full year or more,* then *words. That's normal. That's what to expect – according to Ubaid, and Kira, and Sari and anyone else who has experience with children. We were talking about it in group, just the other day.*

He bent to pick up some of the twigs and branches that littered the spaces between the rocks. She started as the movement disturbed a gang of brown lizards. Although they were striped vivid blue and orange, she hadn't seen them until they scuttled away. The whole group paused on a nearby formation to watch. Their heads bobbed restlessly.

There's no aggression in them, Huldar assured her.

She held out her hands to weave a net of energy and he piled an ever growing stack of sticks onto it.

Bonfire? she asked acerbically.

Enough to keep us warm for a few hours at least, he replied.

As she worked the sticks into a cohesive bundle, she noticed some had an unpleasant, musty smell. She pushed them further from her nose and looked again at the lizards.

There's something primal about flame, Huldar said. *Comforting. And when Casco –Archerran Casco, wakes, he'll be hungry as a lean rada. I know I was. We'd best have hot food ready.*

For him and Daric both, she said. *And tea. Tam packed extra galano. Perhaps that will help Malena.*

Maybe, he replied. *I hope so.*

Andel's chest constricted painfully. Her undercurrent of worry swelled. She tried to keep walking, but her head began to spin and she stumbled.

Huldar turned sharply. *Put the wood down.*

She hesitated, then did as he asked.

Now, *look at me.* He lowered his head to meet her gaze. *Together, just as Ubaid taught us.*

Tears stung her eyes. *You are angry with me.*

I'm not, he said. *Not anymore.*

He smiled a little and reached for her hands. *Come on … it's alright.*

It's happening again, she said. Panic rose in a choking tide. *Like with mother …*

No, he said quietly. *No, it's not. You held this situation together. You were their anchor, just as they'd intended. They chose you for this because you are strong.*

She nodded compliantly, but the tears spilled over, chill against her face. She had failed her mother; she had inflicted terrible harm. *What if I …?*

You didn't, he said gently.

His soft touch gave her the strength to look up. Slowly she let herself be immersed in his regard, and he in hers. Together, they took several deep and measured breaths … in through the nose, out through the mouth, just as Ubaid had taught them. With each exhalation, anxiety abated.

I was angry, Huldar admitted. *I was afraid. But it's the circumstances; this need for secrecy – it goes against my nature, and when I thought you and our daughter might be in danger and I couldn't be there to protect you … yes, I was angry. But not now.*

She nodded, more convincingly this time. The pain in her heart eased. *I was afraid I had let them down, that I wasn't strong enough, and that I'd made you angry …* She analyzed her responses as she'd been taught, and felt herself unclenching. *But I didn't let them down,* she said to herself. *I didn't cause things to go wrong.* She looked up at him again. … *And your anger was understandable, if not justified.*

Not justified?

She almost missed the subtle laugh in his words. The corners of his mouth lifted. *How is our own little Blessing? Has she had anything more to say?*

Andel gave a small smile in return, and with the faintest of gestures suggested he come see for himself. With his awareness in tow, she felt for her daughter's presence, careful not to wake her – still soundly asleep.

She seems … contented, Andel said.

Yes, she does. Huldar murmured.

His touch on their infant's mind was as gentle as if he thought she might break, his fascination for her extraordinary abilities, tightly reined.

Andel immersed him in the memory of what had occurred when her unborn child had reached out to Alis'. Maybe if they reviewed it together, they would find something new. Huldar was, after all, used to dealing with alien entities – had even spoken to the Went; and in some way, her daughter might be one of them. But apart from the astonishing, fully formed words, there was little else to see. Andel hadn't even realized the full extent of what had happened until Alis and Huldar's arrival.

She took more breaths. His hand was warm on her belly. His touch was rich with love and curiosity.

Was it real? she asked quietly. *How did she do it? I had no idea. For a sickening moment, I truly believed I'd failed.*

I guess we'll know soon enough, he whispered. *She seems exhausted now, and pleased with herself, and no wonder!*

A cold gust tore sticks from the top of her wood pile.

"We'd best get back," he said.

She gave the skies a worried glance and let him help her retrieve her firewood before he hefted his own.

When they returned to the platform, it was as if they stepped back into reality. Malena still huddled over her unborn baby, and Casco still lay in Daric's lap. The Djan'rū was an invisible presence between them. Only Alis had changed position. The healer gave a tight-lipped smile and indicated for Huldar to hurry with the fire.

He tipped his head toward Daric. *I'll sing one of those shelters he makes, but I find it difficult to make the full dome.*

Hmm, she answered, and looked at the pile of branches. *Best stick with what you know.*

The pun went over his head. She felt bad for even making it.

He wandered the platform until he found a suitable site, then encircled it with large stones. The fuel he'd gathered was set in the centre, ready to burn, then closed his eyes and sang a clear semi-circle into being. It wobbled for an anxious moment, then found the anchor points and solidified. He nodded in satisfaction as the dome took shape then turned to the sticks and conjured a flame.

As Huldar helped her up, the edge of the rock scraped against her palm and knees. She hated feeling so awkward, but he gave a good-humored snort and led her closer to the fire.

She fed sticks to the flames until it became a healthy blaze. Soon, water was set to boil and talemgal tubers put in the coals to cook. Smoke swirled around their shelter before escaping to the boisterous winds. Its fine, herbal smell lifted her spirits, and she made a mental note to ask about its healing potential.

Alis eyed the shelter appreciatively and after a few words of encouragement, left Malena at last. As she entered, she closed her eyes and took a deep sniff. *I agree. This smoke may have medicinal properties,* she said. "I feel almost cheerful." She glanced back at the navigator.

Andel followed her gaze.

"Out of danger - for now," Alis said, but her tone spoke of a crisis ongoing.

Huldar bowed his head. I'll go make a shelter for her, and one for the other two.

Andel's vision blurred with fresh tears. "Will she be alright?"

"Who?" Alis answered. "Malena or her child?"

"Both," Andel answered, confused by the uncharacteristic harshness in the healer's voice.

Alis sighed. "I am sorry, Andel, I'm just tired. And what has happened here? ... There is so much to process. Malena panicked. She has taken a deep emotional blow. But for her blessing's sake, she must bury her guilt and deal with it at a later date."

Guilt? Andel asked.

Huldar paused before leaving. "And her Blessing?" he asked softly.

"Stable for the moment, but the balance is precarious. The next few hours will be critical." She glanced sadly at Malena's huddled form. "There are no guarantees, and until the child is safely born, we won't know the full extent of the damage."

Andel's sharp intake of breath was involuntary.

"Yes," Alis said. "She will need all of your support - and none of your judgement."

"I don't judge her," Andel said.

Huldar gave Alis a warning glance. "Breath has blown," he said, "and we will deal with the consequence as best we can."

Alis shook her head. "My apologies. You are right, of course."

"Consequences?" Andel narrowed her gaze at them. "Right about what?"

The healer bowed, a small bob of her head. "It is not for me to judge, either," she said. "It is for me to heal."

A thin sliver of light bled between Casco's eyelids, but the pain of that small admission of life was almost too much. To say his head hurt was an understatement. The itch beneath his scalp was like fire.

Casco! Beloved!

Part of him rejoiced to hear Daric's voice, but the vibration rang white-hot against his bruised synapses. He squeezed his eyes shut against the torment.

Wind blew chill over wetness on his face. To wipe it dry was too much effort.

... "I suspect that for the time being, voice only might be appropriate."

The new comment floated through his ears. Gradually, sounds acquired meaning. He recognized Alis' soft tone as the one she used only for the most direly ill or injured. Recall was slow and non-linear. He had a sudden sense of balance gone wrong. Was he going to die? Better himself than Daric - or Malena and her child.

In another short episode, he saw Daric's throat contort, sensed his supreme effort ... streams of energy spun around them in a spiraling vortex. His heart leapt with a feeling of triumph ... but what had he triumphed against?

Fresh pain drew a gasp as it lanced behind his eyes. With it came memory of Malena's attack ... had she really done that?

There had been a subtle flaw in their design - but he'd seen it in time. Malena should have let him continue. The work had passed the stage where it could be dissolved without danger. Daric had supported his idea for repair, but Malena had not.

He turned his head, heard Daric murmur, but the vision - the memory - was behind his eyes and could not be avoided.

Don't! he warned.

Caring hands held his shoulders, but he barely felt them. His alarm renewed, as strong as if events had yet to unfold. Malena pushed him aside, filled with fear for her unborn child. She unleashed her Shamkar - a voice so strong it could drive connection between stars and planets … but because of her pregnancy, it was skewed - imperfect.

Why had she done that? She'd sung despite his warning, despite knowing her power would be awry.

He'd shown them what he saw, and how it could be mended - he remembered the split-second transfer of ideas. *Do it!* Daric had said.

Although he'd been at the brink of collapse he'd had no doubt in his newly realized ability. A shred of pride had come through - what shred could be spared from the energy it cost to maintain the construct. Daric had been proud of him. He would take that with him to the Breath - But Malena's mind had exploded with a snarl.

Kareski! She'd wrenched her mind from Daric's, nearly killing him in the process, pushed Casco aside and tried to use Shamkar on her own.

… Could one weep through death? Would the Breath of El heal his hurt? Her mistrust … He squeezed his eyes tight against tears. He'd had no idea how much she despised him. She hated him for being half-breed. For being half-breed and successful … for striving above his station.

Daric's rhythmic heart-beat calmed him. Daric's love was real.

Slowly but firmly, his anguish abated. He could not afford it now; he could not afford it then. He saw again the full might of Daric's power, weaving bright ropes of Tsemkar through the holes she had wrought, singing at the same time to give him space to work the fix he'd envisaged. Malena's attack had almost cost Daric his life …

And that other voice, supporting, weaving its own design – had it really been his? Strong … complex. Its depth had surprised him. He'd not known he could sing that way. It was almost as if the Djan'rū itself had taken over, wanting to be born, showing him what to do.

Singing the final chord, and the tying of the knot – that had been the triumph! … Then victory cut short by a blinding flash, agony's grip and the welcome fall into darkness.

Was the gate sung? Had his plan worked? He needed to see for himself.

He cracked his lids open again and the dark blur above soon resolved into Daric's face. A bright droplet fell towards him. In it, he could see every detail of their surroundings. Alis talking with Andel and Huldar. A window-shelter. Blankets and bright cushions. Planar shards of orange light knifed through the falling liquid. Beyond it, Malena looked his way. He could almost taste her fear and self-loathing.

The tear fell on his cheek with a dull splash. Hypersensitive nerves registered its continued downward trail. His own tears swelled the flow.

"What happened?" he croaked.

Daric's joy touched him – so fierce, but respectfully muted. His lover's mind was closed, but judging by the pain Casco still felt, he thought that was probably for the best. He cast his gaze toward the flames and felt their rhythmic hum through the rock.

"Here's Huldar to sing for the pain," Daric said gently.

Boots scrunched on rock as Huldar crouched beside them. Casco welcomed the familiar essence of his long-time friend as he closed a strong hand around his.

Eyes the savage blue of the sky swept his face. Had he not noticed their depth before now? Piercing, velvet-dark pupils studied his head as if boring through bone to scrutinize the pain within, yet when they came to rest on his, he could see love, and presence, and a deep, abiding care.

"Am I going to die?" he asked.

Huldar's laugh surprised him. "Far from it! I'll leave the explanations to Alis and Daric." *Now, let me in,* he asked softly, *so I can sing this charm.*

Casco wasn't aware he'd closed him out. Had he closed Daric out too? Was that why he couldn't share his thoughts, and not the other way around? It seemed improbable.

"Did it work?"

"Whether it did or didn't, you are in no fit state," Huldar said gently. "Let me help you. We are going nowhere, and when you wake, we'll study what you've built and see whether it will work to plan."

Casco nodded as best he could through the scream of his nerve-endings. He took a careful breath to center himself and examined his defenses. There was something different about them - about him ... but what it was eluded him.

Thank you. Huldar's soft voice was balm on his burnt mind, but there was a note he hadn't heard before - was it reverence? And a hint of worry ... perhaps he was more badly wounded than Huldar let on. He tried to compose his thoughts into coherent questions but the effort hurt too much, so he asked aloud, "What's wrong with me?"

Huldar smiled. *This will take the pain away. You will sleep, and when you wake, you'll feel better. Then will be the time for answers – I promise.*

The golden tones of his familiar voice came like light to chase the dark away like a new story he'd not yet told, but all too soon he could follow its patterns no more.

Andel leaned back against the makeshift seating, a thick blanket, a rug and a few cushions made all the difference – and watched Huldar sing Casco to sleep. She was struck by Daric's reverential touch on Casco's sleeping face. How could this brilliant and loving person have become an assassin?

Daric's gaze flicked to Huldar's, just for a moment.

Huldar shook his head and beckoned toward the fire.

Daric shrugged, but was reluctant to leave Casco's side.

How long will he sleep? Andel asked.

For a few hours, just till the worst is over. No one prepared him for this. I believe he thinks he's dying and I'm just too kind to tell him.

She smiled. Her fingers brushed her forehead as she remembered the intense pain of her Tsemkar's manifestation, and the joy, knowing she'd been Marked. How would she have felt – what would she have thought was happening if she hadn't known? She looked at Casco with renewed concern.

What is its appearance – the Archerra?

Huldar shared an image of restless lines of light curving over Casco's skull, half hidden beneath his hair. The formation fell like a pendant jewel from his hairline to the centre of his forehead.

So beautiful!

We'll have to hide it, Huldar said darkly.

Why?!

She felt a burst of anger directed at the Host, and Olatu of Faytha in particular. *How do we explain this?* he asked shortly. He made a sharp gesture toward the secret glimmer of the almost-Djan'rū. *This is our last hope if things go bad – and despite your efforts, a slim one at that. We can't tell anyone. No one!*

She looked up as he came to her side. *But Casco!*

He bowed his head. *He will feel hurt without doubt! But he would not want the mission endangered.*

A low gasp turned their attention toward Malena. Alis looked on sadly as the navigator rocked back and forth. Her hands moved over her belly's roundness as if unable to settle. Her features were twisted in sorrow.

Alis hurried to her side.

Andel felt the blood rush from her face. *The baby!*

At the healer's gesture, Malena leaned back and let Alis lay her hands against her abdomen. Neither could sing, yet Andel saw a glow encompass Malena's haze. It brightened momentarily, then seemed to drain in a flash toward Malena's child.

The two paused, silent and still. The healer's hands remained in place.

Alis? Huldar asked.

Alis lifted her hands and used them to brush tears from her eyes. *She's not dead, not yet. Dear little one is fighting so hard … It may be that Malena's Blessing will survive. Impossible to guess the outcome if she does.*

Why? Andel asked. *Was there too much energy? Ubaid warned us …*

Alis looked at them and nodded.

Andel felt rather than heard the soft tread of feet behind her. "If Archerran Casco hadn't done what he did," Daric said softly, "we would *all* be dead, but now the poor Bless bears the brunt."

Andel peered helplessly at the stricken navigator. Malena's haze showed the continuance of the battle - darkness and sorrow against healing light. It was impossible to say which was stronger.

"What can we do?" she asked.

"It is her task now," Alis said. "Her baby's survival is in her hands, and her heart. Just love her as you always have, and be there for her when she needs you."

Help me up, Huldar. I must go to her.

Huldar lifted her to her feet and she made her way to Malena's side. Hesitantly, she reached out to touch her shoulder. A maelstrom of emotion leapt through the contact. Andel stepped back. Malena looked up but quickly turned back to the battle at hand - the battle to save her child.

She looked at the small shelter Huldar had sung. "Are you cold?"

The navigator nodded miserably.

Andel reached into Qalān for her spare heavy jacket and draped it over Malena's shoulders. Her long, spidery fingers peeped around the edges to clutch the covering more tightly.

"My rug, please." Andel held out her hand to Huldar. "And a pillow? Somewhere softer for her, and warmer than this basalt."

With brisk movements, she arranged the blankets and helped Malena find at least some material comfort.

Alis and Huldar returned to the fire. The healer's haze seemed conflicted.

"Will you be alright?" Andel asked Malena. "Some tea? Or food?"

Malena shook her head.

"We have galano, and Tam packed an extra snack-box - just as well, given the circumstances." She considered for a moment then added, "I'll bring some tea in a little while and leave it close by, just in case. You should have something ..."

She returned to the warmth of Huldar's fire. The pot already steamed above the flames. *What's going on?* she asked him.

He pulled some coals aside and revealed the talemgal tubers among them. They were almost ready and smelled delicious. *That's between Malena and Casco.*

His answer mystified her, but it was clear she would get no more.

ON THE ROCK

Something pushed at Casco's shoulders, and another something at his legs. The movements seemed purposeful. There was no sense of imminent harm. Slowly he registered Huldar's unique signature, and Daric's – familiar and warm. What was Daric doing with his legs?

Ready? Lift!

He felt himself hoisted skyward. One arm flopped over the edge of whatever he was on. Huldar tucked it back toward his body. The difference in temperature beneath his blanket was remarkable. Why wouldn't they just let him sleep?

He's heavier than I thought.

Never wondered where all that food goes? Packed on a bit of muscle too – with the … machete training – that he isn't doing, of course.

Of course, Huldar replied.

A powerful gust rocked them sideways. Daric stumbled. Casco heard him curse.

"This is turning into a blizzard!"

"Nearly there!"

Their voices were shredded by the gale.

Abruptly, the roar of the wind ceased. He'd not noticed the din so much until it was gone.

"Got the blankets ready, and a pillow - here!" That was Lady Andel, he was certain of it. "Nearer to the fire."

His body was lowered. The rocking stopped. Soft hands lifted his head and placed the promised pillow beneath it. Alis put her hand on his forehead and the pain in his head dissipated. He sighed and rolled toward the warmth of the flames.

The smell of hot talemgal seeped into his dreams. He was in a happy place - butterflies, sunshine, soft sounds of a breeze as it ruffled the grass - but the talemgal was insistent. He tried to hold on to wherever he was, but the dream faded and the smell of roasted talemgal took its place.

His stomach rumbled.

Cautiously, he opened his eyes, but no pain stabbed him.

"Ah! The hero returns." A wave of love and relief accompanied Daric's words. "There's hot stew - they tell me you'll be starving, and honey-cakes warming in the ashes."

He squeezed his eyes shut then opened them again. Tilted them toward the top of his skull and saw the worn underside of one of Daric's boots. He lifted himself up on one elbow and saw the rest of him sitting cross-legged on a cushion. His smile made Casco's heart skip a beat, but the euphoria of survival was soon quashed by Melena's wave of hatred. He didn't need to see her to feel it. He kept his gaze on Daric's.

"What happened?" he asked, and was pleased to hear his voice back to normal. "Is the Djan'rū sung?"

Daric's smile quirked. "You already asked that, at least twice."

"Humor me."

"Yes, as far as we can tell, the Djan'rū exists at least in some form or another. We're not sure yet if it's exactly what we planned, but that can wait."

Casco sat up and looked around, letting his gaze slide past Malena's glare. Huldar and Alis were there - he thought he remembered Alis being there earlier. They peered at him as if they were trying not to stare.

"What's wrong?" he turned to Daric. "What's wrong with my face?"

Huldar gave a rueful grin. His eyebrows flicked playfully. "You've been Marked."

"Marked?" He touched his face. It felt no different. He scowled. "That's not funny."

"It's true," Daric said. "Look at me and I'll show you."

Andel and Alis smiled broadly, encouraging him.

Daric held out his hand, and Casco took it.

He'd never quite gotten used to seeing himself through his lover's eyes. The image always seemed slightly distorted - overly large eyes, and sometimes lips - but now his attention was directed to his head, and to his forehead in particular where a pendant of light glowed through the skin below his hair-line. Pale lines shone in waving geometry from beneath his hair. His expression was comically puzzled. He withdrew.

"Why?" he asked. "Why not you?" *You're the brilliant one.*

"El's gifts are bestowed - or withheld, for his own reasons," Alis said. "Had we known how imminent this was, we could have prepared you properly, and you would've known what to expect. I am sorry, Casco."

"But I'm half-breed. Kareski ..."

"So was my mother," Daric reminded him. "She was Marked with a Shamkar."

"I know," he said. Confusion overwhelmed him. "I'm sorry. I forgot."

Alis smiled at him. "Kareski, once Marked, can be accepted into a House and given the status of any other archangel."

Darkness flickered across Daric's veil. Casco knew his family's experience had not been one of acceptance.

He examined his forehead with his fingertips. There was a definite tingle when they passed over the Mark. *His* Mark. He had to say it again, as if that would make it more real.

"I am Archerran?"

Daric nodded. "Archerran Casco ... of Leth?"

Huldar smiled. "I would be proud to welcome you - if that is what you choose."

One by one, his companions repeated the title, all but Malena, who simmered silently in the back-ground. He recalled her flash of hatred while they tried to sing the Djan'rū. His newfound status probably ate at her like a canker.

Daric shoved a bowl of hot stew into his hands. He took his hanta from Qalān and began to eat. Chunks of meat and vegetable vanished all too quickly. "This is delicious!"

He held the empty bowl to his lips and drained the residual fluid.

"There's plenty more," Andel said. "Tam packed extra - almost as if he knew!"

A second helping went a long way to easing his hunger. He took a honey-cake, and smiled. Tam and his honey-cakes! A staple of every communal meal.

Malena glowered at him from opposite the fire. Her hands were wrapped protectively around her stomach. She still hadn't spoken - or even eaten.

Deliberately, he met her gaze.

"Marked!" she spat. "You!"

"Malena!" Huldar warned.

Casco could feel Daric's anger flare, hotter by far than the fire.

"No!" he held his hand up. "I need to hear it." He kept his gaze steady on her green, Maatu eyes.

"My baby, my Blessing," She looked around to engage them all. "She is injured because of what you did. You were supposed to see the bigger pattern, supposed to protect us, but you didn't!"

"You pushed me aside," Casco said. "I did see the pattern. I did protect you. You and your Bless have survived."

"Coward!" she insisted. "You left us!"

"I did not," he countered. "I tried to explain what I had in mind; do you remember? You wouldn't listen."

"You left us. I had to sing or we would all be dead. I saved us!"

Daric shook his head. “No, Malena. You barged in.” He grimaced in anger. “You nearly killed me and Casco. I tried to keep the gate from falling apart after your Shamkar shot it full of holes. Casco saved our lives. His fix was brilliant. You didn’t listen.”

“Filthy Enna! Of course you’d say that.” She returned to Casco. “You pushed me out!”

“Yes, I pushed you out,” Casco said. “I had to! Your actions - do you even remember what you did? … What you said?”

“What I said?” she snarled. “What are you talking about? My child is injured. We barely survived. And you, a … You get Marked? Has El lost his mind?”

Malena! Alis gasped.

“A what?” Casco said stoically. “A half-breed? A Kareski - you used it as a swear word.”

“My Mark is bigger than yours,” she said. “I am a navigator! I know what I’m doing. Tell him, Huldar. Tell the filthy, baby-killing Kalla what he did!”

Huldar spread his hands. “Malena, please, calm down!”

“Get the shawl, Huldar of Leth,” she cried. “I dare you! Try him right here, right now. Do it!”

“If I wear the shawl,” he said, “my justice is final. I don’t think you want that.” He shook his head. “Not really.”

Daric snorted. “Get the shawl, Huldar, if that’s what the stupid Kalla wants. Casco?”

“Please, stop this now.” Alis said firmly. She looked at Malena. “There is a condition, a type of panic. It can happen when we believe we, or one we love, is in imminent danger of death." She turned to them. "This is what has happened to Malena, or so I believe."

"I did nothing but try to save my Blessing. I tried," she yelled. Her finger stabbed at him. Its impact was visceral. "And YOU got in my way!"

He felt like crying. "Malena, it's not true." *It's not true!*

She spun to Andel. "You tell him. You were there. You are my friend. Why aren't you telling them?"

Andel's gaze slid to the fire. "Because, I think …"

"You believe them, not me!" she raged. "How could you? Oh – that's right. Our leader is your husband – is that it? Is that why you're joining them in the lie?"

"It's not a lie," Huldar said. "Listen to Alis. Why would she tell you anything but the truth as she sees it?"

"As she sees it?" Malena said scornfully. "Well, that's not how I see it."

"Malena, please listen," Alis said. "Why don't you let me show you? Let Huldar be a conduit and we can go over what happened from every angle? Like a trial, if you will, but without the shawl. You trust him, don't you? And me?"

The navigator glared, but Casco could see a shred of clarity forming.

"Please, Malena," Alis continued. "I will be with you."

Then Daric stuck his hands out. "Let's get this over with. We have important decisions to make."

The promise of lucidity evaporated. Casco groaned. *Don't provoke her!*

Breathless kalla nearly killed us because you're Kareski!? Deserves what she gets, he said darkly.

Leave her alone! You heard Alis. She couldn't help it.

"And I am not important? Is that what you're saying?" Malena said. "My Blessing, my perfect child is no longer perfect and that's not important? Where's Ariben?" She looked to the horizon as if to see him walking over the rocks. "I want him here."

"He can't be here, even if he wanted to be," Huldar said. "The portal is underwater."

"Why wouldn't he want to be here?" She glared wildly around then started for the door. "You are all against me."

"For fuck's sake!" Daric barked. "Breathless slut! For once in your life, just listen!"

"Daric, please!" Casco removed the shawl from Qalān and handed it to Huldar. "I am ready, Malena. If I damaged you, or your Bless, in any way, I am ready to hear that and receive judgement. Are you ready?"

Her lips curled in a snarl. "I *will* kill you for what you've done!" but she settled back into place.

She'd have to get through me, first, said Daric. Darkness surrounded him, and he realized Malena's life was genuinely in danger.

Casco bowed his head and wondered if that had something to do with why he had been Marked, and not his lover.

Andel leaned back behind Huldar to pull the shawl into place over his shoulders. Outside, a greasy sunset oozed through a break in heavy cloud. Frozen snow scudded across the rock in glittering waves and added to the small drift in the wake of their shelter. Casco was glad Daric had recovered sufficiently to cover their shelter in a second, insulating shell. Being stuck here, weakened as they were and exposed to the elements, may have had dire consequences.

Huldar and Alis joined hands. Their eyes closed. After a moment, Alis held out her hand to Malena.

"You will be safe," she said. "I promise." But Malena's fists remained clenched. Anger juxtaposed with fear in a haze still poorly controlled.

"We call upon El and Asheru to witness this transaction," Huldar said solemnly. "Bey et El a'sien."

"Bey et El a'sien," they echoed, and with that, Huldar's right to judge was confirmed.

A solid flow of energy tingled through Casco's body as Malena relented and the circle was joined.

Outside, darkness fell under its own muted terms. Between them the coals glowed brightly. The faint boom of the surf was a constant note of caution beyond the fitful winds. How long would it be before they'd missed their opportunity to return to the warmth of their tents? Casco stopped his grimace before it could form. This was a question best kept to himself.

We will proceed, Huldar said.

Alis glanced at Malena then nodded. *We are ready.*

Huldar made a small bow. *Daric, can you please share your direct recall of events, starting at the beginning.*

Daric moved quickly and succinctly through the set-up of their experimental work, the practice between himself and Malena, her high praise of the consonance they'd achieved.

But when his review of the actual work began, Casco realized the difficulties of judging any of their actions out of context. His scalp itched. Like pieces in a game of ashut, he could see a way to replay events in real time, as they'd happened. His heart thundered, but he was hesitant to interrupt the flow.

Daric paused and looked at him. *Do you have something to say?*

He bowed in apology. *I am sorry. Alis, Huldar – I have thought of a way I can blend this story together, all three of us at the same time, and repeat it to you as it all actually happened – from a psychic point of view. I can show you, if you'd like.*

Huldar nodded. *Can it be paused for examination at particular points?*

I think so – if we are correctly melded. It could save time if we do it this way, and there is no chance of exaggeration on any part, or the whole thing will dissolve. We each have to replay our parts, emotionally and psychically as they happened.

Alis, what does Malena think?

After a moment's deliberation, Alis nodded - *Go ahead.*

Casco's heart galloped hard against his ribs. This had to work. He was sure it would ... but he would have to touch Malena's mind and accept the hatred she felt for him.

With a few deep breaths, he brought his anxiety under control, then he reached out.

Daric was there for him already, but Alis had shielded Malena from the group and now that arrangement must be breached. He sensed an exchange between the healer and her charge before the contact was offered, then came the impact. Deliberately, he opened himself to it and breathed his way through the worst. He could feel Daric's desire to protect, but warned him off. Malena must feel trust for his technique to work. Once enmeshed, they would be constrained to view their actions in sequence with each other, able to observe but not change or hide any part of what occurred. How would he respond if indeed he was shown to be remiss? If she was right to loathe him?

El had Marked him, he reasoned. He must trust he was able to face the truth, however the experience cast him.

He stopped his procrastination and wove the net - not Shamkar, nor Tsemkar, but just as binding, and at his signal, the reiteration began.

Their recollections fed painlessly into the scaffold he'd made and the whole of the event was replayed from the beginning, when they had first meshed minds. As if it was a dream and outside normal time, sometimes the replay moved quickly, but at others the recitation was slowed so pivotal events could be examined from every viewpoint. It felt quite odd to experience his own actions as an observer. He'd always thought of memory as a perfect replay, but to see his movements played out in context; some parts were vindicated, while others were shown to be skewed.

When Malena broke away and decided to sing, he could see why she thought he'd let her down. His practiced contact with Daric had made it easier to share his idea with him, and Malena had received only a perfunctory sketch of his intentions.

However, in the heat of the unfolding disaster, her reaction had been extreme, primal consciousness had taken over and it had taken all of Daric's strength combined with his own to stop her from destroying them all.

Perhaps the biggest surprise had come when he witnessed his own virtuosity. What he'd shrugged off as improbable was actually true. He had read the disrupted energies and understood them, then merged with them in a way that steered the whole into the expression he desired. In a sense, the Djan'rū *had* sung itself.

The session ended when he saw his own collapse.

The circle dissolved.

Malena sobbed in Alis' arms.

Huldar removed the shawl and handed it back to him. "There are no judgements to be made," he said solemnly. "Malena, do you understand?"

She nodded miserably.

"Do you accept that your child's damage is not due to any action on the part of Casco, nor Daric?"

"I did it," she wailed. "I harmed my own child. I didn't mean it. I am a navigator. We are trained …"

"You are pregnant," Alis said gently. "At this time, our protective instincts are heightened. It is a survival strategy. Blessed, and alone, Malena - you couldn't help it."

Huldar shook his head angrily. "This whole venture! You all could've died … But now we have a secret weapon, a last resort." He stood up, stooped beneath the dome, and prepared to leave. "I don't want to know any more. I will not examine what you have constructed with you. I will wait at the gate and hope Breath blows in such a way that I am not forced to betray you."

Casco sighed. "Malena, I hate to ask, but will you come with Daric and I to look at it? We need you."

She stifled her sobs and nodded.

They gathered their things and the left-over food and followed Huldar to the outside.

Beyond the shelter, the gale hit them with brutal force.

Huldar shouted above the howl of the wind, "Andel, Alis - with me! Daric, take down the domes as you leave. Don't be too long."

Casco watched the faint light cast by Huldar's globe bob into the darkness until Daric touched his arm. *Come on. She's there already.*

At the Djan'rū site, whirling half seen energies plaited in and out of a succession of intricate forms. It was as if they yearned to find balance, but ever and always tumbled moments from completion.

Malena studied the space with eyes half squinted. Her head tilted from side to side. Eventually she turned away.

"I know it's there, but … I can't connect." She turned to him. "Something's gone wrong. How are we going to turn it on if I can't reach it?"

"Can you see it?" Daric asked.

"Sort of - but it doesn't call me like a normal Djan'rū would."

"That's what you wanted, isn't it?"

"Yes, but we do have to make the thing work!"

Casco's eyes widened. Although Malena couldn't, he could see the energies clearly, and he remembered the sound and feel of every strand. Just to be sure, he reached his hand into the edge of the storm. Layers of force resonated to his touch. His skull hummed with it - a pleasant sensation. He had never felt such power. Something had happened to him. He was no longer the Casco he had been when they'd arrived here.

"I can make it work," he said softly.

Daric's shock was well hidden, but he felt it just the same.

"If you do, Kandät Enna will see it," Malena snapped.

Casco smiled. Once, only a short time ago, her attitude would have made his skin crawl with fear he might have given offence. Back in the Realm, the consequences of offending anyone outside the enclave could be dire. But now, he was Marked. His responsibility was to himself and the refinement of his calling.

"It's tuned to my signature," he said calmly. "It wasn't intentional, but that's how it is."

Daric looked at him strangely.

His cheeks chilled. He wiped his eyes. *Must be the wind.*

"That's it then." Malena raised her hands in a melodramatic gesture. "All this, and the mission's a failure."

"No, it's not," Daric said. "Casco, can you show us? Maybe we could imitate something you do, just enough so the thing can be turned on by any one of us if needed?"

Malena looked at him with distaste. "Stay away from me. You'll have to show him."

Casco shrugged. *Daric?*

Their touch was breathtaking. Casco longed to share with him, discuss and unpack all that had happened. Daric's love and pride humbled his heart, yet made it sing in an all too brief flash of joy.

Later, Casco smiled. *For now, let me show you …* but after several attempts to explain what he could feel and the necessary sequence of manipulation, he stopped.

Daric shook his head. *You are Archerran now, and I can't follow.*

Don't be silly. Of course you can. It's just me with a funny hat on … isn't it? I haven't explained well enough.

No, Daric admitted. *When you helped with the invisibility cloak, it took me quite a while to get my head around what you'd done. It wasn't that I couldn't follow, it was the way you understood the forces involved. That was pretty much beyond me. This definitely is.*

But Daric, no! I … I don't understand.

Daric laughed. *Neither do I!*

Then I'm the only one who can activate our last hope?

You are.

A new worry descended on him. What if their survival was up to him and him alone? If a navigator came, he, Casco, would have to survive so he could activate the Djan'rū.

But you were already vital to the project, Daric said. *The trip up north, the message to Saphella …? No one else can do that, either. You are Ziquarra. However young your talent is, you are the only Ziquarra we have. Our secret weapon.*

They can't know. He touched his head. *They mustn't find out. I have to go into hiding.*

Or at least wear a very big hat.

"Have you two finished whatever it is you're doing?" Malena said. "I'm cold, and Huldar is waiting."

"Of course," Casco said. "We should go."

She held up her hand. "So, Daric, show me first," she said. "Easier where I can see it."

Daric shrugged. "I can't. It's tuned to Casco."

"Rubbish," she snarled.

"I assure you, this is the case."

Casco stood firm while she looked at his head, although the main part of him flinched.

She frowned and turned away as if she'd seen all she needed to, yet was still puzzled.

They started for the shore, but in the utter dark and in the teeth of the gale, even negotiating the platform's edge was difficult. Casco got out a large globe and set it alight, not too bright but far-reaching. At least their other senses would not have to work so hard.

Eventually, they saw their three companions silhouetted against a backdrop of shining white spume, and Huldar beckoned them to the portal. Ambitious waves already lapped their feet. The air was thick with the smell of salt spray, and the slush and boom of the waves.

Closer! Huldar said.

They huddled around and in the blink of an eye stumbled forward into a desert evening. The deafening sound of surf was replaced by the throb of millions of hopeful suitors, each singing their hardest in their efforts to find a mate.

Casco sighed as warmth permeated his half-frozen body. He looked around at his bedraggled companions. Hair hung in sodden strings over tired faces wreathed in kressie-fur hoods. The leather was charmed to repel water, but the trimming was uniformly worse for wear.

He took off his coat and several layers beneath, then sat to unlace wool-lined leather leggings. Huldar helped Andel to the ground, then Alis. Malena waved Daric's help aside and half fell in an awkward descent to the sand.

"Only a week before the navigator comes," Daric said. "Then ten more days till the mid-season communication becomes possible. Things are hotting up, my friends. Soon we'll know if our efforts" – he glanced at Malena – "our sacrifices, have been truly necessary."

"For your sake, I hope they have," Malena said darkly.

Huldar closed his eyes for a moment, then opened them again. "I've contacted Gento and Banga. They'll spread the word, if necessary, that we are safe and well and will return to Eastern Basecamp soon. In the meantime, we have to get our story straight. I suggest as much truth as possible. I'll leave you to it. Call me when you're done."

"Wait!" Malena said. "Take yourself to that island near The Hat. Adds authenticity. We'll tell them I fell. That we were investigating claims of a sweat-lizard infestation where the new potential nacrite deposit is. A few of the miners went there – they could've introduced sweaters where they don't belong."

"Good." He nodded sharply. "Malena and Andel, come with me." He deliberately went to help Malena up first. "As you say – adds to the fabric." He turned to Alis. "I'll come and get you in a few minutes. There should be no one else in sight when I do."

"Understood," said Daric.

I'll go my own way. Casco said. *I have an idea.* As if by accident, he tapped his head above the inner sigil Daric had implanted.

He remembered the scene at the Red Weyfal, the harrowing journey with little Kisha, Daric's unexpected gentleness with the child - it seemed such a long time ago.

Daric nodded. *Stay hidden. I'll find you.*

Alis looked at him with knowing eyes. "Don't despair, Casco," Alis said. "It will not be forever."

"What of Sari?" he asked.

"I'll look after her," Daric said gently. "You know I will."

"Can I have some food, if you have any?"

Daric and Alis rummaged in Qalān. Daric had a full supply pack, and Alis, a container of honey cakes. He took them and turned for the gate. It was vital he had absolute clarity to turn the ancient portal to where he wanted to go. Tears could come later.

DELEMÄT

Bai'ah opened his eyes and raised his head. His throat was closed at last. It was time to return to the reality where he existed as Shamkarun Kandät Enna. His Mark burned as the envelope collapsed, but his relief was mitigated by the stench of vomit.

Breath, what a ride! one of his spinners murmured, and he agreed. They were lucky to have survived.

Sheeting rain drenched jumbled cargo, washing the residue of their passage clean. Splintered boxes and strewn goods were peppered with black-clad Ashik, some still bent over, heaving up their guts. He'd warned them not to eat before this final leg, but Ashik - he gave a scathing snort - who could tell them anything? He hoped they'd enjoyed their second helpings.

Of course, General Delemät Ashik stood proud and unscathed among the wreckage, every inch Imperial, although Kandät saw him examine his palms where they'd almost welded to one of the more stable crates. His lip twitched in an almost-sneer. Whatever had brought the God-

Emperor's little brother to slum it on this most remote of outposts, he did not envy him.

He gathered his wits and organized his deeper defences before Delemät had sufficiently recovered to be the danger he was, and turned to his crew. *Well done, all of you.*

In reply, his mind was filled with wordless songs of respect and regard. He inclined his head in a heart-felt bow and gave a tight-lipped smile. *Without you, the chord could not have carried. My thanks to you all for your trust. Double pay from my own account when we return to Giahn.*

The mood lifted immediately. His generous gift would be well worth it, tangible proof of his honest regard for their prowess, and encouragement to make the terrible trip to Went again.

The ether filled with sound as porters hurried to save precious foodstuffs from the rain. Feet squelched rapidly on grass-covered mud as his hardy crew went back into action, ferrying the larger boxes to safety. Why Olatu of Faytha hadn't paved this Djan'rū was a mystery to him.

Delemät turned and gave him a perfunctory nod. Water sluiced down his hard-eyed features. A nose broken and imperfectly healed. Kandät wondered why, when the best healers the Known could offer were at his disposal. The general blew water from his lips as if he found it hard to breathe.

Suddenly, the slouched and sickly troops stood straight and formed ranks. Many were injured, although thankfully none severely. The Host's healer had already arrived and moved along the lines, addressing each injury in turn.

Olatu of Faytha scurried forward, every bit as shifty as Kandät remembered. He looked up at Delemät, obviously completely unaware of his status, although the Tsemkar on his cheek should have been some indication.

"Where are the workers I asked for?" he demanded. "I see only more Ashik!"

Delemät fixed him in an imperious glare. His Tsemkar glowed. Olatu gaped, suddenly unable to breathe.

"You got us, instead," Delemät said sweetly.

Olatu's face reddened. Slowly, he sank to his knees.

Kandät wondered when, or even if, Delemät would relent. Difficult as it was to imagine, Olatu's death at Delemät's behest would certainly top anything in the last report.

Olatu gasped hoarsely and fell to the ground.

Delemät sneered.

Cargo moved hurriedly around them.

"Where are the barracks?" Delemät asked. It was as if he was talking to the air where Olatu would have stood, if he could.

The stricken Faythan pointed down the road.

"Jaldan?"

"Here, lord Delemät Ashik." The nasal voice issued from beneath a black umbrella as it made its fastidious way along a freshly cleared path. Beneath it, a pale, blade-thin figure in a vomit-stained robe.

Kandät shuddered. Delemät was an arrogant, entitled brute, tortured by proximity to the throne - but Jaldan of Trianog, 'the mind bender' made his skin crawl. The master of mind-manipulation and reverse healing - no true healer would have anything to do with him. There were several reasons why he might be part of Delemät's company. The only one Kandät could endorse was that they planned to leave him here, for good.

"Go with my troops to the barracks," Delemät said. He kicked at the still gasping Faythan. "Olatu here will set you up. I'm going for a look around."

Kandät shook his head. He, at least, was immune from Delemät's thuggery, but as for the others - here on Went, there were no constraints, and no Imperial brother to cramp his style.

Delemät's burning bronze eyes fixed on his. "What's your problem?"

Kandät's eyebrows flickered upward. "Nasty weather," he said.

The general grunted.

Olatu had finally struggled to his feet. Delemät pushed him aside and stalked off to familiarize himself with the encampment's layout.

The Ashik troops waited patiently while the Faythan got to his feet again. Mud dripped from expensive robes. Farushael of Cantori, Olatu's aide, stepped forward, but after a moment's hesitation, Olatu waved him away and led the troops to the military precinct himself, as Delemät had directed.

Kandät signaled the careworn aide. "Greetings, Farushael of Cantori. Where is Shamkarun Huldar?"

Farushael bowed. "Busy elsewhere, my lord Shamkarun Kandät Enna, but I'm sure he'll have nothing but good to say about Olatu of Faytha's conduct these last six months - when he gets here."

"I hope that will be the case. Let him know I've arrived. He knows where I'll be."

Farushael bowed and left him. His stomach ached with emptiness, but he would wait for his crew before finding a meal - and besides, it would give Shen more time to make some of those excellent pies.

Rain trickled down his back and dripped steadily from his nose.

Kattist? he called, but there was no reply. Perhaps she was out of range.

The crew had just begun to assemble when his senses pinged with a strange sensation he couldn't quite place. He squeezed his eyes shut and opened them again, but his vision remained blurred. Flying creatures took to the skies in their thousands.

He looked around at his equally startled crew and saw Farushael running towards them, waving his arms. *Get down! Get Down!*

A rhythmic banging in the ground beneath them quickly grew to a roar. The aide dropped flat to the mud and Kandät immediately followed suit. Rocks tumbled and bounced down mountainsides. The ground shook like prey in a predator's maw … then a deep silence fell, broken only by an occasional deep pop or thump.

Farushael lifted his head and motioned them to wait. After a few minutes, satisfied the quake was over, he got to his feet and gestured for them to do the same.

Kandät looked down at his clothes, sodden with rain and now stained with mud and grass. He would have to throw them away.

Several larger tents sagged with poles askew. He hoped the refectory was still intact.

"Sorry sir," Farushael said. "Earthquake. There's been a lot of them just lately."

Around him, his crew were also regaining their feet. They were a bit wild-eyed - and no-doubt he looked the same.

"What does the diviner say?" he asked.

Farushael shrugged apologetically. "Err - Olatu won't ask. I heard that she thinks it's something to do with volcanic action."

He looked at each of the several cinder-cones on the horizon. None seemed to be smoking.

"Which one?"

"I don't know, sir. Shen said that she said to him that magma is on the move. But you'd have to speak to her."

"I will," he said.

"That's why we don't pack things up so high these days. Whole load of nacrite lost to the skies when the box it was tied to fell and broke apart."

"It was tied to a box?"

"We'd run out of weights."

Around them, songs resumed as angels carted precious stores to the stores. Already a group had gathered, looking for personal deliveries and mail from the Realm. Tents were straightened. Rain continued. The recovery seemed calm, as if this truly was an everyday occurrence.

Kandät sighed. He definitely felt queasy. "Thank you, Farushael. We are going to the refectory now. I hope it hasn't fallen down. I need food - or at least a cup of tea, or something stronger, before I hear any more."

"Oh, the refectory will be fine," Farushael assured him. "But they dowse the fires as soon as they feel one coming, so hot tea might be delayed."

He nodded and summoned his crew to follow. There was no need to heat a mug of ale!

As promised, the refectory tent remained unscathed, although remarkably empty.

Shen hurried from the kitchens and bowed. "My lord Shamkarun Kandät Enna! And crew! You must be exhausted. Sit down, sit down, please." He quickly guided them to the same table they'd used on his last visit. "I've made your favorite pies especially, but I'm afraid hot tea will take a few minutes. Meantime, maybe an ale or two might not be amiss? These tremors are unnerving, yes?"

"Indeed," Kandät replied. "Good to see you, too, Shen. I've been dreaming of your excellent pies since Parsay."

"Only since Parsay?" Shen said cheekily. "Then I'll have to lift my game. I have omosa to start you off - if you'd like? Omosa, pies and a few jugs of ale - then easenberry tarts and tea to follow."

Kandät smiled through a hard-hitting wave of tiredness. "Excellent."

The cook signaled, and food and drink began to arrive. Shen bowed and returned to his kitchen, but to be honest, with the first omosa and slug of ale, he barely noticed anything more than his need to eat.

IN THE DARK

Casco sat on the rock he usually sat on. There was a folded blanket to cushion him from the cold, and a perimeter charm to keep curious creatures at bay. The sandy cave floor was scuffed with evidence of martial training, and his sword still lay at his side. No need to hide it down here.

It was the silence he found most unnerving. He could hear his heart beat steadily in his chest. For the first time in his life, his mind was consistently empty of touch.

Lind's hollow expression came to mind. Even after they'd found her, she was never right. It was the silence, she'd told him, and the nothing. She'd not known where she was, up or down, falling or still … at least he didn't have to face that. At least he could get to the surface if he wanted to – and there was time to practice the Ziquarra techniques Alis had shown him. he couldn't interact with anyone, but it was easier and easier to check on his friends, even Shen in the Hosts kitchens.

He remembered Saphella of Hermes, her smile, her fine, light-blond hair, her pale yet vibrant eyes – neither blue nor green. How different they'd looked when she was absent from her body, remote and empty, as if she was dead. Did his have the same look when he was travelling?

They say like calls to like, he thought. How different his life might have been …

The nearest inhabited planet seemed too far away to attempt unaided - but he would have to try to reach Saphella in barely one week's time.

The portal chimed. Anticipation made the light brighten a little more than he'd intended. He rushed over the sandy floor and up the rocky ledge to crush Daric's hard-muscled chest against his own. His distinct odor filled his senses. Where their skin touched, love tingled through - but there were also images of the daily life Casco missed; Sari at a pregnancy class, Malena crying, Huldar addressing a meeting in their main Marquee in the East.

Daric pushed him back to look at him. "You have been missed," he said.

"The navigator has arrived," he said. "Who was the unpleasant one he brought with him?"

"Ahh, well done! You observed without being caught." Daric looked around. "Is there somewhere we can sit?"

Casco's buoyancy faded. Daric's guarded haze told him the news was bad.

He tipped his head toward an alcove in the side of the cave wall where he'd had laid a rug over the sand. He'd emptied his Qalān of cushions and spare blankets and used them to adorn appropriately sized stones in readiness, in case the mothers actually arrived.

He took Daric's hand and was shown an image of Delemät Ashik. "Ishät's own General," Daric said. "And you saw the troops?"

"I only looked the once. Too risky. Delemät's Mark is extensive. If it hadn't been for that earthquake … "

Daric nodded. "Wise choice."

"So, it's true then?" His words echoed, soft and portentous - *true then, true then …*

"I'm afraid so."

"Who is Jaldan of Trianog, and why did Delemät Ashik bring him?"

Daric shuddered. *A bad combination. Very bad. Did you know that Delemät is the God-Emperor's younger brother, the only surviving sibling.*

Casco frowned. He'd been right to be cautious. *Four, weren't there?*

Two now, Daric said. *And our dear Delemät doesn't dare mention his relationship to the throne. I think that may be the only reason he's still with us, although the Breath might be too good for him. And as for Jaldan – I'd like to see what either El or Asheru could find to love in that one.*

Why? You think even less of him than Delemät?

The mind-bender. Daric grimaced with distaste. *Even in my profession, he makes people shudder. He's a reverse-healing expert. And – as the moniker says, he bends minds. Hideous. I've seen his handiwork – had to put a few down. An insult to sentience – to life itself.*

Put them down?

No longer able to function, or be healed. It was a kindness.

Casco gulped. The images Daric furnished were deliberately sketchy, but no less horrifying for their lack of detail. Any romantic aspirations he'd harbored for this reunion faded.

"It's true, isn't it?" he repeated. "They're here to kill us."

"Yes, I believe they'll try."

Casco studied Daric's eyes - their tawny shade so typical of the Tiamäti, shot through with blue-silver strands. There was no mistaking the deep intelligence in them, but for every shining highlight, there was a shadowy counterpart.

"You were right. And Huldar was right to trust you."

Daric shrugged and dropped his gaze. "At least we are prepared."

He nodded, but as the reality of their situation dawned on him, cyclic thoughts echoed inside his head as his words had earlier in the cavern.

"More gossip," Daric said brightly. "Kandät Enna has been asking after Malena, but she's refused to see him."

"I saw her crying," Casco said.

"You spied on her?"

"The image came through when we touched."

"She's struggling," Daric admitted. "I feel sorry for her - in a way."

"You?"

He snorted. "You've infected me with empathy. What can I say?"

"And Ariben?"

"… Has been more than attentive. He must truly love her - poor fool."

Harsh! Casco grunted.

Yes, I suppose it is, Daric agreed.

"Andel? And Sari?"

"Missing you terribly, as do I."

Casco shook his head. "Poor fool."

Daric gave his shoulder a playful thump.

"Just saying!"

"And the earthquakes are getting more frequent. Olatu tried to get Andel to divine beneath the Host Encampment - I think Kandät Enna had something to do with the request - or Delemät. I convinced Huldar to tell them she couldn't possibly work so close to the birth. Don't want Jaldan anywhere near any of them."

"Are they in danger?"

"Who, the blessed or the Host?"

"Well, we know the blessed are!"

"The Host? If it was me, I'd move - but I'm the cautious type, as you know."

Casco huffed a laugh. "When we very first arrived here there was an eruption in the ranges across from Basecamp. Andel's first mission. I went with them, and Cobar and Lind." A vivid image of the tough, yet waif-like explorer came to mind. "When she smiled, her whole face changed. It was as if the sun had come out of the clouds. She didn't like Andel at all - at first. But then Andel saved our lives."

"The Lahar?"

He nodded. "You've heard the story?"

"I have indeed," Daric said. "Several times. An amazing feat."

"Pure brilliance," Casco agreed. He took Daric's hand and let the memory of that first excursion pass between them in a series of detailed vignettes, although he couldn't help wondering how much of this recollection was … not quite accurate. His experience with the Djan'rū had left its mark in more ways that the obvious. "Lind," he said sadly. "I think you two would've gotten along. A shame you never met her." He paused to clear his emotions. "And our trip up North?"

"Malena has given me a message for you to get through to Saphella," Daric told him. "She said it has to be delivered exactly as she's given it. She's wrapped it in a similar sort of package to one I've used from time to time. Can't tamper with it, or it's obvious it been breached."

Casco gave a slow nod. "When?"

"Six days from now."

His heart plummeted. "Six more days? I'll go mad! There's only so much training I can do in a day, and I've explored the cave as far as I dare on my own. If anything happened …"

"No more exploration!" Daric said. "I'll be back as soon as I can, but with Delemät and Jaldan snooping around …"

Casco sighed. "Got more food?"

That I can do.

He watched as Daric unloaded a pile of bags and small boxes. "Fresh stuff from the new shipment," he explained. Last was a bowl of ripe golden wheel fruit. "Picked them myself," he said proudly. "And Shen sends his regards."

Casco bit into one of the orange-yellow fruit with relish and wiped the juice from his chin. "Where do they think I am?"

"The story is that you stayed down south to capture every last sweater and relocate it back to the Eastern swamps."

He imaged the tiny flying pests. "That should take some time!"

"Gotta love them! Fortunately, everyone is busy with cargo, stores and dodging the Ashik. No one has time to worry about a lost planetwalker. Kandät leaves tonight," he added.

Casco chewed more thoughtfully. "And just like that, we're on our own."

"We always were," Daric said. "Can't stay much longer." *Delemät's on the prowl.*

Does he know what you are? – Who you are?

An unmarked Enna with a wide range of abilities? Safe to assume he suspects. Ugly kalla suspects everyone.

What about Sari? How is she?

Worried about you, of course, but she's a smart one, isn't she? Just rolls with the Breath – accepts me as her Casco surrogate – just till the real one gets back.

Casco bowed his head. After going through so much, he hoped he would be there to help deliver his son. He touched the Mark on his head. At least he had something to offer, now. He was no longer a simple Kareski – like it or not.

I'm sorry, Daric said. *I know how much it meant to you. But the way things are going – there's no way you can show yourself while Delemät's here, and he'll be here for some time.*

How so? I thought he'd leave with Kandät Enna.

Sadly, no. "Kandät's off into the Chime today, but he's only going as far as Parsay, or Mecca or some-such then heading back. Another navigator's taking over to finish the cargo run to Giahn. But it will still be ten weeks before he's back to pick up that Breathless piece of shit, and the rest of the cargo."

"Ten weeks?" Casco heard the squeak in his voice but was too alarmed to care. "We have to get to the North. What if he finds me? Or interrogates you? ... Perhaps we should arrange my 'death,'" he laughed. "At least then he wouldn't be looking for me!"

He laughed again, but Daric didn't smile. Casco's head slowly tilted. He could feel Daric's thoughts whirling, but couldn't tell what they were about, and that made him nervous.

What did I say?

"It's a bit extreme," Daric replied thoughtfully. "... It would have to be convincing. No one else in on it at all. Absolute belief." The look he gave Casco was calculating and a little remote. "It would be very painful."

Casco recalled the time spent looking for Lind – the planet-wide search and sleepless nights worrying what might have happened to her, and then Radätel Gok, the overlord. The thought of his friends deliberately made to suffer in that way over him was outrageous. "Sari ..." he began –

"– Should get your death-cry," Daric interjected.

"Daric, no! It's not fair."

"No, and for that reason, no one would expect it of you."

"She would know it wasn't real. How can a death-cry be faked? It's impossible!"

"Training," Daric said thoughtfully. "And practice – perhaps."

Abruptly, Daric got to his feet. "I'll be back as soon as I can," he said and started for the portal.

Sand and pebbles crunched over-loud as Casco hurried behind him. Why did it seem he was being abandoned?

"I will be back," Daric said gently. The words echoed ever more faintly, *be back … be back …… be back* . At the foot of the portal, he turned and drew him close at last for a lingering kiss. The taste of him filled Casco's mouth. Afterward, they stayed close, forehead to forehead, reluctant to relinquish the warmth.

I'll come back, Daric whispered. *I'll sleep here with you tonight.*

Danger?

Minimal. Daric gave a lop-sided smile. *He might be Tsemkar, but there's no way he could find or sing this gate.*

The portal chimed softly and Daric disappeared.

Casco turned back. There was a distant splash. Beyond the light of his globe, the dark pressed in. It wasn't till he let it fade that his bio-luminescent neighbors became visible, like galaxies of stars in their own, sacred universe. He lay back to watch them, busy on the ceiling, oblivious to his presence - or so he believed. Were El and Asheru watching the Uri'madu in the same way? If so, what would they make of them, or the Host? Or someone like Jaldan of Trianog - the Mind Bender? He frowned as a dark, triangular-winged shape flowed over a patch of luminescence. All around, the lights went out and he couldn't tell where the predator had gone.

DELEMÄT'S PURPOSE

At the edge of the Host's encampment, spinners hurried to and fro around massive crates of minerals and ores. The load was as much as they had ever lifted, and its balance critical for a successful departure.

Between this and the first rows of tents, Kandät Enna stood with Delemät Ashik and looked him in the eye. They were metallic bronze in color and every bit as hard as the metal they resembled, but the navigator did not flinch. Delemät's Mark flared softly, but Kandät was ready for that also. There was heat from a two pronged attack - conventional Tsemkar, hence the visible flare, and a second, more subtle lance that sought to get in behind it while he was distracted. It was very sophisticated - the influence of the Mind-Bender no doubt, but a life-time of extreme focus made it easy for Kandät to keep the Delemät Ashik's of the Realm at bay.

Delemät grunted.

"What were you going to do?" Kandät tilted his head. "You can't threaten me. At least I can claim my own heritage."

A minute muscle twitch around Delemät's lips was all that said the barb hit home. “I am Ishät’s brother,” he rasped.

“Good for you,” Kandät retorted. It was the first time he’d heard the truth from Delemät’s lips since the death of his sister at Ishät’s own hand, so the admission, although hesitant, had a certain defiant charm.

“You will forget what you have seen,” Delemät continued, “or I will kill you. Understand?”

“Given that my niece - your dear brother’s wife - is also with child under dubious circumstances, it will require more than a hard look and a botched attack. She needs to know.”

“She already does. The rest of the Realm does not, and I am directed to ensure it stays that way.”

Kandät felt the blood drain from his face. “You can’t be serious!”

“Oh, but I am.”

Around them, the screech of bugs reached fever pitch. Delemät’s cold insouciance filled Kandät with anger. He thought of Andel of Trianog, the only one of the blessed he had glimpsed, although his spinners had heard plenty from the miners. She had seemed very pregnant indeed - perhaps not far from giving birth. Anywhere else, she would be considered sacred; Breath’s vessel. To deliberately harm such a one was unthinkable. He let some of his rage burn through. “If, when I return, I find a single one of Went’s Blessed has been hurt, I swear I will leave you here to die.”

The General’s eyebrows gave an arrogant lift. “My brother may not thank you.”

“But there are so many more who would.”

Delemät considered him for a moment as if amused by his anger. "I have not said I am going to kill them. My orders are to ensure their silence. There are other ways."

"Such as?"

"Jaldan of Trianog may be able to help."

Suddenly, the monster's presence and the Ashik troops made sense. "No." he said flatly.

"Better, perhaps, than death," Delemät said. "With Jaldan's help, they will remember nothing of their child's unusual … engenderment, and nothing of each other. He assures me this is possible, and nowhere near as painful as some procedures. As I see it, and as my brother sees it - and, by inference, how El himself sees the situation, their lives are not worth the chaos that would erupt if the Realm realizes it's been duped. That El was not the one who Blessed them." He paused as if to give Kandät time to absorb the enormity of this situation, then added, "That would be bad."

"How El sees it?" Kandät saw an enormity of a different type. "You think El endorses the God-Emperor to pretend he has his blessing?"

"Yes," Delemät replied firmly. "I must. My brother's will is paramount."

"What if your own daughter, Charäel, was caught up in some Imperial intrigue through no fault of her own. Would you kill even her at your brother's command?"

"She is not part of this story," Delemät said darkly. "You are."

"Do you even believe El is real?" he said incredulously. If the God-Emperor no longer honored the deity who had made him, chaos truly was inevitable. It had happened before, millennia ago; civil war – thousands killed before order could be restored, and the life of the errant Emperor had ended very badly. He had read the last remaining account in a fragile tome in the Guild's library. "This will be the downfall of everything," he said. "You must speak to him! Stop it now!"

"Speak? To him?" Delemät looked around. "Have you forgotten where we are? And as I said, Jaldan may be able to help." He studied him for a moment, his lips poised on the edge of a sneer. "He may be able to help you too, old one, and your precious niece – if you don't do as I say."

"You dare threaten the Empress?"

Delemät nodded slowly. "Maybe, maybe not. It's up to you. – And Kandät Enna, I may not be able to openly send you to the Breath, but I could make what remains of your life utterly miserable. And as for your crew, new spinners are easily come by."

"Don't you touch them!"

Delemät bunched his massive shoulders and rolled them, each in turn, as if loosening for battle, then gave the smallest of bows before stalking back towards the barracks.

Kattíst? Kandät breathed, *Kattíst, where are you?* Did she know the danger she was in? If her pregnancy was as advanced as Lady Andel's it was too late for them to leave. He would have to rescue them, if any remained alive, on his return. They expected him back in ten weeks, but if he went direct to Mecca he could do it in nine. It would push their abilities to the limit, and the advantage was small, but under the circumstances, it may just be enough. If only he could contact

Malena and let her know! But then he remembered the Mind Bender. Perhaps her silence was El's will. Perhaps secrecy was best.

As if Huldar had intercepted his call to Malena, the tall Lethian strode toward him. Kandät marshalled his scattered thoughts, thankful for the firmness of his haze and veils. At least his many years of proximity to the Imperial court had given him this much.

He bowed as Huldar approached, and greeted him, "Beloved of Leth."

Huldar masked his moment of confusion well, but to Kandät, not well enough. That small opening would have been ample for Delemät or Jaldan to lay him low. How to warn them?

"I am expected in ten weeks for the next cargo." He tried to imbue his words with urgency. "… Please, take care!" *May we talk?* He imaged Delemät. *Eyes and ears are everywhere.*

Huldar flashed him a look to show he's understood, before bowing politely in return. "I look forward to it. Perhaps I could walk with you back to the gate?"

Kandät smiled and indicated the way forward with an overly elegant gesture while saying, *I know this may sound extreme, but there is no time to say it any other way. Delemät is here to kill you.*

Huldar gave a short smile and inclined his head as if acknowledging Kandät's gesture, then took the first step. *I know.*

Kandät's surprise was not as well hidden as he would've liked, but Huldar remained silent.

The return trip may not take as long as anticipated. That is the best I can do.

Huldar nodded slightly. *Much appreciated.*

And Jaldan –

– *The Mind Bender,* Huldar finished for him, and Kandät almost smiled. The Lethian was not as naïve as he seemed.

They reached the Djan'rū all too soon. The space seemed empty of its massive load already, the shimmering envelope had already been sung. But if one knew where, and how, to look, there was a small break through which the cargo could be seen, a doorway through which he could enter. How he wished he could spirit this noble annangi away with him, and his equally lovely wife, but Huldar would never abandon his people, and Andel's pregnancy now imprisoned her. He looked at him long and hard, committing his features to memory, then bowed low.

"Farewell, my friend," he said earnestly. "May the birth of your First be a joyous occasion, and Breath blow you and yours good fortune until I return."

Huldar bowed in return and raised his hand. "Until we meet again."

Kandät could feel him watching as he entered the envelope, then he put the situation out of his mind as discipline demanded, warned his crew of his decision and focused his entirety on singing them safely through to Parsay on the shortest chord possible.

BLESSED CONFUSION

Huldar stood alongside the majority of the Host and watched as the navigator's huge envelope was sucked into the Chime. Afterwards, in mental replay, he could almost see the exact moment when the shimmering bubble vanished - almost.

His reverie was disturbed when he felt, rather than heard Delemät Ashik's approach.

"Shamkarun Huldar, a moment of your time."

Huldar's spine chilled. The General's voice was deep and cultured, his clipped Ashik accent unmistakably regal. How was he to deal with such an opponent?

He turned and bowed politely. "Of course, Lord Delemät Ashik."

Delemät looked coldly through him. "I will interview your wife and several others with this strange new affliction. Bring them to my pavilion tomorrow, here, at this time."

"They are not my possessions, lord Delemät."

The General stared at him, his expression as empty as the southern ice. "You may call me Lord Tsemkarun Delemät Ashik."

Huldar tipped his head in acknowledgement. "And my correct title is Lord Shamkarun Huldar, Beloved of Leth, but here on Went we do not stand on ceremony.

Delemät's gaze burned into his own, but Huldar knew he was correct in this. Daric had assured him that as unbelievable as it was, strictly speaking, his new title coupled with his far more extensive Mark made him Delemät Ashik's social equal.

This truth dawned on Delemät slowly. His brow furrowed as he wrestled with it. Huldar couldn't blame him. It was a hard one to swallow, but they had based their gamble on Delemät's lifetime conditioning in the protocols of the Imperial Court, and it seemed Daric was once again correct.

"I will suggest to my team you are interested to talk with them," Huldar said briskly. "And I have a request of my own. Jaldan of Trianog is a known criminal, and I will not allow him anywhere near any of the Uri'madu. Whatever reason you saw fit to include such a one in your contingent, I expect you and your team to respect my will and enforce this."

"I am no peace-keeper!" Delemät's frown deepened.

"Then what are you here for?" Huldar asked. "Olatu requested replacement miners."

Delemät frowned. His head twitched as if worried by a buzzing insect. "Tell them. Tomorrow. Here." Abruptly, he turned and walked away.

"I will tell them no such thing," Huldar said quietly after him, but his comment was not acknowledged.

It was later that same afternoon when Huldar stepped through into the southern desert. Daric stood and beckoned him to a tent pitched under the cover of a rugged group of rocks. He'd used a portable screen to protect it, but skillfully set so no anomaly showed.

The sides of the tent were raised to allow welcome air-flow, and somehow, a group of desert sweaters had found them. The persistent little lizards flickered around their faces trying to find somewhere to land.

Huldar smiled. *Just put out a tray of water – not too deep, and they'll go there.*

Daric snorted. *Why didn't I think of that?*

Because you're not 'Beloved of Leth', Ubaid said jokingly.

How did it go? Tam asked. His hand flicked and caught a persistent sweater so hard it landed with a tiny thud and lay unconscious by the fruit-bowl. He looked at it with concern. *Sorry little one!*

Huldar picked it up and held it in the palm of his hand. *No harm done,* he said after a moment, and placed it gently near the shallow water dish Daric laid out. Within moments, the sides of the makeshift pond were covered in a shimmering carpet of tiny, iridescent wings. Tam's swatting victim got groggily to its feet and was soon squabbling for a place.

If they could smile, I'm sure they would be now, Huldar said. He took the lid from the bowl between them and swiped a golden wheel fruit, then sat cross-legged on the sand.

Link with me. Better if I show you, he said, and held out his hands.

Daric watched his interaction with Delemät very closely. *You kept your nerve, and the whole thing went more-or-less to plan. Well done,* he congratulated him. *You've at least brought us a little more time, although now, the risk to the miners is greater.*

Tam shifted uncomfortably. An image of Tashel flickered through his veils.

"To tell the truth, it was almost fun," Huldar said. "But terrifying just the same."

"While he is confused, he will procrastinate," Daric assured him. "If we can keep him off-balance, we stand a greater chance of survival."

"I have warned the miners," Ubaid said, "or tried to, during our most recent pregnancy-class meeting. Tashel seemed to understand. She's very clever. I had to be so cryptic, I don't know if I would've understood myself!"

Huldar nodded. "They should go into hiding as soon as we can get them safely out of harm's way." He turned to the cook. "Tam?"

"I've told her that already – in not so many words, of course. She's meeting me at East basecamp tonight for a 'special dinner'. That's *her* tonight, which will be this afternoon. Quite soon, actually. I've made casten for her – saroo casten, then honey cakes with golden wheel sauce. She likes casten."

Ubaid nodded. "Once she's here, I will inform her team she is too unwell to continue at work and will remain under my care until after the birth."

Tam gave him a short bow. "Thank you."

"What about Farrel and Tish?" Huldar asked.

"At Top End copper mine," Daric replied. "They insist they are in no danger, and safe from unwanted contact. I can't convince them otherwise."

"Then they are prime targets," said Ubaid.

Huldar gave a solemn nod. "And Gael?"

"Already with us," Daric said. "She's working alongside Sari at the moment as an advisor on Eastside Gold."

"Advisor? I thought she was a miner."

"She works with Shamkar, so she's useless in her normal capacity - but what she doesn't know about extraction methods ..." Daric shrugged. "She's working with Sari on an environmental mitigation issue."

"The moss-creepers." Huldar nodded. "That's right. Sensitive to by-products of the third song-cycle."

"Do any of the miners know details of our plans?" Ubaid asked.

Tam shrugged. "Only that the Uri'madu camps will be a safe-haven when the time comes."

"Not even Tashel?" Daric asked.

"Of course not! We agreed!"

Huldar opened his palms, "Of course we did, Tam. Daric meant no offence."

Daric frowned. "When did you expect her?"

Tam looked at the sun. "Should be at Eastern basecamp any time."

"Have you heard from her?"

"No, but that's not ..."

"Try to contact her," Daric said. There was an edge to his request. "Now would be good."

Tam grimaced. "But she doesn't like it if she thinks I'm keeping tabs ..."

Huldar gave Daric a worried glance. "Please, Tam," he said.

"And she'd contact me if something was wrong - I know she would."

"If she was able!" Daric said.

Tam gave an exasperated sigh and closed his eyes, twisted his head about as if trying to settle on a direction, then opened them again. His brow wrinkled. "I can't find her."

"Try again," said Ubaid. "She might be in Qalān."

Tam nodded once and repeated his actions.

Huldar slumped, head in hands.

"Nothing," Tam said. "I can't find her! They've got her, haven't they! They've taken her!"

Daric's mouth twisted. "He'll try to force your hand with threats. It's what I would do."

"Threats ... are you sure? He doesn't look like the sort to waste time bluffing."

"Tam - he will only kill her if we do nothing."

"Then what should we do?!" the cook cried. "If you knew this might happen, why didn't you do something to stop it?"

"I tried to warn them!" Daric snapped. "I'm not omniscient!"

"Calm down, please," said Ubaid. "Huldar, what should we do?"

Huldar projected what calm he could, but beneath his own veils, anxiety roiled. What if Andel was missing? What should they do? He looked at Daric. They must try to anticipate their enemy's next move. "Tam, go to the mine, just to be sure," he said. The cook seemed relieved to be given some way to take action. "Trace her movements, but be as quick as you can. We will wait for Delemät to contact us," he said. "And one thing is clear. It's time to enact our plan."

Daric turned abruptly. "No! Stay here Tam. My advice would be to wait. She has gone. He has her. It makes sense. There will be a message, and until then we can't act. We can't give him control. We should go with your original thoughts, Huldar. Collect the Blessed and get them into hiding - but gradually if possible."

"But what if he hurts her?" Tam cried. "He could be hurting her right now! Why can't I reach her? For all we know she could be dead already."

"I don't think so," said Daric.

Ubaid nodded. "I believe Daric is correct in this, Huldar. It would be foolish for Delemät to spook us too much in the early stages. If the Empress is blessed, and she must be, or why send Delemät and the Ashik at all?, he will want to come home with as much useful information as possible - including what happens with the births. He won't kill or hurt her yet, Tam. We'll get her back. It will be alright."

Shamkarun Huldar, Sacred to Leth. Huldar winced at the thinly veiled sarcasm in Delemät's tone. *I have a message for you.*

Speak then, he replied. *What message?*

He waved them over and held out his hands. *Listen to this …*

Huldar of Leth – if you value life as much as you say you do, you'll send more subjects for interview. This one is tired already. The sending included an image of Tashel, lying as if unconscious on the ground. A sense of Jaldan's presence bled through.

"Tashel!" Tam cried. "My Tashel! It's her! What has he done to you?"

Daric gave him a warning glance.

Return her unharmed, Huldar said, *and we'll discuss this further.*

Bring more and this one goes free … otherwise …

I must have your word she is unharmed, and your assurance for the safety of my team. I will not put them in danger.

Delemät's presence dimmed momentarily. *Very well, you have my word.* He sent amusement. *But it's not like you can go anywhere, is it?*

Huldar chose not to respond to his implied threat. *I will come to the Host encampment tomorrow. Make sure Tashel is in perfect health when we get there.*

There's no way you can enforce that, Delemät sneered. *I can take who I want, any time I want. This is just a courtesy.*

His presence abruptly vanished.

"We must trade someone?" Tam said. "Who? How can he do this?"

"Who is there to stop him?" Daric answered cynically. "Best we do this as much as possible on our own terms."

"We must be very careful who we send, Huldar," Ubaid warned.

Huldar nodded. "We'll call a meeting."

Daric frowned sharply and put a warning finger to his lips.

The group were instantly silent and still. Huldar's eyes found Daric's. The assassin shook his head minutely as Delemät's farsight ranged back and forth over the site. Huldar swore beneath his breath. Of course, he'd pinpointed their location from their interaction. He gave Daric a congratulatory nod. Thanks to his expertise with portable screens, they were safe.

Delemät's presence faded.

Huldar began to speak, but Daric's ferocious frown stopped him. He motioned his hand for the others to remain still, and moments later, his neck shivered again as Delemät's farsight returned.

Daric grinned. *He must've been so sure,* he whispered.

Eventually the Ashik's presence moved on, but Huldar was wary of relaxing too soon.

"What was that?" Tam whispered.

"Delemät Ashik is one of the best farseers there is," Daric said quietly. "By now he'll know we aren't at either base-camp either. I suggest we leave immediately and split up."

"We should meet somewhere it's logical for us to be," Ubaid suggested.

Huldar nodded. "I'll contact each of you when the meeting is to be convened."

The low murmur of conversation was punctuated by sudden laughter as Topper related his version of the latest birthing class.

Huldar looked up to where the string of moons had coalesced into a narrow, switch-back serpentine formation that seemed to join the purple glow of the nebula to the indigo of the southern night sky.

Patience!

Huldar glanced at his wife, then Daric, then back to the fire. The Fjords picnic site was beyond Delemät's range and an ideal location for another secret meeting, but his head spun with plans, counter-plans and damage mitigation strategies as he waited for the Uri'madu to assemble. Outwardly, he took care to appear the very essence of calm leadership, but of course, Andel knew the truth.

At last, there was movement, and he looked up as Cobar and Daric rushed to help Gael and Sari scramble downslope. As Sari shepherded Gael to sit beside herself and Andel, he wondered if the capable Cantori had any idea she could never return to her former camp. Apart from Malena and Ariben who were yet to arrive, but he had Ariben's assurance they would, the Uri'madu were assembled.

Gento threw another branch onto the cheerful blaze. Sparks swirled beneath Daric's sheltering dome before exiting into the dark.

Andel's focus seemed to be on Sari and Gael, but in the same way as she could feel his mood, he could feel the questions in her heart.

He stifled an unexpected yawn. It seemed as if he'd been on the go forever.

How long since you slept? she whispered. *Three days? Four? Because if you did, it wasn't with me!*

He sighed and acknowledged her truth with a slight nod. He would make time for sleep soon, but right now, there was a fresh crisis to be solved.

He frowned at a small ringing in his mind. Another symptom of extreme fatigue?

"Tam, how's the stew coming on?" he asked.

"Arko's in charge of stew," Tam snapped. "I'm doing cakes and they'll be ready when they are."

"Nearly done," Arko said.

The ringing was persistent. He glanced upslope. Had he really heard the portal chime - through the dome and despite the continuous moan of wind off the sea? Below them, breakers boomed against the long row of slotted headlands jutting unapologetically into their path. He closed his eyes. It was as if he could feel the planet's endless roll through space. The tiny tug of each individual moon resembled a crowd of siblings each vying for their mother's attention.

Had he really communicated with her, this vast, improbable entity? Why did she care about him? Why had she shown him such a terrible future was possible, even probable? Surely such knowledge would skew his judgement - or maybe she'd shown him what he needed to see in order for his judgement to be skewed a certain way? The way she saw as best-outcome? There were no answers.

The small ringing took on a softer edge. It was her. He was sure of it. But why? What was he supposed to do? Was this the sacrifice she'd mentioned? The blessed ones? How was he supposed to know? Time was the only way he would find out.

Ariben shuffled sideways downslope. Malena slapped his hand away as he sought to help her with the rocky descent, then grumbled when she tripped and nearly lost her balance. Memories of the situation on the rock platform down south swam dangerously close to the surface. He must sleep soon.

Daric had assured him this meeting place was as safe as they'd get without retreating underground. There was nothing to stop Delemät trying to track them physically, but it was unlikely he would even see the ancient trackways they'd used, and even more unlikely he would be able to make those portals work for him, and even his prodigious farsight could not reach this far.

When Malena and Ariben settled quickly. He looked around at expectant faces and felt a pang that Casco couldn't be here, at least not physically. What a celebration that should have been! He could almost see the happy, firelit faces, drinking, eating, story-telling …

Again, he stopped himself. That information should be so deeply buried it was forgotten even to him, but it was almost as if the planet herself was dragging it up. And no doubt he'd be watching from a safe distance. He shook his head. His oldest friend was Marked, had a talent for Ziquarra, that most esoteric of gifts, and it had taken the love of an assassin to make these extraordinary accomplishments manifest. Time was a wonder indeed!

"Stew's up!" Arko announced. "For those of you who haven't eaten, can't talk on an empty stomach. And for those of you who haven't slept, there's a bit of a sting in this one's tail."

He ladled out of a second bubbling pot and held a bowl out to Huldar. "Kanth. Savior of many a rough situation. The other's just plain stewed kressie."

"Thank you, Arko."

The bowl was warm in his hands. The first mouthful a revelation. Not only had he not slept, he hadn't eaten.

Andel smiled at him encouragingly, the kanth worked its magic, and soon he was holding out his bowl for seconds. The resonance in his ears faded somewhat, and he knew it was time.

"Uri'madu," he began. "My friends, we have decisions. Important, dangerous choices."

"Where's Casco?"

"He couldn't be here tonight," Huldar answered, "but I have already discussed what is happening with him. The seriousness of our situation cannot be understated. Tashel has been taken by Delemät Ashik and Jaldan of Trianog."

There was an upsurge of anxiety, and anger from some.

"Tashel? Why?"

"He took her because she was one of the Blessed!" Tam said.

"And she happened to be an easy target at the time," Daric added.

Huldar held his hand up for silence. "Delemät has said, that in order to get her back unharmed, we must give him more subjects to study. Tonight we must decide whether or not to comply."

A deep silence fell as the group grappled with implications that before now, had only been theories.

"We can't just abandon her!" Tam said angrily.

"But who would go as a willing sacrifice to those two, Jaldan of Trianog and Delemät Ashik?" Daric asked.

"Are there any guarantees that no one will be hurt?" asked Calen.

"How could you trust any promise of his?" asked Ariben. "Who gets to police thirty Ashik? Trained warriors?"

"We have our own trained warriors," Nachiel countered. "I know they do practicing. I've watched."

"Not thirty of them!"

Huldar held up his hand. "There will be no fighting. Not at this stage."

"What then?" said Ariben. "We just lie down and take it?"

"She's not one of us," said Calen quietly.

"She is one of the Blessed!" Kiri snapped. "Tam is her trusted other. We must protect her if we can."

"I'll go," said Sari.

"Not without me," said Andel stoutly. Huldar gave her a tight smile, but there was no way he could let her anywhere near their enemies. She knew far too much.

"And me," said Gael. "Tashel is my friend."

"Count me in," said Rosheen.

Gento and Cobar nodded approval.

Kiri stood up. "I can handle that low-life bully."

"Maybe you can," laughed Banga. "Kalla better watch his balls!"

"He's no lightweight," Malena cautioned. "He's Ishät's brother, for those of you who didn't know – and the only one who's managed to stay alive." She snorted derisively. "Must be a nervous sleeper."

"Never mention who he is," said Daric. "Not to his face. Never go there."

"Well, brother or no, there's safety in numbers," Gento said.

Ariben sniggered. "Yes, and he's the one with the numbers."

Huldar held up his hand for silence.

"So, are we agreed thus far? We will comply with more subjects for him to interview?"

"So long as they don't have to go alone," said Gento, "and it's only an interview. No one gets hurt."

There was a murmur of agreement.

"I will accompany them," Huldar said. "And Gento and Cobar if you're willing. There was no stipulation preventing this."

Daric gave him a clandestine nod.

"Are we agreed?" Huldar repeated firmly.

One by one, the Uri'madu gave consent.

When it was done, Huldar felt his pulse elevate. In truth, there was no way he could ensure the ones he chose would be safe. "As to who will go," he said, "I thank those who have volunteered with all my heart, but there is no need to put all of you in danger at this time. We will all get to play our part, never fear!" He looked around the fire-lit faces. "I will come to each of you Blessed ones in turn, and we will decide on three."

"When?"

"Our agreement with Delemät - tentative agreement - was for tomorrow." He turned to Tam. "If you could serve the honey-cakes and tea?"

"Might need something a little more potent," Bush suggested.

Topper nodded vigorously.

Huldar gave a grim smile. "And besh if you have it, Tam."

While food and drink was laid out, Huldar turned to Andel. *You can't go.*

Why not?

I know you want to, and you are strong and capable and loyal to your friends, but I would think it was obvious. You know too much, beloved. Things even I don't know. He is a brutal master manipulator. One sniff of our escape plans and he will follow the trail to the end. He is too strong. ... how much does Sari know?

Only that we had some idea this would happen – as much as any know who were there when Daric first mooted the idea.

Who else should not go? he asked her.

Malena, of course, and Alis – if a healer could even be considered. But no other Blessed have been involved. That was our deliberate choice.

He nodded his thanks. *Once he realizes we've second-guessed him, he will surmise we have plans in place. When he can get no further useful information, he will go after me and possibly Casco.*

What about Daric?

He has no idea who Daric really is. With that, an image of Pieru, the Guild-Master came to him. He had suggested quite strongly that Daric's 'other abilities' might prove useful. How horrified he'd been at the time ... He flushed the sequence from forethought as quickly as he could. Any hint of outside assistance, no matter how slight, should be completely hidden, and he would not want Shamkarun Pieru's life endangered. Another thought chased it to oblivion – If Pieru was also 'Beloved of Leth', perhaps he had some level of safety ... But no one outranked the God-Emperor.

Pieru? Andel said.

Huldar sighed to himself. He really was too tired. *I wonder what he would think, if he knew our situation?* he told her, and it was no lie.

Slowly, he made his way around the group, engaging each of the Blessed in private.

Most were scared, and not just of Delemät. They were tired, ungainly, and unsure. Gael in particular was terrified she would split open like a Went and give birth to a hair-covered monster, yet she was adamant she should go to save Tashel who had become her friend. Huldar realized that whatever happened, she expected death.

"Do you know about the island," he lied gently. Daric had prepared him for this. He didn't like it, but her eyes seemed huge and hopeless, ready to clutch at any shred of relief.

She shook her head.

"There is an island, part of a chain to the north-west of the Central Continent. There is a cave there. Food and warmth. We will be safe, Gael. There is hope."

In another part of his mind, Daric congratulated him, but nonetheless, he felt tainted.

Sari was another who would not be stopped, and neither would Rosheen. He could think of no reason why either of them should not face Delemät. Sari, especially, could be a tactical asset as she was Andel's best friend and yet knew nothing of their cave system or the portals they'd created through ancient Qalān. He hated thinking this way, playing ashut with people's lives, yet he understood the necessity. Daric and Delemät had made that abundantly clear.

I know Qalān can be difficult these days, she said, *and some gates it's best not to trust without either Casco, or Daric or you to sing the way. Should I try to keep that from them?*

If you can, he replied. *But if they do find out, don't stress. They've probably already noticed as much for themselves.*

So, you're not going to stop me?

Do you want to be stopped?

No, she said, and a wave of sadness washed through him - a pulse oddly resonant with the sound of the planet's ongoing connection.

At length, he stood in front of the dying coals. Some needed to be roused from sleep, others were anxious about their daily schedules, but there were no complaints.

Arko wiped his eyes tiredly. "Breakfast for those who want it, and the water's still bubbling. Tea things," he waved his hand. "You already know all that."

Huldar waited for their attention. "Sari, Gael and Rosheen will be exchanged for Tashel," he said. "They will be accompanied by Gento, Cobar and myself at all times for the duration of any interaction with Delemät Ashik or Jaldan of Trianog, or anyone else, for that matter, and I will personally ensure their safe return.

Bold promise, Daric whispered.

He knew it was, but it was one he intended to keep if at all possible. If these mothers were the planet's sacrifice, he knew in his heart she would not get them without a fight.

THE DEEPEST OF LIES

Casco shivered. Here in the cave, he never felt warm, even though intellectually, he knew the temperature was always the same. Water plinked rhythmically in the distance, and for the moment, that was the only sound. The dark, as always, seemed to press against the light of the globe, the larger one from Radätel Gok's collection. He would have to return it to Radätel's family when they returned to Giahn … if they returned to Giahn.

She has to feel it in her soul, Daric insisted. *This is a golden opportunity. With Ziquarra, you can make that happen, and right at the most advantageous time.*

He shook his head. How could he bring himself to do this? What of Sari, the gentle soul who had been there for him so many times, and Huldar, his best and oldest friend? Then there was Shen, Lady Andel, Tam … how could he do this to them?

Because you must, Daric said. *It will not be forever. This is not your real death, just a convincing fake that will go a long way toward buying us a future.*

How do I know that? How do I know this is the right thing? What if I cause all this pain, and for nothing.

Daric gripped his shoulders. *That won't happen. You would never let that be. We will take our moment and use it. They will forgive us when they understand the necessity, I promise.*

Casco snorted, the sound overloud in the quiet of the cave. *You can't promise for the likes of Gento and Cobar, or Arko ... he can really hold a grudge.*

But he seems so –

– quiet? And level headed? He is. But ask him about the bander fruit-bugs.

Bander fruit-bugs?

Just ask. And take a few bottles of besh with you.

Daric chuckled obligingly, but Casco was serious - about the ale at least. That particular story was a long song indeed.

He could feel his resolve weakening. Daric's argument was strong. The enemy was unaware of his status as Archerran, and if no one was looking for him, he could move beneath their notice - he and Daric, to keep Sari and the other Blessed ones safe. They might be angry when they found out what they'd done, but the price would be worth it if the Uri'madu could be kept alive until they could be rescued, or until the ice covered them over and there was no more need to hide.

Punch the words into her, Daric encouraged, *then drift away. She has to have a sense of emptiness. All bonds broken.*

What bonds?

Daric shook his head. *There are so many. Friendship is a shared experience. Energy is traded. Small threads stick and form conduits. One reason why skilled assassins have no loyalties and must always work alone.*

Casco frowned.

It's a lonely life, my love, and ultimately unrewarding. Daric took his hand, so he could feel the truth of what he said. "I am glad I found you, Casco. Glad I am no longer alone."

"And I – my life has changed since I met you, and for the better." He touched his scalp. "This would never have happened without you."

His love flowed through their joined palms, and Casco frowned as he met a new wonder. How could he have missed it? Daric had never believed himself to be loveable. Not truly, for what he was. Darkness ducked and wove through the Enna's soul like elusive fish, each one the seed of a potential monster, yet he was good, and Casco did love him.

He recalled their indescribable moment down on the beach when the sea creatures sang. *We did see the Bel Nishani, didn't we?* he said wistfully

Daric shook his head. *You're not going to actually die.*

Their hands slid apart.

So, how can I do that? Break those bonds?

Daric's mood closed down. *I've seen it often enough. I'll show you. You've only got one chance, so get it right.*

The assassin helped him visualize the myriad small ties he shared with Sari, some the gold of her hair, others the color of her eyes. More esoteric ones were inspired by the sound of her voice, the feel of her presence, even certain movements and habits. The strongest were remnants of shared memories, and he wondered how he could tackle such a web of connection all at once.

Don't sever them from her, Daric told him, *cut them from yourself. There is a song based on the maneuver one uses if one*

wishes to end one's life – except you won't kill yourself, of course. It slices through unwanted bonds. … There is some pain involved, and you'd best be prepared. It will be proportional to the depth of your regard.

Casco sighed. This was going to hurt a lot then. *So, death-cry then bonds?*

It should appear simultaneous, so bonds then cry. Be watching from close by, have your cry cemented in your mind, sing to cut the ties, then send it.

What should my Death-Cry be?

What is the one thing, the most important thing you would have to tell her if you really were dying?

He remembered Lind's Cry – and Sari's reaction. *Duvät Gok has eyes …* It didn't make sense for quite some time. Anger came unbidden. He had seen the creatures now.

"Why wouldn't my cry go to you? They'll suspect something's not right."

Daric shrugged. "We are not blood relatives or Dabaku." He paused as if considering what to say. "Yes, while I hope never to hear it, I also hope you would honor me with your actual cry – should it ever come to that. But Sari is important to you, and she does wish, in her fantasies, that you were really hers. She would never want you dead, but she will be too overwhelmed by your cry to question it."

Casco grimaced as the import of those words sunk in. "To play on her hidden emotions that way, it is so unfair!"

"Not so hidden that I can't see them, or anyone else who cared to look more closely," Daric retorted. "This is war, Casco. We are at war for our lives and those of our children –

your own child. This will give us freedom to carry out the mission to the North."

INTERVIEW WITH THE MONSTER

Huldar, Gento and Cobar stepped through the portal on the hillside above the Host Encampment. Between them, Rosheen, Sari and Gael stood strong, but Huldar could sense their fear.

First Gento, then Cobar kissed Rosheen, and for a wonder, she didn't push them away.

"Are we ready?" Huldar asked. "Sari? Gael? Rosheen? There is still time to back out."

"And leave Tashel to die?" said Sari.

"I understand your suggestion comes from love," Rosheen said, "but don't underestimate us."

He gave a sharp nod. "Point taken."

They started down the grassy trail toward the outskirts and came to a newly erected pavilion-style tent. Delemät Ashik and Jaldan of Trianog stepped from beneath the door. Delemät looked the Blessed up and down as if they were goods at market, while Jaldan's dark eyes glittered in his skinny face.

"Delemät Ashik," Huldar said. "Where is Tashel?"

"I wanted at least one archangel," Jaldan said. "The navigator would do nicely."

Huldar frowned. Jaldan's haze had an overlay of darkness. Something was very wrong. The planet's ring changed, clearly a warning. His spine gave an involuntary shudder.

"Delemät Ashik?"

Delemät regarded him with stony eyes, devoid of emotion. "Yes … where is Malena of Maatu?"

"Shamkarun Malena is unwell," he said smoothly, and it was no lie. "If you must have an archangel, Van can come with Calen of Leth to accompany her."

Jaldan glanced Delemät's way, his expression petulant, and spoke mind to mind with Delemät, or tried to.

As if also shocked by his rudeness, Delemät's eyes narrowed. "Your substitution is acceptable," he said.

Jaldan looked away as if the middle-distance had suddenly developed a fascinating alure.

"Bring the miner," Delemät commanded him.

Jaldan scurried to do his bidding.

Huldar nodded. "I must contact Van. It will not take long for them to get here."

Delemät nodded in return. "Very well. In the meantime, perhaps we could discuss the missing portal?"

"The one mentioned by Farushael of Cantori?"

Delemät inclined his head. His expression was politely genial, but his haze was completely motionless, and to Huldar's mind, his inner veils were as glacial as Went herself could be.

"As I said to Farushael," Huldar replied, "Qalān can be tricky on this world."

Delemät's eyelids flickered, momentarily narrowing. "Yet I am told you are a master portal maker. Skilled enough, perhaps even to make a gate vanish."

Huldar snorted lightly. "If this feat were indeed possible, I'm sure it would take some time to achieve - and time is precious these days."

The fractional quirk of Delemät's chin was Huldar's only warning. His defenses were sluggish from lack of use, and on their own would have been barely enough to ward off the Ashik's attack, but he felt the planet's voice swell in his soul, and the darkness shattered on impact.

"Sir!" Huldar said angrily.

Delemät grunted as if surprised by his strength.

The Rukh stepped forward, murder in their gaze.

"Apologize!" Gento demanded.

"What's happening? Sari asked.

Delemät's lips shrugged. He gave Huldar a nod.

That's no apology, Cobar snarled.

"Enough!" Huldar snapped.

After a slight hesitation, Cobar bowed and stepped back.

The planet's voice receded. Huldar tipped his head as if listening to the portal on the slope above.

"Van and Calen of Leth have arrived," he said coldly. "Once Tashel is returned to a place of safety, we shall accompany your current subjects to wherever it is you have planned to hold these interviews."

"We want to see them alone," Delemät said stiffly.

"No doubt," Huldar replied. "But that will not happen."

"I was rather hoping … " Jaldan cleared his throat. "That is to say … the diviner - your wife …?

Huldar stared at him coldly.

"- Yes …" Jaldan's voice dribbled into a pause. He turned toward Sari. "Leth by the look of you - mostly Leth." He toyed with his stylus and studied the blank page before him as if it already held the answers he sought, then abruptly took aim and swept it delicately across the paper.

He paused, still looking at the paper. "And you claim your pregnancy resulted from eating a 'berry'."

"Yes, sir," Sari said. "Although we later discovered they weren't berries at all, but the eggs of one of the creatures here …" She glanced at Huldar for reassurance.

He nodded. This was nothing the Imperium did not already know.

"- The Went," she continued. "Such beautiful souls. They are sentient, you know. Citizens. And they deserve our utmost respect. We would never have eaten the eggs if we had known!"

Jaldan nodded absently. His hand went still.

Sari scratched the hair above her forehead as if her scalp was suddenly itchy.

Huldar noticed an aberrant thread of energy and signaled Cobar and Gento. The Rukhs' expressions barely changed, but almost immediately, Jaldan's probe thinned and snapped back to its origins. Rosheen gave each of them a strange look, as if something unexpected had happened. Cobar gave a small shrug and the pair returned to silent watchfulness.

Jaldan rubbed his head. "I was merely attempting to ascertain the nature of the bond between parasite and host," he said indignantly. "As it was, I could barely penetrate!"

"Parasite and host?" Sari glared at him incredulously. "Is that how you see us?"

"Ask your questions verbally, as agreed," Huldar said.

The mind-bender turned to Delemät. "This is most unsuitable! How can I work under these circumstances?"

"You fancy yourself intelligent," Delemät said coldly. "This is your chance to prove it."

Jaldan gave each in turn a narrow look, then began writing again as if nothing had happened. Eventually, he turned to Rosheen.

As the interviews progressed, Jaldan's nasal voice grated. It was clear his talent was not as a singer. Huldar watched Delemät and Jaldan in the same way he would watch wild creatures in the field, every sense hyperalert but unobtrusive. His haze flowed with less than average intensity - too still and he appeared as a predator, too active and his presence may cause alarm. His inner veils were schooled to complete opacity, yet without the mannered formality that might seem artificial and engender mistrust. Beside him all three Rukh stood watchful. Sari, Gael, Van and Calen stood as close together as possible without actually touching.

He waved his stylus in Sari's direction. "Children?"

She frowned. "Only this one."

The pen left more fine marks on the paper.

"What was the nature of your interaction?" he asked dispassionately.

Sari's frown deepened. She gave a puzzled blink. "What do you mean?"

"Your sexual interaction, of course," Jaldan said rudely. He turned to look at her. "I'd heard you weren't quite bright, but really? Need I elaborate? Was there one partner or many?" he snapped. "Male or female? Was it pleasant? Was there ejaculate? If so, how much?"

Huldar's head tipped firmly sideways. "Are these questions relevant?" he said coldly. "I suggest you rephrase."

Jaldan scowled up at him. "I need to know!"

"Just answer," Delemät said.

Calen stepped forward. "How would you feel if this monster asked similar questions of your own daughter?"

Delemät's eyes flashed. "My daughter would know better than to get involved in a drug induced orgy!"

"More likely she'd be too frightened to tell you," said Rosheen. She turned to Huldar. "I, for one, will not answer such personal questions. We should leave now."

Sari and Gael nodded, but as they seemed about to turn away, Jaldan's power flared in a tightly woven attack.

Gael gasped, her eyes wide with terror.

The Rukh grimaced as they tried their utmost to sever the link, but this time, their efforts were in vain.

"Tell me everything, "Jaldan sneered silkily, "or she will suffer - I promise you that." He turned to Huldar. "Your own dear wife taught me this trick. I call it the White Terror."

"Make it stop!" Gael screamed. She clutched her head and pressed as hard as she could. Her eyes squeezed shut then opened again unseeing. *Make it stop!*

Huldar paused, shocked by the intensity of the attack, and in that void the voice of the planet swelled. Rapid power filled every pore, every corner of his being. Latent energy was there for the taking. He felt alive as he never had.

He pointed to Jaldan. Light seemed to stab from his fingertip. "Delemät! Control him!"

Delemät studied Gael's agony with interest. "Why should I?"

Sari knelt by Gael's side. "Stop it!" she shrieked. She caught Gael's arms to stop the miner from punching her own head. At first, it seemed Gael would be too strong, but suddenly, she stopped and clung to Sari's arms as if she dangled above an abyss and only that grip could save her.

"Stop this now!" Huldar roared.

Sari turned to Delemät. "Tell him to stop!"

"You should have answered his questions, little angel," Delemät sneered. "This is all your fault."

Huldar felt the planet's voice overwhelm him in a tide of anger, and he welcomed it. He opened his throat. Sound poured out in a cohesive stream and wrapped around Delemät's neck. He lifted his arm and the Ashik was raised skyward. It should not have been possible to lift a living being so, but he had no room for wonder.

Stop this now! His cry punched directly into Delemät's brain.

As if the link between Ashik and Trianogi was immediate, Jaldan's attack ceased.

Delemät still dangled in the grip of his rage.

The Ashik's Tsemkar flared, but his attack was absorbed and neutralized.

Huldar watched his enemy writhe. As panic set in, his anger grew. The Planet sang in his veins. Its child had been threatened. *You!* he cried. *The Chosen's own brother. You wield your pet monster like a sword. A tool with which to destroy another's life!* He lifted Delemät Ashik higher. "Why?" he hissed. "She is helpless! A pregnant mother. Annangi's most sacred form!"

How could the God-Emperor allow this – El allow this? he asked himself. *Asheru – where was she?* His raging song tightened its grip.

The hated visage purpled. Terror tinged its bulging yellow eyes.

… *Huldar,* a gentle voice intruded. *I think you should stop now.*

He looked at Sari's terrified face and dropped Delemät like a sack.

The planet receded. *Now is not the time,* she conceded. *Soon you must choose, but not yet …*

Delemät Ashik lay in a fetal position and gasped for air. Jaldan cowered in the corner, arms raised as if they might ward off a blow – but despite his pathetic show of fear, one eye peered between his fingers and studied Huldar with interest.

Sari and Van helped Gael to her feet. Calen stood side by side with the Rukh and glared at Delemät, her expression every bit as ferocious as theirs. It was if they dared retaliation.

Outside, feet drummed rapidly uphill as all available Ashik ran to their general's aid.

The tent flap was torn aside by a sword-bearing warrior.

Huldar opened himself to the planet again and braced for the worst.

"Stand down!" Delemät commanded. His voice was hoarse. One hand rubbed his throat.

The Ashik stopped. Their leader gave a doubtful bow and backed away.

"The interviews are over." Huldar said coldly. "From now on, you will leave us alone."

"You know that cannot be," Delemät rasped. "You will never –"

He was interrupted by Sari's anguished cry. "Casco!" she screamed. "Casco! No!" and with a look of utmost horror, she collapsed.

Huldar dropped to her side. *What! What has happened?* But although his heart doubted, her reaction could mean only one thing. Somewhere on this planet, his long-time friend lay dead.

Rosheen and Gento stood as if stunned while Cobar swept Sari from the ground. Tears rolled down his craggy face. Sari sobbed against his neck, incoherent with grief.

Huldar motioned for them to leave, then with a last look at their defeated antagonists, followed toward the portal. An eerie silence wrapped his mind. He struggled to comprehend the chain of events. How had he done what he'd done? How could it be that Casco was gone? Their footfalls were soft on the grassy path. He felt Delemät Ashik's gaze on his back. Could almost feel the rasp in his throat. Ashik warriors parted and lined the way as if they were a guard of honor, but Huldar felt no pride in what he had done, only fear and overwhelming sadness.

THE BROKEN TRAIL

Heralded by the long buzz of a lone red-winged tree-hugger, the rising sun eased slowly above the horizon. As if to congratulate the hugger's bravery, the soft chirrup of a potential companion soon joined it.

Dawn air stirred through sharp edged fronds. Light filtered boldly through clumped tree trunks. Blurry shadows trailed like ribbons down hillsides. The song and counter-song of the hugger pair drifted on the breeze, filling space above and below with their plaintive call - and a poignant balance was struck.

Hnarse Stargazer paused to absorb the moment. Its heart beat strongly. Tears dribbled from its nose. How could one ever commit such exquisite totality into words?

The balance altered as another hugger signaled interest, then another, until there were thousands, and their sound swelled to a shriek that seemed to take on a life of its own. Carmine wings clothed strap tree trunks in pulsating shrouds. Above them, foliage shimmered softly in the milky light of morning as if captured by the overwhelming voice of this particular moment.

With great reverence Hnarse bent its head to the ground and droned. Its attempt to frame such beauty in a song to the planet's Heart would take time. Each vivacious tone, every exuberant variation of color and touch of vagrant breeze must be encoded lest such an event be lost and never repeated.

But as the Went knelt on the grass a new sound intruded - or was it merely a vibration? Either way, it interfered with its recitation in unpleasant ways.

At first, Hnarse pressed on, but its song quickly lost impetus.

The strange noise pushed up through Hnarse's forehead, dark and alien. Something terrible was happening!

The strident buzz of the huggers abruptly ceased. Inside his head, screams of the herd reverberated. Terrible cries! Went milled about as if unsure or lost. Some crashed into trees or stumbled over rocks as if, like Nielli, they had been blinded.

Nielli bumped against Hnarse's side, *We must flee this place!* It wrapped its trunk tightly around Hnarse's and lurched sideways, dragging Hnarse with it.

Hnarse followed in a sudden jump, then shied again at a loud, blunt crack. Ground gave way where it had been standing only moments ago. The diameter of the newly existent hole grew with alarming rapidity. Rocks and dirt cascaded downward, first with a hiss, then with a thunderous roar.

Hnarse leapt aside, but was not quick enough. There was a short sense of falling before a solid thump knocked the wind out of its chest. The rim was within reach, and as soon as it could, reared up and got its front legs over, then pulled itself forward so the mid-legs were on the rim, but its hind legs scrabbled vainly against the disintegrating wall. It closed its ears to the cries of more Went as they tumbled against the rocks below, but its eyes could not un-see the bodies that fell past it to their doom. How could their souls ever be recovered? They would be lost to the great circle and know nothing but darkness.

Nielli still held tightly to its trunk, but the ground lurched again and with a tumbling crash, Hnarse's footing disappeared. Nielli's feet skidded closer to the chasm. Hnarse reared up again and tried even harder to drag its rear end over the edge, but soil gave way and every shove dragged them both closer to disaster.

Then it heard a new kind of thunder as Neetha bellowed galloped to their aid. Its coat rippled wildly, "What can I do?"

"Help Nielli!" Hnarse rippled back.

Neetha's trunk joined Nielli's and Hnarse used the extra leverage to try and hoist itself upward, but its trunk became one long rope of pain as more of the fragile ground slipped away.

It cried out in agony as Nielli let go. The small Went knelt down close to the rim. Its trunk felt for the edge. It lay down and inched forward. Fresh rock and dirt hissed by as if in warning of fresh collapse.

What is it trying to do? Hnarse thought wildly. *Help me! Go back and help Neetha now!*

But the blind Went continued to push forward until its forelegs dangled in space. Air moved rapidly in and out of Nielli open mouth as it extended its trunk.

After a few wild swings, Hnarse felt it wrap firmly around its flailing mid-leg, and finally understood.

As it pushed its leg forward and up, Nielli heaved backward in rippling waves.

The limb found firm ground. Neetha threw itself into the task and managed to pull backward a few steps, but Hnarse's scrabbling had eroded the lip into an overhang. It would only be a matter of time before the treacherous shelf gave way.

"Go now!" it cried. "We are all in great danger. You can't die because of me!"

But even as it spoke, Nielli almost dove over the precipice to dangle its trunk down and down again toward Hnarse's hind leg.

A clump of grass fell from the brittle overhang.

It kicked reflexively as Nielli contacted its hind leg, then the young trunk encircled it with a tight grip, just above the foot pad. Together with Neetha, the two Went gave a gargantuan heave.

As Hnarse rolled up and over, it felt the edge give way.

Neetha and Nielli tugged furiously to pull Hnarse's body to safety as the overhang thundered into the abyss.

Hnarse felt the cool rush of air thick with the smell of dirt.

"Keep rolling!" Neetha commanded.

It tucked its legs tucked tight rolled as Neetha commanded. Clouds, dust and sky spiraled. Its already bruised trunk hit a rock with force, but all it felt was percussion.

When it stopped, the sensation of movement continued. When the ground shuddered again, Hnarse stumbled upright and ran. The drumming of its heart resounded with the thud of its feet. On and on it galloped until eventually, its body failed. Limb by limb it collapsed onto the forest floor, resigned to whatever terrible fate awaited. Sweat oozed from its battered foot-pads. Heat enveloped its aching body. Air roared in an out of its lungs. How could it get enough?

Slowly, other sounds intruded. The wind in the trees. The creak and crackle of dry leaf-litter. The screams were gone.

One by one it dragged its legs beneath itself, then with an almighty heave, pushed itself erect.

The pain in its footpads was like nothing it had ever experienced. Every part of its body hurt. Tears dribbled from its torn and beaten trunk. It was thirsty and tired, and when it looked around it realized it had no idea where it was. The canopy was too dense for a reading of the skies. Hnarse started to lift its nose and scent the air, but the pain caused an involuntary cry.

For one to die so far from the trail was a disaster akin to the one it had fled. No one would find its soul. No loving mother would come to carry it to the sacred caves.

Hnarse knew it should sing this event to the Heart, its agony, and that of the other Went now gone forever in the cataclysmic event it had somehow survived. The Heart should know of its terrible fear; but it couldn't bring itself to tell. Nielli and Neetha were the only reason it still lived, and yet it had run away without them, heedless of their fate. How could it sing until it knew they, at least, were safe? Elders were supposed to lead. To be pillars of the herd. How could it sing their bravery … its cowardice?

Tears landed in a small, dark pool at its feet. But then, as if in answer to its distress, a single ray of sunshine illuminated a veil of tiny white flowers. Like a sprinkle of stars, they sprouted from a small clump of leaves at head-height on a tree-trunk. When the air moved, a radiant scent washed through its injured nose.

Hnarse sniffed back tears and shuffled closer. Each star resembled a little rearing Went showing its colors. How had this particular wonder remained hidden until now - unsung, yet here it was, growing and thriving? Truly, life was more mysterious than a simple Went could understand. Perhaps it was enough just to sing what was seen and leave the rest to the Great Cycle itself.

At last, Hnarse bent its hairy head to the ground and droned. All of its hurt and fear poured out and down. Shame for its panicked bolt, gratitude for its friends existence, hope that they would forgive. It translated the sound of the rumbling ground into song; sods and clods falling amongst the lost Went - how many it did not yet know. But through it all was woven the joy of its discovery, the shining miniature Went-flowers, each connected by a thin, fine stem to the whole - and it sang the heroic efforts of its friends. They were the reason this exquisite discovery had been made.

When it was done, the light was fading, but the veil of flowers continued to shine with light of its own. Another marvel! Had his two-leg friend seen it, Hnarse wondered, but the alien had been absent now for many days.

Then Neetha's loud trumpet sounded through the forest and Hnarse's heart leapt with gladness as Nielli's soft voice came into its mind, *We have found you!*

"Hnarse! Friend of my Heart!" Neetha's coat rippled like waves to shore. Nielli trundled at top speed behind it. How the blind one could travel with such confidence over the uneven terrain was another mystery Hnarse knew must be committed to the soul of the planet.

When they came close, Neetha reared up, legs held wide. With great effort, Hnarse mirrored the Grassmover's gesture, but although it was a moving reunion, the most wonderful of its life, most of all it longed to show its friends the glowing plant on the tree trunk.

Step by step, Hnarse threaded its way through the pathless forest. How had its body managed to run so far? Interest in its surroundings waned. All this new information must be committed to Heart, but to place one foot haltingly after the next was the best it could do for the moment.

Neetha was also nursing damaged foot-pads, but not be as bruised as its own. Hnarse had no sound limbs. Neetha still had four.

"Not far now," Neetha said stoically. "Just over this rise …"

Nielli bumped into Hnarse's backside and it realized it had stopped again.

With supreme effort, it limped toward the rise. Ahead, Neetha assured it, was the trail at last, but when it reached the top it paused, confused by the scene below. Nielli nudged its rump again. No doubt the youngster was also tired and hungry, but blind as it was, how could it understand?

An enormous circular hole now bisected their ancient pathway … as if a giant Went had stamped its foot and the ground had given way.

"Neetha," it asked. "Have the others … gone ahead?"

"Some ran, as you did, my friend." The Grassmover's trunk moved softly over its back. "Others have yet to be found."

"But – there are so few."

A nagging doubt caused Hnarse to search its memories. What it found chilled its soul further.

"There was one instance, so many cycles distant …" it said quietly to Neetha. "A great hole such as this one opened up, not far from here - where the trail does a large meander and sour tharis fruit sustains us?"

Neetha nodded. "The tharis is sparse and unpleasant. I often wondered why the trail sends us there."

"It was once more direct, but Went were forced to deviate. Elder Motharn Singteller was there also - even in earlier incarnations we were never great friends … but Motharn will definitely remember, history is what Singtellers do best. We must tell the herd of this together."

Hnarse started toward the gathering below until Neetha placed its trunk on its own. "Motharn Singteller is gone."

"Gone?" Hnarse tossed its head. "But its wisdom is needed!"

"Three younger Singtellers remain," Neetha said. "One of them must become Elder."

"Motharn was there! It is the only other who may remember the shorter path."

Nielli tried to huddle closer, but Hnarse's agitated movements bumped it away.

"The shorter path?" Neetha's coat rippled in confusion. "I didn't know there was one." The sway of its coat communicated concern for Hnarse's health. "Maybe the ordeal has confused your thinking?"

"Then others must search themselves and corroborate my memories," Hnarse told it. "Heat and flowing fire pouring down mountainsides as if from many wounds. We are stranded, cut-off from our home!" It hobbled onward, impatient for action. "Many are lost - returned to the planet, never seen again." It motioned to the remnant of the herd. "We cannot afford to lose any more."

Went clustered in tight groups. The smell of fear was strong. There were nervous snuffles as Hnarse and Neetha rose to show their undersides. Hair movement was tight. No other Elders rose to greet them.

Hnarse stayed upright for as long as it could in an effort to assess how many of the herd had survived, and locate more Stargazer brethren. Perhaps if it showed itself in this way, more would emerge from the forest - surely that's where they were hiding ... lost and afraid.

"Come down, Hnarse," Neetha said gently. "This is all who remain."

"But that cannot be!" His coat whipped back and forth in pain. "My Stargazers? ... and the Mothers? Where are the rest? If they are swallowed, how many are gone with them?"

Neetha stared mournfully at the pit. From where they stood, it appeared a line of darkness had cut their time-worn trail in two. There was no going back. High above, the skies above wheeled as they normally did, but here ...Hnarse shuddered. "Not a circle at all," it said fearfully. "An ending. A break in the flow of all we knew and have sung to Heart." It gave Nielli an involuntary glance. "What did we do wrong? What was there? What happened that we didn't we see?"

"Hnarse Stargazer, you are now the Eldest," Neetha said. "You must guide us."

The remnant gathered around. A young Singteller rose unsteadily to face them, then the last of the Enders followed.

Neetha also stood, followed by another Grassmover to represent Mothers who showed their colors but once, at the last cave. Then the oldest of the three Stargazers, an earnest three year old called Rathe also bared its chest.

First Mother survived, but only one of these most precious herd members stood beside her. The others had fallen to their deaths, and the souls they had nurtured – those lost on the trail, would never come again.

"If we stay on the regular path, further disaster will overtake us." Hnarse told them decisively. "This I know from lives of old, and the planet itself has made it clear." It knew beyond doubt's shadow this was the route they must follow, yet the decision was a hard one. "Has anyone else access to these memories?"

The new Singteller Elder returned slowly to its feet. "I remember," it said.

Hnarse bowed its head with relief. It was not alone.

"I propose we deviate from the trail and head to Selly Farn," Hnarse said.

"The place of the foretelling?"

"Yes. Selly Farn lies on the rises beyond the shaven waters. It will be the final trial of this cycle."

"Went do not swim well," the Singteller said slowly. "But I agree it is the best way."

As if to spur them into action, a new tremor quivered through Hnarse's bruised footpads. Went trumpeted in alarm.

"Stay close," Hnarse called. "Follow me!"

It looked back and saw Nielli, an island of stillness buffeted by the rush of panicked Went.

Hnarse! It waved its trunk in an effort to catch a familiar scent. *I can't find you!*

Nielli! Hnarse was gripped by fear that the bravest of all would be lost. *I will not leave you! Wait there.*

Then Neetha pushed through the milling crowd to Nielli's side. The youngster's trunk curled around the Grassmover's.

"Go!" Neetha said. "Lead us. We are all your special responsibilities now. I will make sure this particular new purpose is safe until you have time for it again."

Hnarse turned and took the lead. Although their departure must be hurried, it would not allow panic to enter its heart again. No pain showed in its strong and rhythmic steps - there would be time to tend to its injuries later, when the ground had stopped shaking.

Memories of the alternative path were elusive at best, but a large outcrop shaped like the head of a Went indicated they had turned at the right time.

The way led downward. In the distance, the mountainsides were covered in patches of deep scarlet. The distinctive color jogged Hnarse's memories further. These were blooms it knew to be dangerous - even deadly, but their fruit was tasty and nutritious, a true delicacy. If they proceeded with caution and avoided the thorns, at least they would do better than the detested tharis pods they usually subsisted on at this time.

It pointed them out to Grueth Singteller, and together they began to spread the word. Good food was at hand.

As they neared the final rise, Grueth came to Hnarse's side. Its hair waved in thoughtful swirls. Ends flicked - almost apologetically. "I seem to recall an additional danger. Something to do with rocks?"

Hnarse paused. The task of leading the herd had driven its past-life memories deep again, and as Grueth had just pointed out in the most delicate of ways, this was a mistake. "Rocks?" It turned to Grueth. "Can you …"

Grueth's hair moved with greater definition. "There is a song … If you are in agreement, we must stop and connect to Heart."

"Connect?" Hnarse knew its hair control was nowhere near as refined as young Grueth's, but Grueth was, after all, a Singteller. "I have not thought of our observations as going both ways." This fascinating concept must be discussed with Neetha as soon as the opportunity arose. "Is this how it is for you, Grueth Singteller? Does Heart communicate back to you?" If Nielli could communicate without sight, could this 'planet speaking' skill also be learned?

Grueth's follicles showed hesitation. "I – I know the concept may seem …"

"No, not at all," Hnarse assured it. "What do you hear?"

"Nothing, really. But there is a strange feeling I have, and when it comes, I can connect more fully with past lives. I believe the planet remembers what we have shown it. Everything we commit to Heart is retained."

Hnarse considered this. The idea certainly made sense. How else could each cycle be perfectly recreated? "Let's stop right here," it said. "While we sing to Heart, can you ask for details of this song? Determine the full extent of this new trial we face?"

"I will try," Grueth said, and Hnarse was sure it would.

Went paused to drone. Despite their fear, they needed little persuasion. Hnarse could barely concentrate, and its communion was soon done, but its feet enjoyed the rest and it was difficult to force itself fully upright again. When it did, it found Neetha peering thoughtfully ahead.

Many Went still rested their heads against the ground and droned. Hair swished and rolled. Sound reverberated around and through them.

Neetha used its trunk to move Nielli closer. "So," it said quietly. "We go to the place of foretelling?"

Hnarse nodded.

"Then shall I take the part of Enzo Grassmover?" Neetha said, "and you, Shaartuhn Stargazer? Are the days of the broken circle truly upon us?"

Hnarse did not know how it should answer. The poem about those two most memorable Went, The Prophecy of the Broken Circle, was always the last to be told before the white waste and the long sleep was upon them. Hnarse remembered the great Fesneeth Singteller, and a much younger self watching in awe as natures gifts of snow, wind and failing light had been employed as props to color the Singteller's words.

"Maybe," it said softly.

Light played over the backs of the gently seething group of Went - all there were left to lead. Dribbled tears stung its damaged nose. Its mind rang with the prophecy. Was this the strange sensation Grueth had mentioned? For a moment, it could almost see the master Singteller's coat ripple again … rhythmic and portentous.

"The time of the broken circle will come," Hnarse murmured, "when the circle of winds will sniff in vain, and the circle of skies will turn on emptiness …" *Weep for the purpose betrayed,* it continued in its mind. *They will wait in the dark to mend what is taken. Blue of sky, gold of sun, white of dark in dark of night. Sing the rise of the purpose reborn.*

Nielli huddled close against Neetha's chest and looked up as if the sky it could not see was already darkening.

"We will trust the circle to find its ends," Neetha finished quietly, as if it had heard also. "As we must. The circle continues, dear friend of my many cycles - friend of my heart."

Hnarse bowed its head to the ground and droned again in an outpouring of grief and uncertainty which swelled and was carried by the long sound into the planet's Heart. Those who were lost must know they were mourned. Their observations would no longer guide the renewal, and those who were left must do their best to ensure all would be regenerated as it should be. That was their purpose. It must be fulfilled.

What if we all die, Nielli asked. *What will happen if there is no one to recover all the souls of the lost.*

I do not know, Hnarse answered sadly. *Sometimes, it has happened that Went who are not Mothers can become so, but if too many mothers are lost, the souls who cannot be carried back home remain where they fall, to be recovered on the next great trail.*

But what if we all die? All of us? And there is no one left to tell the Heart how to regenerate after the white waste?

That I can't say. It got creakingly to its feet again. Neetha watched them, knowing they communicated, but unable to hear. *Maybe nothing will regenerate and all will remain white and cold forever. So it will be best if at least some survive, or who will help the next cycle of new purpose find the trail?*

NAVIGATORS

A subtle change in pressure on certain phrases in his chord would have made Kandät Enna smile if the discipline of his craft had allowed it. The Djan'rū on Oris, one of the guild's most remote outposts, was close. Kandät had always thought of its interaction as seductive; reflective of the isolated nature of the far flung moon and its desire to find companionship - or so he mused. He was certainly keen to arrive there, at any rate. Despite its famously meagre comforts, thanks to the efforts of the Navigator's Guild, there would be good food, vermin-free sleep, and most importantly for him at this time, a small contingent of expert Hermes.

When the change came and their chord resonated fully within that of Oris, Kandät Enna let his voice fade. Time-honed senses probed the tone of the envelope and found it satisfactory. He opened a tiny window - just enough to check their successful arrival with absolute certainty, then signaled his spinners.

He recalled the first time he'd returned from Went to here. The chord had rung in his mind for hours afterwards, leaving him in a 'state of grace' as his navigator brethren termed it. A feeling of connection to deity, of oneness with the known ...

of utter access - a beautiful thing indeed. He hadn't wanted to let it go. He never did. But true to his promise to Huldar, today they were on a tight chord and there was no time.

They stepped into silent bays. It seemed they had the place to themselves, which suited him very well. No prying Imperial sensitivities.

Sama will rustle up a meal for us in no time, he said to his crew. *Don't wait for me.* And indeed, the aroma of Sama's wonderfully filling pastries already wafted from the refectory. He watched his crew vanish through the plain double doors. Hunger gnawed his belly with the claws of a trapped rada, but he turned to a passageway with Hermes House Rune carved above the lintel.

The Hermes waiting room held only a few plain chairs, but before he could sit down, a tall, craggy faced Archangel stepped from behind a wooden partition and bowed.

"Lord Shamkarun Kandät Enna of Tiamät, how may we be of service?"

"I need to contact the guild at Hesh. Is there such a one in residence?"

The Hermes bowed again. "I can assist you." He waved his hand with elegant economy toward the room behind the counter. "Although the distance is too great for a face to face meeting."

"That will be no problem."

A choice awaited him. A modest yet superbly crafted divan was set opposite a small table. Beside it perched a straight-backed chair, similar to the ones outside. He eyed the divan, but chose the chair. It would keep his senses sharp.

The Hermes smiled knowingly, and with a wave of the hand, the divan slid silently back into the wall.

"Thank you, Hermes," Kandät said as he took his seat. "I trust I need not ask for your discretion?"

The Hermes bowed his head. "Confidence is maintained, my lord Shamkarun Kandät Enna. It is my honor to serve. With whom do you wish connect?"

"Mael of Maatu."

The Hermes gave a single nod and closed his eyes. *May I?*

Kandät nodded in return. *Of course.*

While Kandät waited for the connection to be made, he couldn't help massaging his knees. Time to see a healer. His circulation and cartilages needed more and more maintenance these days. He barely noticed while he was singing, but once his Shamkar faded …

It is early morning on Hesh, the Hermes said. *Guild Lord Shamkarun Mael of Maatu awaits. Speak without fear of interception.*

Kandät nodded. *Dahj,* he began. *I am sorry to wake you.*

Bai'ah, Mael responded. Among navigators, to commence communications with an exchange of nicknames was a sign of urgency, and despite the lack of imagery, Kandät felt the spike in the Guild-lord's attention. This Hermes was a master.

I hardly know where to start …

At this next piece of code, Mael increased the security around him to be doubly sure no eaves-droppers could attend.

When he was done, Kandät sighed. *Mael, it is worse than we thought – far worse. The replacement miner staff were cancelled at the last minute, and instead I have delivered Delemät Ashik and Jaldan of Trianog to Went, along with a troop of Ashik fighters – I wouldn't call them warriors.*

Mael sighed. *I already knew some of this, or suspected – but not about Jaldan. I was on Giahn the day you departed. Delemät came to my office. Warned that Went was now off limits. Confiscated the crystal. As if it would ever be a joy trip or holiday destination! I know Ishät wants to keep all of Went's resources to himself, but this is extreme, even for him.*

I don't think you fully understand. Kandät paused. He'd been so sure Mael would have figured it out. *There is another thing you need to know. The translation to Went is more difficult every time. Lives have been lost.*

The song itself needs work?

Mael seemed to leap at the chance to change the subject. Was that a good sign? *Maybe, but I feel it is the planet herself that rejects us.*

Have you asked Huldar of Leth about this?

An image of the tall Lethian flowed between them. *Huldar's gift is certainly an interesting phenomenon, but no,* Kandät replied. *I have not asked. My interaction on Went has been mostly to keep Huldar and Olatu from each other's throats.*

He could feel Mael's eyebrows lift. *Surely it's not that bad. I have never heard anything adverse about Huldar's character. He may be quite driven, and a little obsessive, but those are desirable traits in his profession.*

Kandät snorted. *Olatu is a waste of El's good Breath.*

Oh? Mael barely hesitated. *Surely your judgement is somewhat harsh?*

Not at all. He was somehow involved in the death of the Uri'madu's Imperial Overlord. I've avoided making a report about it ever since. Huldar chose to keep him on Went, even knowing his guilt. I think he thought Olatu of Faytha would not be brought properly to trial if he sent him back – and I can't help thinking he's right. The Faythans have the Imperium on a tight leash indeed.

Mael grew thoughtful. There was a short silence. *Then I certainly won't ask Anu to examine the existing Chord. He is an absolute genius with those things, as you know! But maybe it's best left as it is.*

Thanks! Kandät said sarcastically.

Your skills are also legendary, Mael said with a smile. *And if you are the only one who can make the journey …*

This was something Kandät had not thought about. A chill ran down his spine. *Does that put me in danger?*

I hope not! Mael said lightly. *I was thinking more by way of your greater worth. The resources there are rumored to be exceptional. Which reminds me – how is my charming niece?*

Kandät bowed his head. *So like her mother – may she rest safely in the Breath.*

Mael grinned sadly. *How my dear sister stood still long enough to be Blessed is a mystery to all who knew her. So how is Malena? Is she truly with child?*

I am worried for her safety, Dahj. She would not see me while I was there.

Mael sent a pulse of amusement. *She hates you.*

I know, he admitted, *but last time we spoke I think some bridges were crossed. She trusted me with that message …*

Well, said Mael. *I should hear from her any day now.*

The communication window? Should have opened days ago, and if you haven't heard from her yet, I wouldn't be surprised. Kandät let a mix of negativity and speculation concerning the role of the Ashik flow through the conduit between them.

Mael frowned. *She is Maatu's niece, and a navigator. Huldar is Sacred to Leth. Surely no one can prevent their access?*

Delemät Ashik can and will – by force if necessary.

But why?

The Empress.

Mael grew quiet again. At last, Kandät could feel some consonance.

The Empress is also Blessed … Mael said.

Exactly.

But what does that have to do with Malena? The Empress Ishiquel has made her announcement – delayed so she could be absolutely sure. She did not want to disappoint her subjects with a false or fragile alarm … admirable, I thought. The whole Realm is consumed by excitement. And Malena? She has secretly married. She must have. I've been wracking my brains trying to work out who. I expected her to return with you on this trip or the next. Yet you say you haven't seen her?

Kandät paused. The truth *was* unbelievable, and if he hadn't seen it with his own eyes, he would be as skeptical as Mael clearly was. But Malena had told him the truth. And he'd glimpsed Lady Andel of Trianog and one of the miners – both hugely pregnant, far beyond what would normally be expected. If Malena was at a similar stage, she would not be able to return despite her wishes to the contrary. And she would know that. That would be why she wouldn't see him.

He thought back to when he'd last returned from Went - how long had that been? They thought they'd found all the stolen eggs, but had they? Were his spinners loyal? He was sure of it. But he'd become aware of his niece, Ishiquel's Blessed state only four months later - and now, a bare six weeks further on, she'd made an announcement. And while he was away? Why hadn't she waited until he could be present? He could think of only one reason.

He looked at the Hermes blank expression. There had never, to his knowledge, ever been a breach of Hermes confidentiality, yet this information had the power to break the realm. Delemät's warning replayed in his mind, and not for the first time, but his path was sealed now. The truth must be shared.

Kandät? Mael prompted. ... *Bai'ah?*

Dahj. How should he frame this? *There is something I must tell you, but if I do so, I may, after a fashion, be accused of betrayal. My spinners lives ... put at risk.*

Betrayal of whom?

Ishät Ashik, he said quietly.

Now it was Mael's turn for silence. He could feel the Maatu's confusion, and although they had a history of deep trust, he knew the Guild-Lord was alarmed indeed. And so he should be.

Mael's emotions firmed, no doubt behind the strictest of veils. *Alert the Hermes to the need for utmost secrecy, then you'd best tell me. Well decide where our loyalties lie after that.*

The Hermes nodded, and Kandät felt the crush and prickle of a raft of very powerful screens indeed.

When the air had settled, he started again. *It's about the Blessings.*

What Blessings? Malena's?

Malena is not the only one, Kandät explained. *The Uri'madu ate the eggs of the Went.*

The species up for citizenship?

Yes.

Well, that's awkward, Mael said, *but I take it they did not realize?*

Of course not! Kandät said. Why was his old friend making this so difficult for him? *But the result was the pregnancies. All those females who ate the eggs and had sex with a male soon after, became pregnant. None were married - except Huldar and Andel, of course, and the two healers.*

But that's not possible, Mael said simply.

I assure you it is, Kandät insisted. *Malena is not married, and yet she is Blessed. She told you the truth.*

How many babies are we talking about, here. And what has this to do with the Empress? Mael asked, but Kandät sensed he'd already worked it out.

There was a Faythan plot to bring the eggs to Giahn, he said, and sent him a summary in an expertly controlled thought-package. *Their worth would be incalculable – as you might imagine! At the last minute, the Uri'madu stopped it. We thought we had recovered them all …*

The Empress?

I now believe she was gifted with at least one of the eggs.

He showed Mael the pregnant miner as he had glimpsed her. *Ishiquel has not delayed her announcement, Dahj, I believe she is carrying a hybrid child. It seems they develop more quickly.*

Kandät waited. Mael's moment of panic was short-lived. The Guild-Lord was as fine a statesman as his Brother Manu. Kandät was sure his mind would be whirring with play and counter-play like an endless ashut tournament and whatever shock he felt would be well hidden.

At last, he reengaged. *Delemät plans to kill them all,* Mael said flatly. *You know what's going on there,* he appealed, *– the players involved. Can we save them?*

I have warned Huldar I will return one week earlier than expected, Kandät said. *Delemät won't dare kill me. I am the only way he can get home. … Dahj, If any of the Blessed remain alive, I feel I must try to bring them to safety. But if I do, what then? If the God-Emperor has ordered those deaths, he will not just stand by and forgive us … and I can't imagine Delemät is there for fun. If we save them, Ishät will find out. He will know that we know about his child. And how do you think he'll respond?* Kandät said sarcastically.

I don't know! Mael said. *This is all wrong. Blessings are the gift of El, not the result of ingesting another species' egg!*

Kandät put his head in his hands. How could he make Mael understand? The Realm could be ripped apart. Ishät Tiamät, already unstable, could be tipped beyond what shred of sanity remained him, and if that should happen, there was no way to evict the Chosen of El from office, nor to control what might be the outcome.

Perhaps, he said slowly, *painful as it may be, it would better to let the thing play out as Ishät intends.*

A child is a child! Mael hissed.

On one level, Kandät agreed, but was one life worth more than another?

If we could bring them to Ekeridu, Bai'ah. My brother would give them sanctuary, Mael continued, *– I know he would!*

But the consequences, Kandät said. *How many will be lost if Maatu incites the Imperium to war?*

And the balance between Maatu and Tiamät is already delicate … Mael said softly. *You are right, my friend. This must be handled as diplomatically as possible – although how that might be achieved when the planet Went is so distant and beyond contact, I do not know. Perhaps we could make the silence of Went work for us,* he said slowly, *as Ishät Ashik no doubt expects it to work for him.*

Unless the Breath blows something completely unforeseen … He rubbed his forehead. His thinking seemed ponderous, weighed down by the difficulty of the situation. He shared an image of a tall Maatu with a kindly, yet weather-beaten face and measuring green eyes that seemed to look right through you. *Perhaps Manu Maatu may have some ideas?*

Perhaps. I will tell him, of course – with your permission? And what of Arien Leth? Surely he deserves to know?

This must be kept quiet, Dahj. Arien loathes El's Chosen with a passion. He'd have the Realm polarized and at war before anyone else had time to think. … And don't discount Huldar's own abilities. He is resourceful and intelligent, and so are his crew. They may have made plans of their own.

Mael's mind clenched tight. *I've met Casco – the Kareski. He is certainly a cut above.*

That he is, Kandät agreed. *And Huldar's closest friend.*

Sacred to Leth … can he really talk to planets?

Yes, he can – to Went at least, Kandät told him earnestly. *Malena assured me it is true.*

Then maybe, if the planet truly does resist our incursions, if it has that much power, he will be able to use it to protect them. A stream of doubt was followed by a sense of resolve. *We will not leave them stranded, in any case. Delemät need never know. Either you or another can pick them up, if they are known to have survived, after your next scheduled visit.*

But what if they haven't?

Mael met this with a deep silence.

Somehow, his lack of comment made the situation seem all the more real. The prospect of losing the Lethian caused a painful knot to form in Kandät's chest, and to lose Malena, and her Bless – all those innocent mothers and babies – how could it be borne?

I have told Huldar I will return one week earlier than expected, Kandät said eventually. *I hoped he would be somehow able to use that … that I might have a chance to get them to safety. And how can we send another to pick them up? What of the stolen crystal?*

I'll work something out, Mael said.

Kandät nodded, although he knew Mael could not see him. *I fear for Ishiquel's life also,* he realized. *And for the life of her Blessing. What if it is obviously different? How will Ishät explain a hybrid child? He already hates half-breeds …*

Kareski, Mael corrected absently. *How is Ishiquel? Do you know?* he asked. *And how is young Aqumät taking all this?*

Last time I saw Ishiquel, she told me of her Blessing. She looked radiant. She told me to tell no one, and so I did not. Now, I expect, she's is in complete denial. But how else would one adjust to what she must be going through? Aqumät – I saw him not long before I left for Went. Poor lad barely copes with the ludicrous assignments Ishät gives him. His father wishes to see brutality, but Aqumät avoids such traps with increasing agility. He paused to think. The First's face was shared between them. Burly and strong as most Ashik elite, but with the wary look of a hunted creature. *Marriage is the one card he truly holds. He has the right to refuse any potential bride his father puts forward, and so he does.*

Strength, Mael said.

Although the thought had a disconsolate tone, Kandät knew the complement was genuine. *If there was another child to choose from,* he said, *I doubt he'd get away with it. His uncle and aunt …*

And that devious kalla, Delemät, survives! Mael snarled.

Thank goodness for Aqumät Ashik, Kandät said, *or the brute might get his chance.*

Delemät? Mael said scornfully. *He'd never risk death at the Throne of El. He knows what he is. Revels in it. Breath alone knows what he might do now he's alone on Went and no big brother scrutinizing his every move.*

His own miniature empire, Kandät retorted. *I doubt it will bring out the best in him. I wonder if he realizes Huldar is technically his equal …*

Despite a slight nervous nausea, Kandät Enna's stomach rumbled in earnest. If he didn't eat soon, his body's reserves could be depleted enough to delay his promised return to Went.

A wash of contrition came through as Mael sensed his hunger. *I am sorry, Bai'ah. You came to me immediately on your arrival, didn't you? Go. Savor Sama's wonderful cooking before you faint. Leave this with me for now and contact me when you reach Parsay. I may have some answers for you by then.*

Kandät hesitated. *Tell me this, Dahj; if the worst should happen, shall their deaths go unremarked?*

No, Mael said, and with that, the session was ended.

DARK DAYS

Huldar sat on a strap-tree log above the Central Continent campsite. He was aware of the warm, humid air flow that presaged the incoming evening storm, but was unable to enjoy it. Sunset glowered beneath towering clouds, green with hail and lit from within by flashes of lightning. Several second later, the slow, dull rumble of thunder reached him, but he picked an exploratory clicker-bug from his leg and barely noticed.

The bug clicked indignantly and waved its multicolored paddles. He set it down on the fibrous trunk of a neighboring tree and watched it scuttle away.

His soul ached.

Below, in the clearing before the main marquee, the Uri'madu had lit their fire. Despite the heat and humidity, it was a tradition they would not forgo.

Beyond the fire, standing stones surrounded the simple Djan'rū he had helped build, then the wide view across the valley to the spectacular volcanic ridges.

He remembered their first time here - the eruption - how Casco had saved Andel's life after she had saved theirs.

He saw his beloved friend's face again and curled in on himself and wept.

How could he be gone?

How could he be gone?

How could he go back to the Uri'madu and their campfire and comfort them when he could find no comfort himself?

Perhaps if they had a body. Maybe it would be easier. But search as they might, no corpse was found.

The prickle of surveillance touched his neck - Delemät Ashik, no doubt. What did their grief matter to him? How could a soulless creature understand the nobility and joy that was Casco. Kareski, he called him. Half-breed. As if there was fault inherent.

"Yes, take a good look," he said aloud. "Casco was twice the annangi you, the God-Emperor's own brother, could ever hope to be."

The prickling receded.

Huldar looked over his shoulder. It was as if he'd felt Casco's presence ... as if he'd tried to comfort him. Huldar snorted and shook his head. His friend's song had been sung. His death cry issued - 'Remember me to our son'.

In the distance he heard the west portal chime. Farushael of Cantori arrived, stayed briefly to convey his respects, then departed. Huldar knew he should have been there to receive him, but could not bring himself to join his team. Too many had been lost already, and who knew how many more would return to the Breath before this assignment was done.

He started when his neck prickled again. It was almost as if someone had touched his shoulder. *Nice of Farushael to put in*

Daric looked around, his movement silken and dangerous, but relaxed when he saw the latest arrival was only Shen come to join them. The cook shuddered as he stepped through the screen. Although he'd never shared the knowledge with anyone other than Andel, Huldar knew him to be Kareski like Casco and surmised that was the reason he'd helped them so often and so kindly.

"One moment," Shen said, and trotted off to the Marquee. When he returned, he didn't sit with Tam, as Huldar expected; instead, Daric moved closer to Sari to make room with them. The action seemed natural, yet Huldar had never noticed a particular friendship between them.

When they were settled, he straightened up, ready at last, and prepared his best storytelling voice for the ordeal to come.

"Casco is gone," he said strongly, and was surprised by how easy it was. "He is gone from us." He bowed his head. Not so easy after all. "He was my oldest and dearest friend," he continued. "Breath wove our paths together. Many of you may wonder how that happened, and the answer may surprise you. I first met Casco on the back streets of Giahn. I noticed him lift a pair of boots from a market stall, but I was not the only one who had seen. A pair of peacekeepers followed him, and as they moved in, I stepped in their way and thanked Casco for picking up the boots for me. He played along as if we were already life-long friends.

The peacekeepers apologized and left, and afterwards, I asked Casco why he'd done what he did.

He told me he wanted the boots so he could leave Giahn, go on an adventure, change his life. He told me those particular boots of all the boots in the Imperial City, were the best made, longest lasting and most comfortable.

'They're not the most expensive,' I said to him, 'and Higga's, two blocks up, have the best clientele.'

He gave me that look – you know the one, sort of a mix of patience, pity, and trying to hide the laugh. "If'n be suckered by yon crappyshit, uns be kennin dem starry blisters sho'nuff."

He looked at Shen… "I don't know if I got that exactly right."

Shen nodded and gave a small laugh, but it was clear he struggled.

"I offered him a job," Huldar continued. "I needed a logistician. Said he'd get all the adventure he could cope with and never have to risk stealing again – if he didn't want to.

"We grew up on assignment together. Travelled the known in between times. I watched Casco face every hurdle, every one – physical, mental, psychological – with dignity … except for the bander-fruit bugs."

Arko laughed, a soft huff. "I was there."

Cobar and Gento nodded. "Before our time, but we've heard the yarn more than once," Gento said.

"I am not going to tell that story today," Huldar said. "I don't think I could, and there are better ones to tell. But sometime in the future, when Sari's boy, Casco's son, is sitting with us around a campfire much like this one, I'll tell him that story among many other, far more edifying ones. Stories about his father's courage and honor. About how much he wanted to meet his child, how much he loved Sari as his close – very close friend and team-mate, and Daric, as so much more. How Casco was one of the Uri'madu, and how, through no fault of his own, their opportunity to meet was lost."

Sari bowed her head and hugged her belly as if it was the only thing that could give her comfort.

Andel put one arm over her shoulder and flashed Huldar a glance. The sense of deep sorrow that came through their marriage bond was penetrated by a small frisson of alarm.

Healers? he asked. He'd heard grief could trigger a baby to be born prematurely.

Andel shook her head, a tiny gesture. *Tell you later.*

He nodded, relieved. But the Blessings would come, and soon. Daric had stepped up to take Casco's roll in the birthing. Huldar was certain this was a situation the assassin could never have prepared for, yet he knew Daric would do his best, and behave with utmost honor.

"How strangely Breath has Blown," he said. "This part of the Divine Tapestry … where threads are confused; in one moment, gloriously changed, then ended before anyone has had time to prepare - ended just when new filaments in colors unimaginable are about to make their appearance. From the outside, this part may well seem as if it's one of the most thrilling and exciting designs yet. But to us, who are those strands, all we can do is endure.

"Appreciate each day, stay strong in our trust for each other, and hope that there are brighter times ahead."

He steeled himself, and looked up at the stars. "Farewell, my dear friend. May El and Asheru bathe you in the love you deserve - you have always deserved. May Breath Blow you peace and return you to us refreshed and ready for yet more adventure."

"Em barahn ash sel do et El a'sien," Malena whispered brokenly. *He saved us, Huldar,* she said privately, *and I rewarded him with anger. Blamed him, when … And now, we cannot speak openly of his achievement – the honor bestowed on him, even now when he's gone from us, and it makes the hurt so much worse.*

He nodded miserably. That his friend should be denied the recognition of his Mark, of his title as Archerran … It was so wrong. Hatred for Delemät Ashik and all his kind flared loud in his heart. If the Host and their Ashik had not been on this world, if the Uri'madu had been left to do their jobs as they always did – peacefully cataloguing and studying, Casco could have announced his gift to the world and worn it proudly home to Giahn.

How would the Tiamäti have dealt with that, he wondered. A Kareski with irrefutable status. Unmarked archangels would have been forced to bow and show him respect.

He shook his head. *Why did they eat the eggs in the first place?* he asked himself. *Why had Breath blown them on this path?*

All threads continued … he reasoned sadly. *Maybe the Went would help the God-Emperor discover a capacity for love and tolerance – something he lacked. Maybe this was the event that would turn him back to the ways of El and Asheru … and there would be no more persecution of Kareski, no more raping of planets …*

He turned at Andel's sudden laugh and saw her involved in a conversation with Arko.

"No! Really?" she said.

Gael winced. "It mated with his fingernails?"

"Each and every one," Arko said seriously. "And that's Breath's own truth. … of course, had he been sober …"

"You got him drunk," Daric said quietly. "Deliberately."

Arko froze when he heard Daric's voice behind him. His eyes widened.

The assassin bent his head around and whispered against Arko's ear. "Seven hundred years later … and that's the best you can come up with?"

Arko spun to face him.

Huldar stood straighter, ready to intervene if necessary.

"Daric Enna" Alis said sternly. "That was uncalled for"

Daric turned to face her. "Uncalled for?" His face twisted in sadness. "If he was an archangel, or even an angel, is this the first story that would be told of his life?" He glared at Arko, then slowly around at the gathering. "A story of shame?"

"He's right," said Malena. "Casco was infinitely more than that. More than any of us."

"It's just an old story," Arko stammered.

"I loved that one too" Tam said bravely. "That moment of weakness. A crack in the shell of perfection. It was as if he felt he was on show and had to do everything right, every time, or there would be consequences. I think it was because he was Kareski. He was so brave and there when we needed him, without fail. He tried so hard, never stinting - but deep down, he was always afraid."

Nachiel nodded. "And some of the things that scumbag Olatu has said …"

"Huh! And what about that miner … " Bush started.

"She got hers." Topper said. "Can't even remember her name."

Huldar's gaze followed as Daric walked to the fire and stood where he had, only a short time ago.

"I loved him the first time I saw him," Daric said, as if to the flames. When he turned, others grew quiet, perhaps shocked, as Huldar was, by the tears that flowed down his cheeks. His eyes seemed haunted. "I was assigned to assist him in a delicate matter … the rescue of a child and her mother from persecution at Ashik hands. There was … something about him - bravery, empathy … and kindness, such kindness - qualities I lacked. Tall, capable, beautiful … so full of unrealized power, and so hurt inside. For the first time in my life, I wanted to heal someone. He was, and will always be …" He took out a soft white cloth as if to wipe his face, but his hands held the cloth against his eyes as if he could no longer bear to show his grief.

"I'm sorry," he said brokenly. "And Arko, please forgive me. I didn't mean to be so harsh. It's just that …" He shook his head. "I can't stay."

Huldar watched sadly as he left the fireside and walked quickly toward the eastern gate.

"Leave him," he said when Sari went to get up and follow. "Give him the space he needs."

Alis' head tilted sadly as the gate softly chimed. "Two such injured yet beautiful souls intertwined," she said reflectively. "He has done surprisingly well just to be present."

Daric stepped through the gate to the eastern basecamp, and put his handkerchief away. No sooner had he arrived than his neck prickled, and Delemät Ashik's farsight grazed him again. It was tempting to follow the stream back to the source and do his antagonist an injury, but the time was not right to reveal his full range of capabilities.

Let your target think they are the one with the power, he heard his old mentor say. *Let them underestimate you, the more the better. The opportunity will present, the strike will be easier to make; and if their defenses are down, send it deep and relish the moment their swaggering life is cleansed from its shell.*

He released a light huff of breath. If she could see him now, what would she think? That he had gone soft? That his life would soon be over? She may have thought that way, died that way; but his life had changed. He had grown. And it was thanks to Casco in the main part, and Huldar - and the Uri'madu.

He bowed over, as if in great pain, then slowly, as if every limb was forced, made his way along a short track to a favorite viewpoint. In reality, the act was not difficult. Casco's trauma over the action they'd set in motion was real and extreme. He only hoped he would stick to the plan and not reveal the truth to his friends - not yet.

Again his neck itched. Why was the general so keen to follow his every movement? A saying of the Trianogi came to mind - *'How distrustful are those incapable of trust?'* If there was an answer to that, it would have to be 'Delemät Ashik'. He was very glad Huldar had seen sense early and they already had plans in place. Anything they tried now would likely be doomed to failure, but with Casco 'dead' and the invisibility cloak at hand, at least they had a chance at getting their message through to Saphella of Hermes. After that, it would be a matter of simple survival, whether help came or not.

He gazed out at the bare plains below. Once he would have viewed them only for their qualities as a space in which to hide or hunt. Now, they sang to him of life and adaptation. Now they were a place of beauty, one of endless other such sites - whole worlds yet to be seen, an endless treasure to be held in his heart. A love that would never betray.

Above, the stars pressed down, brilliant and alive. He reached up as if to touch them, as if their flow would wash away Casco's pain. He arched his fingers as if to scoop a few from place. He longed to smell them, to bathe in them. He remembered his sister's early passion, all those years ago in Giahn. … Was this how it had been for her? But she'd said she could hear them calling, that their songs were like kanth for her soul.

Something else occurred to him - more of a realization … Delemät must know who he was. It was the only reason the constant surveillance made sense. His enemy expected him to go north and try to contact either his navigator sister or the Explorer's Guild.

He sat carefully on a rock to reconsider their mission. Many possibilities played out in his head, but in the end, only one sequence consistently succeeded. He should stay easily detectable to Delemät's farsight at all times - although not overtly so. He would try to get to the North and fail. Delemät Ashik must appear to win, even if merely in principle. Only then would Casco be safe to go on and make the attempt alone. He hoped Casco would understand how his sacrifice truly was essential to their survival.

Another strategy occurred to him - hiding in plain sight. Surely there must be ecological studies to be made now that the northernmost lands were accessible? He would ensure

Huldar sent him on such an assignment, a legitimate reason for Northerly travel.

The risk was great, but this plan gave the greatest chance for the message to be delivered, and their only hope of rescue.

He looked up as another viewing buzzed him. Delemät must know he would feel each and every one. Slowly, as if in great pain, he shuffled to his tent, but as he crossed the threshold, his own, powerful screen hid him from surveillance, and at last, he could lower his guard.

In the early hours of the morning, after a fitful snatch of sleep, he wrapped himself in the cloak of invisibility and slipped outside. To use the gate at night was a calculated risk - there would be a brief shine and alteration in its tone. The indicators would last for only a moment, but if Delemät saw, his suspicions would be aroused.

Hidden beneath the wondrous cloak, he was completely invisible, but neither could he sense another's farsight. He stationed himself at the brink of the portal and composed his emotions before taking the step. It was approximately two before midnight on the central continent. Surely even Delemät had to sleep?

Then Breath blew a stroke of luck. The gate chimed softly as Calen and Van arrived, and while it was still in flux, he sang himself through to the hidden portal in the desert. Resistance was strong, but there were no surprises. He was sure Qalān recognized the Uri'madu and let them pass. After a few bad scares, miners and others of the Host had taken to traveling in groups and singing in tandem. Many chose to walk overland unless travel was unavoidable.

The desert air was chill. Nocturnal creatures scuttled across his path. They could see his feet, but nothing else and while some saw the strange moving objects as a threat and ducked for cover, others he had to avoid.

He headed southeast. There was no trail to follow, and as he walked over coarse sand and pebbles, he was careful to leave none. To someone who knew what to look for, the gate in ancient Qalān was detectable, but on this starlit night even he had to squint into the darkness to see the disturbance that pinpointed its location.

He schooled his emotions to naught and made sure the song was clear in his mind before stepping through to the hidden cave.

Dry skin on his face eased. He breathed deeply of cool, moist air. Bioluminescent creatures lit up in a galaxy of welcome. It was beautiful, but normally his arrival was lit by one of Casco's lightsinger globes.

Casco! he called, but there was no reply.

Surely his friend hadn't ventured outside? They'd agreed.

Casco? he called again.

The globe above Casco's sleeping place gave off a dim glow. He hurried forward, thankful for the work they'd done to smooth the path.

As he got closer, he could make out a figure curled in the bedroll, pale face upturned.

He called again with a pulse of vague alarm, but Casco remained unresponsive.

Damning thoughts rushed through his mind. He hadn't warned him of his imminent arrival – hadn't even spoken to him since they parted that morning. But that was because they couldn't risk it. Casco understood that.

Stones rattled overloud as his walk became a run. Regret added weight to his plummeting heart. His way was traced by glowing points on the cave ceiling but all he could see was the motionless bundle amid the blankets.

He threw himself down to kneel at Casco's side. His lovers eyes were closed. The Mark on his head was dull. His hand was so cold … cold as death. He put his cheek close above Casco's nose. Breath brushed it in the faintest of disturbances, and at last, he understood. Ziquarra! Casco had left his body, probably to view the funeral gathering, and now he'd been gone too long.

His first thought was to call for Alis, but he stopped himself just in time. No one must know what they'd done. The risk of capture and betrayal was too great. Delemät and Jaldan as an interrogatory team could possibly even be a match even for him.

Casco lay limp as death in his embrace. He wrapped blankets around them both and held the body close, all the while sifting through what little he knew of Ziquarra and its dangers.

There was a thread, he'd heard, the same thread that connected body and soul. The longer a practitioner was gone, the thinner the thread became. The most vital thing a Ziquarra learned was how to preserve that connection, and how to follow it home.

He rocked Casco's slack form back and forth. He'd had no one to teach him, and now he was lost.

Think, Daric Enna, he berated himself. *Think!*

He knew how to find and sever that thread, it was a trick essential to his trade, but could he find and follow without breaking it?

Casco! he cried, *Come back to me! Casco, please!*

Far away, Alis buried her head in her pillow and wept.

Is it Daric? Ubaid asked tenderly.

She shared what she'd heard and he held her close. *Don't listen,* he whispered sadly. *You know you shouldn't …*

I can't help it, she replied. *You know how much he means to me.*

All the more reason to leave him alone. He must work this out for himself. He is in process –

– He is always 'in process'.

Ubaid smiled softly, *And when there are – if there are,* he quickly corrected – *consequences to be dealt with, we will be ready. … You know he will come to you if he needs you. He trusts you … Breath knows you're the only one now that he does.*

But why hasn't he been to see me yet? Why hasn't he asked for my help? He knows I'm there for him … is he really so …

Self-reliant? Ubaid's brows lifted. *Alis, my love, Daric's self-belief is complete. I doubt his personal dictionary contains a term for failure. But his emotional intelligence is – how to phrase it … on a steep learning curve. Maybe it hasn't occurred to him this may be something he could need help with.*

Back in the cave, Daric held on and waited. He extended what healing he could into Casco's failing body, keeping it alive for when he should return, but he could not penetrate his mind to find the thread – the shields, his own designs he'd taught Casco to safeguard against it, held fast. This had been the only thing he could do to help him, and now it may be that he had inadvertently killed him for real.

Time passed.

He waited with dread for the moment, that one moment where he may be able to save Casco's life.

Tears slid unnoticed down his cheeks.

He was so tired, but he dare not sleep.

A sudden change in Casco's shield strength snapped him back to alertness. This was the moment of death; the chance he'd been waiting for. He slid beneath what remained of the barrier. The thread he found was a mere filament, fragile as spun glass, but he grabbed it and pulsed his own life-force into it regardless of what that might mean for their future.

Casco! he called *Casco, where are you? I need you! Don't leave me …*

The thread brightened.

He tugged, just a little. If the tether broke, there could be no repair.

Finally, he sensed Casco's presence.

Daric?

The relief he felt at that contact was like nothing he'd ever experienced, but it was short-lived.

Perhaps this is best, Casco said. His voice seemed remote. *You should let me go. My friends have mourned me. I didn't understand how it would be for them. I have hurt them deeply. How can I face them, ever again?*

"Casco, please, come back," he whispered aloud. "This thing we've done, this sacrifice, it's the only way we can succeed in getting a message out to the Realm – to Saphella."

He twisted their life-threads more closely together and showed him his reasoning, and what it meant for their plans.

Casco's presence strengthened until suddenly, it was as if he stood before him. He could see every feature of his face, every hair on his head, every shade of color in his eyes. There were no barriers between them. He felt Casco's tumult as if they were truly part of each other – as if it was his own. But now there could be no subterfuge, Casco could see that what he said was true.

The silence between them stretched out as what Daric had deduced sunk in, then he felt Casco's mind reengage.

Daric? he said wistfully, *I think you've married us.*

Daric barked a short laugh. A fresh bout of tears moistened his cheeks. "Are you angry?" he whispered.

The avatar smiled and shook its head. *A bit surprised. It's usual for people to ask first – or so I'm told.*

"Luckily I kept your body warm," Daric said with a lightness he did not feel. "Please, come back."

The body in his arms twitched. Slowly, Casco's eyes fluttered open. He opened his mouth as if to speak, but no sound came out.

"Shh …" Daric stroked his face. To feel Casco present in his body once more was overwhelming. Where they touched, love tingled through every pore. "Don't try to talk just yet. I don't know how long you were gone before I got here, but it was as if you were dead - in fact you almost were. It may take time."

He took a flask from Qalān and tipped it up so Casco could drink.

Casco smiled his thanks, but there was no need, and no need to say how tired they both were, since each could feel the other quite clearly. Instead, they simply let go and fell asleep.

TIME TO RUN

It was high summer in the foot-hills at Eastern base-camp, and heat shimmer rose off every exposed surface. Some distance from the empty tents, Andel sat on a cushion where a rocky overhang provided much needed shade. Nachiel and Sari had been with her until a short time ago when they left to find Tam and get a fresh supply of galano sticks - the only thing, it seemed, that could ease the blessed ones' constant nausea.

Sari was quite cheerful, overcompensating perhaps, but she didn't - or couldn't - believe Casco was dead. Every few minutes, she looked around as if she expected to see him. It was unnerving.

Andel glanced at the empty cushions around her and sighed. She wished Casco was still with them too, but not to the extent that she couldn't deal with the truth of his absence. But then again, she was not about to give birth to Casco's child.

Slowly the silence seeped in. Tension in her shoulders relaxed. She thought of her father and smiled. If she were at home right now, how he would fuss. Once she might have enjoyed the attention, but she had grown to love the isolation, and the peace and freedom it offered.

Her excuse for staying behind was the finalization of her notes on new silver deposits north of the central ranges, and crisp sheets with diagrams and map-references soon covered the empty cushions. But after a time, fatigue set in, and the characters seemed to swim across the pages. She hadn't realized how bone-tired she was, and the heat didn't help. Perspiration dripped onto one of Nachiel's delicately drawn maps and blurred its carefully inked edges. She tried to wipe it off before it could do more damage and succeeded in smearing the lines even further. Moisture oozed down her face, her shirt clung to her back, and her pregnant bulk made every movement feel as if she was wrapped in sweat-soaked sand-bags.

Nearby, the portal chimed.

Footsteps started toward her.

"That didn't take long," she muttered. The guilty map lay across Nachiel's cushion. He would not be pleased! But when she looked up, instead of Sari and Nachiel she saw Jaldan of Trianog's disturbingly cadaverous form. Two Ashik had arrived with him. She supposed they'd accompanied him to ensure the portal song had sufficient strength, but when he stopped, they arranged themselves on either side like body-guards.

Huldar? she called worriedly, and sent him an image.

Stay put! he cried.

Her frown deepened. She knew there had been some sort of problem with Jaldan's 'interviews', but the trauma of Casco's death had been overwhelming, and she hadn't thought to ask.

Don't go anywhere with them. Promise me! Huldar's mood suggested extreme caution. *I am on my way,* he started, but a heavy screen settled around her, then dense silence as her senses were cut off from the outside world. Apparently Huldar was right to be concerned. She recognized the configuration as one Daric had taught them. It was in common use by the Ashik, and the counter attack was a simple reverse pattern she could easily perform. Perhaps they'd forgotten that unlike Shamkar, Tsemkar abilities continued as normal during pregnancy. There were no additional shields she could detect, and Huldar knew what was happening, so she played the wide-eyed captive. Daric said it was better for an enemy to underestimate one's capabilities, and if she could keep them talking, there would be more time for Huldar to get here.

"Jaldan of Trianog?" She waved her hand at the disturbance around them. "What is the meaning of this?"

Jaldan made a careful bow. "I merely wish to have conversation with you, my dear."

My dear? She echoed to herself. He may be one of her House, but his presence made her skin crawl.

"How dare you!" she snapped. He blinked in surprise. "We may be far from home," she continued, "but you will address me correctly."

Jaldan bowed again, more deeply. His haze rippled. Almost she thought she sensed nervousness - then it cleared. His mouth curved in a smile, but his eyes glittered intently. "My apologies, Tsemkarun Andel of Trianog, but I have studied you for so long, it feels as if I already know you."

Studied me? Again, she repeated his words to herself. She drew on her physical discomfort and hid her growing alarm beneath valid annoyance. "You don't know me at all." she said brusquely. "And the screen? There is no need, and I see none for these Ashik, either."

"The screen?" He turned his head as if he could see it. "A mere precaution. A habit I have. I like to feel … private."

"Then surely these good folks can go." She pointed to the Ashik.

He gave an unctuous smile. "So you agree to converse with me?"

She indicated her notes. "As you can see, I am busy, but send them away, drop the screen, and I'll give you a few moments."

His head tilted slyly. "And if I don't?"

She looked at him in a manner she hoped would convey both strength and confidence.

He appeared to consider her offer, then surprised her by dismissing his entourage. With barely a grumble, the Ashik stepped back through the gate.

"As you can see," he said carefully, "I mean you no harm."

She wondered at his sense of caution. What threat could she possibly pose? She decided to push her advantage - whatever it was. "And the screen?" Without it, at least Huldar could hear if she called.

Jaldan bowed and waved his hand as the screen evaporated. "I have done as you asked, Tsemkarun Andel," he said politely. "May we talk now?"

He blinked as sweat dribbled through his sparse eyelashes.

"Why are you so nervous?" she asked.

"Ahh," he said. "You see … that is the reason I wish to talk. Delemät desires information about your …" he flicked one finger toward her belly, "parasites - for want of a better term. Well. They're not annangi, are they?" he said defensively. "And since the Empress is also afflicted, he seeks knowledge to help his Imperial brother decide what to do. A family matter, you see, and one that barely concerns me. No. I have come to learn from you. This is my sole reason for accepting this dreadful assignment. Terrible conditions! Yes, if you would be so kind as to enlighten me," he paused as if weighing his options, "I … promise … to make things easier for you at the end."

Andel felt her face twist into a confused frown. "Easier for me?"

"Yes," he said firmly. "I want to know how you do it."

She shook her head in confusion. Huldar was closer, but not close enough. "How I do what?" she asked. The connotations were too awful for her to grasp. "And what did you mean, easier at the end?"

"Why, the terror, of course." He looked at her with some surprise. "The white terror, I call it, though no doubt you have a more sophisticated, more wonderfully mystical term for your abilities, and I am happy, no, proud to change my nomenclature in your honor. I can induce the terror - that, I have mastered, but how do you shape it into a lasting, even permanent structure in the recipient's mind?"

Andel paled. "How …?" she stammered. Her stomach clenched. Nausea redoubled as she recalled the scene of her capture, the imprisonment of herself and her mother, and the haunting retribution she'd exacted.

"Ah, I see your consternation," Jaldan said encouragingly. "Yes. Well, you see, I was called upon to heal a certain operative - impossible, of course. You were much too thorough for that, and I bow to your consummate skill! But it would be a shame for those skills to die with you, as I'm sure you agree?"

"Please leave," she said firmly.

Jaldan sighed and with an air of reluctance, closed his eyes.

She struggled to her feet. "I asked you to leave!"

His lips pursed, and suddenly it was as if his fingers touched her hair, as if thick fluid ran down her scalp. She tried to speak, but couldn't. Fear … did she feel fear? Should she be afraid …?

"Yes," he whispered, "yes, yes - you do remember."

Her baby kicked with some force and self-awareness returned. She threw off Jaldan's probe with a Tsemkar pulse so strong she surprised herself. A protective energy remained to shield her mind from further attack. It was her own power - she could feel the heat in her Mark, but she had no idea how the formation had been achieved. A sense of satisfaction drifted upward from her unborn daughter, and she smiled. Her 'parasite' was far more than this monster assumed.

Jaldan cowered, and her anger was triggered into a calm, but almost blinding rage.

"You want to learn about terror?" she asked.

He nodded rapidly. It was as if he drew pleasure from fear.

"Then I'll show you," she said. "Come with me."

All thoughts of Huldar and rescue had vanished. She turned for the gate.

Andel?! Huldar cried. She shut him out. It was her responsibility to save the Known from this obscenity, and knew exactly what she must do. The sacrifice must be made.

I am sorry, my Blessing, my beautiful gift, she said to her daughter. Grief flowed like a river through her mind. Thoughts of Sari … first Casco, then …

All will be well, her baby replied.

Love emanated from her unborn child, and that confidence, unmarred by the doubts of life-experience, permeated her senses. But as she stood before the portal, tears fell from her eyes.

I do not deserve such love, she said. *Not anymore.*

You do, the child assured her. *You are mother. You are … perfect.*

Before she could change her mind, Andel grabbed Jaldan's robe and drew him into the portal with her.

The whiteness closed around them; horrifying; empty. She bucked with pain as her marriage bond went dead. Jaldan shrieked. She gave him a push. If this was the way she was to die, she didn't want his perverted soul anywhere nearby.

His torso vanished first, then his face - swallowed by nothingness. Last to disappear was one, long-fingered hand, curled into a claw as if to grasp at its final hope of salvation. There was no swirl, no eddy to show where he'd passed.

Monster gone? her child said. *Home now?*

Andel's heart ponded, leaden and futile. *I don't know how,* she replied. She looked around as the reality of their plight set in. But with the inevitable grief came a feeling of peace, as if a long torment was over and at last she could rest. The space where she held Huldar so close to her heart was now empty – a dark void in the whiteness of Qalān. Maybe she would pass to the Breath, or maybe not. Her baby was with her. She was not alone, and as for the cost? No price could be too high if it prevented the weaponization of her terrible ability.

She was shaken from this morbid reverie when her child giggled. Her whole body vibrated, starting from her belly and working outward. As if from a great distance, she heard Jaldan's screams. A sense of freedom filled her, and she giggled too.

I do, her Bless laughed. *I do!*

Suddenly, it all seemed so funny. *What do you do?* she asked her baby.

I know! the little one said. *I know the way.*

There was a bump as they landed on the ground. Andel's senses were flooded by the sight of her wind-scattered notes on the cushions, the sound of the breeze in the trees, the sweet, sharp smell of the air, and the cooling feel on her skin. Her marriage bond sprang back to life. Her mind sang once more with the myriad vibrations that comprised the planet Went.

She started in fear as the portal chimed, but it was not Jaldan. Instead, Huldar, eyes wild with panic, bounded through and almost landed on top of her.

He reached down to scoop her into his arms and buried his face against her neck. Love and fear flowed through the contact in equal measure.

Where is he? He looked at the notes, now scattered by the breeze. *What happened?*

"He's gone," she said simply, and joy welled up with fresh tears.

Huldar pushed her gently away so he could see her face. "Gone?"

She nodded. Her eyes flicked toward the portal.

"Jaldan?"

She nodded again, unsure how to best frame her thoughts.

"Where has he gone?" Huldar asked. "Has he hurt you? If he has, I'll kill him myself, I swear it!"

"No need," she said.

He gave her a puzzled look.

"I took him into Qalān." She stifled another giggle. "He got what he wanted."

Huldar bowed his head. She could sense his fear as recollections were released into his conscious mind. Memories of the interviews came through to her, and of what Jaldan had done to Gael.

I meant to warn you, to tell you, he said frantically. *But then Casco, and Sari, and – please, forgive me ..."*

But far from the recrimination he expected, or even felt he deserved, Andel felt herself unclench. Knots of doubt evaporated. She put her finger to his lips. *Of course I do.*

He kissed her forehead, and eyed the portal again. "But how …?"

"– am I here?" she finished for him.

He nodded.

Her hands cradled her stomach. "My Bless, my beautiful Bless … She knows how to move through Qalān." She let her head fall against his chest. *I thought I would die with him.*

"But why … you risked your life! You and I, we released Lind together. The song the planet gave us – it took our combined power to do it, and even then …" He shied away from his memories of how damaged Lind had been, but the image of her eyes, huge and haunted in her emaciated face, lingered between them.

"I know," she said sadly. "But it was what I had to do." She looked up into his face. "He would have made what I did into a weapon, a hideous torture no one would be safe from. He even had a name for it." She paused to wonder at the strength of her conviction, but even in hindsight, she knew her actions had been justified. "He wanted to know – said he'd give me an easier death."

So, he is in there? In Qalān?

Gone, she said. *Now mother can … and the babies will be safe.*

You would have died! You knew you would die …

She nodded and began to retrieve the maps. Emotions tumbled through their bond. As she gathered the last cushion, a wracking sob shook her frame. She remembered

Jaldan's scream, distant, hopeless, terrified, and turned to Huldar. *What have I done?*

Huldar pulled her close and held her as if he wished they were welded together. She opened her heart to him, and he to her, and she saw his respect, his pride in her strength and his overwhelming love - but now, there was a tinge of fear. Was it of her, or for her? The two were so closely intertwined it was impossible to say.

They turned as the portal chimed and the two Ashik who had been Jaldan's bodyguard started towards them.

Huldar's arm remained protectively over her shoulders. She wiped her eyes and stood tall.

The warriors gazed around the site. Narrowed eyes flicked over them while the minds behind them searched.

Huldar tilted his head in enquiry.

The Ashik made a perfunctory bow. "Jaldan of Trianog is not here?"

"As you have no-doubt ascertained," Huldar replied.

They focused on Andel. "You were seen to enter Qalān with him," one of them said. "Where did you go?"

"As you can see, my wife is distressed," Huldar said firmly. "Jaldan attacked her. She barely escaped with her life. My report will be in Olatu's hands within the next few hours, I assure you."

"Where is he?" the Ashik insisted.

"Find him yourself!" Huldar retorted.

The two looked at Huldar for a moment, then at each other. A few hardy insects made desultory calls, as if practicing for later.

Finally, the Ashik turned and marched back to the portal. A faint cloud of desiccated plant material and flitting wings swirled in their wake.

As the portal softly chimed, Huldar tipped his head toward the tents.

She nodded. They needed a screened and protected space.

The air inside was cooler than out, but stifling and close. She watched sweat bead on Huldar's forehead and trickle slowly down his face.

"What should we do?" she asked. "They'll keep looking!" She placed her hands on the familiar tent pole and rested her head against it. "Delemät was watching," she said as if to the pole, then she turned to him. "Why didn't I feel it? I made Jaldan lower the screen!"

"Don't blame yourself," he said soothingly. "Under the circumstances …"

"He will want to interrogate me!"

She lowered herself awkwardly and sat on the bed. Her head gravitated to her hands. The future closed in on her; a future in which Delemät Ashik's presence loomed large. Her heart pained.

"Daric is on his way," Huldar told her. He held up an empty mug.

"Yes please," she sighed. "Sari and Nachiel …" She sent a precis of their mission to get fresh galano.

He reached into Qalān for two more cups. "Tea always helps, doesn't it?" he said calmly, but his hands fumbled slightly as he set water on to boil.

For some reason, this simple action reminded her of Casco. She could almost hear his voice - calm and practical, with the little bur that only showed when he was nervous, or very relaxed. A single tear scrolled down her cheek as memories passed between them.

Sari can't accept it, she whispered.

I know. He shared with her Ubaid's belief that Sari would, eventually, in her own way, come to terms with Casco's death.

"I know Daric will do his best," Andel said, "but the birthing will be difficult for them both - even more than it would already be. He loved Casco too, with all his heart."

Huldar nodded.

The flame beneath the tripod burned steadily.

Small tendrils of steam wound lazily from the water's surface.

Andel felt, rather than heard, the portal chime. For a moment, she held her breath, then Nachiel's familiar voice called to her.

In here, she said, then the portal activated again.

Nachiel's reply was overridden by Daric's urgent voice, *Quickly. We must leave NOW!*

Huldar flicked his hand at the pot and extinguished the flame. He left tripod and mugs behind as he pulled Andel to her feet. With one arm wrapped securely around her for support, they rushed from the tent.

Daric stood by the portal and waved them on. Sari and Nachiel waited anxiously beside him.

What's happening? Andel asked. *What's wrong?*

Ashik! Daric said. *Delemät. On their way. Be here in minutes.* He beckoned again. *Come on!*

Before they stepped through, Huldar's and Daric's eyes met. A moment of understanding passed between them, but Andel had little time to wonder. The two archangel's voices united in a powerful sequence that sent them into the complete darkness of an unfamiliar cavern.

Huldar lofted a globe. It brightened quickly, but the light was slow to find a surface.

Andel shivered in the sudden cold. *Where are we?* she asked. The silence - like the darkness - was absolute.

Daric turned to her. "Remember the lava tubes you and Casco spotted, all that time ago?" His voice, although hushed, seemed incongruous; it's edges deadened.

"A lava tube?"

He looked around as another globe brightened. Features on the nearest wall had begun to appear, but the ceiling was still shrouded in darkness.

It's … enormous!

"Why?" Sari asked. "Why do we need to be here?"

"Is this part of our escape plan?" Nachiel asked.

"Yes, it is," Huldar said. "We'll be safe here. Daric and … they've," he paused again as if unwilling to say Casco's name.

Daric nodded. "I think that time is upon us. We have to get everyone here."

"If we don't act quickly enough, they'll take hostages," Huldar said worriedly.

"Hostages?" Nachiel said. "Would they do that?"

"No time to lose," Daric said to Huldar. "You'll have to go back. Head them off."

"Head them off?" Sari repeated vaguely. "But how did you know?" she asked. "Are you sure?"

"There's food and supplies in the storage area yonder," Daric told them. "Huldar, you'd best return to camp. There's not much chance he saw us leave – I expect he was too busy yelling."

"Can you manage the evacuation alone? I'm sorry, Daric, but who will help you?" Huldar frowned sadly.

"Best you don't know."

Daric motioned toward the portal and the two stepped through with alacrity, leaving Andel with Sari and Nachiel to make the vast cavern ready for the imminent arrival of its new inhabitants.

Andel dragged her gaze from the empty portal and started for the dim piles of supplies.

"Don't worry, lady Andel," Nachiel said. "We'll have this place looking homely in no time. Might I suggest we pitch some tents?" He peered up into the gloom. "Might make people feel a bit more secure."

"Good idea," she said.

Sari waddled closer to one of the supply caches. "Nachiel, if you could light a fire first?" she said. "There's a huge pot here. I'll get some water on to boil."

The cavern's gate rang with a lower tone than any above ground, perhaps as it was part of the ancient system, and for the main part, buried under millennia of soil deposits and rock formation.

Andel looked up as Rosheen, Tisha, Gael and Tam stepped through. She had a brief glimpse of Gento and Cobar's faces before they vanished, presumably back to where they came from.

Rosheen bustled toward Nachiel's attempt at a fire. "Let me do that."

He stepped aside.

"Nhadu," she scolded. "You need Rukh for proper flame."

"Sorry, but she's right," Tam said. "Have you located the food stores yet, Lady Andel?"

"Over here," she said, studying neat rows of crates, bags and boxes. Daric and Casco … how had they found the time? And without anybody knowing? "We'll be quite well fed, at least."

Tam nodded appreciatively and started up the first aisle. "When Arko gets here, we'll make an inventory, but in the meantime, I think this," he reached for a bag of talemgal, "this and this," he marked several more items, "will get us started."

EVACUATION

As they stepped through to the Eastern Foothills campsite, Huldar gave Daric a brusque nod. “Breath blow us survival.”

“Indeed,” Daric replied. “Stay strong, my friend. See him for what he is, a very big fish in a tiny, tiny pond, and such a one quickly runs out of air.” He looked back to the gate in alarm. “They’re coming!”

Huldar sprinted for the campsite. *What now?* he whispered, but the assassin had already gone. *How did he do that?* he asked himself. The gate had not sounded - he was sure of it! His eyebrows were still raised in shock as he pushed beneath the door-flap.

Almost immediately, the portal did chime, and Delemät’s powerful farsight punched against his tent’s screens. If Daric was anywhere close … *Stay safe, my friend,* he whispered.

Footsteps marched in heavy unison.

He composed his screens, straightened his veils and opened the tent-flap just as ten Ashik stamped to a halt outside it. They shuffled aside as Delemät pushed through, his demeanor as perfectly neutral as it would be in his brother's Court.

"Tsemkarun Delemät Ashik." Huldar gave a very correct bow. "To what do I owe the pleasure?"

Wariness flickered in Delemät's gaze, then vanished. He bowed in return. "I am searching for Jaldan of Trianog and Tsemkarun Andel of Trianog, your wife. Where is she?"

Huldar frowned.

The ashik shifted uncomfortably.

Delemät bowed again. "My apologies. My language may seem overly rough, but I am in fear for my assistant, Jaldan of Trianog's, life. Your wife was the last to see him alive." He gave a brusque nod. "I'm sure you understand."

"She was here this morning with two of my team." Huldar said. "They left her alone when it seems your assistant attacked her. She escaped and returned here."

"Maybe so," Delemät replied, his tone fractionally sharp. "But I would still speak with her. She may be able to shed light on his sudden and complete disappearance."

Huldar nodded slowly. "Your abilities with farsight are extensive, as I have noticed on many occasions."

Delemät snorted impatiently. "Contact your wife and advise her of my request. Given her delicate condition, the most appropriate way for me to achieve my goals is with your help. As you say, I could proceed without it, but that would be rude, don't you agree?"

"Yes, quite rude, as you say. So, you request an interview?"

"Yes."

Huldar observed the instability of Delemät's haze with some trepidation. "May I ask how you know this?" he said politely. "What leads you to the belief that my wife, Tsemkarun Andel of Trianog, may harbor some evidence pertinent to your aide's disappearance? And why all these Ashik, if your intent is so … innocuous?"

Delemät took a sharp breath. "Come now, Huldar. Tell me where she is and we will leave you in peace."

"Stay away from my wife," Huldar said firmly. "You have already proved your propensity for bullying behavior. There will be no more interviews. I thought that was made clear to you at our last meeting."

"Jaldan has disappeared after a disagreement with your wife!"

"What are you suggesting?" Huldar said sharply. "Maybe Jaldan's investigations have led him astray. Find somewhere else to lay blame. Qalān is notoriously difficult here. Perhaps he has accidentally taken himself to the other side of the world, and merely awaits your legendary farsight to locate and retrieve him. Should you need help, I believe Farushael of Cantori is familiar with most portals."

Delemät nodded slowly. "Ah yes, the legendary vanishing gate."

His opponent's smile sent alarm bells ringing in Huldar's mind. He closed his eyes and let the planet's energy find him.

"You will no doubt be pleased to know we solved that issue - just a bit more of an overland trek."

Huldar's head tilted fractionally as he calculated the distance between the next available portal and the sacred shores. The journey would have taken days at best. He watched his opponent's eyes, and waited.

"A shame you were so busy studying those useless behemoths ..."

"Citizens," he corrected.

"Potential citizens," Delemät conceded. "Anyway, my ... the God-Emperor will be pleased with the result. We discovered where the fish were cocooned and dug them up."

Huldar went cold. "You what!?"

"Smelly business, or so I'm told, but plenty of gems to show for it. All in all, we recovered just over two thousand of them. Dug until none remained."

"You killed them all!?" He fought back tears. "An entire generation? You have critically endangered the only new Citizens to be discovered for a thousand years!"

Delemät smirked. "Narrows their candidacy, I imagine - and should they become extinct, the planet and all its many assets will once again become my brother's undisputed property."

Huldar felt the rage building in him. Energy flowed upward through his feet, his legs, and filled his torso to bursting. Should he try to control it? The question barely registered.

"Find Jaldan yourself!" he roared. "And may you and all your kind join him! She will eat you! Eat you! There will be no escape!"

Delemät took a step back. His sword flickered from Qalān.

Huldar swiped with his flattened hand, and the Ashik toppled in its arc like hurricane felled trees. With another blow, the remainder also staggered. With a flick of his wrist, the whole group were sent tumbling toward the gate.

He turned his attention to Delemät.

Delemät's Tsemkar flared to life, but whatever fearsome charm he loosed had no effect on the planet's wrath. With a snarl of frustration, the God-Emperor's brother raised his sword and struck.

With blurring speed, Huldar gripped the blade in his hand. Its fine-honed edge bit deep, but the planet drew him on.

Delemät's eyes widened. He could neither complete his strike, nor withdraw without releasing his weapon and admitting defeat.

Slowly, Huldar forced it down, then with a simple song, snapped it.

Delemät dropped what was left and ran. The look of terror on his face should have been satisfying, but all Huldar could see were the decimated cocoons of the Went. The Elders would come to welcome their newborns, and find only silence.

Blood pooled at his feet, but he couldn't let his piece of the sword go. He stared after Delemät and his limping Ashik as if rooted to the spot, long after the portal quieted. Energy pulsed through him, white with anger, stained with blood. He could hear nothing else, see nothing else. The pain seemed fitting.

After some time, as if from nowhere, a figure appeared and made its way hesitantly forward.

Huldar barely noticed. His gaze was still fixed on the portal. His agony, indescribable.

Huldar?

The name - his name, had a strangely dual quality, as if echoed from within him.

Huldar – let go.

Slowly, his gaze lowered to Daric's.

"Andel needs you," Daric said softly. "We all need you." *Please …*

Let go, the planet whispered. *Our time is not yet come.*

The energy drained so quickly, he stumbled. Daric's hand was there to stop his fall.

He peered at the fractured blade in his hand. How had it not been severed?

Let me help, Daric said.

Huldar nodded.

With surprising care, he felt his fingers unwrapped, one by one.

The metal clattered free.

Folds of clean cloth were placed in his bloody palm. Daric closed his hand back around it.

"They killed them all," he whispered. "Destroyed them when they were at their most helpless. Why?"

"Let's get you to Ubaid," Daric said, and started for the portal.

Huldar followed. His soul seemed empty. A burned out husk.

Father?

His face twitched. Was he hearing things now?

Father? The small voice came again, and he understood – the voice of his child. Love and peace flowed from her small heart into his, rebuilding him from the inside out.

Daric paused by the portal. "There is nothing more we can do, or could have done," he said sadly. "But the Uri'madu, your people, are safe."

Huldar grasped at his daughter's consciousness, but to hold it was impossible. Slowly, her presence faded. He shook his head. "And the miners?"

"All but one."

"He must not have her!" he cried. What Delemät might do to her didn't bear thinking about.

"He won't," Daric assured him. "They will be safely with us before nightfall."

Daric sang them through to the great cavern. Huldar stumbled against him, barely conscious.

Ubaid! Quickly!

Andel rushed forward, but Ubaid reached them first. Expectant faces, pale in the gloom, watched in silence as the healer shouldered the burden and helped him to a bed. Andel held her husband's good hand while Ubaid bent his head over the other.

"What happened?" he asked quietly.

"I don't exactly know," Daric admitted. In his mind's eye he could still see the broken sword - Delemät Ashik's own blade - and the dreadful wound as he prised the shattered end from Huldar's grasp. "When I got to Eastern Basecamp, he was surrounded by some sort of glow." He recalled the white fire, burning as if fueled by Huldar's own soul, but felt reluctant to share.

"A glow?" Andel repeated anxiously. "Did Delemät do something to him?"

Daric shook his head. "I think it was the aftermath of something he did to Delemät," he replied pensively. "When I left him earlier and went to start the evacuation, he was alone. There were ten Ashik coming his way, led by Delemät. There was a fight. I saw signs. And he … seems to have snapped Delemät's sword. I recognized the Imperial insignia on the hilt."

Ubaid studied the savage wounds on Huldar's upturned palm and fingers. "Snapped a sword?"

Daric shrugged. "That sword of all swords should have severed his hand cleanly - but it was still wrapped around the broken end. He couldn't let go."

Ubaid put two fingers on Huldar's palm and closed his eyes. The Healers' Mark seemed to writhe with effort. Slowly, the various parts reunited, a process Daric always found fascinating. Huldar remained unconscious. When skin, tendon and bone had knitted back together, Ubaid placed his fingertips on Huldar's forehead.

"He will be alright," he said slowly. "He's been through quite an ordeal, but … he just needs sleep."

A whisper of relief sped through the cavern.

Andel burst into tears. Sari and Alis moved closer to comfort her.

Daric looked around at their new home. Topper put a mug of tea in his grasp, but before he could thank him, he'd smiled and turned away.

He looked up at the gloom and wished Casco was here; lighting was one more thing his husband excelled at.

Gento and Cobar left Rosheen's side and came towards him.

"Well done," he congratulated them. "Everything went to plan?"

"I'll feel better when Banga gets back with Shen," Gento grumbled.

"I'll go in a moment and keep watch," he told them. "Any chance we could get a few more fires going? And some more globes?" He looked up at the dark. "It would be nice if we could see the ceiling."

"I'll get onto it," Gento assured him. "And don't worry little Enna, I'll keep an eye on the boss while you're gone."

Daric smiled and bowed with heartfelt intensity. These two had saved the Uri'madu as much as he or anyone else had. They had kept the secrets he'd charged them with. They owed him nothing; yet he knew without doubt he could trust them with his life.

SONG OF FRUSTRATION

Tent leathers, impossible to tension in the tropical conditions, gave a desultory flap. Outside, the standard of Tiamät gave a half-hearted flutter. Delemät Ashik scowled. Sweat dripped uncomfortably down his back. Although it was pointless, he continued to pace the rug. Four Ashik stood on guard, swathed in careful neutrality. Each one as irritating as the last.

What were they thinking?

"How can anyone function in this heat?" he barked.

Not one of them so much as twitched.

He turned to a disturbance in his tent's lobby.

"My lord Olatu of Faytha," one of them announced.

"I know that!" he snapped. Did they think him such a fool? "Bring him in."

The Faythan simpered forward. Delemät just had to look at his poorly managed haze to know the news was not good, but he asked anyway. "Well?"

"No sign as yet, Lord Delemät, but they must be somewhere."

"Do you think?" he said sarcastically. Tent leathers flapped as he looked Olatu up and down. "No, maybe that's too much to ask!"

The Faythan had the effrontery to appear offended by his comment.

"Has self-control entirely escaped you out here in the wilderness," he barked, "or are you merely tempting fate?"

Too late, Olatu's haze and inner veils firmed to a more seemly aspect. The bow that followed was irritatingly precise. "I am doing my utmost, my lord."

"Not utmost enough!"

"But there are quotas yet to fill."

Was this idiot giving him excuses?

"Surely my lord's farsight …"

Delemät knew his glare would have had any of his officers quaking in their boots, but the Faythan continued to speak.

"… could be ably augmented by a few more eyes on the ground?"

The idiot admitted that despite his express orders, he'd not thrown his entire Host at the issue? And now sought to appease him through flattery? Fascinated as much as appalled, Delemät watched Olatu dig his hole deeper.

"The Uri'madu know this planet," Olatu blathered on, "the terrain – their reach is global. Of course, we will continue to do our very best to find them, and our cook, there have been reports of an anomalous smell, but …"

Olatu paused, completely misinterpreted his incredulous silence and even continued as if it had been meant as encouragement.

"… I'm sorry, but I fail to see how we, a simple group of miners can we hope to find one as wily and dare I say it - powerful as …"

Before he could say the name, Delemät's Tsemkar flared to absolute brilliance.

The Faythan fell dead at his feet.

"… Lord Huldar?" Delemät finished nastily. "I told you never to mention him again." He turned to his guards. "Clean that up. Get the Cantori - Frashel, or whatever his name is."

"Farushael of Cantori?" The one closest to the exit bowed and left, while another departed with the blubbery body in tow.

Delemät looked at the remaining two. A shiver of nervousness tightened his shoulders.

"Four guards at all times!" he snapped.

One of them looked at the other. Was that an eyebrow lift? How could he be sure? His Tsemkar flared again, and his Ashik troops numbered one less.

WHAT NOW?

Huldar lay curled around Andel, warm under their blankets, and listened to her soft, regular breathing. Harmony flowed between them wherever their skin touched. Her leg twitched, then her arm, and he smiled when she made a snuffling noise in the back of her throat. Dreaming, no doubt. For the first time in ages, despite the evacuation and all that had gone on, she had no trouble sleeping - not since Jaldan had been dealt with.

She twitched again and the baby moved. Did they share each other's dreams? He'd often wondered at the privacy of the subconscious. What Andel had done to save herself and her mother - 'The White Terror' as Jaldan had called it - maybe the reason he'd not been able to reverse-engineer it was because it was a dream-state. A constant, waking nightmare ... in which Jaldan 'the mind-bender' of Trianog was now fully immersed. Would he be dead yet? Probably not, although time might flow differently when there were no reference points to measure it by. Lind had survived for weeks, but she'd had no idea how much actual time had passed - maybe for her it had only been days - terrible, terrible days.

He stroked Andel's arm and kissed her soft hair. Even though their bond was strong and clear, the mystery of her fascinated him every day.

He smiled again. He owed a lot to Went ... but she had taken her toll. He remembered the song the Planet had given them in order to breach Qalān. Should they save Jaldan? But the thought of such a monster further demented by his stay in complete sensory deprivation made him shudder. His wife had been willing to sacrifice herself and her child to rid the Known of the threat he posed. He would honor her decision.

Elements of the demanding charm trickled through his mind. It had not been passed on to anyone except the Guild-Lord; but who could be trusted with such power? Casco had been the only one besides himself and Andel to have any inkling of its working, and now ... his friend was gone.

He shied from the pain as best he could.

Andel moaned. The quality of their bond changed slightly and he rolled away, reluctant to infect her sleep with his grief.

He mused on Sari's belief that Casco was still alive. When he'd asked her why, she said her baby knew it to be true. At the time, he'd thought her delusional, but now, he was not so sure.

He recalled his daughter's voice in his mind, so sweet and pure. He'd been frozen in rage, his own and the Planet's. There had seemed no escape, but she had understood, disentangled them and brought him home. If Casco's son had spoken to Sari in the same way ... perhaps ... it was true?

He let his senses range through the walls of their tent toward Daric's. Powerful screens shielded it from intrusion, but he knew it to be empty. To the best of his knowledge, Daric had not slept in it since their occupation of the giant cavern, just on a week ago. Huldar trusted him completely … but where did he go?

The portal chimed in its soft, distinctive way and Huldar sensed Daric's arrival. It was as if the assassin had been called by his thoughts. Hope grew so strong, it almost made him itch. What if Casco was still alive, and the whole thing had been some sort of Daricesque ruse?

The rest of the Uri'madu were asleep. Soft footfalls paused by the fire.

Huldar slipped out of bed, and as quietly as he could, pulled trousers up his legs and threw a shirt across his shoulders.

Daric, silhouetted by the dull coals, juggled an awkwardly curved log into place. When he let it go, sparks puffed lazily upward. The local timber, a structural variant of the strap-tree, burned long and hot, and its smell - slightly peaty, but more sweet - drifted slowly up the length of the gigantic cave. No one knew yet where it exited.

Orange light bounced off the planes of Daric's fine Enna features. Haunted eyes shone with reflected flame. They warmed with a brief smile of welcome, then returned to the fire.

"How are you feeling?" Daric asked.

Huldar flexed his hand. "Better than I did."

His true question pushed to be voiced, but how could he frame it? If he was wrong, Daric's own grief would be triggered - and if he was correct, the answer was best kept hidden.

Daric tipped his head. His gaze took in the tents and the vast darkness behind them. "It must be strange for you, cooped up here, no work to do."

He gave a rueful smile. At first, there'd been the camp to set up and a myriad small tasks. Now things were running smoothly enough, and he longed to at least check the progress of the Went, try communicating again, but he knew he couldn't risk it. Delemät's gaze was constant. He must sleep sometimes, but to date, they'd noticed no pattern and even that small observation was risky.

"What's on your mind?" Daric prompted.

"The North." He nodded slowly. "With things the way they are - I don't know what you have in mind, but I feel it would be best not make the attempt on your own."

"No?"

"I could go with you," Huldar said. "Delemät is afraid of me. We'll go, do what we have to do, then leave. Quick and simple. Use the gate we made in ancient Qalān. It's only a few steps from there. No one will stand in our way."

Daric shook his head. "Quick and simple is good, but you're forgetting - if Delemät knows we've contacted a someone, his scrutiny will be constant - even more-so. One slip and our lives will be over. Our new Djan'rū would no doubt be found and any unexpected navigator killed the second they stepped from the chime."

"Oh."

"He's an entitled brat," Daric said. "but he's not stupid."

Huldar glanced at him. "And I am?"

He received shared imagery of the broken sword, accompanied by a half-cheeky smile. "Maybe you had a knock on the head?"

Huldar snorted. Maybe he had! Delemät's farsight kept the major portal trails and many of the minor ones unusable. At least they still had ancient Qalān. The work they'd done there had really paid off.

"... Can you tell me what happened?" Daric said carefully.

He shrugged his lips. Where to start?

Coals cracked and released a fresh cloud of embers.

Daric drew a breath, as if to speak, but fell silent again. "What was that ... 'fire' around you," he said at last.

The picture he shared made Huldar's brows knit. He'd had no idea of any changes to his haze, or that there had been some sort of bright light around him, but there it was. No wonder Delemät had been disconcerted! He remembered the force with which he'd felled the Ashik troops - as if the wind responded to his anger.

"And the sword?" Daric glanced at his hand. "How did you come to break it?"

Huldar's frown deepened as he tried to compose events into words. "I opened myself to the Planet," he said, "as I did when the interviews started to go wrong." He paused, staring into the coals as memories of that event returned to him. Had he really lifted Delemät Ashik by the neck? He could still see the terror his eyes - and the anger in his haze. "I knew she would help if I needed it. But then he told me about the Bel Nishani ..."

Pain stabbed through his chest.

Daric looked away. *If it's too much ...*

Huldar shook his head. He'd explained to Andel. Maybe it would be easier this time.

... I was so ... 'angry' hardly seems strong enough. Incensed! It was as if I held the planet's rage inside me as well. Her children had been violated and killed – and it was as if those were my children too; if that makes sense? I didn't know about the fire, or whatever it was.

Daric shrugged. *I mentioned it to Ubaid, but he was more concerned with getting your hand to stick back together.*

Huldar looked down at the scars, still livid. It was as if they were Marks of a different kind, brought on by the vast emotion his hands had wielded. He flexed his fingers – almost as good as new. There was no sound but the slow creak of the coals and the inaudible hum of annangi presence. Daric waited, patient, attentive. High above, he could just make out the cavern's ceiling.

And the sword? He shrugged, trying again to make sense of the enormous power that had flowed through him. *She did it, I think – made me impervious, sort of. Although I still got cut. ... I wanted it to break, and it did.* He could still feel the shock as the metal snapped. *... Now is not the time,* she said. *Soon you must choose, but not yet ...* He met Daric's gaze. "It unsettles me. I don't know what she means."

Daric poked the fire. "She's a planet, so confusion is not surprising," he said wryly, but his tone was thoughtful – even distracted. They watched small flames spread along the darkened log. "What I do know is that you should keep absolutely clear of Delemät Ashik. He has lost face – serious face, for perhaps the first time in his life. He will want revenge. His fear demands it."

Huldar nodded. Daric was always right about such things. "And you? Will you go North alone? I can't help feeling it's a bad idea."

"I have my ways," the assassin said cryptically.

"And it's best I know nothing," Huldar smiled laconically. "Well, that secrecy has served us well so far, and I trust you know what you are doing." He sighed. It was so hard not to ask the question that tormented him. Instead, he said "Let me know when you're back and safe."

Daric's head tilted in affirmation. "I most certainly will." He dusted his palms together and stood to leave. Huldar's senses followed as he made his way to his tent, but his screens were impeccable, and there was no anomalous sense of Casco's presence to be gleaned.

NO SMOKE

Casco sat beside Daric and compared the array of supplies laid out before them with the list in his head … Waterproof coat and jacket, two each; Mitts, four pairs each; heavy-duty scarves, four each; several pairs of spare socks and full-body underwear. There were several warm blankets each, two sets of water repellent leathers for emergency shelter; and two sets of eye-shields - Daric's invention - in case of blizzard conditions. Two of Ariben's faceted chasite screen-stones twinkled amongst the hoard. First aid packs, two each; Food packs, enough for ten days - way more than they would need for a 'quick trip', but there would be no immediate help if they got into trouble, and it was best to be prepared. High energy snack-packs, twenty each … had he forgotten anything?

The list in his head started over.

Daric laid a hand on his arm. *It's time.*

Casco turned to study his face, and was captured by details of his sculpted lips, so mobile in love. Broad forehead, narrow nose and high cheek-bones with planes that caught the light just so. Fine creases, new since their sojourn on Went, had grown at the corners of his amber, Tiamäti eyes.

Tell me again? Why take that risk?

There it was – that half-smile he found so hard to resist. *Because it will keep you safe.*

Casco sighed. *I don't like it.*

I know, Daric said, but an unhealthy level of excitement joined the warmth that flowed through their bond. With some dismay he admitted to himself his husband thrived on danger.

How will I know you haven't been captured? Ziquarra is out of the question. I can't exhaust my reserves before I reach the target.

No need. Daric touched his forehead playfully, just below his Mark.

He nodded. Their marriage bond would be visible and traceable to some, but not the sigil. He tried to quell his apprehension. An armory of doubts, many of which he would normally have kept to himself, had already been aired. Daric had answered all with absolute confidence; it seemed he had guessed and second-guessed each possible action and reaction. But the lump in the pit of Casco's stomach persisted. He had been to the far North and knew first-hand the conditions they would face. Hostility from any unfortunate Ashik stationed there could only add to the difficulties of traveling alone at such latitudes.

A water-beast in the back of the cave moaned prophetically. Although large and territorial, they survived on thriving colonies of tiny pale invertebrates in the subterranean lake system. He had discovered that this particular area was a long island in a dark underground river, perhaps an analogy for the turn their lives were about to take.

Daric snorted softly, and Casco realized he'd unwittingly shared.

It's hard to get used to, he shrugged.

I know, but …

They smiled at each other, and his confidence returned. With movements unconsciously synchronized, they wrapped themselves in their warmest jackets, stowed their various packs in Qalān and started for the gate.

You sing it, Daric said. *She likes you better.*

I doubt it, Casco replied. Since Jaldan's fate had been enacted, none of the Uri'madu had trouble with any level of Qalān. It was as if it recognized them, and they had somehow proved themselves. Had it seen Jaldan as a gift of appeasement? The idea made him shudder a little. They had so little understanding of the medium through which they traveled, or even what it actually was, but it was true the ancient system seemed to welcome his presence.

They stepped through to the most Northerly exit as if it was the shortest and simplest of actions. He shook his head and thanked the planet in his heart. He'd seen the trouble the Host were having. Songs were difficult to manage. People taken to unexpected destinations. Others had found simple steps to take an alarming length of time. No one had been eaten by it yet - except Jaldan, but all were disconcerted.

Biting cold hit the exposed skin of his face. He closed his eyes against the blinding whiteness of snow, then eased them open and squinted into the distance, expecting to feel the prickle of Delemät Ashik's farsight at any moment.

Relax, Daric told him. *He doesn't know this gate exists, remember?*

But Casco could feel the tension in him, and knew the moment when the danger of the mission they were about to undertake actually registered.

It won't go wrong, Casco assured him. *You have thought of everything, planned meticulously and brilliantly as always. And don't worry. I won't be taking any unnecessary risks.*

I'll come for you; always.

I know. He gave a small smile, but inside he was filled with wonder. It was true. If he needed help, Daric would always be there. Daric loved him utterly, with all his flaws.

And the good bits!

He snorted. "I will get better at this."

"You love me too," Daric said softly. "And I know beyond doubt you would do your utmost for me also." He gave a gentle smile. "You have saved me, Archerran Casco of the Uri'madu, and I could never be whole without you in my life. Our marriage was unplanned, but deeply desired, and I … could not wish it any other way." A single tear fell from Daric's face like a frozen jewel into the snow. "Breath blew us together, and blows through us together."

Casco covered his eyes in case his own tears froze and enmeshed his lashes. "You're only saying that because you think you might die," he said brokenly.

So might you … Daric's lips shrugged. He turned for the next portal, over two miles away. *Into the unknown. It's what I do best.*

He trudged through thick snow in Daric's wake. Every fifty steps, he sang to cover their tracks, and deep as they were, the marks of their progress vanished. The going was slow and exhausting, but they had no time to rest.

He was jolted from a kind of walking stupor by Daric's hand signal, and quickly sang to cover all traces of their presence.

The sigil in his forehead warmed as he was sent a message of extreme caution. *Too soon to get caught yet,* his partner whispered.

A heavy screen settled over them, then a lighter, more cryptic one above that.

They waited. His breath steamed. His legs ached with cold. He wriggled his toes inside his boots and flexed his calf-muscles rhythmically, but it was not enough. Then a small alarm sounded – the sensation shared from Daric's mind, and he knew Delemät Ashik had passed them over.

He's nothing if not thorough, Daric said quietly.

'Obsessed' is more the term.

Daric's response was a cloud of huffed breath. He dissolved the screens and moved toward the portal they both sensed, only two hundred paces away.

Casco nodded apprehensively. This led to the second-last gate before the North Comms portal, and was the only one through which the area could be reached. He had viewed eight Ashik stationed there, as well as the six bored warriors stationed at the final destination. The plan was to never alert them, and if the storm they expected rolled in, that would at least be a possibility.

Four Ashik looked at each other through the faint shimmer of a portal. Light snow peppered their shoulders. Frost collected in furry icicles on the fabric shields that covered nose and mouth. From time to time, one would glance at the hut where warmth and food waited, along with four miserable replacements awaiting rotation.

Some distance away, sluggish waves broke on a shingled shore, but they were hard to see through the falling flakes.

"I've heard he can walk through walls …" one, a gnarled veteran, ventured.

"Don't be stupid." Their leader rubbed the back of his neck with one thickly mitted hand. "How could anyone walk through stone?"

"No stone here," another quietly commented, then looked nervously over her shoulders. Opposite her, another, taller than the others, hunched his shoulders and rolled them.

The leader snorted. "Breath you lot are thick! Gotta come through this gate, don't they? That's why we're in this shithole, isn't it!"

"Not if he can walk through walls," the first responded. "An assassin, or so I heard …"

"He's no assassin! You just gotta look at the piss-weak kalla. Typical Enna! Soft as feather bed. Not an ounce a sneak in 'im, let alone fight!"

Undaunted, the gnarled one continued. "So what about that Huldar? I saw him lift the boss. Right off his feet he was. Fuckin terrifying, that's what it was."

"You were there?"

"As Breath be true," the speaker assured him. "Leth was burnin - had like flames an shit. Never seen anythin like it."

"Breath!" the tall one murmured.

"No wonder boss be safe back there in his nice warm tent, then, eh?" the female said snidely.

There was a guarded snigger, then silence.

The only sound was the snow-muffled crash and hiss of distant breakers.

They jumped to attention as the gate chimed. Four swords sprang from Qalān. Four pairs of eyes gazed into empty space.

"… Where are they then?"

"Chimed," the female answered. "I heard it."

"We all heard it, shit-for-brains!" the leader shook his head. "Be some sort a glitch. You know how Qalān is these days."

"And that's the truth," the veteran said with a snort. "Took a full minute to step through to the latrine the other day. Thought I was gunna piss my pants."

The gate chimed again.

Once more the space remained empty.

The guards looked at each other.

"Well I'm probably gunna piss mine if that happens again!" The female lifted her chin toward the hut. "How long before that lot take over?"

"Hour, or thereabouts," the leader answered.

She stamped her feet up and down in the snow. "I'll be frozen solid!"

The leader looked at an outcrop not far from beach. "We should take it in turns to run around that and back."

"At least there's no earthquakes here," the tall one said timidly.

This comment was met with pitying silence.

"You are joking, aren't you?" the leader said. "Go on then, get running."

The tall one gave the leader a nod and started for the icy shingles of the beach. When the gate chimed for a third time, the remaining three barely noticed. But soon afterward, it activated again. Before they had time to react, a shrouded shape appeared in their midst, stepped behind the nearest Ashik and slit her throat. At the same time a stun-charm immobilized the veteran. In the next heartbeat, he fell to the snow, stabbed in the neck. The leader, groggy from the backlash, vanished with the figure through the portal.

When the runner returned, he saw two bodies lying in lightly trampled snow - now stained red.

The tent in the valley shook as reinforcements burst through the door.

The tall one waited beside the bodies, as the mission leader, a captain in the Ashesse, or so-called peacekeepers, led three others over the rise and frowned at the scene.

"El's Breath!" he murmured, and pointed to two of his team. "You and you, remove the bodies. Cover them with snow. We'll attend to them later. You," he pointed to the survivor, "clean up." He studied the bodies again. "Where's Dätmar?"

"Maybe he's run off?"

"No tracks," the captain pointed out, then closed his eyes and let his senses range.

"Dätmar?" Their calls seemed deadened by the falling snow. "Dätmar Ashik!" But there was no answer, and no sense of the missing fighter's presence.

They looked at each other and stepped away from the portal.

"Have you told the boss?" one asked.

A look of panic crossed the captain's face. "No need for that just yet. Why were you not at your station?"

"I had permission to go for a run. We were to take it in turns. It's freezing!"

"You abandoned your post?" he retorted angrily. "Colder for your comrades! How do you think Lord Delemät will feel ..." His sentence was stopped by the chime of the portal. At his signal, the Ashik leapt into formation, weapons at the ready. But as before, nobody stepped through.

The captain nodded. "Toying with us."

"Who?" another asked. "Is it Huldar of Leth?"

"Not him," the captain said firmly. "He'd come right out and do what he had to do. This one's sneaky."

The survivor looked around. "The assassin?"

"That or the Rukh," the captain agreed. "All Rukh are warriors - even on Went."

He turned his gaze skyward as if checking the time, then used the point of his sword to indicate the messy snow. "Didn't I tell you to clean this up?"

The survivor scuttled to obey.

"Here's what we'll do," the captain said to the others. "Guard the portal as before. I'll stand back, stun-charm at the ready.

Boss wants whoever it is alive; remember that. Needs it to find the rest of them." He looked at the sky again. "Hurry!"

No sooner were they in place than the cold rush of Delemät's farsight brushed the site. The captain smiled grimly and kept his eyes on the portal. At least the arrogant lump of shit probably wouldn't make the effort to see inside the shack and find it empty.

Casco returned to his body, kept warm beneath the snow-covered leather shelter by several layers of blankets and furs.

He took a deep breath, sat up and immediately began to draw the configuration of captain and guards with his finger in the snow. *Four, here,* he said, *not so close but a bit more nervous, and one behind – about here? The captain. Stun charm defense.*

As he drew, he also shared everything he'd seen.

Daric nodded. *Delemät's done his pass, so time for this bruiser,* he looked at the Ashik they'd abducted – *Dätmar is it? to be useful.*

Casco looked up. *You'll wake him?*

Stand him up and send him through.

You won't have to step through with him?

"I will," Daric said. *But I won't stay long. Need to take out one or two more before my big finale.* He stood and dusted the snow of his pants, gave Casco a wink, then dragged Dätmar outside and gave him a solid punch to the face. The Ashik stirred to life, but was dazed by the blow. Daric wrenched him to his feet and held him firmly. "Keep warm till I get back," he said cheerily, then he was gone.

Casco watched the portal and waited. If this attack went as smoothly as the last, he should be back within moments. The temptation to look was strong, but too much Ziquarra would render him exhausted, and the main part of his mission was yet to come.

When his nerves were stretched almost to their limit, Daric stumbled back through the gate. He held his left forearm. Blood seeped between his fingers. Casco reached for a first aid pack.

It's not too bad, Daric said. *Bit of a cut is all.*

Plenty of blood.

I'll close it in a minute. Get that antiseptic powder, and a bandage.

Casco nodded. It wasn't the wound that made him nauseous, it was the thought of what might have been.

The captain got in a lucky blow, Daric explained.

And?

He shrugged. *Another down, two if you include Dätmar.*

"A good result then."

Daric winced as Casco dusted the cut with brown powder, then the assassin passed his hand above it and sang what repair he could. Afterward, a livid line remained. He motioned for Casco to bandage the opposite arm. "Keep them confused," he explained.

Casco gave a short huff and did as Daric suggested. "Ubaid can look at it when we get back," he said. *How does it feel?*

Daric pumped his arm up and down. *Workable.*

But Casco knew different. *Residual pain, and it feels a bit tight. Maybe you should wait a bit and give the healing time to set in?* "Not everyone can heal themselves."

Daric sighed. "A necessary skill in … the work."

"Did he see you?"

"Yes," Daric nodded briskly. "And recognized me. So now for the finale!"

"Chasite is set, just as you asked." He flashed a visual of the screen's placement, the only way Daric could know for sure where it was. "What if Delemät comes too soon?"

"He'll use this gate." He gave a doubtful glance in the crystal's direction. Casco felt some tension through their bond, but exhilaration still dominated. "I'll lead as many here as I can, hopefully all of them, but if not … be ready."

Casco fastened the insignia given him by Embar of Rukh to his left shoulder, the exact spot it had first been pinned. '*Draga, third stage on the path*'; he could almost hear his instructor's deep, rumbling voice.

They both flinched as accumulated snow crashed from a nearby tree.

"Wasn't so cold back on Haas," Casco said quietly.

Daric grinned. "Got your brush knife ready?"

He whispered his sword to hand and weighed it in his palm His wrist turned back and forth as he tested its balance. "I loved you the first time I saw you," he whispered to it. As if of its own volition, it cut a complex arc through the air.

"Embar would be proud," Daric said.

Casco grimaced. "Let's hope the third stage on the path is not my last."

It will be worth quite a few ales at the Imperial if it's not.

He snorted. *I'm guessing the Weyfal's out of bounds for the foreseeable. How's your arm?*

Daric drew his own fine blade and flexed a figure in the bitter air. "Good as it's going to be."

Their eyes met. How far they had both come, Casco mused. How precious this archangel, this Enna was to him. Adoration poured into him, equal in measure to the deep love he poured out. Their kiss was almost blinding in its intensity, then it was done, and without a backward look his one true love stepped back to the fray.

The snowfall paused. It was as if all of Went held its breath. With precise tones, Casco firmed the screen over their rough shelter. It would be hard for the Ashik to breach, but they would try and eventually succeed - or so it was assumed.

With two quickly sung sequences he'd covered all traces of their presence. One barely discernable hint was left to lead their enemies to the shelter.

He crouched by the portal. No sooner had he thrown the invisible cloak over himself, than Daric jumped into view. Blood from a head wound spattered the ground as he sprinted for the chasite screen. He scooped a handful of snow as he ran and held it against his head.

They're coming!

Casco lifted the cloak just enough to sing, and within seconds, all that remained was a light crystal frost that hung in the air, too fine to dampen.

His heart thundered. Would the cloak be enough to hide the sound? He tried to focus on his breathing, but it was hard to make his mind comply. His legs and feet ached with cold. How badly was Daric wounded? Both screen and cloak were impervious to thought transference, so he couldn't ask … until he remembered the sigil.

His forehead warmed - similar to the feeling his Mark gave him but deeper inside.

A sense of relief was returned to him. He knew the pain of Daric's head wound, and the ache of the snow packed onto it, but the sensation was remote.

Then the gate activated, and Casco tensed in readiness.

Three Ashik rolled from the portal into a trine fighting stance and released a strong stun-charm. Sound echoed across the clearing. More snow slithered from trees.

They looked around with wary gazes. One pointed to the trace deliberately left in the snow. They maintained their crouched formation and followed.

When they'd located the shelter's screens and were turned from the portal, Casco drew himself slowly to a standing position, cloak furled tightly around him.

Should he step through while two more guards remained on the other side? As if Daric had understood, he got a feeling he should wait.

His feet pained, but he dare not move them.

The Ashik's first counter charm flared and fizzled against the top-most screen.

Daric sent a sense of amusement, but Casco was not entertained. His boots and socks were best quality, but frost-bite was still a risk.

His hopes rose when the gate chimed, but only one of the remaining Ashik stepped through - a tall and muscular individual.

Casco frowned at him. Was this the same young warrior he'd seen before?

"What's the problem?" the newcomer said. The voice sounded similar enough. He decided it was the same one.

"It's this screen. We think he's in there, but coward won't face us."

The tall one tilted his head. "Ahh! Let's try this ..."

I'm going! Casco thought at the sigil. One extra would be easy to hide with the other bodies.

As the Ashik's next attempt was voiced, he dropped the disguising fabric and sang himself through to the north, stun-charm poised.

He released it the instant he felt the gate engage, and was surprised to see a tall Ashik fall. Another shook her head and with a disconcerting snarl, leapt into the air and swung her blade at his head.

Their swords met with a sharp clang. Without hesitation, he landed a swinging round-house kick and activated a second charm. He could almost see Embar's image superimposed on his opponent's, except this time, the point of his sword continued its drive through her throat. There was a barely audible crunch. Her body jerked and shuddered.

He had to put his foot on her chest to withdraw his blade.

Behind him, the second warrior scrambled to his feet.

Casco swung reflexively.

Blood sprayed from a gaping wound as the tall one's neck opened up. The young warrior slowly toppled. Heavy fluid spattered Casco's face with warmth. His knees went weak. He forced himself to watch, then doubled over and dry-retched as the young Ashik gurgled his last.

He wiped his mouth and straightened up. Where the extra fighter had come from, he had no inkling, but he could sense no other presence. A flaw in his fledgling Ziquarra capabilities? Perhaps he should be grateful there were no more surprises.

The bodies were still warm. Snow became transparent as it landed on their faces, as if they still fought his designs. But now they were lifeless, he could use Tsemkar to stack them beside those Daric had dispatched earlier, and cover them with the same level of snow. Then the site must be cleaned and tracks erased before he could head further north.

If one of them had thought to alert the final outpost, he'd best be prepared to fight again.

A quick excursion told him what he needed to know. The area around the final gate was clear, the expected storm imminent.

An extra level of cold assaulted him as he stepped through. He remained motionless as Daric had directed, until he could find the alarm, or alarms, and disarm them.

Frozen snow scoured his face. He turned his back and covered his nose and mouth with a scarf while his senses poked carefully about. Daric's blizzard-protecting eye-wear was somewhat successful, but had a tendency to fog up.

Encircling the site was a single sophisticated loop, fortunately one of the designs Daric had schooled him about. He followed the trace, careful not to touch more than one thread at a time, and inserted a mitigator large enough for him to fit through.

His footfall crunched lightly as he turned to repair his handiwork and reset it. Then he tackled the second alarm which was less than two boot-lengths away and even stronger. It needed a delicate touch, and he was pleased with himself when it too was breached. Beyond it was nothing but open snow.

Broken light flickered dimly from the small valley over the rise where the Ashik encampment was situated. He could almost feel its warmth, but he resisted the instinct to scan its occupants and continued up the shingle toward the headland around the bay where he hoped to find shelter of sorts.

Walking against the wind, every step became a battle of its own. The cold ate at him like a living thing. Wind screamed in his ears. Without Daric's eye-shields, he was certain his eyeballs would have frozen. He scanned the path ahead carefully, a trick Lady Andel had taught him, but every rock or uneven surface must be negotiated with care and slowed him further.

He was almost on top of the rockface before he actually saw it looming through the storm. In the icy lee of a narrow crevasse he paused to take stock, and after a brief look around, conceded this might be the best he could do. His first attempt at a window failed, but the second was successful, and relief from the wind was instant.

He spread an emergency shelter beneath the transparent charm, and once he was sure no light could escape to betray his presence, he ignited a small globe.

Drifts of slick sea-weed piled like frozen tentacles on the back of the fissure. Small life sang from it, sluggish and disinterested.

He laid a waterproof blanket over the snow and frozen shingle, then set a large fire-pot atop a tripod of stones. When a confident flame licked its edges, he arranged himself in the most comfortable position possible, covered himself in bed-roll and blankets and prepared to leave his body.

The message Malena had given to Daric … and Daric to him … was a small parcel in his mind. He didn't have to understand it, he just had to find Saphella of Hermes and pass it on.

The sensation of Ziquarra was a strange one, as if his outer form was an item of clothing he simply stepped out of. He looked back at it before committing to the search. The sealed space seemed secure and warm enough, but if anything went wrong, if his body grew too cold, there would be no returning. What if he never saw his own child, never saw Daric again, he asked himself, or Sari, or Huldar … ? Emotional weight increased with every name he recited. His spirit sagged, unable to leave. Fake death was bad enough. He was not ready for the genuine event. But his friends would most likely die, and himself with them if his mission was not completed.

With that in mind, he firmed his intention and shed the sadness, leaving it behind with his body.

Saphella!

Darkness surrounded him. He brought to mind the light in her pale golden hair, her unusual, crystal blue eyes, the smell of her skin and its feel beneath his fingertips … despite the intensity of his love for Daric, he found he'd forgotten nothing.

Saphella of Hermes!

He freed himself to the call and let mind and memory carry him. Distance was immaterial …

Saphella, he whispered, and suddenly, there she was.

She looked up from a client at the table. *Casco? You are Ziquarra?*

A clever retort was a luxury he had no time for. *Please,* he said. *I have a message you must deliver for me.* Already the strain was telling. *I can't hold this for very long.*

He felt her attach to his essence. An enormous sense of relief filled him as the psychic bundle was transferred. Whatever happened, now they had a chance.

I will come to you, she said. *I have nearly finished here.*

He left her with a sense of thankfulness and let himself return.

The crevasse seemed dimmer than when he'd left it, and the fire had nearly gone out, but the thrill of survival after such an epic excursion helped his body warm more quickly. Saphella's connection remained as a miniscule thread through the endless darkness, and he smiled. He doubted anyone but a Ziquarran master could detect it. He'd forgotten how intuitive she was.

Carefully at first, he got to his knees, put fuel on the fire and set a pot to boil, then retrieved a snack-pack and emptied it of honey-cakes. Hopefully, Saphella would contact him before too long. The plan was for him to leave as soon as he was able, however, the storm outside had strengthened alarmingly. The window was proof against it, but couldn't stop sudden draughts that made the fire flicker and the roof-leather creak. In a guilty moment, he tried to sense Daric, but he seemed to be asleep. He remembered blood pouring from his scalp. Not serious, he'd said … but why did he feel nothing? He tried the sigil. Perhaps Delemät was there and he was in deep hiding? He withdrew his probe and tried not to worry. Daric may have tried to contact him while he was absent – in which case he'd have no idea.

He hunched by the flames and sipped his tea. Cold pressed through the rocks and his breath steamed despite his proximity to the heat.

At last he felt a tell-tale pressure on his mind, but it was Saphella, not Daric.

Casco of the Uri'madu? One awaits communication.

He smiled at her playful formality, and opened himself to their communion.

Précises of the past few years flashed between them. It seemed she was still serving the Kareski and considered somewhat of a specialist, but on Hesh now rather than Giahn.

Without revealing too much of their current situation, Casco reiterated the importance of the message, stressing its urgency and the need for complete secrecy.

Bein nary well acieved, ja, she said with a smile. *Way wishin ye'd kennin un neider fore … bin starry, sho la.*

He nodded. *Dreamin naught but hale an gliden great silvery wings o'fetch. Bein so?*

She smiled again. *Naught be changing wid un. Heart yet beatin pure an fera. An disn lad, Daric Ja? Starry fella. Ben true friend and sackin strong!* Her silvery laugh eased that particular tension from his mind. *Bein home soon, ja?*

Hopin, he said. *Hopin true.*

With a last, loving touch, he let their contact go. The ether was empty again.

The weather outside had not abated, but Daric's silence worried him and he could not stay. With a last look at the glowing fire, he replaced his mitts and head-scarf, donned his warmest jacket and propelled himself into the ferocious winds outside.

Pure and wild, Saphella had called him. He looked into the storm and almost laughed aloud. Was this how he appeared to her?

Where is he?

I - I don't know, sir.

"There were traces - tracks leading to here." The captain indicated the remains of the shelter. "This is where he was holed-up - or so we thought. Took us a while to breach the screens. We found a few spots of blood, and more over there."

"His blood?"

The captain nodded. "Baros sliced his head, but not enough to kill him."

Delemät stalked toward the aberrant spatter. "And what did you find here?" There was something about the space ahead, but he couldn't quite make sense of it.

"Nothing, sir. We found nothing."

"He must be here!" He scowled into the distance. "This is the only gate he could use. The next nearest is one hundred and sixty miles south-east, and I doubt even an ecologist would hike that!"

"There's another, four hundred due south," the captain said.

"If I need your input, I'll ask for it! Delemät snarled. "Find him! … Of course, I'm assuming he didn't double back on you dim-wits and get to the comms window despite your astonishingly effective efforts?"

"No," the captain stated confidently. "Troops stationed there at all times, as ordered. Alarm set. No one passed."

He studied the speaker. At least that much was true. Their resistance must have scared him off. The Enna - he assumed it was Daric Enna, was injured and could not have gone far, but under these conditions he could have fallen and died and they'd never find a body.

He flinched as a presence flickered over him. The guild had been forbidden access by Imperial decree. There were no Ziquarra among the host or the Uri'madu - wherever they were; so who would breach that embargo? The energy hinted to him of that sly old Ziquarrudjan, Ulisharu of Trianog, and his scowl deepened. She was not bound by the Hermes code. No one had the right to live that long. Generations of secrets in one, withered body.

His Ashik milled around and tried to seem busy, but there was nothing to be gained by searching further. The perpetrator had failed. … And what did it matter what the old spider saw? A few Ashik hunting in the snow? Some miners at work?

“Enough!” he ordered. “Return to your stations. Expect reinforcements within the hour.” It would give them something to do for the next eight days before the comms opportunity was over. Then it would be a matter of throwing all available resources into finding the Uri'madu.

Driving snow covered Casco’s tracks as he slogged toward the portal, but he’d travelled only a short way before a brief chime warned him it had been activated. Normal farsight showed him four fresh guards stationed around it.

“Shit!” he murmured. Should he wait? Surely they would not stay out in this? They looked inward to the portal rather than out toward him, but he could see was no way to get to it A fresh gust knocked him sideways. He decided to go back to the shelter.

By morning, the guards were nowhere to be seen, and the storm had passed. He donned his most cautious screens, but although he managed to get near, twenty paces out from the portal site he almost triggered a new alarm.

A squinted appraisal showed him six more, and none of them the same as the two he’d disabled the day before.

AN ANSWER TO THE CALL

In Ambo, the principle city of Hesh, spring sun beat down on packed market stalls ringed by tall buildings and stylish homes. Although allocated to House Nhadu only eight hundred years ago, Hesh had already developed a reputation for its artists and crafters, talents the Nhadu excelled in.

Down a quieter alley, Shamkarun Anu of Maatu let his fingers push beneath the luxurious pelt of a snow bear. His lips twitched into a dreamy smile as he imagined his lover's face framed in its silver-tipped glory, or on the floor of their hidden villa, lying in the glow of the fire …

Anu noticed the Hermes approach at some level. The messenger's pale head bobbed from view then rose again, but silken fur nestled around his long fingers, and his vivid imagination had taken wing.

To Shamkarun Anu, First of Maatu, a message requires your attention, the Hermes said, and bowed again.

Anu's brow lifted. This one was nothing if not determined. He shook his head for him to wait while he completed the purchase then led him to a quiet corner.

"My apologies," he said. "Should we find somewhere more private?"

The Hermes peered calmly toward the vast complex of the Navigator's Guild Hall.

Anu nodded and started back, retracing the Hermes path until he reached a rainbow striped tent decked out with ropes of nursery ornaments and children's toys and ducked behind it to take a short-cut. The messenger followed calmly in his wake, as if stepping over guy-ropes and rubbish in a dignified manner had been part of his no-doubt extensive training.

They emerged not far from the stone steps below the translation bays. Anu skirted round the bottom to a side door used by staff as entry to the kitchens.

The morning-tea atmosphere was one of chatter and exotic aromas. Anu walked unremarked, one tall, green-eyed navigator among many, and led the Hermes to a padded booth at the back, where they settled opposite each other. A faint blue light pulsed as the Hermes erected a screen – a traditional precaution, but Anu nodded appreciatively when a second, tighter configuration closed around them, neatly disguised by the first. It was difficult to stack screens from the outside in. This Hermes was no simple back-and-forth repeater.

May I begin, my lord Shamkarun Anu, first of Maatu?

Please! Anu said, then closed his eyes and waited.

From Shamkarun Malena of Maatu, the Hermes began, and Anu was surprised again. He hadn't heard from her for ages. *Please come to me cousin* the message continued. *As the wind in the grass we need your help. The Navigators Guild have the necessary information for you to Kattíst a chord.*

Besides Malena's private seal, the full content contained an expertly compressed packet of geographical information. Anu recognised his cousin's touch and quickly unravelled it, but the details concerned a planet he had no knowledge of.

He returned to the Hermes. *Kattíst a chord? Those are her exact words?*

The Hermes gave a single nod.

Alarm circled beneath Anu's perfectly schooled screens. For Malena to frame a plea in that way, her situation must be dire indeed. 'As the wind in the grass' was a phrase he had not heard they were very young. Then, it had been code for secret excursions and disobeying of rules. Was this some sort of elaborate game?

Before he could think how he should reply, the Hermes bowed again.

The whereabouts of the sender are unclear, my Lord, and the need for continued secrecy, paramount. The path was indirect. No reply is possible at this time.

Anu nodded, "Thank you Hermes. I trust I need not ask for your respect."

The Hermes bowed with correct deference and delivered the ritual reply. "Confidence is maintained, my Lord Anu, First of Maatu. It is the honour of my House to do so."

Anu watched as the white-robed messenger was reabsorbed into the food-hall crowd. Noise and colour faded from his attention as he calculated the adjustments he must make to his plans.

Charäel would be cross, but their bear-skin adventures would have to wait … and his crew deserved a well-earned break, tired, as he was, from a series of tight translations. He realised he was still holding the pelt, and with a last, regretful touch relinquished it to Qalān.

Mael, he said privately. *Could I have a moment?*

Of course! the Guild Lord's replied. His sending communicated a feeling of relief and included the notion of a mountain of paperwork – no doubt only slightly exaggerated, and an image of Belät Gok of the basket weaver's guild. *You're the perfect excuse. Five minutes and she'll be gone.*

Anu passed Belät Gok in the corridor, not far from Mael's office, and acknowledged her overly elaborate bow with a polite nod.

The double doors opened to admit him.

"Dahj, I have a problem," he began.

Mael sat up, surprised by his informal entry. "What problem, Shak'ri? How can I help?"

"Kattíst. I need to go to her."

Mael tilted his head and gave a thin smile. "Kattíst is often a problem."

"I need to know where she is." He shared the full message with the Guild-Lord, since she had said he must in order to find out where she was.

"On 'Went'," Mael said. "Half way through a lengthy Imperial contract."

"Went?" he frowned. "Strange name."

"Beyond the Belt," Mael explained. "Elliptical orbit, long one. It's reached the zenith of its habitable phase and will freeze again over the coming months. Anyone stranded there would face certain death." He crossed the room to a tall cabinet, whispered a short song, and withdrew a small wooden box from one of the myriad drawers. Inside the container were several quartz crystals beside an obviously empty slot. "I'm surprised she managed to get a message to you. The place is only able to be contacted for a brief time in its entire cycle … around about now. But several weeks ago I had a visit from Delemät Ashik."

Anu's eyes opened wider. "He took the crystal?"

Mael closed the box. "Warned me not to attempt contact. Imperial decree."

"Really?" Anu felt his head begin to tilt.

"Yes. However Kandät Enna managed to get some information to me - very circumspectly of course. Most disturbing. I would have dismissed it, except he is the only navigator besides Malena herself to have made the journey to Went … as yet; and as you know, he is not given to exaggeration."

Anu waited. Whatever it was, it seemed Mael needed time to choose his words.

"Malena is pregnant," he said at last.

"What!?"

"This she had already told me, again through Kandät."

"Who's the unfortunate one?" Anu said sarcastically. "And why keep it secret?" He stood up. The view from the window barely registered. "Married? I thought she rejected the Enna – whatever his name was. That's what I heard!"

"She did reject him," Mael snapped. "You may not realize, but that was the reason she was sent to Went in the first place – to go some way towards patching up Imperial ill-will toward our House."

Anu leaned forward. "I couldn't take my father's place! How could anyone work alongside that ..." He spun away and began to pace the room. "I don't blame father for bowing out, but I can't be an aide – a general for Breath's sake? I'm a navigator! Look what he did, has done, to the Kareski, and that's just one thing. There are so many others! He's forgotten who he is, thinks he *is* El!"

"Calm down!" Mael said strongly. "This is not about you, your father, or anyone else but your cousin."

Anu looked away, ashamed of his outburst and the heat in his face.

"Sit." Mael leaned back. He motioned to the chair. "Please."

A few moments later, when his emotions had stabilised, he bowed in apology and sat as his uncle had requested.

The gaze Mael returned was businesslike and not unsympathetic ... but there was an uncharacteristic edge to his haze. The more carefully Anu looked, the more worried he became. Something troubled his uncle deeply indeed. He braced himself. What could be more important than House Maatu's ongoing troubles with the Imperium? His suspicion was confirmed as Mael gestured additional screens into place.

You must speak of this to no-one, he said at last. *I must have your promise.*

I promise, Anu assured him. Mael's switch to a very private thought-mode added an unexpected layer of solemnity, and again, he wondered what it was he was about to hear.

Kattíst is not married, Mael said at last.

Anu almost smiled, but his uncle was not given to joking. *She must be!* There could never be Blessing without the exchange of a marriage bond.

Mael shook his head. *I can assure you, she is not.*

Forgive me, but perhaps there has been a misunderstanding? Malena can be … overly dramatic at times.

Not this time. The news came to me from Kandät Enna, and he assured me it was true. He is deeply concerned, but dares not speak out. There are others who are pregnant in the same way … and it may even be that our own Empress has …

But she is definitely married!

Yes, but in need of a second Blessing.

How?

The properties of the egg of a certain species discovered by the Uri'madu – the ecologists assigned to the planet Went. They had their work cut out for them even without this!

Hybrid pregnancies? What do the healers say? Are they normal? Are they …

– Annangi? Mael shrugged. *We have no further reports. Went is closed to us – which worries me greatly. I have met and worked with Shamkarun Huldar, Sacred to Leth, the leader of the Uri'madu, and with his friend, Casco, his second-in-charge. Casco was a leader in the Kareski Rebellion and evacuation. Brave, kind, determined … You have not met him?*

Anu studied the image provided, and shook his head.

Both great people, Mael continued. *The team is one of the Guild's very best.* His gaze roved his office as if searching for answers. *We have no idea what's going on, how many pregnancies, or even if they still live; only that the gestation is much accelerated – as it seems with our Empress.*

Mael cleared a space in front of himself. Anu had the sense he lifted something heavy from beneath his book-shelf, and sure-enough, at his uncle's soft word, a plain calcite box regained visibility. He opened it, selected a clear grey double-pointed crystal and passed it across the desk.

Anu closed his palm around it. Vibration seeped into his hand.

Only Malena and Kandät have had access to the working chord, but what you have in your hand is old Senlätu Enna's original registration – may she rest sweetly in the Breath. A direct reference from collaboration with your friend, Ulisharu.

You want me to design a new chord?

Mael nodded. *See what you can do with it. There are few scryers as talented as yourself, Shak'ri, maybe none. Go there, save Malena and the Uri'madu as well, if you can, but make no mistake. This is no game. This is not just another chance for you to demonstrate your prowess as a navigator – an opportunity to show evidence to support your rejection of the Imperium, your father's wishes or the needs of your House. He will kill you if he finds out what you have done,* Mael said. *Squash you like a bug.*

Anu frowned. *Ishät?*

Mael nodded grimly. *Delemät Ashik is there already. I'm not sure which of them would relish the chance more.*

Anu closed his hand more tightly around the crystal and let its encoded information flood his system. The planet Went was far distant from Giahn, and the Djan'rū described as a possible access was no more than a possibility and had no relation to the configuration Malena described in her message. The proposed chord was a mere outline of ideas, but it had promise, and he could see ways already that could speed the journey.

You'll be on your own, Shak'ri, his uncle said. *If any should ask, our conversation was about a new Faythan contract – Tith to Arnika, which sadly you have refused.* He held out his hand for the crystal, and replaced it in the box which promptly vanished from sight. When it was back in place, and the dust rearranged to where it had been, Mael dropped the extra screens and leaned back in his chair. "I warned her that a Guild member with strength enough to meet her requirements would command considerably more coin," he said aloud. "She has conceded her offer may need revision, but I haven't heard back as yet."

"Faythans!" Anu rolled his eyes. "She would have known the costs." He shared a natural-seeming smile, then shook his head. "Always have to try. Tell her to get back to me when she's doubled her offer."

Anu returned to the refectory, picked up a meal and commandeered an office in the guild complex so he could examine the Enna's work without distraction. Within a few hours, the meal had gone cold. He'd fleshed the framework into a viable chord of translation, but it was morning of the next day before he'd streamlined it and made it singable.

He went for another meal and ate it this time – then a second. He'd need all his strength to hang the chord together and make it work, but with the right amount of focus, and only himself to transport, he estimated his time of arrival at three and a half, or four weeks allowing for the unexpected.

Once within the planet's vicinity, he planned to construct a way-station - a stationary envelope in Qalān, and attempt the rescue from there. Mael had also passed on Kandät Enna's warning about the planet's difficult and dangerous entry. If anyone else had said as much, he might have ignored them, but Kandät Enna had been his first mentor, and he knew him to be extremely powerful and experienced. If Kandät said it was bad, it was bad.

With a full stomach and ample supplies packed and ready, he settled down for his last sleep for quite some time. Did he have everything he'd need to cater for an unknown number of tiny infants? He doubted it - but hopefully their occupation of the waystation would be short.

The next morning, he messaged his spinners and crew-boss. They would find their pay at the Guildhall, and bonus enough to take a good long holiday. Beyond that, they shouldn't wait around for his return.

HOME

The cave was silent but for the occasional splash of a water-beast, and lit only by the bioluminescence of its native inhabitants.

Huldar kept watch over the portal, but couldn't help following the gliding trails of slugs as they crisscrossed between clusters of ceiling stars and hazy rock-jellies with long, phosphorous green tentacles – or were they roots? Even after a week of study, he couldn't decide. They seemed to fulfil the function of both.

This was the third 'night' he'd stood vigil. There had been no word from Daric, and he was beginning to worry, but even so, his eyes slowly drooped. Perhaps if he rested them, just for a moment …

He started from a convoluted dream when the portal chimed at last and Daric half fell into the cavern. Blood and worse seeped from an angry scalp-wound. Bleary eyes peered from a caked mask. Huldar rushed to his aid, but was too late to prevent his ungainly collapse.

Ubaid!

He felt the healer wake and flashed him an image.

"He did it," Daric murmured. "You are safe now … safer …"

Huldar bundled his head onto a soft pillow and threw a blanket over his shivering body. "The message?" he gently prompted.

Daric nodded. "So brave …" Tears left pale lines through the blood on his cheeks.

Ubaid ran forward and knelt at his side. "We need to wash that blood off," he said sharply.

Huldar ran to get hot water.

"Daric! Stay with me!" the healer murmured. He placed the fingertips of one hand on the assassin's bloody forehead while the other passed over the oozing wound in his head. "What happened?"

"… Got me," Daric mumbled. "Distraction … I hid. Passed out. Chasite ended. So cold …"

Huldar laved his face with warm water, but Ubaid signaled the scalp wound so he turned his attention there. Dried clots slowly softened in the water and yielded to Ubaid's song. Huldar winced as skillful fingers parted blood-caked hair to expose a section of pearlescent skull. There was a distinct cut into the bone. Lines of shatter ran from it.

"You've had a go at this already," Ubaid said quietly to his patient. "Good work …" but the look he gave Huldar was far from confident. He turned back to Daric. "You'll have to let me in now, or I can't fix it … please?"

Huldar held the bowl and waited. Crimson-stained droplets fell slowly from the cloth in his hand.

Ubaid's expression grew more distant. "Please, Daric. I won't hurt you …"

Eventually, he shook his head. "I don't want to move him, but he won't let me in."

"Alis?"

Ubaid nodded reluctantly.

"He would never hurt her. You know that."

The healer exhaled. "Granted, but in this state? He doesn't know what he's doing."

"We can't lose him!" Huldar said.

"Are you saying his life is more important than my wife's? Our Blessing's?"

"No, of course not!" Huldar said. "But he feels safe with her. She is aware of the dangers and can protect herself."

Still Ubaid hesitated. Then there was a heavy tread behind them, and Huldar was surprised to see Alis already on her way. One hand held her immense belly, the other was held wide for balance. Ubaid flinched at the naked anger on her face.

"I am not your possession to be told whom I can heal and who not!" She hobbled closer. "Get out of my way. Help me get down!" she said crossly.

Ubaid stood hurriedly and held out his arm.

She smoothed her palm over Daric's forehead. The intricate Mark on the back of her hand flared strongly. "There is infection here," she said sharply. "As you no doubt noticed."

Her head lowered toward Daric. Her eyes closed. With almost imperceptible changes, his features softened. After a long moment, she nodded and waved her hand for Ubaid to take it.

"Shh ..." she murmured, and clasped her husband's hand tightly. "This will hurt. Are you ready?" She nodded at Ubaid. His Shamkar pulsed then steadied. The tone of his voice was thin and delicate, and very clear.

Daric's screams began almost immediately – a terrible sound Huldar had never imagined he would hear.

What's happening? Andel asked.

It's Daric. He sent a compressed visual of what had happened.

He will be alright, she said stoutly. *He always is.*

Huldar nodded, but this time he was not so sure.

"Encephalitis," Ubaid muttered.

"I can see that," Alis shot back. It seemed she had yet to forgive, but the look she gave Ubaid next was odd indeed.

Her partner shrugged.

They continued their work.

A small crowd gathered at the foot of the track, held back by Andel and Sari. Huldar sent her a smile of thanks, but it switched off as Daric's body began to shudder.

Ubaid's song paused, but the Mark on his hand brightened to near incandescence. "Hold him steady," he said. "But be careful! An assassin's muscle memory? There's no telling what he'll do. Touch him as little as possible." He gave Alis a worried glance. "Any contact may provoke a reaction."

He fixed Huldar in his gaze and gave a nod. *Are you ready?*

Huldar nodded to say he'd understood, but had little idea of what he should do.

More cautiously this time, Ubaid began to sing again.

Daric's arm moved so quickly, Huldar almost didn't see it. He managed to stop the bunched fist a hair's breadth from the side of Alis' head. She continued as if nothing was amiss.

Slowly, he pushed Daric's arm back to his side. Daric's eyes opened and rolled blindly back and forth. He muttered and his left hand sprouted a knife. Briefly, Huldar noted the neat bandage around his forearm, then with the speed of a striking snake, the blade came at his eye.

He dodged it, but too slowly.

Blood trickled down the side of his neck.

He struggled to hold the knife away. The stun charm came from him instinctively, the same one he'd use on any aggressive creature, and for a wonder, Daric's arm was halted. But his eyes bulged alarmingly as he fought.

"Calm him!" Ubaid said.

Huldar sang a soothing chain.

Daric still strove against him, but his efforts gradually weakened.

"It's me, Alis," the Naghari crooned. "You are safe. You are among friends." She stroked his forehead lovingly.

"Nearly there," Ubaid said softly.

"Shh, little one, brave soul, shh now," Alis murmured. "It is me, Alis. I am with you …"

"Casco?" Daric murmured. "Where is Casco?"

"I am with you for now," she said. It was as if she spoke to a child.

Daric moaned and despite Huldar's song, tried to get to his feet. "He is trapped," he said. "I must go to him!"

Huldar pushed back as gently as he could.

Alis glanced at her husband. Ubaid frowned, but whatever passed between them remained private.

"Shh …" Alis soothed again. "We will go there soon. First, you must recover."

"No time!" Daric cried brokenly. "He is …"

But whatever he was about to add was lost as his eyes rolled back and his body went limp.

Huldar looked at Alis then Ubaid, but it was as if this was what they were waiting for. Ubaid's song increased in speed and intensity, while both their hands pulsed with light.

Finally, their Marks dimmed.

Daric lay pale and unconscious between them.

Ubaid lifted the bandaged arm then went to the other which was actually scarred and examined it briefly before returning it to his side. Again, the healer's comments remained uncharacteristically private.

Huldar frowned, but if Alis and Ubaid had information they were reluctant to share, he was sure they had good reason.

"He will sleep now," Alis said. "He must be kept warm. No loud noises."

"He will recover?"

Her head wavered from side to side. "And if he does, there may be complications. His brain is injured, Huldar. His speech may be impaired, and his movement to some extent. He will be very weak for some time, and use of Tsemkar will cause extreme pain. He must be kept quiet." She turned to her husband. "Best tend that cut on his face."

His skin crawled as Ubaid began work on the wound Daric had given him.

There is something you should know, the healer said carefully.

Alis nodded. *The bond is unusual but – Daric is married, still married – to Casco.*

Huldar glanced at Daric's bandaged arm, then at the other. How to make sense of this?

Casco lives? he asked.

Yes, it seems so.

His heart began to sing. *Then I was right! … But I didn't dare ask! How could they do this to us! … And Sari's child told her the truth.*

She was right to trust, Alis said, *but Daric and Casco must be allowed to reveal themselves in their own time.*

Casco must know how dire his husband's situation is, Ubaid added, *but for whatever reason, can do nothing to help. We fear greatly for his safety, but until we know more, we should not risk intervention.*

Huldar nodded understanding. Whatever plan the two of them had concocted, it was bound to be convoluted. Everything with Daric always was. But he was usually successful.

"Help me here," Ubaid said aloud. "Roll him onto this blanket." He produced two poles from Qalān, and when Daric was in place, secured the blanket on either side. He helped his wife to her feet, then indicated for Huldar to take the other end of the stretcher. "Careful, now. Let's get him to bed."

CASCO

Casco kept his presence high, as close to the cavern's ceiling as he could be and still in it. He was undetectable to those below, but had to strain to see what was going on. There was no cold where he was, and no physical pain, but to watch Daric's struggle for survival was agonizing. He could feel his confusion through their bond; experience his frustration as if it was his own. All he could do to help was offer encouragement and continue to love, but that seemed so little.

An inner alarm told him he was reaching a limit of endurance.

With a firm will, he forced himself to reinhabit his aching body. It was not easy, but his technique had improved with practice.

A small globe slowly came to life. Its warm yellow light brought his surroundings into focus. Snow had covered the leathers again - they bowed beneath its weight. He needed to clear the air-vent, but his mind seemed thick and heavy.

That's because the vent needs clearing, he told himself, and he knew it was true. But he was so tired. The effort seemed beyond him. Maybe it would be better if he truly was dead.

Stop feeling sorry for yourself and clear the vent.

His lips twitched into a tiny smile, remembering how grating he'd found that upper class Tiamäti accent - before he and Daric had met. With a few tiny movements, his lover's expression would become almost pitying, as if he wondered how an organism so devoid of intelligence could manage to survive at all.

Just a few more minutes, he said to him. *I need to get warm.*

Now! Daric-in-his-imagination snapped.

He sighed and gathered his wits. Soon, a wash of icy fresh air fell against his face. He shivered, but it forced him to move.

A white cloud steamed from his lips. Was it the divine Breath of El?

Just ordinary breath, he answered himself.

He checked the vent again and extended the stasis charm. It was a risk, just as the dome had been. If anyone thought to examine this area, they may detect it.

Enlivened by a dose of fresh air, he conjured a small flame, then fed it with a few bits of dried driftwood and sea-weed. Soon, his small pot bubbled above it, and a hot mug - painful at first - warmed his hands.

How many days had passed?

He counted back five, but couldn't be sure. Each day was an interminable blur.

Would the Ashik never leave? In four more, if he was correct, the window would close. Maybe then, if he was still alive …

Loneliness slumped over him - cold and heavy like an ice-slush breaker. Tears chilled his cheeks. What did he care? There was no one to see. Daric had regained consciousness days ago, Casco had seen it from above, but his beautiful, once limber body now labored to walk. A visit to the latrine was pure embarrassment. He'd tried speaking to him, but his injury … had damaged his ability to communicate.

He knelt before the fire, bowed his head and closed his eyes and filtered what he had witnessed in the cavern through his mind one more time. Every tiny detail was available to him - events fully reconstructed in the virtual reality of a memory far too acute to be his own. Time could be slowed or even stopped, viewpoints altered. His ability seemed almost supernatural, most likely the influence of his Archerra, although it did not cause his Mark to warm.

Again and again he examined Daric's movement. When compared to the past few days, it was definitely more confident. Ubaid supported his elbow. The healer seemed pleased, but his Mark glowed the entire time they were in contact. It was just as well he hadn't tried to speak to Daric at that time - the healer could have sensed his presence.

Sari was a constant at Daric's side, caring for him in every way she could. Her presence was both a relief and further torture. If she came to term while he was still trapped, who would help her through the birth?

Unable to bear it any longer, he opened his eyes and let his vision be taken by the lick of small flames and the glow of the coals.

Sari did not deserve abandonment. He put his hands over his eyes and rubbed his face hard, as if the action could ease his predicament. In only four more days, the communication window would close, the Ashik would leave, and he would be free to return. She believed him dead - they all did; but when the way was clear, he would return as he and Daric had planned. He would tell them what they'd done and why.

But what if the birthing began before that? he asked himself. What then? What if she, and or their Bless, died - because neither of her trusted others were there? 'Trusted' was the word that tortured him most. Sari had chosen him; the first and only male he had trusted with her body. She had not had any idea it would make her pregnant - how could she? Yet, she'd continued to love him. Even when he'd ignored his responsibility - actually made her ask him to be her birth assistant … she still loved him. And now she gave Daric the same unstinting regard.

His fists ached from being clenched.

He knew he should eat - keep his strength for further excursions, and just to stay warm, but the thought of food in his mouth made him feel sick.

What would Daric do?

The answer was a dull pain in his head. He needed sleep. He needed action.

"For Breaths sake!" he yelled. "I can't even stand up straight!"

Daric! He poured all of his need and longing into the call.

Snow creaked and fell with a small, dull smash.

There was no further sound except his breathing, raw and ragged with emotion.

He threw himself back to the ground and crawled into his bed-roll. *Daric,* he whimpered. So much for the promise of never being apart. Even his sigil had gone dead. He pulled his blankets over his head and dreamed of being warm and asleep.

Casco? A familiar voice invaded his slumber. *Casco, wake up. I know you're there.*

It took him some time to realize the voice was real - but it was not Daric's.

Casco, respond, please.

Ubaid? he replied. *Is this a dream?*

No. Listen to me. I know you and Daric are married. The presence of your bond told me you were alive. Alis and Huldar also know, and Sari has never believed you dead. You must return now, if you can. Her birth process is beginning.

I'm trapped, he replied with a rush. It felt so good to communicate.

Are you hurt?

No, but Ashik guard the portal night and day. Delemät paid them a visit just the other day. We killed several of them, earlier, me and Daric, and they want revenge.

They're Ashik, Ubaid said. *Of course they do. Can you see no way past them? Daric is …*

I know how Daric is.

His words fell into silence.

Of course you do, Ubaid said quickly. *I am sorry. He will recover, I'm fairly sure of it – just a matter of time. His higher mind is comatose … healing … Has he spoken to you?*

No. Casco found it hard not to cry.

I found you when you called to him.

You heard?

Felt it and followed the trace. I wouldn't have interfered but for Sari.

Casco's face was wet with tears. The pain in his chest had grown until he could hardly breathe. He tried to continue his conversation, he wanted to so badly, but no words would come.

Take a moment, Ubaid said. *I know this must be hard for you. I won't leave you, not now that I've found where you're hiding. We've missed you so much. I have missed you.*

He took deep, regular breaths and tried to control his emotions as Daric had shown him.

Will they welcome me back? he managed at last.

No doubt of it! Ubaid assured him. *Of course, there will be anger. They have been deeply hurt. But when they realize why you did it and what you and Daric have achieved, they'll understand. Even now, they don't know about the message.*

But you do, Casco said.

Huldar asked Daric about it when he got back, Ubaid explained. *I put the clues together. And why else would you be stuck at the North Pole? Now, how can we get you here? Have you thought of using your Mark?*

How?

You can weave the abilities of others. You don't have to have the talent yourself. Perhaps you could link with Huldar?

Casco's mind whirled with possibilities. His first action should be to neutralize the guards ... *A sleep charm. Huldar told me about it. Banga gave it to him. He said it would knock out a kadderin.*

Good! Ubaid's tone was encouraging.

It's important that no one knows I have been here, he explained. *They must think they've prevented us from getting through. If I could get close to the guard on duty – there's only one there for a short time between shifts – I could knock him out and he might believe he just dozed off ... but what of the next portal and the Ashik there?* His spirits plummeted again.

We should link you up with Huldar, yes?

He knows?

He was overjoyed, Ubaid assured him. *Could hardly believe it when I told him. He wants you back, Casco, with all his heart.*

Ubaid's contact dimmed while he spoke to Huldar.

Casco's heart raced. What should he say? He remembered how sad Huldar been at the funeral. How he'd tried to comfort him and almost given himself away. How could he ever be forgiven? Casco shook his head. How could he forgive himself?

Huldar's anger hit him like a wall. *You complete and utter arsehole! Breathless kalla!* he yelled. *How could you do that to me? To us? Have you any idea what you've put us through?*

I ...

And you were there, watching, weren't you! Huldar cried.

I ...

Why? By El's great design – by the Ineffable Song of All, why?

Casco found himself crying again. *I'm so sorry. I had to. With my Mark and Delemät Ashik … It was the only way. … It was hard for me too. I've been alone all this time. I could only watch you from a distance. And here in the snow …*

His voice faltered as the wall fell and Huldar's familiar presence flooded into long-empty ties. With it came the truth of the love they felt for each other but also the agony of loss. Now he saw it from the inside and understood – no apology could mend that. Things could not be as they were.

What can I do?

Huldar's anger abated. *You have already done it, my friend. Just continue to breathe. That will be more than enough. The rest will take care of itself. And now, for Sari's sake, we must hurry. How are you situated? What do you need?*

Casco gave him a précis of what had happened – Daric's audacious plan and its execution. Then his own lonely mission and consequent position, trapped on the other side of the portal.

It's a lot to take in, Huldar said quietly. *And your new style of situational analysis … breathtaking.*

I thought about that sleep charm Banga showed you, the really powerful one?

Huldar gave a virtual nod.

Will it work on two separate individuals at the same time?

Maybe. Huldar paused as if thinking. *Can you enhance it with your Mark?*

Maybe, Casco echoed. *If we wait another hour or so there's just one guard. For some reason, the other is always a bit late – but he'll be fresh and alert.*

And Ashik are trained to detect screens, Huldar added.

Casco imagined the approach. *If I'm careful, I'm sure I can get close. Just like stalking any other creature – just have to time it right. But can Sari wait that long?*

Ubaid? Huldar asked.

She is still in the early stages, Ubaid replied, *but hurry just the same. She is the first, but others will follow and we can't be sure how the birthing will progress … Are you sure you should risk this?*

He tried to think, but Sari's need overcame all. His body ached with the desire to be home. *I'll get ready to go, then take a quick look. Ziquarra,* he reminded them. *I'm getting quite good at being unnoticed. Their roster is somewhat flexible. We have to take the chance when it comes.* He paused. *Huldar, can you sing the portal to exit at a different location? The current exit is as heavily guarded as this one, but the alternative is the one you made with Duvät Gok.*

I'd almost forgotten!

I was thinking about those early days and it came back to me. Casco flashed him a memory of his frost-burnt face, Duvät Gok in his lap, both near dead from exposure.

Huldar smiled. *You saved me.*

We never used that particular portal again. Casco's heart raced. *And it'd be rough for sure …*

And very dangerous!

Can you remember the song?

Huldar hesitated. *Any mistake would be disastrous.*

Maybe we've reached that point.

I've just got you back!

We have to try, Casco told him. *The need is now. I'm no use to anyone stuck here. Already dead, remember?*

That's not funny.

The spectre of Lind passed between them, and he saw the similarities in their plight – except Lind had no hope of rescue. All he had to do was endure … and at least he'd been able to do things, see things. Was he ready to die that way?

Can you remember or not? His tone was more abrupt than he intended.

I'll know when we get there, Huldar replied.

Then that will have to do. If you can't, be ready for the guards on the other side. Four of them. If we knock a couple out with the sleep charm, I'll fight the others off as best I can and make a run for it.

He began to gather his belongings. Huldar's internal battle was his own affair. He had to leave now. Not for the first time, he wished he hadn't dropped the invisible cloak. It was somewhere by the second gate, but to plan on finding it in the snow with armed Ashik trying their best to kill him was idiocy. When the guards had gone, he'd go back and search. Ariben would kill him if he didn't find it – or worse still, hate him forever.

He lay back in readiness to leave his body and assess the situation with the portal guards. His Mark spread warmth through cold skin. Huldar's mind was connected yet distant, as if his friend had become an implement to be used – and in a way, he had. The Archerra warmed further as he prepared to do something he'd not tried before - integration of Ziquarra with virtual real-time observation. If successful he could keep a safe distance and wouldn't have to strain to see.

A deep breath cooled his lungs then was exhaled, and with it, his spirit floated free. He concentrated on his proposed path to the headland. Time slowed as minute details filled his mind - each hump and drift, each wind-blown snow-flake was visible. When he came to the headland, this new vision revealed the advantages and pitfalls of every potential path. He chose one, and continued toward the portal where two bored Ashik, swathed in fur and leather, faced each other.

One stamped his feet up and down in an effort to keep warm.

They looked tired. The snow beneath their feet was dirty and bruised. He glanced sunward. The shift would be over in less than half an hour.

"Think he'll come back?" the stamping guard said offhandedly.

His comrade shrugged. "Who? The boss?"

"Not him," the stamper said. "Sent his report back home and done with it. Too cold for royalty up here!" He looked back and forth over his shoulders. "I'm talking about the assassin," he hissed.

Casco had seen enough. It was time to retreat, but at the mention of Daric, he hesitated and let his spirit form drift closer.

The other guard snarled. "If he does, he'll get what's coming."

Stamper shook his head. "Can't be killed. Baros got him fair in the brain-box!" He acted out a forceful blow as if his sword was in his hand. "Didn't drop him."

"You saw it? … Didn't think so. Baros! Song sung a bit too loud."

"Were blood on his sword! Saw that clear enough."

"Grazed him," the skeptic said. "An he's not been back …"

Casco realized he'd come too close and stayed very still. This was something he could tell Daric when his mind came out of hibernation - how his myth had grown!

"… Yet!" the skeptic added. He watched his fellow's expression for a moment then laughed. "Scabby Enna won't be back, you fool. Waste of Breath. But if boss comes back and finds you slackin off - I'd be more worried about that."

Scabby Enna? Casco felt the words, rich in derision, resonate as they travelled through the frigid air. Waste of Breath? Pure scorn tightened the speaker's facial muscles. Lifted one edge of his upper lip.

Casco's anger slipped his screens.

The Ashik rubbed his neck and looked up. Casco's enhanced vision was filled with the soldier's suspicious gaze. Without thought, he leapt to the relative safety of his body. A flurry of snow settled around him. The sky above shone down a merciless blue. His mark was so hot it almost burned.

Across the snowfield the guards still peered skyward. One still rubbed at his neck.

Screen, quickly! Huldar said. *What was that? What's happened?*

Casco lay flat on the snow and let Huldar's song camouflage him. His heart raced. How had he ended up here? He steadied his breathing and replayed his observation of the past few minutes. The study of potential routes, the headland path, the Ashik's discussion, his rage … then his retreat. That particular sequence was a little more difficult to unravel, and even more difficult to understand.

It seems that when I fled, instead of returning to my body, my body came to me, he said slowly.

It what?!

I was using my Archerra to help me observe, he explained. *It was a new idea I had. I got a fright, tried to jump back into my body – and this happened.*

He glanced toward the guards again and was relieved to see them relaxed but vigilant.

What am I supposed to do now? he asked.

Follow the plan, Huldar replied. *There's little else we can do. Take over the screen …*

Casco examined the configuration. It was less a cover and more one that strongly discouraged observation. When he had the sequence cycling neatly he added a trail-erasing component and began his slow, crouched advance.

Fresh cover crunched beneath his gentle foot-falls. The trail he left was still just visible, but there was nothing he could do to reconstitute snowflakes to their original form.

Anxiety aside, he continued, with movements controlled and steady.

One of the Ashik looked his way. He stopped. His heart thundered so loud he wondered if the sound would betray him, but the guard's gaze moved on and Casco continued his slow trek forward.

He'd studied the alarms from afar. The first was easily disabled, then the next, but with each advance, the risk grew.

When the odor of unwashed guard tickled his nose, he paused. At last, he was close enough to close his eyes and let Huldar sing.

It was a delicate moment as the sleep charm began to insinuate itself beneath the Ashiks' personal defenses. Casco could feel its vibration running through his own head, but thankfully couldn't hear it. Gradually, the guard's eye-lids drooped.

One guard stumbled to his knees. His head sagged forward. The other somehow remained standing, face bowed to his chest.

The plan was working, but Casco couldn't help glancing in the direction replacements would come from.

The vibration stopped. *Is he asleep yet?* Huldar asked.

Everything was still. All he could hear was the guards' rhythmic breathing.

As Casco took his first step toward the portal, his heart-rate surged. The final two alarms were easier to tweak than their predecessors. He stepped through each gap in turn then pushed the flows back into their original form.

The portal hummed beneath him. His own head bowed as he waited. Would this be his last moment on Went?

Here goes, Huldar said.

The portal blurred and chimed. He stepped out into a steaming marshland. The ground beneath him shook alarmingly. Ash and sparks belched from a mountain in the not too distant ranges. The air smelled rotten.

He turned to view the escarpment and shed his furs for the first time in a week.

You did it! he said happily.

Of course!

He could feel Huldar's smile and knew his relief was shared. All that remained was to climb the cliffs unobserved and hope there was no guard on Central Basecamp.

After days of enforced rest, physical exertion was welcome, and he scaled the steep path to the plateau in record time. Just below the edge, he paused to take stock. Above was the field of standing stones. The nearby Djan'rū hummed heavily against his senses. He ducked as a wave of farsight passed by, then made a run for the stones.

He stopped in the shadow of a squat boulder and laughed to himself. He hadn't thought he'd welcome coolness again so soon.

A brief bout of farsight showed the camp was empty, and he gave a grim smile. With so much attention on the North, maybe the Ashik were spread a bit too thin.

He closed his eyes to better enjoy his release, but frowned as words came to him; *Father, hurry!* He cocked his head at their strangeness. Had he imagined them?

Ubaid has told me Sari's birth process proceeds more rapidly than expected, Huldar said. *It seems there are complications. You must hurry!*

Remnants of spring wild-flowers crunched as he climbed to his feet. He jogged toward the camp, but that strange voice stayed with him ... Father? It could only be his child! A heady mixture of excitement and dread filled him with fresh energy. He saw the east gate ahead and sprinted for it.

Two steps from safety, the gate shimmered and chimed. "The most corporeal light-spirit I've ever seen," Delemät Ashik said silkily.

Casco froze.

Delemät took a step closer. Every part of him reeked of malice. "And Marked? Astounding. Where are you going, little spectre? Would you mind if I came along?"

His Tsemkar flared.

Casco's Archerra answered with a blinding flash. The smell of ozone filled the air, and when he opened his eyes, he saw Huldar looking at him, right in front of him, eyes wide with astonishment.

"Casco?" he said hesitantly.

"Casco!" He turned to see Sari hobbling towards him. Her smile was enormous.

"He told me you would come," she said happily. It was as if she'd expected him. "Brought you here himself. Saved you from that monster – that dreadful person." She tilted her head as if listening to an inner voice. "Yes, yes, my darling. Of course!"

He frowned, but then the voice he'd heard at the campsite spoke to him again, and the mystery was confirmed. *Father, I will be … born?*

He touched Sari's face. "I have missed you so much …" He knelt and placed his hands against her belly.

The small voice came into his mind again … *I am afraid.*

"Afraid? I told him not to be," Sari said brightly. "I told him you would keep him safe, and Daric too, when he's able." She glanced quickly at Daric's tent - somewhere he dreaded to look. *But Delemät Ashik terrifies him,* she added privately.

"Terrifies me!"

She reached for his hand and held it firmly to herself. *Talk to him, Casco. Tell him it will be alright.*

Others of the Uri'madu had begun to arrive. He didn't want to look at them. He could hear Nachiel sobbing. Most seemed too astonished to speak. Malena rushed forward but Ubaid said something quite forceful and she backed down. Her haze was brittle with anger.

He shut them out and focused on Sari in the way Ubaid had taught him - her musculature, emotions, and sensations, then the small, separate awareness she contained. He found all in order, the child's position perfectly aligned, yet Sari struggled. Her face was slick with sweat. She gave a low moan and gripped his hand more tightly as a contraction clenched her abdomen.

Breathe, he said … *just breathe it through.*

Kira came forward, Here, let me …" and began to move her hands in healing passes across her lower back. "Shh," she said soothingly. "It will pass, and soon you will have a beautiful son to hold in your arms. Imagine that!"

But when the contraction was over, Casco was aware the baby had not moved. He could feel the little one's tiny heart racing. Fear clouded his infant's presence. It seemed their child was determined to stay safe in the womb.

He got to his feet, looked tenderly into Sari's gaze and saw her again as she'd been the day she'd asked, sweat-sheened face beneath the shade of her wide straw hat while she fended off a cloud of fluttering lizards. Now, as then, her eyes were huge and trusting, and this time he vowed he would not disappoint.

"Somewhere more private?" he asked her.

"More private?" She gave a weary smile and imaged the inside of her own tent.

As he took her elbow, the look Kira gave him was strange, even a little afraid. She reached out as if to touch him, then snatched her hand back.

"Just checking," she muttered, and returned to Sari. "I won't be far away."

"Far away." Sari nodded. "Thank you."

The Uri'madu parted to let them through. Their shuffled footsteps were the only sound. Fear and anger tainted the air, but there was also wonder, hope, and a welcome from some.

They'll get over it, Sari told him.

I hope so, he replied.

They moved slowly down the path between a row of tents. Daric's was set on the outskirts. He tried not to look, but he could feel Daric's presence and knew his husband's sleep was unnatural.

You should go see him, Sari said. *I'll be alright for a while.*

He have her elbow a gentle squeeze. *You two are my focus for the next little while.*

Sari smiled weakly, then returned his grip with a vengeance as another contraction began.

He stood in front of her and held onto her arms. She pushed her head against his chest.

"They're getting stronger," she gasped, "but he doesn't want to come. You have to speak to him. I've tried, but he is too afraid, and any comfort I offer makes him more determined to resist."

Casco frowned at her belly. "Have you told him you both could die?"

"Die?" She shook her head. "He has no concept of death."

He tried not to frown and kept her walking toward her tent. Although it wasn't far, every pace was considered and the journey seemed to take an age. He pushed aside the tent-flap just as another contraction ripped through her body. The pain was intense, but thanks to the birthing classes he could shunt it aside and continue his support.

When it was over, he helped her lower herself onto her bed and propped her up with thick cushions.

Talk to him, she said.

He nodded and put his hands against her belly. The small consciousness rushed to greet him.

Father!

You saved me, Casco said gently to him. *You brought me here. You wanted me to help, and I am so looking forward to holding you, loving you, watching you grow. You are our Blessing, but you must be born to the world for those things to happen. … Can you understand?*

There was silence. For a long moment he doubted a reply would come – but then … *It will hurt,* the baby said.

Casco was beyond surprised by the maturity of his son's word-making, but the flow seemed too natural to question. *Not as much as you think,* he said. *If you will let me, I can help you through the difficult bits.*

Bad things will happen.

Yes, they will, he countered, and wondered if they spoke of the actual birth process, or what might come after. *But there will be more good than bad, I'm sure of it.* He let his love trickle through the baby's natural defenses and smiled as antipathy dissolved and trust blossomed in its place.

Mother is scared.

Casco nodded. *Of course she is. Neither of you have been through this process before. You must allow it to happen.*

Did it happen to you?

He nodded again. *Yes it did and I survived. All creatures must be born in some way.*

This is different for me. I don't know how.

Just let her push … here comes one now. He took the baby's mind firmly in his own. *I will help you. Let yourself be moved …*

Sari cried out as the baby shifted. *Are you with me or him?*

Both of you! … Rest now until the next one. Everything is fine.

Fine? she snapped. *Easy for you to say!*

In the hours that followed, there was a small opportunity for Casco to take a break.

"Sang him to sleep," he explained when Ubaid noticed him outside the tent. "And Sari is between contractions. I just needed some air."

"I'd like to say that this is what every father goes through," Ubaid said to him, "but it isn't. Your son - all of our Blessings - are psychically and emotionally developed beyond anyone's expectations. You are doing an amazing job. We are all learning from your experience."

"Thanks," Casco said sourly. "You're assuming we'll survive."

"I hope so!"

The line was delivered with sincerity, but Casco could hear the wry under-thought, *One funeral is enough!*

"Lady Andel's process has begun," Ubaid continued, "and Gael and Rosheen are very close."

"Alis?"

"Soon. Very soon." He paused as if receiving a message, then said, "If you are able, after your son has been born - which I'm sure won't be long now," he added encouragingly, "could you visit some of the others?"

"Of course. If I can, I will." He shrugged, then rolled his neck to relieve some tension. "But they won't exactly be pleased to see me."

"A good opportunity for reconciliation." Ubaid gave a small smile. "I've been filling them in with what I know to be true. It won't be as bad as you think."

Casco turned back to the doorway as Sari's body prepared for a fresh contraction.

"Don't worry Casco," Ubaid said in parting. "You are doing a wonderful job."

Casco! Sari called.

I'm here, he told her. *Do you need to get up? Walk some more?*

Walk? I need to get this baby out of me is what I need!

He's on his way, he said patiently. *You're nearly there. And you're both doing so well!*

She looked up at him. he could see her exhaustion - feel it as if it was his own. *What if he hates me?* she said quietly. *What if I hold him, and he doesn't want me to be his mother?*

He wiped her face with a cooling cloth. *Why would that be?* he said tenderly. *He loves you already.*

Did he say so?

He wanted me here to protect you, because you needed help. Of course he loves you.

But all this pain I've put him through ...

He's handled it well, Casco assured her. *And he won't remember.*

What if he does?

Here it comes ... There was no more time to ponder. He held her arms again and let her brace against himself. She cried out, and with a mighty push, the baby moved to the very edge of the outside world.

Finally Casco saw the end of their struggle approaching. *Ubaid!* he called. *Help, please! I think I missed this particular class.*

He's coming! Sari cried. *Casco! I can't stop it! I can't!*

He knelt in front of her. *Put your hands on my shoulders!*

With a gush of fluids, their son was delivered into his hands.

He's here! he cried. He didn't care who heard.

Their son gave a cry of discomfort as his first breath filled his lungs, then opened his eyes and looked straight into Casco's. A vast energy passed between them, as if all of time was captured in this one instant. Casco gazed back at the child, overawed by the amount of love contained in this one small body. Tears flowed down his cheeks, dripped from his chin. How he wished Daric could be here.

Hurt, the baby said accusingly. *Hurts me.*

I'm sorry, Casco said. A smile warred with the pain his soul as he forced his sadness aside.

Is he alright? Is everything alright? Sari asked.

Perfect, Casco replied. *Can you stand?*

He winced as she slowly pushed herself upright. They were still connected and he could feel everything.

She looked down. *The cord?*

Oh! Yes. He sang at the umbilical cord and watched it fizzle to nothing, then wrapped his child in a warm, soft blanket and held him up to his mother.

With a soft sob, she took him into her arms. The wonder as she gazed into her Blessing's eyes for the first time seemed to fill the tent with its own special light.

Ubaid rushed in. "May I?" He held out his arms. "I just need to check …"

Sari nodded and somewhat reluctantly handed him over.

Ubaid laid him on the bed and opened the blanket. With a delicate pass of his hand, the vernix crumbled and blew away, leaving the baby's skin exposed for the first time. Casco marveled at its soft golden color; not metallic, but rare and beautiful. His hair was thick, but exceptionally fine – a cap of white-gold fuzz. His eyes were as yet uncolored, but deep and focused. They took in their surroundings in a studied way.

"You've definitely been here before," Ubaid laughed.

"Is he …?"

Ubaid smiled. "Usual number of fingers, toes, limbs and eyes. The skin coloration is something I've not seen before, and he certainly has a head of hair, but apart from that, and his advanced cognition, he seems a completely normal annangi, both inside and out."

Casco couldn't help the sigh of relief – not that he could have loved his Blessing less.

"Now let's look at you," Ubaid said to Sari.

While Ubaid tended to Sari's exhausted and bruised body, Casco bent to rewrap the baby. His smile steadied as he noticed the child's hair moving.

Happy, the baby said. *More love.* His wise little eyes studied Casco's.

Casco smiled back. He had no idea what the baby really meant to say, but he couldn't help it. Then the tent door moved and Daric stepped inside.

Casco's heart stopped. Sari and Ubaid froze in astonishment. Only the baby seemed unmoved.

"Daric?" Ubaid said.

More love father, the baby said smugly.

Casco needed no further prompt, and rushed forward. "El's Breath! It's so good to see you," he murmured into Daric's neck. His embrace firmed as he breathed in Daric's smell and relished the physical substance of him. Their bond reanimated, gently at first, then with a rush.

"Careful!" Daric gasped. "Still a little fragile."

"How?" Ubaid demanded.

"How?" Sari echoed. "We thought you would die."

Daric looked at the child in Sari's arms and shrugged. "Must be space for me in the Great Design after all."

Suddenly, it was too much. Casco's legs began to fail. He sank to the bed and sobbed into his hands. Daric knelt beside him and started to reach out, but Casco stopped him. *I can hardly control myself as it is,* he explained. *If you hold me now …* He looked up at the radiant new mother, and the storm began to pass. *This is Sari's moment.*

Outside, a crowd had begun to gather.

"Does he have a name yet?" Ubaid asked gently.

Casco forced himself upright. Daric stood beside him.

Sari gazed into her baby's eyes. Her head tilted.

"Chalah?" she murmured. "Cshyaladth …?" she said slowly, then shrugged. "I can't seem to get it right." Her quizzical expression slowly melted. "Calath, then," she said with some satisfaction. She smoothed the blanket around him and held him toward Casco and Daric. "Meet Calath."

Casco looked around as others repeated the name.

"– Calath …" he heard Ariben say.

"Welcome, Calath," Huldar said reverently.

Feet shuffled. Interest pressed but did not intrude. It seemed the whole settlement had assembled, even those who's birthing had begun.

"Calath," they murmured to each other. "… Calath."

"Go to them," Ubaid suggested. "Show the Uri'madu their newest member."

"Newest member, yes." Sari got to her feet and stood between himself and Daric. "Come on. We'll do it together."

THE GOD-EMPEROR

Ishät Ashik's gaze drifted around the walls of the Trophy Room. It was the one chamber in this vast palace he'd never felt was his own, yet he often came here when his thoughts were troubled.

He sat at the simple wooden desk, its edges rounded by the arms of so many of his ancestors, and pulled his journal from Qalān. His fingers moved restlessly. Enamelled blue fingernails drummed on the open pages, but the stylus lay idle. What should he write about? As Chosen of El, he should have few fears, but right now they crowded his thoughts like the long-dead monsters on the walls around him, preserved and displayed for his vicarious glory.

His gaze stopped, as it often did, at the weyfal. The huge beast's niche took up the entire west wall. Its reddish fur was matted around a gaping, blood-soaked wound in its neck, the death-blow delivered personally by his great, great grandfather, Tsemkarun Barisät, Thirty-Second God Emperor of the Realm. The weyfal's head was lifted, mouth open, forked tongue curled into the air as if its agony continued long after its death. Wicked, tusk-like prongs, each as long as his arm, jutted from gums filled with curved and venomous fangs, each one sharp and yellow. After all this time, its eyes still glittered with malice.

On a small plinth beside it, a ball of yellow spines inside an impervious crystal dome seemed almost comical. It was small enough to fit into his cupped hands, but to attempt to touch it would be foolish indeed. The dark stain on the tip of each spine was dried poison. The mere touch of a silant's spine would leave its prey paralysed within moments. He imagined the horror as one lay helpless while the creature's tubular feeding apparatus pierced their body and drained them to a husk.

This silant was unreachable, but he knew the poison to be available – if one had the contacts.

Another wall held a display of scaly hulmittu hides, each bigger than the last, each with the name of a God-Emperor inscribed below it. Even after so many millennia, their oily smell dusted the room.

Ishät gave a short nasal huff. He did not wish to be remembered as a lingering odour.

He looked at the vacant space he had set himself to fill. The dapinar was the trophy he wanted; all but one of its phases was represented. His father, Zohrät Ashik, Thirty-Fifth God-Emperor, had killed the latest addition, the extremely rare blue-phase rastin, but the red-phase torath, the rarest and most savage of all, was yet to be procured. If only he had the time …

He snorted again. The Kaskarudjan Kariiel Enna might be a worthy substitute. He would have her displayed … just so.

Ishiquel sent an irritable thought, *Stop worrying and come to bed.*

A vision of his wife's pregnant body eased his tension, but his own emptiness would not subside. He tapped his palms against the arms of the chair, sent a soothing flow back to his wife and left the doubts of the trophy room behind him.

Within their bedchamber, a nest of crystals suspended below the central cupola illuminated the room with soft yellow light. The placement of the crystals represented the sun and planets of the Tiamät home system. Giahn hung above the bed, fourth from the sun, slowly turning in its orbit.

The God-Emperor sprawled among the cushions on his wife's purple velvet lounger, watching as an oiled slave unpicked the fastenings of her dress. She turned to watch herself in her mirror. A cool, flower-scented breeze wafted loose hair from her shoulders. Her fine robe dropped to the floor, then her chemise. He stepped towards her and ran his palms over the warm bump in her belly. This was his daughter, the Second of Tiamät. Ashik. He saw her grown with a sword in hand, graceful and deadly - a warrior empress wielding the power of Tiamat as he did.

He saw himself over Ishiquel's shoulder and dwelt for a moment on the pleasing grandeur of the image.

Since the announcement of the pregnancy, precious ores had arrived from Went. Trade deals had gone as planned, and his armourers were busy. The forging of nacrite infused weapons was the work of specialists, and those who were trustworthy could be counted on one hand. Revenge had been slow to come, but now it was nearly here and he could almost feel its sweet and sudden release.

He had barracks full of new recruits. They thought of themselves as peace-keepers against the Kareski. He scoffed inside. As if that rabble could ever pose a threat. It seemed the populace were as easily manipulated as Delemät had claimed they would be. They saw the arrival of their Second as confirmation of El's mandate. All whispers of El's divine displeasure had been stilled. He would be a banner for them to rally behind; stamp out any who opposed him - Maatu's disrespect erased ... The Leth's vile threats made null and void.

Ishät smiled on the outside, yet disquiet passed beneath his veil. He withdrew his hand from his wife's belly as once again, the spectre of Kariiel Enna invaded his happiness with its own style of torment. ... So much power in her lithe form, and temper! At the time of his matrimonial choice, Kariiel had been too young and impetuous for tradition to be satisfied, whereas Ishiquel had been of a more compliant temperament and suitably older.

Kariiel's relief had been ill-concealed, almost to the point of rudeness. Abrasive. Yet brave. Confident - or defiant. He had often speculated what path his life might have taken had he chosen her rather than Ishiquel.

His wandering thoughts brought on a gentle snort. *Kariiel Enna ...*

In the mirror he saw his wife's sharp glance.

Thoughts of Kariiel scurried into the depths. He gave what he hoped was a loving smile. Ishiquel countered with apprehension about their pregnancy. Why was their daughter's development so rapid? ... he could sense, rather than hear her thoughts. Was El or maybe Asheru, the eternal consort, helping them make up for lost time?

"Aqumät says she spoke to him. Imagine!" Ishiquel gave an indulgent moue. "So keen for his baby sister to be born."

"He is a strange one," Ishät replied. His words were coloured by knowledge of his son's weakness as a warrior; his seeming inability to take harsh decisions. A shame he threw more to the Enna ...

"He believes she is a gift to us," Ishiquel prattled on. "An odd notion, don't you think?"

His head twitched sideways. "From El and Asheru?" How could his First be so simple? If the divine couple existed, he'd seen no proof. And the Marks? He flexed his shoulders. Even his own - they could be anything – perhaps even parasites like the Kaskaru and nothing to do with divinity at all.

He fought the frown that loomed on his face. He'd thought his inner mind well veiled, even from her, but Ishiquel's brow wrinkled.

"Ridiculous!" she said. *El brought the berries to us. He knew our need. Wanted us to use them. Otherwise he would have stopped us.*

"You are right, beloved," Ishät soothed. He stroked his wife's shoulder. "She is proof of El's great favour." *Remember what the eggs did for us? I have never been so consumed by lust.* He sought his wife's gaze in the mirror. "So close to the divine ..."

For a moment, her gaze smouldered into his, then she looked away. *What if they should guess?* She studied her face in the mirror. *What then?* "When will Delemät return?" *When will we know?*

But our populace have no idea, my precious one. He shrugged. *And even if they did, we represent El's divine will, and you are the embodiment of Asheru herself. Who will fault us?*

He felt her relax again, but when he tried to touch her naked shoulder, her energy firmed against him. A current of apprehension traversed their bond. He saw thoughts of stone and metal bars, and the discomfort his new prison caused her.

He shrugged again. She would never understand the needs of state. Again, he despaired of their First - Enna to the core, just like his mother. But their daughter would be different - fierce and proud - as she should be. "A small charm worked into something much bigger," he said aloud. "And it is your own invention. Your cleverness. I only had to adjust it a little, and …"

But why? I sought to make slaves lives a little easier, but … Why do we need such a prison? The Realm loves us now. No one will harm us …

So you would like to believe, he said darkly, *but there is jealousy, my magnificent one, and not all are so loyal.*

Manu should not have left us, she said with a stab of spite. *There has been a Maatu at El's Chosen's side since time immemorial.*

Yes, my love, he answered. *And the Leth should not have threatened us.*

The planet Went is ours, to do whatever we like with. It is not up to Leth to limit El's will. The proof is with our precious daughter. El has Blessed!

"And the beauty of this new prison my love," he continued. His hands moved lower down her body. "Is that no one can see into it, and no one can get out. Arien's treason will have consequences." he mused. "The Realm must know our strength."

And Kariiel? she said defiantly. *Will she remain a thorn in my side?*

He fought to keep his mood stable and buoyant. Soon, Delemät would return with the information they needed. All would be well. His hands found her breasts and cupped them gently.

Kariiel? What of her?

They will be here! At the palace. Ishiquel covered his hands with her own. *Daniel should send someone else. I don't want her anywhere near me … or you.*

He could come alone, he suggested, and hoped she would not sense the wound this would cause him.

And tell her everything when he returned? She turned from the mirror and drew his head down for a lingering kiss. "She would never have been enough for a great Emperor such as yourself."

"You are my strength," he crooned. "And now our Second will be an incontrovertible statement of your superiority."

"Kariiel has no Second," she said smugly.

"No indeed."

She eyed a jar of perfumed oil, and he picked it up. The glass was round and smooth. Her hands imprisoned his. Their eyes met in the mirror.

He could assign another, she said firmly. *A birthing specialist. I'm sure you can think of something?*

But …

You are El's Chosen. Nothing you do or say can be taken as an insult … not to them.

His gaze took in her swollen breasts and voluptuous belly. His wife should be able to decide who attended her during the birth of their child. He owed her this much. And someone more … expendable than Daniel himself may actually be preferable.

She smiled into the mirror. His hands were freed. Drop by drop the unction fell and oozed over each breast in turn. With a flash of Tsemkar, pink heat-trails appeared in its wake. She closed her eyes and guided the smoking stream to encircle her nipples. As the delicious sensation was shared through their bond, thoughts of anything but carnal pleasure slid aside.

Ishiquel guided his hands to swirl the oil with palms and fingers. The dense, swollen globes were fiercely attractive. He pinched her nipples hard and relished her gasp.

The Kaskaru should be mine, he whispered. *If she died, they might come to me. The ultimate power. Her death should be a statement. Hah! Then none would dare oppose me.*

Her head tipped sideways. Pleasure slowed. *You would end Kariiel's life? Send her to the Breath?*

"Breath blows," he whispered forcefully, his voice thick with arousal. "It does not discriminate. The power of El should not be divided in the mind of the Realm."

His erection pressed firm against her back. Her acceptance of pleasure became outright desire.

"But Kariiel is your niece," he murmured. "Your blood. Surely you would not want her to suffer?"

Ishiquel turned to him, lips parted and moist. Pleasure flooded their bond. He kissed her deeply and the scent of fragrant oil swam through his senses.

With delicious self-control, he disengaged from his wife's embrace and signalled a slave to turn back the bed covers. As a ripe young bottom bent to do his bidding, he gave it a savage tweak.

The slave stumbled. Her lips closed over the painful barbs embedded in her tongue. Her collared mind was an enticing display of all the terrors his action had engendered.

Ishiquel's mind intertwined with his in a lascivious flow, but her eyebrows gave an infinitesimal lift.

He smiled and gave the slave master curt instructions; El's Chosen would have no desire for physical enhancements tonight.

Slight feet pattered the floor. The door closed with a bare whisp of scented air, but Ishät Ashik's senses were already deep in his wife's wonderfully trained grip. `

MALENA

Malena threw her head back. Her efforts ended in a mighty cry, but she knew nothing had changed.

It's alright Malena, you're doing fine …

She shook her head. Ariben was an absolute gem, but intertwined as they were, he couldn't hide the truth. Her body was ready, but the baby would not come. Without the help of a healer, or maybe even with it, they would both die.

Call Ubaid … please.

Ubaid is attending Alis. He can't be here. He stroked her face with a cool, damp towel. *Maybe Casco?*

She shook her head again. *That lying scum? Pretending to be dead? Who does that?! Only an Enna could come up with such a sick, such a depraved … such a … a*

Her diatribe dissolved into another cry of pain, even deeper than the last. When it was over, she slowly released her grip on Ariben's arm. His breathing was ragged, his concern heartbreaking.

She won't come because she fears me …

Malena …

She fears the life I offer. I know she does. I'm hopeless. I hurt her – I did, and I … I can't undo it.

Ariben lifted her hand and kissed it. *Casco was not at fault.*

I know, she snapped. *I know that! And now she wants to kill us both!*

Has she said so?

Of course not! She sighed disgustedly. *Why am I surrounded by idiots! She hasn't said anything. You know that. Nothing! Not since …*

Then trust her, Ariben said calmly.

How could he be so calm? Malena thought to herself. Was he that stupid?

Trust yourself, he went on. *You are a good person, Malena. A gifted person. You told me she enjoyed it when you showed her the stars. That at that time, you thought you had a special connection.*

That was before. Now she hates me.

She felt Ariben withdraw to greet someone at the door.

"Ubaid?" she said hopefully.

"No."

She recognized Casco, and disappointment came with a jolt. "Get away from me! Half-breed!" she snarled. "I don't want your help. I don't need your help!"

She reached out for Ariben as another contraction began, but found Casco's arm instead. Her rage screamed through the pain of another failure.

"Get away from me," she wept, but their hands remained clenched wrist to wrist. Ariben held the other firmly. Love and warmth eased through both contacts as Casco worked with Ariben's to release locked and fatigued muscles.

"I don't know what to do …" she said, and turned to bury her head in Ariben's chest, ashamed of the whimper in her voice.

"Let me in," Casco squeezed her hand kindly. "Please?" He tapped the Mark on his forehead. "I might be able to help."

Too exhausted to refuse, she gave a wan nod. But although the place where their skin touched warmed, there was no sense of Casco's mind in hers. His eyes were open, but remote. His head slowly tilted, his Mark flickered with light, and he nodded as if in conversation.

"What's going on?" she said.

"Shh," Ariben replied. "Give him a chance."

"A chance to what?"

"I think he's talking to her, or trying to."

She gasped as she felt the stirring of a new contraction. Ariben's grip firmed in readiness. She knew he would endure with her, but they were both so tired.

Wait – Casco said firmly. *Resist the urge to push, if you can.*

She nodded.

The pain swelled.

Ariben squeezed her hand. "You are a navigator. You can do this."

His caring eyes filled her gaze. How had she ever thought them dull? She puffed in and out in strict rhythm, while her failing body screamed, *Just let this be done!* To silence it, she sent her mind as close to her beloved stars as she dared.

When it was over, her breath came in ragged sobs. Sweat dripped from her chin. She followed Ariben's gaze to Casco and was surprised to see that a dome of bright linear patterns had formed around the three of them. The Mark on Casco's head flickered with blue-white flame. He touched her stomach and she felt a familiar warmth spread as tired and torn muscle was healed and strengthened.

She glanced back at Ariben, who seemed more than a little awestruck. "Ubaid?"

Ariben nodded. "Working through him," he whispered.

"Try and touch her now," Casco murmured.

"My baby?"

"Yes," he said. "I think she is ready … but time is short."

Malena blinked back tears. "But she won't let me … not since …"

"Try," he insisted. "Please. For both your sakes. She is beautiful, so beautiful. She is your gift Malena, and she deserves her chance."

"But I have tried, I have!" she cried. "What do you think I've been doing these past months? There's been nothing else to occupy me."

"It's not about you."

She could hear curtness behind Casco's patient tone, and a true sense of urgency.

"She wants to trust you," he said. "She doesn't understand the whys and wherefores, or the intricacies of your doubt. She is … waiting. Now is the time."

She glanced at the web of light surrounding them and his eyes smiled.

"What should I do?"

Navigate.

She nodded. There was only a short time before the next contraction, but her heart beat strongly again and she felt ready. She extended her mind to the closest line of song, and after the slightest pause, touched it. It embraced her eagerly, as if it had indeed been waiting, and she let herself be taken by the flow.

Stars… a view of the cosmos was the last thing she expected, and she instantly recognized the perspective of her home-world, Ekeridu. She could almost feel the old rug beneath her, the smell of worn fibre and damp rock, as if she was actually laying on the stone-paved courtyard of her childhood villa, deep in the mountains, and looking up. The feel of those stars came back to her in a rush - the sound they made - as if they called her home.

A small presence watched with her. Was it her daughter? She reached out, but like a small silver-scaled fish, the watcher slipped back into whatever depths it inhabited.

A sense of loss filled her, and she was suddenly in her parents kitchen, waiting - waiting for them to come and say goodbye. She'd sat alone in the sitting-room for ages, and gotten hungry. In her hand was the letter of acceptance into the Navigator's Guild for apprenticeship under Shamkarun Nasaku of Maatu. She'd been told Nasaku was one of the greatest of mentors - and that she had asked for Malena specifically. It was a great honor. She knew it was. But as a close relative of Manu Maatu her acceptance was a foregone conclusion, and the best of tutors was her right … wasn't it?

Part of her thrilled to be answering the call at last, but where were her parents? Eventually she tucked a few easenberry tarts into Qalān and left for the bays alone.

The scene shifted, and she was back at 'the wall', a vast rock edifice constructed to stop the plateau on which the Maatu palace was built, from slow, crumbling subsidence. She peered upward. Cloud obscured the top, almost eight hundred feet above. Water dripped steadily from the massive blocks. Her cousin, Anu, was already twenty or so feet into the climb.

Come on! he said impatiently. *It'll be murder when the sun hits.*

We're not allowed to do this, she reminded him.

Who'll know – if you don't let on?

His grandmother, the great Kariiel Enna, was an avid rock-climber. She'd seen her scale this artificial cliff as if it was no more than a pleasant walk in the park. Anu adored her. Wanted to be just like her. Maybe he thought this climb would impress her.

It's a long walk back, he said, and it was. There were no nearby portals.

There was a long silence. She could hear his feet scraping for footholds. *Go on then,* he said. *Go home. If you're too scared, you'd probably fall anyway. Some navigator you'll turn out to be.*

I'm not scared! she lied. *I'm just picking my path.*

He laughed.

She reached for the first hand-hold, then the next …

Two hundred feet from the base, Anu slipped.

Shit! he said. She could remember it as clearly as if she was there. A rock skimmed past, barely missing her head. For a terrifying few moments he scrabbled for footing, then found it. After a short rest, he continued, but she froze.

I can't do it, she said.

Yes you can. You must – otherwise you'll be stuck there forever. He climbed on, leaving her further behind with every reach and step. She focused on the rock in front of her face, to terrified to look anywhere else.

After a few minutes, he called back again. *Maybe one day you'll be just bones and old skin still clinging in place and people will say, look! There's the Maatu who couldn't make it.*

That's not funny! she screamed.

He hesitated. *What, you really can't move?*

No I can't. She started to cry.

Shit! he said again.

After a while the sound of feet on rock grew louder. Nervously - so nervously, she looked across into Anu's grinning face.

Don't worry, sis, he said. He always called her sis, back then. *Down or up, you choose, but we've got to go somewhere.*

Down, she said - *no up. I don't know.*

Well, if I were you, I'd decide quickly. This is no picnic! You have a little Tsemkar, don't you?

She gave a small nod.

Then use it like this … it's a Zaikhanun trick. Father taught me. Song and mind together. Shapes the rock so you can hold on.

That's cheating!

I'm not doing it! he said. *But if it means you survive, please, cheat! I promise I won't tell.*

She used the charm, shaped the rock, and made it to the top. He stayed beside her all the way, and never said a word about how. It was their secret still - how they had scaled the wall together. Not even his grandmother knew. For ages, she'd lived in fear he would tell, and ever since, she'd been determined to do everything herself, with no help and no short-cuts … no fear of recrimination …

He had been at the Bays in Giahn to welcome her to her apprenticeship. A week later, her parents arrived, full of congratulations and genuine pride - but why hadn't they been there when she needed them?

She experienced a vague sense of activity, a pulling and pushing around her body, but it was remote and unimportant for now.

Then a small voice said - *Will you be there for me?*

All sense of the outer world evaporated. *Of course! Of course I will!* Her heart raced.

Your mother was not, the little one said firmly.

I am not my mother, Malena replied, and it was as if a light exploded softly through her mind. *I am not my mother,* she repeated, *and you are not me. But I love you with all my heart.*

I am different, her daughter said bravely.

Yes, she agreed. *You are my gift, my wonderful, sacred gift, and I want you. I want you to be with me. We can learn from each other, protect each other, and I will always be there for you – I promise.*

The solemnity of her vow surprised her. It was as if whole new chains of events had been initiated, new threads in the great tapestry of being.

Like Anu promised? her daughter asked.

Just like that, she agreed, and again, the truth almost overwhelmed her. Why had she been so antagonistic towards him? He truly was her spiritual brother. He had always been there for her, and it was to him she had called when she needed help most.

My name is Shameera Stargazer, her daughter whispered. *I am a stargazer, like you.*

"Push now," Casco said. "Push as hard as you can! Keep going!"

Shameera Stargazer, she repeated reverently, *Be ready, now.*

With great determination, she bore down, then after a short gap, she pushed again.

"Here she comes," Ariben said. "Oh Malena! She's here!"

In the ensuing silence, there it was, the sound of her daughter's first breath. Then came her first small cry, her voice in the song realized at last.

Casco handed her to Ariben, who after a moment of rapt fascination, handed her to her mother.

Clear, pale eyes regarded her.

"Shameera Stargazer," Malena said softly. "You are most welcome."

SMOKE TRAILS

To Delemät Ashik, life in the Host's encampment seemed even more ghastly than usual. Mud was everywhere. Incessant rain beat against the pavilion's leathers. The floods had abated, but the heat and humidity was like nothing Delemät Ashik had experienced, and the camp healer had become somewhat of a specialist with fungal infections. How his brother would laugh - if he could see him.

Farushael of Cantori stood awkwardly by one of the tent-poles.

Delemät frowned. "Where did you say the miners detected smoke?"

"I can show you ..."

He pulled a map from Qalān and without even asking permission, cleared a space on the desk and with an annoying flourish, threw the painted vellum onto it. "Central continent," he mused, while his index finger trailed over mountains and plains."... Yes, around about here - somewhere." He made a circling motion. "Smell of talemgal."

"The northern edge?"

"North east," the Cantori corrected. Delemät quelled another stab of irritation. "Yes," Farushael continued hurriedly. "Not too far from the silver mine."

Delemät's shoulders raised. The furrows in his brow deepened. "But there's nothing there!"

"No, Lord Delemät," the Cantori agreed. "So it would seem."

They braced as the ground rumbled. As the shaking worsened, Delemät gripped the edge of the table. Farushael clung to a tent-pole. Small items fell from shelves.

When it was over, Farushael dusted himself off. He was breathing heavily. "We should move," he said.

Delemät found the hopelessness in his tone repulsive. "Rubbish," he sneered. "We are Ashik, not kreth. We do not flee from the slightest disturbance."

Farushael nodded a bow. "As you say, my lord."

"That's the first real tremor we've had for a week," Delemät said pityingly. "The threat of eruption is just that - a threat with no real substance."

"Miners say differently," Farushael said defiantly. "The ones closer to home insist the danger is real."

"Look around you! A full community. Piles of ore ready for shipment. No other Djan'rū capable of such a volume of cargo. Our navigator is due back soon. We stay."

"And afterward?"

"As Breath blows." He studied the map and placed his finger where Farushael's had been. "How long will it take to get to this … place of talemgal?"

"With Qalān the way it is … a day? If we are careful."

He gave a curt gesture. The Cantori bowed and departed. Delemät did not look up from his study of the diagram.

The district indicated was mountainous and difficult to access, and with few portals close by. He'd watched the area before, but seen no unusual activity. Was that where were they hiding? His fists balled in frustration. When Kandät Enna came, his time was up and as yet he had none of the vital information he'd been sent to procure. His mission had failed completely. Even Jaldan had somehow managed to vanish before any advances on weaponizing his mind-bending ability could be made. How could he face the Empress and admit he knew no more about her pregnancy or the what-ever-it-was she carried than she did? All he could ensure was that no one remained alive who knew what they'd done - besides himself, of course, and Kandät Enna.

He thought again of events at the North. The Enna's attempt to reach the communication window had cost him almost a third of his Ashik contingent, but at least no message had been sent. He should have brought tougher, more seasoned soldiers, but the God-Emperor had been unwilling to waste such valuable assets. He could only hope the renegade had died as a result of the injuries he'd received.

Visions of the divine tentacles haunted him, and his brother's growing madness. El's Chosen spent hours obsessing over plans for revenge against the Maatu, yet Maatu were synonymous with navigation; the rulers of travel and transport, honorable and impartial, and ferocious warriors besides. The actual management of the Realm was left to bureaucrats and toadies.

Then another memory … his brother's terrifying rage when a Nhadu ambassador praised a Lethian wine. His Tsemkar had flared – the representative killed in a messy heartbeat … yet the Leth provided over eighty percent of Giahn's staple foods. The only viable native industry Giahn could boast was a small fishing industry. The Kareski had fielded a strong black-market fruit and vegetable trade before his brother chased most of them from the planet. Since then, the price of fresh goods other than fish had seen an exponential rise, and any mention of Manu Maatu or Arien Leth in his presence was mere foolishness. Did he intend Giahn to starve?

He shook his head. Subversive thoughts could blossom now he was beyond Ishät's reach, but soon he would have to return. Would he be welcomed by El at that point? The thought of re-birth, refreshed and cleansed, was not altogether distasteful.

In a flash of rage, he swept his desk clean. The map flew through the air like an over-large autumn leaf and landed with a soft rustle.

Where were they!

How could an entire company of utterly useless ecologists disappear from the face of the planet? How could they hide their psychic emissions so completely? The babies had doubtless been born, but were they born dead? There had been no sign, so perhaps they had. He thought again of the Empress. How she most worry!

The only clue was this anomalous smell of smoke. He gave a short huff. Even he couldn't far-see an aroma.

Farushael! he yelled. *Argushät!* It was time to investigate in person.

HIDDEN GEMS

Deep underground in the Uri'madu sanctuary, the campfire flame's slight flicker gave away the slow passage of fresh air. Above the fire, the unfamiliar warmth repelled the ceiling's wildlife, but beyond that circle, bright creatures peppered and flowed in a vast living tapestry.

Beneath its vault, Malena sat close beside Ariben and nursed her baby. A strange contentment had come over her since the birth. If, during her previous life as a navigator, any one had said this would happen, she would have reacted scornfully. How could the extra work and responsibility of a child be good? How could being a prisoner to another's whim be pleasurable? She couldn't help smiling at the thought of her younger self - so impetuous! She would never in her wildest imagination have expected to be here, with a new Bless and a loving partner, stuck underground and in danger for their lives. Yet life was good, and the strength of the love flowing through her was another whole new world.

Shameera Stargazer stared wonderingly into her eyes. Her shock of pale hair flowed and flickered in calm, regular waves that followed the cycle of her suckling. The effect was deeply soothing, almost hypnotic.

Slowly, in what had become a morning ritual, other couples came to join them.

Kira sat beside Banga and handed their small son to him. He eased the lip of the bundle down to view the little one's face.

"They're so quiet," Kira said. "Makes quite a change. It's as if they understand the need."

Casco nodded. "They do."

"They still speak to you?" Banga lifted his brows and touched his finger playfully to the baby's nose. "Little Nareth ere's said nothin since he was born."

"Just his name then nothing," Kira agreed. "Does Shameera talk to you?" she asked Malena.

Malena nodded. "Sometimes." She almost felt guilty. "But I talk to her all the time. I know she's listening." She smiled into her daughter's face. "… Aren't you?"

"Where's Sari?"

"She'll be along soon," Casco said. "And Daric's with Huldar."

He waved as Shen started toward them.

Ariben gave a gloomy sigh. "Yes. Another meeting. If he could give us some good news for a change …"

Banga nodded. "Somethins up."

Shameera's hair waved pensively.

What is it? Malena asked her.

Her baby's gaze rolled inexpertly toward Casco.

"Shen!" Casco called. "Where's Gael and Alsha?"

Malena and Shameera's eyes met again. Malena raised her eyebrows and gave a little shake of her head. They would get no insights about the meeting from him.

At last, when they were all assembled, Huldar and Daric made their way forward.

"I won't waste time telling you how well you're doing now our Blessings have all been born - you already know that," Huldar began. "But we do have a problem. There has been some interest in the area at the very end of our cave system. Smoke from our fires had to exit somewhere, and unfortunately, it has been noticed. This means we'll have to move."

Ariben groaned.

Malena fought to get her head around what that would mean.

"Where will we go?" she asked.

"South," Huldar said. "And there's not much time. Those of us who are familiar with the necessary portals will sing the mothers and babies through. Pack what you can into Qalān, the rest will be picked up later, once you're all safe."

"What about our supplies?" Shen asked.

"We've already started to move them, as of this morning, and we have other stockpiles. It's a shame, I know, and a bit of a shock, but we haven't actually been discovered yet, and with luck, this situation will remain the same. I would ask you all to gather back here within the hour so evacuation can commence."

"What of the navigator, Shamkarun Kandät Enna?" Tish asked. "Has he arrived yet?"

"Not as far as we know, but it should be any day now."

"Will you contact him? Ask for safe passage? Escape?"

"I have no plans to do so," Huldar said. "The risk is too great."

"But how will we survive?" said Gael. "Seven years? Do we have enough food?"

"We'll freeze to death!"

"That's his plan," another said darkly.

"Hopefully it won't come to that," Huldar reassured them. "The southern caves are almost as large as this one and geothermally warmed. We have seeds. We will grow what we can to supplement the food we have set aside. When we don't return, the Guild will start looking for us. Someone will come."

"Someone?" Banga said. "Someone who?"

"I don't know," Huldar said patiently. "But I am certain they will."

Malena nodded. Anu would come. She was sure of it. But when? And when to activate the new Djan'rū she'd told him to use? It would have to be soon, but afterward, it's presence could be no longer be hidden. Kandät Enna would sense it when he arrived, and even Delemät, if he looked hard enough, might find it.

"If you could please get ready to leave?" Huldar continued. "Tam and Arko, and Tashel, of course, if you could be in the first group? We'll need heat and food as soon as possible."

Tam glanced Arko's way and nodded.

"Me an Gael will join them," Shen said.

Tam gave Shen a nod and turned for his kitchen while Tashel headed for their tent.

"You seem distracted," Ariben said, and gave her shoulders a gentle squeeze. "It will be alright. It's just a move. We knew it would probably happen."

She nodded, and arched into the contact, surprised and secretly quite pleased he'd noticed. "Sorry. It's just that something's not right."

"Shameera?"

"She seems sad." Malena's head tilted slightly as she studied her baby's infant haze. "And her hair is waving oddly - as if she knows something but won't say."

Bad come. Mama go?

Malena hugged her precious bundle tight. *Yes, but nothing will happen to you. You are the most important thing in my life, my Blessing, and I won't let anything or anyone hurt you ever again.*

Love mama. Love Casco, Shameera began to recite. Her hair swayed happily, as if it had its own separate entity. *Love Riben, love Darry, Love Sari, love Dar* ... the list went on in a rhythm all its own.

"She seems more cheerful now," Ariben said. "What did she say?"

Malena stood up and waited for him to join her. "She said 'Bad come.' She understands we have to leave here, so I assume all the babies do." She started for the tent they shared. "And now she's singing, reciting all our names – or versions of them." She smiled down at her child. "Clever little one." She turned back to Ariben. "But she never sings the babies names ... odd, isn't it?"

"She *is* only a few weeks old," Ariben replied indulgently. "I think she's extremely clever."

Shameera gave a happy coo. Images of the various creatures in the cave began to pepper her song, and Malena realized she had a name for each type and was including them in her song, one by one.

"Beyond clever," Malena murmured, and looked at Ariben again. "Truly, I think she is."

Ariben wiggled his finger over the baby's face. "Kaskarudjan Shameera?"

The new cave was not as vast as the one they'd just left, but Malena felt more comfortable and it was definitely warmer.

When the tents were up, the additional stores placed and the babies asleep, the Uri'madu began to gather around the fire.

Malena gravitated to where Andel stood with Sari and the Rukh.

"Geothermal," Andel was explaining. "It will be warm in here even when the whole planet is frozen. There's a stream further in and a hot spring, and soil, so we can grow food."

"Better all round." Malena looked up at the ceiling. "And not so many shadows." She'd never liked the shadows. "Are there any creatures to contend with?"

"Huldar said to watch out for the aquatic lizards. About four feet long. He assures me they don't hunt in packs, but if you go paddling they'll try and eat your toes."

"No good for babies then," Ariben said.

"The water quality is good," Sari said. "Just finished testing."

"And you didn't get eaten?"

"Eaten? No, I just shooed them away. Quite pretty," she shared an image of pale green and brown patterned reptiles with spiny orange crests that broke the water when they swam. "But sluggish and not too bright."

"A bit like my Tashel," Tam muttered. He continued to stir a huge pot suspended above the flame.

Ariben chuckled. "Malena thinks Shameera is so clever she'll be Kaskarudjan someday."

"Ariben!"

"Well," he shrugged. "... I was the one who said it. But she's so ... It's hard to remember she's just a tiny baby."

"Until you see her," Malena said. "You should look more often."

"Come on," Arko called. "Eat it while it's hot."

Nachiel responded with a sigh. "Stew?" he muttered darkly. "There's a surprise."

Ronnin rolled his eyes. "Such luxury."

"I heard that!" Tam growled. "Come on everyone, while our blessings sleep."

"Before Huldar and the others get here?"

"They will be some time yet," Andel said. "They won't mind," she glanced Sari's way, "- so long as they don't go hungry when they return."

"They won't," Shen said. "We'll make sure of it."

"Then let's eat," Cobar said.

With a belly full of plain but tasty food, and the first offering of honey cakes in weeks, Malena sat on a log looking into the flames and rested her head on Ariben's shoulder. It would be a few hours before the babies woke up. The strange tendency they had to all sleep at the same time was odd, but at least meal-times were still an opportunity to relax – at least for some. She couldn't help wondering when Anu might arrive. The activation of the gate was critical, and the effort of hiding her worries added an extra level of stress to the demands of a new baby

"We need a story," Topper said. He turned to Minna and Tala who sat between himself and his brother. "Huldar tells the best stories."

"Anyone?" Bush said.

To Malena's surprise, a story floated to the surface of her mind, perhaps triggered by Ariben's earlier comments.

Ariben gave her a speculative look. "I think we have one here."

"Malena?"

She took a deep breath and nodded. "Do we have the shawl?"

"You have a shawl?" Tish, one of the miners, asked.

"Indeed we do," Topper replied. "Huldar is a master, but he lets us use it too. Tam?"

The cook grimaced. "Actually, Casco still has it at the moment, but I have this one. Not quite as venerable, but it was woven by Salat of Nhadu."

Ronnin eyed it appreciatively.

"Didn't he weave the Cantori wedding shawl?" Nachiel said.

"The very one," Tam said proudly, and withdrew a bundle of white fabric from Qalān.

Warmth seeped into Malena's back as Ariben arranged the stole across her shoulders.

"What's the story?" asked Van.

"Kattíst," she answered. "This is the story of Shamkarun Kattíst, the Weaver of Stars."

"A new one for me," Andel said with a smile.

"New?" Sari echoed. "Yes. Thank you, Malena."

Malena nodded thanks. "Are we ready? Good then. I dedicate this story to the memory of those we have lost, may they rest sweetly in the Breath, and to the bravery of all here. May the Breath of El's Great Design blow us to warmth and safety soon."

"Breath blow truth," her audience responded.

She nodded again. Her heart beat right to her fingertips. The fire crackled as if it, too waited.

"Long ago," she began, "a lonely young Maatu looked up at the night skies, and like so many of us, felt the song of the stars in the core of her being." She shrugged. "All fairly ordinary, you might say. She's a Maatu. Maatu are navigators. Where's the story in that? Well, the tale begins when you find out she was an angel, and therein lay the difficulty."

"But the first navigator was an angel, wasn't he?"

"Yes, Banga, he was, but that was a very long time ago, and since then, the vast majority have been archangels. Despite this, Kattíst presented herself to the Guild Hall at Ekeridu. No one would consider her for apprenticeship, except for a few who wanted coin in return - coin she did not have. However, the call of the stars consumed her. She felt that if she couldn't be a navigator, she didn't want to live. So she waited in the bays, constantly listening, talking to spinners, and trying to learn what she could. After some months, she believed she had mastered the chord from Ekeridu to Giahn and decided to give it a try.

"On that night, when the bays were quiet, she gathered the chord to herself and began to sing. An envelope formed, just as it had for the real navigators. The shimmering bubble, ready to speed her to her longed-for stars, encompassed all she ever wanted to be ... but seconds before she could attempt the actual translation, she glimpsed a handsome archangel running towards her, his arms waving frantically.

"Stop!" he yelled. "Stop!" and something about his urgency made her pause.

"It's too dangerous!" he cried. "You'll be lost to the great between!"

She tied off the envelope as she'd seen countless real navigators do and tried not to seem surprised when the variation worked.

"I can do it," she called back. "I know I can."

"That may be," the stranger said. "But you have to book your space - otherwise you could interfere with another's arrival. We are all on strict schedule. Didn't you know that?"

"Kattíst blushed and shook her head. Her heart fell. How could she book a time if she wasn't an actual navigator?

"And sorry, but your accent was just a mite sharp," he said. "I assume you were headed to Giahn?"

“She nodded.

“I can show you if you’d like?” he said.

“She nodded again, and as simply as that, their partnership was formed.

“Shamkarun Luca of Maatu,” he introduced himself.

“Kattíst,” she replied. “Kattíst of the stars.”

“Although they were angel and archangel, the love between them was instant. He took her on as a spinner at first, so they would not be apart, but she learned so quickly and grew so powerful, it wasn’t long before he was spinning for her – just as it would be in an official apprenticeship.

“He borrowed books for her from the guild’s great library and taught her to read both modern and ancient languages. As she progressed to longer runs and larger cargo, he taught her how to negotiate a contract and made sure she was paid appropriately for her work.

“But although the Guild knew who she was and what they were doing, Luca could not get them to accept her.

“She is an angel,” the Guild-lord of the time, Aron Enna, said. “She will not be Marked, and thus you have made a rod for your own back.

“Angels have been Marked,” he countered. “She is powerful and skilled. She should work with other tutors, have the same protections and opportunities as any other talented apprentice.”

“Exactly why she cannot be left to sing alone!”

Aron Enna, the Guild-lord, would not relent, and Luca was worried by the truth of his words. He could not let Kattíst sing alone for fear she would be Marked in transit. With no one to support her and take over the song, she would die, but she could not hire spinners because she was not a navigator.

"But his concern was short-lived. Soon after this, while they were on passage from Haas to Ekeridu, Kattíst did gain her Shamkar.

"She was Marked?" Andel asked.

"Yes, she was," Malena replied.

"I'd heard of Kattíst," Kira said, "but I just assumed she was an archangel."

"Shh. Just listen!" Nachiel said crossly.

Malena adjusted her shawl. "May I continue?"

"Sorry," Kira began. "It's just that ..."

"Shh!"

Malena plunged on. "News travelled fast. Well-wishers greeted her on arrival in Giahn, and a jubilant Luca announced Shamkarun Kattíst's new status to all, but again, the Guild-lord frowned.

"She may be Marked," he said, "but she is still an angel - nothing more than a glorified spinner."

"Luca was furious - as you can imagine! Straight away he made an appointment to see The Maatu herself. Shamkarun Mara Maatu had heard of Kattíst's achievements and was only too pleased to intervene. As far as she was concerned, El had spoken and they would do well to listen. Kattíst was made a full member of the Navigator's Guild, and Guild-lord Aron was replaced by someone less bigoted. By The Maatu's decree, Kattíst was now to be called Shamkarun Kattíst of Maatu, and given the same rights and responsibilities as an

Archangel. But although she was delighted, she always thought of herself as Shamkarun Kattíst of the Stars.

"And at last, the way was clear for the couple to marry. Their union was still unconventional and frowned upon by many, but Kattíst's achievements were the talk of the guild, and the event was a joyous one indeed. And soon, they were blessed with a daughter, Luna."

"And I'll bet it was those who'd refused her that sung her praises most," Bush said.

"You may well be right," Malena said. "And a happy ending? So you might think. But Aron Enna, the ex-Guild-lord, hated Kattíst now, more than ever. He refused to call her by name or title, and despised Luca even more, seeing him as the one who had cost him his position and respect. Bitterness soured his every song, and unbeknown to the new family, every day he plotted more elaborate ways to destroy their happiness.

"Five hundred years later, Luca was commissioned for a difficult contract - a round trip from Cantor to Du Mah, then Manziat, Germane and back to Cantor. Aron Enna discovered he would be carrying maximum cargo-weight through the solar storms of the Manzay system, far from any safe-haven. Because of this, several additional spinners would have to be hired. One of them was new to the craft and the Enna saw his opportunity.

"Aron asked this newcomer if he would take a special delivery to Germane; a tight-woven basket with a curiously complex charm-seal on its lid. It was to be a secret, just between the two of them, and with the promise of generous payment, the young spinner was in.

"The journey began. All was well. The basket lay quiet and unnoticed, hidden among other cargo.

"The young spinner did his best to forget his bargain. The change to their manifest was infinitesimal - but occasionally, the complicated charm-seal found its way into his dreams. He'd never seen one like it.

"On approach to Manziat, the first of the solar storms hit, but Luca's added strength prevailed, and they arrived in the Linsar Bays without a problem. Folks there were excited to receive their long-awaited shipments, and no one noticed when the spinner was approached again with a second secret item bound for Germane.

"Another payment was made. The spinner shoved a plain wooden box next to the basket and carried on as if nothing was amiss - although he did peer at the charm-seal for a moment, unsure if it had changed. But then someone called for him, and he put box and basket far from his mind and returned to work.

"Manzay is a violent and unpredictable sun. I have weathered its storms, with the help of all my crew, and …"

"Huh!" Banga said. "I think we all know that."

"Hard work," Tish agreed.

"Surely not as bad as Went!" Bush said.

Malena snorted. "No, I'll give you that." She paused as the shocking memory of the miner's death filled her mind. "May he rest sweetly in the Breath."

"Thank you for your respect," Tish said sadly. "Dara was a friend. We all miss him."

Malena gave her a small bow. "We did our best, but sometimes ... And as for our brave Shamkarun Luca, yes, he knew this part of the journey would be dangerous, beyond doubt. It takes a strong and cohesive team to exit the Manzay system safely, and navigate the five day journey from there to Germane - itself a tricky prospect due to its twin-sun configuration.

"A strong flare hit before they could leave, then another in the seconds as they prepared the envelope. This in itself was not unusual, and the team were well versed. But with each absorption of solar energy, although they could not see it, the charm-sung lid of the basket altered just a little more.

"As the Chord was sung and the envelope punched through the latest storm, the protection of the planet's magnetic field diminished. The cargo in the basket began to glow. As the storm raged, it grew brighter and brighter. Blazing tendrils arced from box to basket. A cascade of malevolent charms was activated, each designed to amplify the power of the last. Both box and basket contained a hollow ceramic ball, and when the forces directed at these objects reached a certain intensity they burst apart. A loud explosion peppered the delicate envelope with iron pellets.

"The result was catastrophic.

"Several spinners were struck dead. The torn envelope careened off course. Gaping holes appeared where iron had split the song asunder. Air grew short. Cargo was dumped to reduce the strain, but it was not enough. In a last effort to save his crew, Luca wrapped the strongest part of the envelope around the five the survivors and the bodies of the fallen, and let them go, in the hopes they were not too far from Manzay to snap back."

"Why did he do that?" Shen asked.

"Snap-back is a curious thing," Banga explained. "Seven is the maximum number of crew it can work for, but it is never a guarantee - especially where solar energies may intercede. The spinners would have tried to maintain the envelope and hoped Breath would blow in their favor."

"And so it did," Malena continued. "For the five with the bodies. After a day of fear and uncertainty, they safely re-entered the Linsar bays. They told the Guild everything that had happened. Aron Enna was punished with death - but Luca was never seen again.

"Kattíst ... could not accept her loss. There had been no death-cry, you see? She spent the rest of her life searching Known and Unknown for her lost love. It was rumored she found him at last, in the far reaches of the fourth arm ... and they died together, reunited at last."

"Doesn't anyone know?"

"Not really. But their daughter, Luna, felt it to be so, and it is said that Kattíst's Death-Cry included the words; 'We would have returned if we could.'"

"What happened to their daughter?"

Malena smiled. "Shamkarun Luna of Maatu? Mara Maatu herself took her in. Eventually, she and the Maatu's son were married, and she became Luna Maatu, my seven times Grandmother."

Malena bowed to the gathering, then removed the shawl and handed it to Ariben. Cold shivered her back and shoulders until his protective arm took its place.

Maybe she lives in you, he said. *After all, your secret name is hers.*

Malena shook her head. *She was strong, resourceful, and intelligent, and not easily cowed.*

Ariben smiled and pulled her closer. *As I said …*

TRAPPED

Huldar held his finger to his lips. His heart beat loud in his chest. The only sound was the distant whistle of air drawn more vigorously from the natural chimney by a change in the prevailing winds outside

Daric and Gento nodded - the barest of movements. They dare not use mind-speech. Delemät Ashik and his troops were close by - above ground but close to entry.

A bout of quiet swearing and the smell of disturbed soil heralded the removal of the final boulder, then a faint breeze carried the scents of grass and spine-bush perfume as rock and gravel skittered down the incline.

Huldar winced at a distant grunt of effort - or was it pain, and signaled and the other two to move back. Each action must be considered. Screens held smooth and cryptic.

Delemät's keen farsight swept over them, but more from habit rather than intent. It was clear he did not suspect a trap.

When they reached the second bend and the cover of a small outcrop, Huldar quieted his breathing. "So far, so good," he mouthed.

Every 'plink' of dripping water registered overloud. The rock felt coarse and damp beneath his hand.

He motioned for Daric to assess Delemät's position.

The assassin gave a purposeful nod.

Eighteen Ashik, Daric whispered, *plus twenty or so miners.*

Farushael? Gento asked.

Daric shook his head and held up one hand.

Footsteps and curses echoed through the cave walls. They recognized Delemät's brusque tones as he barked an order.

Moments later, Daric's hand came down.

Huldar gave a tiny nod.

The assassin's face lit in an evil grin. He closed his eyes, his head twitched, and as if that action alone had been enough, a planned cascade took effect. One small rock hit another, then they hit more, then more.

"Look out!" someone cried.

"Shit! Landslide!"

But it was the small explosion at a key point in the ceiling that made Delemät's escape impossible.

Done! Daric whispered.

A gust of dust-laden air rushed over them.

Before it had time to settled, they started at a run for their former camp-ground.

"HULDAR!" Delemät's voice was alive with rage. "Breathless fucking waste of Breath! I know he's done this!"

Farsight arrowed back and forth above them. Huldar flinched as it scoured their screens.

Cobar pictured his sword.

HULDAR! YOU BREATHLESS PIECE OF SHIT! I KNOW YOU'RE THERE!

Even less happy than usual, Daric said.

Cobar snorted.

They scrambled over chunks of rock and limestone flows, following the faint natural light from the bioluminescent cave dwellers, galaxies of shining creatures who went about their lives oblivious to the annangi drama below. Would ever see them again, Huldar wondered, or have a chance to understand them better? He conceded it was unlikely. The lake-monster's roar bounced against his eardrums. Did it sense the danger?

He glanced at a particularly bright star formation and felt his footing slide. Seepage oozed beneath his hands as they broke his fall. Loose shale fell over the edge and splashed loosely into the water. Restless fins clawed the surface, hoping for an easy meal.

I'm alright, he said, as he scrambled to his feet and kept running.

Carnivorous? Daric asked hopefully, and sent an image of Delemät 'accidentally' slipping.

Yes, said Huldar, *but mouths too small to worry us.*

Cobar grunted softly and sent a whiff of disappointment.

Huldar took deep breaths of dank, soil scented air and exhaled in rhythm with his steps. The lakeside run seemed endless, the pace steady enough to avoid accident, but brisk enough to stay ahead of their pursuers. They must exit the cave before Delemät could see how and where – just in case.

At last, the going leveled and the deserted camp ground came into view. All that remained was a scatter of talemgal, a cold hearth and a pair of worn-out boots he'd no further use for.

As they ran up the ridge to the portal, Delemät's almighty pulse of farsight laid bare their screens.

GOT YOU! he roared.

They sensed his withdrawal.

"Now!" Daric cried. "Quickly! Before he has time to consolidate his attack!"

Huldar felt recognition in the ancient forces that gathered round them, and calmed himself to let the song flow smoothly.

A ball of flame exploded through the cavern, obliterating all in its path.

"NOW!" Daric cried.

The sequence of notes fell from his lips, calm and sure, and, still heaving with exertion, they stepped into the harsh daylight of the eastern desert.

Heat shimmer blurred the horizon. Deep breaths quickly parched his throat.

Cobar looked him up and down. "A bit singed, my friend."

"Couldn't be rushed," Huldar replied, "or Breath knows where we might have ended up."

Daric nodded. "Well done. And even if he found the portal, there's no one else capable of working it."

Huldar looked at his companions, the lithe Enna and the hulking Rukh beside him, and smiled from the bottom of his being. How fortunate he was to have such a team. He took a purposeful breath and tension drained from his shoulders as the air was released. They would have time to activate the Southern Djan'rū now, if they acted quickly. Their enemy was too deep underground to sense anything above - or to be sensed. He smiled in satisfaction.

"He'll be there a while," Cobar rumbled.

"Hopefully. But he will find a way," Daric said darkly. "He won't care what it costs."

Huldar checked his knees and was relieved to find them merely bruised, and that the cuts on his palms were superficial. Ahead the faint shimmer of the next of their portals in ancient Qalān seemed to beckon. A deep sense of the Planet's approval thrummed through his soul with the now familiar if much reduced, bell-like tone. His life was on its appointed path - wherever that might lead. "Let's go home," he said, "whatever that means at the moment. I've a hankering for stew."

Daric laughed. "A new story for you to tell. The Great Escape - and what a beauty it will be."

ANU AND KANDÄT ENNA

The refectory at Mecca was warm and quiet. Strong windows looked out onto a scene of barren rocks and layered cliffs bathed in perpetual twilight. The dull, orange-tinged sky, equally lifeless, was streaked by high, sulphur-stained clouds. Some found the view fascinating, more found it dreary, but to Anu of Maatu it had always seemed a warning - an illustration of what the galaxy would be like if it was abandoned.

Silhouetted in one yellow window was the dapper form of his old mentor and friend, Kandät Enna, although since his father's departure from the Imperium and his own refusal to take his place, Anu had let their association lapse.

The navigator sat a little apart from his crew, as if needing space.

Anu retreated before he could be noticed.

A little further down the dusty corridor, he opened the door beneath a sign bearing the rune of Hermes. After a brief conversation, the Hermes departed for the dining room.

Anu sat cross-legged on the threadbare divan. The wait seemed interminable. His stomach rumbled.

Shamkarun Kandät Enna will speak with you, the Hermes said at last.

Anu nodded, although neither could see him. *Thank you, Hermes.*

Proceed.

Anu? Kandät said. *What's this about?*

Sorry Bai'ah, but I need your help.

Shak'ri, in case you were unaware, I am rather busy. You've hardly spoken to me in years. What is it you want?

Anu scratched his head. *It is a delicate matter. Could you come with the Hermes to her office? We can speak without fear.*

Kandät sent a pulse of alarm.

Anu acknowledged his response and affirmed it was appropriate. *Let no one know of my presence here, please. No one.*

On my honor, I will not, Kandät replied.

Anu pushed from the cushions to pace the small room. His eyes burned from lack of sleep. His feet made barely a sound. Had he done the right thing? His gaze roved over bare stone walls lit by soft, yellow globes. His stomach rumbled more urgently. The chord had been tight indeed. Four days without pause needed payment in food and sleep, but he'd reached Kandät Enna before the last stretch, and if his old friend was willing to help, he was certain he could keep his arrival on Went hidden from Delemät Ashik.

The door opened at last and the Hermes entered, followed by Kandät Enna.

The moment their eyes met, Anu knew he had nothing to fear. "Bai'ah!"

"Shak'ri," Kandät said warmly. "Why have you kept away?"

Anu's head tilted. "You *are* the Empress Ishiquel's uncle," he said wryly.

Kandät grimaced. "Yes. That at least cannot be changed. Now, what is it you need? You must be desperate if you've come all the way out here to meet me in person."

"It concerns Malena."

Kandät's gaze narrowed enough for Anu to know he'd struck a chord. "What can I do?" he said. "Don't tell me anything, mind!"

Anu nodded. "I need you to make noise when you arrive."

"Distraction?"

He nodded again. "Would be most helpful."

"Delemät?"

"That's him," Anu said. "About an hour's worth, or more if you can manage."

"Lead him away? I'll need a fairly robust excuse."

Anu shook his head, "Definitely not, unless it's further to the north."

Kandät bowed his head as if in thought. His haze barely rippled, but his veils were immaculate and held over-tight. Eventually, the older navigator met Anu's gaze.

"It will be as you request, but you'd best be aware there's more than your cousin will need saving."

Anu's brow furrowed. *How many?*

I'd anticipate twenty or so, some heavily pregnant, or with newborns. Kandät's brows gave a delicate lift. "I wish you well, my friend, and will do what I can." He bowed in farewell. *Look me up when this is done.*

Anu bowed in return. *I will,* he replied.

We will be gone from the refectory in twenty minutes. Can you last till then?

"If I must," Anu answered.

When Kandät's suggested time was up, Anu messaged the cook with his order and made his way to a table. His head whirled with calculations and necessary adjustments and he barely saw the hall or even the food on his plate. He would craft a waystation in close proximity to Went herself. Such structures were undetectable except to those who made them, and untraceable. Its envelope would hold the refugees in semi-comfort while he worked out what to do with them. But the size needed for so many could only be achieved in proportion to energy expenditure. Best to start small, he reasoned, then recruit Malena's crew to assist with its enlargement.

With the waystation as a base, he could wait for Went's Djan'rū to chime and make his own entrance in Kandät's wake. Whatever trouble Malena was in, if Delemät Ashik was involved, he wanted to get there before he could leave and take her with him.

DJAN'RŪ

Andel turned over in bed. It still surprised her how easy it was to do so, now that she and her daughter, Inanna, were physically separated.

She put her face closer to breathe in her Blessing's intoxicating smell, and smoothed her fingertips over newborn skin … soft, smooth and tingling with life. While she slept, Inanna's hair moved in slow, barely perceptible waves. It made Andel smile to think of the times she'd studied the elderly tent-pole and enjoyed the feel of the swirls in its grain. Now her heart rested in similar pattens, but these were kinetic and expressive - a whole new language.

At last, a longed-for burst of love filled her marriage bond.

We're on our way home, Huldar said. There was a great sense of achievement in his tone, and she sighed with relief. Not only had they achieved whatever it was they'd set out to do, they'd survived unscathed.

Careful not to wake Inanna, she slid out of bed. Again, she relished her freedom of movement as she pulled on a pair of much slimmer trousers and a loose, warm top. Beyond the tent, the only light came from the central hearth and the coals of Tam's kitchen fires, and she wondered how long it would be before they saw sunlight and fresh air again. She glanced at the mop of white hair peeking out from under the blankets. Surely it was important for the babies' health?

Tam was already there. "Just heating up the stew," he said with a smile.

"Lucky we saved some," she replied.

"Yes! Almost had to fight a certain miner couple for it."

"Your own fault, Tam. They didn't get such quality out on the workings."

He snorted a laugh. "Hold on a moment, Lady Andel, and I'll get you some tea."

"I'm perfectly capable of making my own, you know." She picked up her cup and a galano twig from a jar on the long wooden bench.

Tam held out his hand for the cup. "That may be! But just this once, let me do it for you."

"And the next 'once' no doubt, and the next," she laughed. "But thank you, Tam. My father has a saying - even the smallest act of kindness refreshes the hearts of both giver and receiver." She gave him an arch look. "So you must be so very refreshed!"

He rolled his eyes and passed the steaming cup back to her.

Casco stood beside her. "If he keeps this up, he may never need to bathe again!"

She grinned delightedly.

Tam lifted another mug toward Casco and began to reply, but the portal chimed and her breath was stolen by deep gladness as Huldar stepped through.

Casco stopped in mid-reach for his tea, locked in Daric's gaze.

Cobar gave a nod of greeting and strode toward the tent he shared with Gento and Rosheen.

"Went well, then?" Tam said cheerily, but he gave Huldar an odd look. "Was there fire involved?"

"Boom!" Daric laughed, and opened his arms in a wide circular motion.

Huldar's hand went to what remained of his frizzled eyebrows. "A little singed is all."

"I'm waiting beside him," Daric said, tipping his head Huldar's way. "Now! I said, we have to leave now! And there's this huge ball of flame coming right for us! Hah! That's living."

Casco's eyebrows lifted. "It was close then?"

"Close?" Daric repeated. "Any closer and we'd have been nothing but ash!"

Huldar sipped the tea Tam gave him. His eyes twinkled above the rim. "And thanks to you, my friend, our mission was a success."

"Another half-second and we might have had somewhat less of a victory!"

Andel frowned at her husband. "Huldar?"

He smiled. "Delemät and his followers are trapped in our last camp-cave. It should take quite some time before they escape." He held out his arm and she moved beneath it and hugged him close. His smell was every bit as beautiful to her as Inanna's, but his ribs were closer to the surface than they had been.

"He wasn't very happy when we left." Daric said gleefully.

Tam dipped his ladle into a simmering pot. "How long? A rough guess?"

"He has a contingent of miners with him," Huldar said, "so not as long as I'd like, but I doubt he'll be out before Kandät Enna gets here."

"Good news," Tam said. "And here's your stew, as requested!"

Huldar disengaged from her arms and began to eat with gusto.

"Any flat-bread to go with that, Tam?" Andel asked. "If he's in the mood to eat at last ..."

"Coming right up," Tam assured her.

There was a hoot of laughter from the Rukh's tent, before it lapsed into an apologetic hush.

"Sari's bringing Calath over," Casco said. "Why don't you bring Inanna out too, when she wakes." He looked around the small settlement. "They'll all be awake soon."

"Odd how that happens," Daric said.

"They're in touch at a very deep level." Casco shrugged. "I don't understand it, can't feel it – but that's how it is. Huldar?"

A slow smile broke over Huldar's face. "I see what you mean!" he said excitedly. "Maybe it's like a forest, or a local biome. I might be able to sense what they're doing ... if ever I get time to simply sit down with them and 'be', he added wistfully. "Casco, Daric, tomorrow - could one or both of you take a look at the Djan'rū site, make sure all is as it should be? We have to be ready to fire it up immediately Kandät Enna arrives. Malena tells me that will be the time he's least likely to sense it. Casco, we'll need your Ziquarra to coordinate the initiation, but, as I understand it, because of what happened during its making, the gate is tuned to you. You are the only one who can complete the song - is that true?"

Casco nodded. "I'm afraid so. But I'll need Malena to guide me through it, plus Daric for back-up.

"Will you need me this time?" Andel asked.

"If you can," Casco said. "I've a hunch things will go more smoothly if all the original crew are present."

"Inanna can stay with you for a while," she said to Huldar. "But it might be hard for Malena to separate herself from Shameera. Perhaps you can talk with her, Casco?"

"She won't listen to me," he said doubtfully.

"Not Malena," Andel said patiently. "Shameera."

Casco nodded in understanding.

"If she understands her mother will be back, maybe she won't mind staying with Ariben for a while, and that will make it easier for Malena to let her go."

Daric nudged Casco as the Rukh contingent emerged.

Rosheen cradled her baby, a tiny bundle safe in her warrior mother's muscular arms, and flanked by two burly, bush-wise guardians.

Andel felt her eyes sting with tears.

Huldar gave her a gentle smile. Emotion flowed back and forth between them in a primal confirmation of their bond. Both turned when Inanna woke. Although she made no sound, the little Bless could certainly make herself understood. Andel wrapped her arms over suddenly explosive breasts and hurried back to feed her.

Huldar gazed into the hearth and remembered the night, many years ago, when he'd used snow and sparks to tell the story of Creation - The Seven Breaths. The atmosphere had been tense but expectant, as they knew the navigator would come soon and take them home.

He could feel anxious eyes on his back. Again, there was a fire in the dark. Again the Uri'madu waited for rescue - but this time, there was no guarantee. The tone was not expectant, at least, not in a good way. That last fire had portended a tragedy. He could not shake the idea that this one might too.

Darling? Andel asked.

He shared his concern.

No, she said firmly. *You're overtired and exhausted and that won't happen. You will keep us safe, otherwise Mother's premonition ... remember?*

His spirit lightened. Their daughter at least would survive. He gave a quiet nod. It had been foretold.

With that small encouragement in mind, he turned to face them.

“There is hope,” he began. “A watch has begun for Kandät Enna’s arrival.”

“Will he take us home?”

Huldar replied evenly, “I don’t believe so.”

“Have you asked him?”

“We can’t stay here,” another said.

“We can, and we must,” he said, “for the time being - at least until Delemät Ashik has gone.”

“That might be weeks!”

Huldar gave a slow nod. They must understand - but they had not looked into the monster’s eyes as he had, and seen the tortured soul inside. “Delemät will continue to search for us, and for our children, for as long as he can - until the last moment he can remain on Went. While he is here, he will not stop. If he finds any one of us, he will destroy them and come for the rest of us. But he will go. He has to.”

“Does he?” Gael said. “He’s the God-Emperor’s brother. He can do whatever he wants.”

Huldar sighed. “Yes, he is, and it’s possible he might stay, but I, for one, don’t believe he will. The fact is, we must remain hidden for quite some time, now and in the future, even after we are rescued. Our babies deserve to grow and develop in safety. The God-Emperor wants us dead. This is a long-term problem, and if anyone has any good ideas about how to solve it, please don’t keep them to yourself.”

“So, why are you watching for the navigator?” Nachiel asked.

Huldar glanced at the ceiling. Disclosure was a risk, but mitigated by Delemät’s imprisonment. “We have made our own Djan'rū,” he said at last. “It is yet to be initiated. Its location will remain secret until we can be evacuated. And a message was sent - at great personal cost, asking for help."

"From who?"

"Shamkarun Anu, first of Maatu."

"He is my cousin," Malena said quietly. "He will come."

"Kandät Enna will sense the new Djan'rū," Topper said. "He'll know exactly where it is."

"Not if we activate it at exactly the right time - hence the watch." He gazed around his audience. "And here is where you can help, if you feel you can. We need a chain of far-sight observers, each on a four hour shift. You'll be well hidden should Delemät and his Ashik release themselves sooner than expected."

"I have some farsight," Bush said. "And so does Topper."

"Can mothers help too?"

"I don't see why not," Huldar replied. "So long as your babies are safe."

"Then count me in," said Gael.

"And me," said Tish.

"Don't be so stupid," said Minna. "What if you get caught?"

"I won't," the miner answered confidently. "We have to do this. The Uri'madu have accepted us as their own. This is the least we can do."

"If it hadn't been for them and their stupid party, none of this would have happened," Minna snapped, "- so excuse me if I don't feel so grateful!"

"The choice to help is yours alone," Huldar said. "There is no obligation. Those of you who feel they can be involved, meet me here in one hour to discuss tactics, range and rosters." He gave a solemn bow. "Thank you all for listening."

Sun beat down on the tiny speck of land, an afterthought lost in the restless dreams of the great southern ocean. Huldar cocked his head to listen to an unfamiliar chirp. It's volume and resonance seemed to indicate a larger vocalist, but a quick glance revealed no unfamiliar creatures. A flash of annoyance creased his forehead. Right now, he could not let his attention waver.

His gaze returned to the supine form of Casco's vacant body. Their vigil was almost a week old. Delemät must emerge soon, but Kandät Enna had yet to arrive.

At last his friend's body stirred.

One look at his expression told Huldar the news was not good. He handed him a glass of water.

Casco showed him images of the Host's encampment. The area around the Djan'rū bustled with activity, but the space itself remained empty. Then he showed Huldar the ground around the open seam where Delemät and his Ashik had entered the cave. *I noticed this ...* He pointed out an anomaly roughly one hundred paces from the initial shaft, where small group of strap-trees had subsided. *I can't see beneath, but I think they'll come out here. Might be a more stable exit. Who knows?*

Huldar glanced sunward. Their brief respite was over. He messaged Daric. *Screens!*

Casco nodded. *He's spread the word. Everyone on high alert.*

But before he could say more, Gael's voice rushed into his mind. *He's here! The navigator is here!*

While Huldar messaged the others, Casco picked himself up off the ground and started for the portal. Two steps later they were on the island in the deep south. The new exit was somewhat east of the old one in the scrub above the bleak beach. Cold wind roared unrelenting in their ears. Huldar tried to pinpoint the old portal, but it had vanished beneath the waves.

They felt, rather than heard the chime as Malena stepped through and hurried to join them.

Casco pulled his coat tighter around his chest and waited expectantly. Soon Daric appeared, pulling on a coat mid-stride.

No time to waste! he said crossly. *Who knows how long this will take and Delemät will be on the loose at any moment!*

Together, the small group began to pick their way toward the nascent Djan'rū.

When they reached the rock platform, they stationed themselves evenly around the central core of energy.

Casco gave a short nod. Ready?

Huldar relaxed his defenses and gave him the access he needed. They had not linked minds for a long time, certainly not since Casco had been Marked, but there was no time for him to be surprised by his long-time friend's smooth power.

The Djan'rū enlivened at their touch. Energy wove around them, light and almost playful at first, but as the four inputs balanced up, its resonance deepened. Casco stepped forward into the flickering waves and stood just outside its coruscating heart.

He turned to Huldar.

Huldar nodded. *Whatever you need.*

Share your knowledge of the planet.

Without question or reservation, he opened himself to his friend and did as he was asked. Energy racketed through him, as if hungry for affirmation. His inner bell rang and rang louder. He fought to stay upright. Although she made no sound, he sensed Malena's presence. Then Casco and Daric joined forces and aligned them in a single pure chord that reached from the planet's core and punched outward as if to be heard by the stars.

Abruptly, the terrifying sound stopped. The light winked out. In the resulting vacuum Huldar finally sank to his knees.

What was that? he asked feebly. He closed his eyes, and the afterburn of a complex fractal shone on his retinas. The forces involved when he'd built the small gate at their first campsite had been nowhere near as intense.

There were rapid footfalls as Daric and Casco rushed to his side.

Are you alright? Casco asked. His concern was deep and comforting. Huldar felt his chest loosen. Breath once more began to flow. *I'm alright,* he said to Andel's frightened query, *just a little drained.*

I had no idea that would happen, Casco said. *It was what the gate wanted.*

Perhaps somewhat more of an ancient flow than we suspected, Daric said.

It seemed to need the planet's permission, Casco continued.

Malena stood back and stared as if dazzled by their handiwork. "It's magnificent," she breathed.

Huldar was surprised he could hear her. Inside, his mind still reeled, but he felt the planet's approval in a gentle, continuous chime.

"The whole of Went must have heard that," he said.

"No," Malena corrected. "The sound was psychic and localized until the final chord. Hopefully Kandät Enna missed it."

"We'll know soon enough," Daric said.

Huldar accepted Casco's hand to help him to his feet. Strength flowed through their contact, and although the love they exchanged was different to what it had once been, it seemed more fully realized.

They smiled into each other's eyes. So much had changed, yet …

"Let's go!" Daric said impatiently.

Casco grinned. "He's become quite pushy since the Bless."

They started for the gate, running as best they could. Hope shone bright in Huldar's heart. They had set the stage. Now, all being well, they just need wait for Anu of Maatu to make his appearance.

He will come, Malena assured him.

He could feel her confidence. The planet sang to him … yet there was a small niggle he couldn't quite put his finger to, a slight dimming of the light. He paused before they stepped through the portal to the safety of their cave and said to Daric and Casco, "Make sure everyone knows to keep their screens up, and get home as quickly as possible." Perhaps the darkness was Delemät Ashik?

END GAME

There was a flash of light, deafening noise, and Delemät knew even as he fell, he'd fallen victim to Huldar of Leth's cunning again.

Angels screamed, doubtless some of his Ashik among them, but their pain flew over and around him, sensed but unheard, an inconvenience similar to the dust from the cave-in.

Huldar of Leth. He had to be here. Every ounce of his vaunted farsight trained on his quarry. Every detail of the system ahead was exposed to him, each rock and crevice, every stupid glowing creature. There was a shimmer, a trace. No matter how clever his quarry thought he was, the stench of Leth oozed through it.

"HULDAR!" The name seemed to emanate from a deeper, rage-filled place.

To me! he commanded his Ashik. If he followed the trace, he would find the way out. And once he did …

Of the troops he'd brought with him, only eight came to his side. A quick scan showed the rest trapped or dead. A group of miners lifted rock in an effort to free the survivors.

Leave them! he snapped. Broken bodies were no use to him.

The miners continued to work. *We won't leave our brethren,* one replied.

His self-righteous tone was insufferable. Delemät's Tsemkar flared – a ripple of heat across his forehead, and the insubordinate rabble was dead before he hit the ground. The rest of the miners looked at him in horror.

"Who will be next?" He asked. Inside, he seethed with impatience. He had no time for this.

Stones clattered as the miners made their way down the mountain of debris.

He returned his attention to finding Huldar. The lay-out was simple, a long tunnel with a high, curved ceiling – a lake in the middle. They would be forced to skirt its edges. Then, far ahead, he saw Huldar and two others paused on a ridge. Without waiting for permission, he sucked as much energy as he could from those around him and with a roar of absolute fury, propelled a lethal blast toward his nemesis.

The writhing ball of flame exploded toward the ridge. When it was done, he felt light, almost weightless. There had been nowhere for his enemy to run. No screen he knew of could protect against the intensity of what he'd conjured.

He followed its path with his mind, teasing himself with slow anticipation. There were no more fatuous glowing slugs on the ceiling. A soft rain of fine ash was all that remained. Long-necked carcasses smoked on the lake's steaming surface. The smell of roast swamp was strong. … And there it was. The ridge. He recalled Huldar's look of shock – his opponent's last moment now just a pleasing image Delemät could hold dear for the rest of his days.

But the ridge was empty.

Clean.

He focused more intently. There must be some remains. Had they been completely incinerated? Had his blast been so powerful? It was possible. Two dead miners lay behind him, their empty husks mute testimony to the strength of his will.

He signaled two Ashik to accompany him.

"The rest of you work with the miners to clear a way out."

The looks they gave were far from cordial. Boots crunched resentfully. The remaining miners hurried upslope, still hopeful there might be survivors under the rubble. Ashik followed more resolutely. Delemät left them to it. Success was doubtful. Try as he might, the surface was beyond his perception, but his command would keep them busy while he found the exit Huldar had been making for - probably a vent somewhere near that ridge.

He followed faint footprints fired into the mud. The track seemed tortuous in the extreme, but he found any deviation was a waste of time. Huldar had certainly known the terrain.

When the fateful ridge came into view, his pulse quickened. A plan to capture the rest of the group had already formed. The one thing the ecologist cared about more than any other was those hairy lumps he believed to be fully sentient citizens - and although the location of the Uri'madu might be elusive, maybe he could lure them out with a threat to the Went.

He positioned himself exactly as Huldar had and pushed his face to mimic that comical look of shock. At his suggestion, the two he'd bought with him stood where Huldar's shadowy companions had been. But although the scene was gratifying, a thorough search failed to reveal any charred remains, or any clues as to where their exit might be.

The cave continued on. He followed to where the scorch zone ended - a clear transition between glowing creatures and sterile rock. There were no footprints, no sign of any annangi ever having been there. Beyond that point was another long, narrow lake. He could see no way around it, and farsight showed the water eventually vanished in a roaring cascade through a narrow slot. Below that came yet more caves, but these deeper cavities were bifurcated and rough, with little head-height.

He brought his vision back to his immediate surrounds. Where had they gone? The glowing creatures ahead of them emitted a steady, shadowless light. He looked back into the dark. It didn't make sense.

Progress report!

Back at the rock-fall, the most senior of his remaining troops snapped to attention. *Slowly, sir,* she replied. *No survivors as yet.*

Her despondency bled through. She did not believe they would escape at all, yet to kill her now would be wasteful. Maybe he should try to lift his troop's morale. He'd heard people often worked better if they felt valued, and if he could not find an alternate escape route, they would have to make one.

I will return soon and reassess our plan, he said.

The reply was a sense of obedient affirmation with undertones of terror. Perhaps his technique needed work.

IMMINENT ERUPTION

Farushael of Cantori stood on the hill above the Host's encampment and surveyed the Djan'rū site in despair. Although their quotas had been met, they were not yet loaded. His staff had been halved by Delemät Ashik's vendetta against the Uri'madu, and after five days neither the miners, the Ashik, nor the general himself had returned. There had been no word, and he could not make contact. If Delemät was dead it would be cause for joy, but there were others to consider.

Bags and boxes ferried to and fro along rain-slick tracks. From this vantage they looked like insect trains, each group loaded with far more bulk than anyone had the right to expect, yet Shamkarun Kandät Enna could arrive at any moment and they must continue to do the work of twice their number.

He started as a flock of lizards screamed skyward. The warning groan beneath his feet sent him clutching for the rough bark of a nearby tree. Moments later, the ground began to buck beneath his feet. He watched in dismay as a load of boxes tumbled downhill along with several over-tired porters.

One of the boxes broke open. Small rocks peppered the fallen.

Medic! he cried. *Is everyone alright?*

The team-leader picked himself up off the ground. *I think so.* He bent to help another to his feet. Both were covered in mud. *Just another tremor. A few cuts and bruises. No need for the healer to attend.* They looked up as the rest of the team skittered downhill to join them.

Farushael realized he was still gripping the tree quite hard. When he let go, his palms were corrugated with the impression of strap-tree nodules. He was certain this level of personal stress was above his pay-grade. He remembered Lady Andel's initial appraisal of their imminent danger and wished she was available now - but even if she'd said the site was about to blow, they would have to keep at it. This was the only viable Djan'rū. The one at the ecologists base-camp was just too small.

When Delemät Ashik's farsight finally cruised over the site, he didn't know how he should feel. Life without him in the camp was more pleasant, but perhaps now there was a chance they could be ready in time.

Halfway through the following day, Farushael steeled himself when the east portal gave a portentous chime.

He hurried closer and bowed low. "My lord Tsemkarun Delemät Ashik." Only a remnant of those who had accompanied the general had returned with him. He hid his dismay as deeply as he could. "There was no contact. We feared you dead."

"We will have food and rest," Delemät grated.

He tried not to cringe. "A hot meal awaits in the refectory," Farushael assured him. "Although I fear it may be plain fare, since most of us are otherwise engaged in preparation for the navigator's arrival."

"And that Breath-forsaken cook defected."

Farushael bowed again.

"Very well. After four hours rest, those of us who are able will assist with transport of goods." He looked the Cantori up and down. "Good work."

Farushael tried in vain to keep astonishment from jarring his haze, but the shock journeyed to his deepest veils. *Good work?*

One of the miners raised his eyebrows, just a little, as he passed.

A small tremor struck, but he hardly noticed. Something was very wrong.

Two hours later, the Djan'rū chimed. Workers scurried from the vicinity, then stopped to watch as Shamkarun Kandät Enna released the envelope and strode toward the kitchens. His exhausted spinners trailed behind him.

Farushael hurried forward.

"Where is Olatu of Cantori?" Kandät asked him.

"I'm afraid he has rejoined the Breath," Farushael replied.

The navigator rolled his eyes. "I wondered how long Delemät Ashik would endure him. And why is our fine general not here to greet me?"

"He has only just now, almost this minute, returned from an arduous mission. I am sure he will be here soon," Farushael assured him.

"I want to see him now." Kandät waved his spinners on.

"Can it not wait?" Farushael blurted. His cheeks flamed. He bowed low. "My apologies! But the general's mission was taxing indeed."

"Ah, I see," Kandät said knowingly. "You wish to survive where your predecessor did not. Very well, if you will direct me to his quarters I will see him myself."

Farushael watched in disbelief as the elderly Enna marched purposefully down the street. *Shouldn't he be famished?* he asked himself. Navigators needed to eat immediately after arrival on-world - everyone knew it. He thought about what such hunger might mean for his state of mind and decided he wouldn't like to be Delemät Ashik right now.

He assumed a casual air and walked as if on some errand or another, to the vicinity of Delemät's tent. As close as he dared, he held paper and stylus as if checking a list, and began to listen.

The screens around Delemät's tent were of the highest standard, so when the muffled sound of voices bled through, he knew they must be very loud indeed. He thought he heard Huldar's name mentioned, but couldn't be absolutely sure. Delemät's deeper pitch responded defensively. Then Kandät Enna yelled something about 'Ishät'. The God-Emperor's name was so startlingly clear, Farushael nearly dropped his stylus. Things seemed to degenerate from there.

Soon afterwards, the ground shuddered as if in protest. Farushael took it as a sign and proceeded to the Djan'rū to continue checking lading lists. Last time, the navigator stayed for at a few days to catch up on food and some much-needed sleep before reentering the chime, but in his estimation it would be at least two more days before the full manifest could be delivered and secured.

Delemät glared after Kandät Enna as the tent-flap closed. He felt the navigator's steady, over-confident tramp as if those steps were a continuation of the trampling he'd just received. No one else spoke to him so rudely. No one else could - except for his brother, of course. And what a shit-storm that reunion was shaping up to be. And it was all, in every way he looked at it, Huldar of Leth's fault. The babies, the humiliation, the loss of his troops. One full week spent below ground, dirty, dark and always under threat of a fresh landslide. He looked at the roughened skin on his hands. He'd even had to shift rock himself. He'd been caught in a mini cave-in and nearly died. Had it been planned that way? There had been losses amongst the miners and they resented him greatly for it. Him. They resented him. Why not Huldar - the architect of all their problems?

And was he even dead? How could he tell? He could think of only one way, and if his nemesis fell into the trap .... if there was one thing he must do before the insufferable Kandät, uncle to his brother's wife, could whisk him back to life in the Imperial Palace, it was to make sure that Shamkarun Huldar of Leth would never laugh at him again. If he could assure Ishät that without question, the leader of the Uri'madu had rejoined the Breath, maybe he would not be so angry about his many failures.

ANU ARRIVES

Shamkarun Anu of Maatu released his Chord and looked around. Despite the difficulties of working with the planet Went's energy, now he was here, he felt good … accepted - if that made sense.

In the distance, a grey, polar sea heaved and sighed, its wildness nearly as breathtaking as the icy wind.

He reached into Qalān for an extra jacket and pulled it quickly over his head. Pebbles rolled beneath his feet as he jumped down the leeward side of the rock platform. Stale muscles relished the movement, but it felt better still to rest his back against the solidity of stone and let his long legs stretch. With a tight screen in place, he demolished a few handfuls of dried fruit and biscuits and wondered, *what now?*

Kattíst, he whispered. He knew no one else would hear. It was a game they'd played when they were young … the wind in the grass.

Waves roared. Icy gusts whistled between stones. He waited. There was no way for him to know if she was able to respond, or if she'd been captured by Delemät and held hostage somewhere, or even if she was still this side of the Breath.

Fifteen minutes later, he'd surveyed his surroundings enough to know there were no nearby portals. *How was he supposed to help if he was trapped there?* He asked himself. Cold ate at his bones. To be at such a pristine location was exhilarating, but far too close to the planet's south pole for comfort. He could not stay much longer. He tried again. *Kattíst!*

Shak'ri!

He sighed, releasing a breath he'd held for too long. His cousin was alive! But as he looked northward where her voice had come from, he had no clue as to how he could reach her. He could only trust that from the relief in her tone, she had a plan.

Sure enough, an image of a tall Shamkarun, whom he assumed to be Huldar of Leth, slipped into his mind, coupled with the sense this person would arrive shortly. Their link was brief and minimal, but just the same he hoped Kandät Enna's promised diversion was ongoing. Delemät Ashik's gift for farsight was well known.

He let his senses range again, but this only made him more certain there was no portal on the island. Was Huldar coming by boat? He studied the heaving ocean again. It seemed unlikely.

He felt rather than heard a subliminal chime, turned, and there was Huldar, Sacred to Leth, striding over the loose pebble scrublands as if blown to him on the wind itself. Anu's pulse quickened. There *was* a portal! He'd heard Huldar was somewhat of a master when it came to their construction, but how had he managed to hide one so completely? Given his sensitivity to Qalān, he'd have thought it impossible.

He jumped back onto the rock platform and waved. The gale ploughed into him with bone-chilling force.

Huldar's smile lit up his face. He lifted his hand in reply and picked up his pace to a run.

Face to face, his eyes were caught by the complex Mark that covered the Lethian's cheek and even extended down his neck. Such growth occurred only in proportion to the bearer's skill and power, and this one shouted vast quantities of both. "Shamkarun Huldar, Sacred to Leth?" He bowed low.

"Please!" Huldar's voice was compelling, melodious, and unashamed of its characteristic lilt. "You are First of Maatu, and hopefully our saviour. There is no need to bow. And besides, we of the Uri'madu hold no place for ceremony and division."

"Am I to consider myself a member of your team, then?"

Huldar's eyes crinkled. "I hope you will come to think of yourself in that way."

Anu found himself liking Huldar very much. Honour oozed from his every pore, and his power was almost palpable, yet his first impulse was for friendship.

"Sir, I must ask - how is the portal hidden? I have an interest in the workings of Qalān, yet have never heard of a way this can be done."

Huldar cocked his head toward the way he'd come. "Then you'll be interested in this. The portal is not hidden, you just don't know what to look for. Daric Enna's invention, really - a portal through ancient energy paths, hungry, strong and hidden, yet susceptible to negotiation."

"Negotiation?"

"Qalān is a living system."

"Living?" His brow creased fractionally. "How did you discover this?"

"The planet herself told me so."

Huldar turned as if to gauge his reaction, and Anu realised this was part of his charm. His emotions were free and far more open than was usual - perhaps a response to long years of isolation from the Realm. Anu envied him.

The ecologist smiled. "You get used to it."

Anu's mouth quirked, and he let his expression develop into the grin he was feeling. "Planets speaking to one?"

"That too."

They stopped above the stony shore-line. Huldar waved his hand a little forward. "Here we are."

Anu allowed his puzzlement to show. He felt sure they had arrived at the portal site, but sensed nothing, only the cold and the wind. A pack of lizard-like creatures watched from the scrub as if waiting to see if he passed some sort of test.

Huldar held out his hand. "If you would allow me?"

"You're very trusting," Anu replied.

Sky blue eyes looked directly into his. He wondered what they saw.

'Malena has told me a little about you, and our lives already depend on your discretion," Huldar said. "I merely wanted to show you how to see the portal. She may not show herself without my intervention, but once you have seen her, she'll be easier to find when you need to."

"She?"

"Another story. Come. I feel we have little time."

Anu nodded. He'd asked Kandät Enna for an hour, and could expect no more.

Through Huldar's invitation, he was shown a vague, yet vibrant shimmer only four feet from where they stood.

"Another few weeks and this too may be submerged, then the freeze will begin to lower water levels again. The coastline is in a continual state of flux. Are you ready? I'll teach you the song when we're safe."

"Ready," Anu told him.

A silvery string of tones blurred their surroundings, and they stepped out onto the edge of a forest. It was close to mid-day here. Streamers of kelp-like foliage swayed upright from gnarled stumps in an ocean of green. Grey-blue skeins of algae dripped from tendrils of curling vines. A myriad small creatures moved among feathery red flowers, and there was a busy hum in the air. But Huldar strode forward and there was no time to marvel. To Anu, it appeared there was no path at all, but his companion never hesitated. They stripped their heavy clothing garment by garment, but when he started on his jumper, Huldar slowed.

"You might want to keep that. Not far now. Can you see this one?"

Anu squinted at the greenness and kept the glint of the first portal high in mind, but he was all too aware that time was running out.

"There?" He pointed to what he thought was a disturbance in the light.

Huldar shook his head and again, held out his hand. Through their shallow link, Anu saw the gate to the left.

"Maybe it's me."

"I doubt it," Huldar said. "One more and we're there."

Anu looked sunward, despite the fact he knew its position here would tell him nothing useful.

The next step took them south again. This time, when Huldar asked, he steadied his mind and recalled the feel of the previous portals. There was a low pitch to the songs, and a certain clarity, a separation of tone. He put the danger of discovery aside and let his mind range a small, specific area. A glimmer caught his eye. The edges of nearby foliage seemed to move - just slightly.

"There!"

"Well done!"

"May I sing us through?"

Huldar shook his head. "She's a bit tricky. Trusts me, Casco and Daric Enna, and besides we three, Ariben and Malena are the only others she'll listen to … sometimes."

He frowned. It was rare for someone to doubt his abilities.

"This is not Qalān in its usual form," Huldar explained. "You did well to find her so soon - or maybe she likes you."

Anu closed his eyes to better absorb the portal's unusual song - short, powerful and multi-layered. Seconds later he opened them to muted light in a vast cavern. All his senses were abruptly still, and he realised he was deep beneath the ground, far beyond the psychic reach of the surface. Rapid footsteps scattered the gravel as Malena ran toward him.

"Anu!" she cried. "I knew you'd come!"

Her relief brought tears to his eyes. "Of course I came," he said gruffly. "How often have you ever asked for my help? I knew it must be serious."

He opened his arms and held her firmly. She was slimmer even than he remembered, and stronger. Emotion, deep and complex, bled through their touch and when he held her at arms-length tears filled her eyes. He pulled her back to his chest. Her shoulders shook with sobs. Whatever had happened, whatever she had endured, had affected his cousin profoundly.

A craggy-faced Shamkarun looked on. He held a baby protectively in his arms, and Anu needed few refinements to his level of perception to see the deep connection between them. Mael had been correct. It was not a marriage bond - but had Malena fallen in love at last?

Ariben, she said in answer to his curiosity. *Shamkarun Ariben of Leth. My chord in a sea of chaos.*

And who is that he's holding? he asked, but he thought he already knew.

Malena hesitated. *My Bless.*

He nodded slowly. *Kandät managed to warn me, but ...* His brows dew closer in puzzlement. *It's real.*

Yes, it is, she replied. *Would you like to meet your niece?*

She stepped away from his embrace and opened her arm to her partner – it seemed strange not to refer to him as her husband.

She pulled the baby's blanket down a fraction so he could see her face more clearly. Pale, gossamer hair formed a cloud around the infant's delicate features. Large, green-gold eyes studied his own in a disconcertingly mature way. Her hair seemed to wave, but there was no breeze.

"Shameera," Malena said solemnly. "Shameera Stargazer, meet your uncle – Shamkarun Anu, First of Maatu."

As if she knew what the words meant, a smile broke over Shameera's little face and, unable to resist, Anu beamed in reply.

"She likes you," Malena said happily.

The craggy Lethian stepped forward.

"Shamkarun Ariben of Leth?" Anu said, and gave a short bow. "A miracle-worker of the first order."

Ariben's brow lowered.

Anu quickly grinned. "My cousin has found someone worthy at last!"

"Anu!" Malena reprimanded. She turned to Ariben. "Don't mind him. He's always been a bit on the flippant side."

"I don't mind at all," Ariben said seriously. "Nice to be appreciated."

Faces came and went in a blur of introductions. Blessings cooed and babbled, each one different, yet all with the same pale, mobile hair and penetrating golden gaze. Daric Enna gave him a wry smile. The expression reminded him of someone he knew, but he couldn't quite place it. He was surprised to find Casco, whom he knew to have been the leader of the Kareski rebellion, had been Marked Archerra - a rare and very powerful set of abilities.

Finally, Ariben waved to him from the central hearth, a mug in one hand, and a bottle in the other.

Anu tipped his head toward the bottle.

"Besh it is!" one of the spinner brothers ... he thought it was Bush, called out. At least there would be no shortage of help when the time came to expand the waystation, and they could take whatever provisions needed ... a full haul if need be.

A crate of alcohol clinked from a shadowy region at the back of the settlement and was opened with a cheer.

"Come and join us," Huldar said cheerfully. "You are the guest of honour after all."

He smiled and caught the bottle Malena threw at him.

"Told you he was good," she said to Ariben.

"What are your plans?" Huldar asked.

He shook his head. Some things remained the same no matter what. "Kandät Enna will stay four days, no more," he said, "and Delemät Ashik will leave with him. After that, we can move more freely. I've constructed a waystation a short chord from here, but I'm not sure where to take you from there - or if that's where we need to go at all." It would certainly be easier to stay put, then use the new Djan'rū to take them anywhere they wanted to go. He gave the babies a doubtful glance. Their appearance was remarkable; too different to ever be hidden. "I fear the Realm will be unsafe for you, at least until after the Empress gives birth. It will take careful thought."

"Indeed it will." Huldar peered wistfully at the flames. "I must admit, for once I looked forward to returning to civilisation, but that song will not be sung."

"We'll come up with something," Anu said stoutly. "My parents will welcome you and protect you, I'm certain of it."

"Against the God-Emperor's anger?"

Anu took a swig from the bottle. "The God-Emperor? Wouldn't be the first time he's been angry with House Maatu," he replied. "We'll talk about it later. At least you're well stocked and secure from detection – I assume that's why you're here? From your message, all I knew was that my cousin needed my help. I was afraid Delemät had her, or worse."

Huldar nodded. "Things are more difficult than is easily explained. The God-Emperor wants us dead and Delemät Ashik is here to make sure that happens."

"Because of the babies?"

"Yes. The story of their beginnings is unique."

"The Empress has announced her pregnancy," Anu ventured. "Yet only months ago there was no sign."

"Indeed. And therein lies the problem," Huldar said. "Our blessings were not caused entirely in the usual way. The eggs of the Went – a remarkable species endemic to the central continent ..." he hesitated. "We thought them just berries, you see. Ubaid checked them and thought them harmless. Euphoric, aphrodisiac, an interesting fruit and nothing more, but all who ate them and had sex soon afterwards were blessed whether married or not, and those babies developed at about twice the usual rate."

He nodded. "Mael, the Guild-Lord, hinted as much, but berries? How could such experienced ecologists mistake eggs for berries? Surely your healer vetted them first?"

Ubaid leaned into the conversation. "We did. To my great shame, we noticed nothing to tell us otherwise. There is endless variation in what constitutes a life-cycle, but the Wentish interpretation is unique indeed."

Huldar shrugged. "And still poorly understood. It was only later we discovered the truth. I can't tell you how shocked we were. It has been quite a journey."

"The Empress claimed she did not announce sooner so as not to disappoint her subjects with false hope."

"Exactly." Huldar shared a quick glance with Daric Enna. "And now Ishät Ashik wants no one to know he's cheated."

Anu shook his head. "The God-Emperor knew what he was eating?" he said doubtfully. He had no love for their ruler, but for El's representative to do such a thing … "It wasn't an accident?"

"He knew," Huldar said firmly. "Some eggs were stolen. Most were recovered. We believe at least two slipped through and were delivered, courtesy of House Faytha, to the Imperial couple."

"I see – I think." He could feel his facial muscles creasing. "A most remarkable situation." Now he understood why Malena's message had been so cryptic, and so urgent. She was not only in fear for her own life, but for that of her child, and those of her companions. "Delemät Ashik has no idea where you are?"

"I hope not," Huldar said. "If we can just remain hidden until he is forced to leave ... If any one of us was captured we would be forced to evacuate immediately."

"You going to drink that thing or just cuddle it?" Malena interjected.

Anu rolled his eyes.

Huldar grinned. "You can imagine how relieved I was to see you." He gestured toward the central fire, where the rest of the company had gathered. "Please, enjoy the party. We can talk more, make plans, and answer all your questions tomorrow."

Anu's free hand shot up reflexively to catch another bottle Malena had thrown at his head.

Huldar clapped his shoulder. "Ambidextrous? You are good!" he turned for the fire and the kitchen trestles. "Time for serious discussion tomorrow. There's hot stew, talemgal, golden wheel fruit, honey cakes and more than enough besh to go round. We've supplies to last the full seven years at a pinch."

Anu looked into the depths of the cavern and shuddered. To be trapped here for seven years? He put the first bottle to his lips and let the cold ale slide down his throat. But as difficult as the situation was, it intrigued him, and to pit himself against Delemät Ashik, the lovely Charäel's father, was always a joy. While part of his mind lingered on the snow-bear pelt he'd tucked safely into Qalān, he eyed the cheerful crowd. Despite the range of power and rank, they were a well-integrated group, and definitely a team. Huldar was their undoubted leader. The respect the Uri'madu had for him was evident in their natural deference; but despite his enormous rank, above even his own as First of Maatu, he fitted into the party as if he was one of them. Remarkable.

THE MORNING AFTER

Anu woke with a start. It took a moment to understand the triangular shapes above him as the ceiling of a leather tent, and to remember where he was.

At first the cavern seemed completely silent, but when he extended his senses there was the rhythmic hush and release of sleep, the comforting reverberation of a snore, muted murmurs, then a welcome clunk from the kitchen bench.

His stomach rumbled. A few more good feeds wouldn't hurt him, and although the Uri'madu's supplies were plain, they were plentiful.

It wasn't until he'd settled with a massive bowl of hot left-overs and a satisfying mug of tea that a peculiarity struck him. The babies made no sound. Not a single blessing cried. He'd heard them make noises while they were out and about with their families, and seen them respond in normal ways to their surroundings … and the Naghari couple, Alis and Ubaid, seemed unperturbed - even proud of their infant's early signs of intellect.

He recalled a visit to a creche, not so long ago, with a parcel he'd been contracted to deliver in person. Five mothers with their infants; swapping child-raring tips, or so his first thought had been. Three of the little ones were adorable - happy and engaged just like the strange children of the Uri'madu. One was more withdrawn - a little shy, his mother said; but the fifth started crying when he walked in - cried with her whole being. It was abundantly plain she didn't was to be there. Her harassed mother fielded the barrage of negativity as best she could, but a baby's passion is unbridled, and its base telepathy strong and often very difficult to control.

Apparently groups of this kind were a time-honored method of teaching overly reactive infants to accept the presence of others, and he'd been an unwitting participant in their desensitizing program. He hoped it had been successful. He'd departed with a sore head and a new level of respect for mothers.

He caught the cook's eye. "Tam, is it?"

"Arko."

The sturdy angel busied himself with chopping a mound of circular yellow fruit into pieces. "Tam an Shen 'll be here soon enough," he said. "They're the real cooks. I just help out."

"Sorry," Anu said. "Timing … I'm a bit too early it seems."

Arko kept chopping. "Must be hard for one of you lot, navigators I mean. Understandable. And here?" He waved his knife around. "No day or night. Wouldn't have a clue myself. It's just routine."

Anu glanced around the campsite. "Arko; the babies … are they always so quiet?"

"Yep. Happy little things. All sleep at the same time, wake at the same time … roughly. It's like they're connected. That's what we think."

"Do you have one?"

Arko shook his head, a little regretfully Anu thought. "Tam, he's Tashel's now - has a little boy. Areth, he calls himself."

"Who, Tam?" Did planet-walkers have nick-names now?

"No, the baby." Arko paused in his chopping. "They all came with their own names. Can't change em. Won't have it. And Shen, he's with Gael - one of the miners from the Host. Theirs is called Aitha." He smiled. "A bonny wee girl."

Anu remembered Andel and Huldar's bless, Inanna - extraordinary eyes, gold with azure veining, focused and bright. When they'd met, he'd shivered. It was as if they had some sort of connection. In fact, none of the infants he'd met had the bland blueish eye-color of newborns, all were variations of gold … as if they truly were already themselves and born that way. His thoughts went to the Empress. How would the Imperial couple deal with this level of composure, with an old soul born with its own name? Would they try to hide its differences, or celebrate their child's otherworldly beauty as the special gift of El?

He eyed the loaves in the coals, and Arko wafted a slab of thick bread his way.

It was warm to the touch, and springy. He wiped it through the juice in the bottom of his bowl and relished its nutty taste.

"Archerra is a rare Mark," he said, and swiped the bowl again.

Arko nodded.

"A sort of combination of abilities, isn't it?" he said around a last mouthful. "Like Sajhar?"

"Believe so," Arko said. "You'd best ask him yourself."

"Of course." Anu put the bowl down. "Just curious."

Arko leaned forward conspiratorially. "One thing he can do, happened once or twice, he can go from place to place." He snapped his fingers. "Just like that. No portal, no song, nothing. He doesn't talk about it."

Anu's pulse quickened. Translocation was an ability he'd recently discovered in himself, but he'd spent years working on the combination of song and Tsemkar, and even what might be Ziquarra, although this was not a true talent for him. The jump had to be to a place he'd already clearly seen. Did Casco's talent work in the same way? He glanced toward the tents.

"How long before they get up?"

Arko glanced upward, although there was no sun to observe. "Blessings'll kick off in about half hour. Have to have things ready by then."

"Of course," Anu said. "My apologies."

"Not at all," Arko chuckled. "I'll bet curiosity's what woke you! But I do have to get on. Huldar'll be here first – or Daric. Don't mind that he's Enna, whatever he was, he's one of us, now. Anyways, they'll be happy to fill you in."

Sari put down her breakfast bowl and picked up her cup of tea. The warmth against her fingers reminded her of so many comforting cups before. She looked across the rim at the tall navigator in animated conversation with her partners. She could feel their excitement; whirring minds spinning out ideas in skeins far too complex for her to follow. Once, she might have felt intimidated by such intellectual prowess, but now it made her proud. Daric and Casco loved her almost as much as they loved each other, and they were more than holding their own with none less than the First of Maatu. She felt protected and valued in a way she'd never thought possible.

Calath wiggled in her arms. Sari smiled into his dear little face and waggled her finger for him to follow. Emotion flowed between them, a love rich and unfathomable, another experience she'd been certain she'd never have - yet here it was. She wished her parents were still alive so she could share her joy with them - happiness where before there had been only empty space. They had died still blaming themselves for what had happened to her. After so many years ...

She pictured her sister's face. At least they still had each other - but would they ever meet again? She had no way of knowing. Maybe, when they were all safe beyond the God-Emperor's reach - if that was possible, and if she survived ... maybe Anu of Maatu would give her sister a message. Let her know how much she was missed and how she wished they could be together again.

Mama?

Calath's mouth moved, but the sounds he made had little resemblance to speech - as yet.

Yes, my sweetheart?

Safe? Love Darry. Love Cass. New person?

His name is Anu. He is a navigator. She sprinkled her fingers to imitate stars, and pictured the skies of Went in her mind for her son to see. *Like Malena.*

Stargazer? Shameera?

She smiled. *Yes. He will take us to safety, far out among the stars.*

The smile in her son's mind faded. *Far?*

Yes, she said reassuringly. *Away from danger. To a wonderful new home …*

Doubt bloomed in his infant thought. *Not safe?*

She held him close. *Casco and Daric will always keep us safe.*

After a short deliberation, Calath nestled back into his customary happiness. *Love Mama, love Cass, love Darry, love Nu, love Regella,* he recited.

Yes, she replied, although the inclusion of the new, unknown name puzzled her - and it seemed fully realized rather than the shortened versions he usually used. *Love Calath too,* she said, and held him so she could look into his face. *Who is Regella?*

A curious sense of flame and heat came to her; the idea of a long path, then a rapid flickering of darkness and light - did this represent time?

Here, Calath said, his expression serious and oddly mature. *She is here, not there.* His arm came up and his fingers wiggled. At the same time, he gave back the image of stars Sari had shown him. *Love Regella,* he said. *Remember …* He paused as if at a loss, then resumed his usual style of recitation; *Love Mama, love Cass, love Darry, love Nu. All safe. Calath safe.*

She hugged him close again and was rewarded with a strong flow of love and trust. Whoever, or whatever 'Regella' was, her blessing's happiness gave her no cause for alarm, and the bubble of their warmth washed any lingering concerns away.

DELEMÄT

Snow-capped mountains, azure lakes, steamy jungles, barren plateaus - Delemät's farsight combed the central continent's varied landscapes, following the path of the Went. Map-like, these vistas passed quickly beneath his gaze. The path was clear, but the Went weren't on it. His fists balled in frustration. They always followed the path!

He glanced at the Djan'rū. The cargo was on the verge of completion. The ground heaved with alarming regularity. A nearby eruption truly did seem imminent. Kandät Enna had been adamant he would not delay his departure, and Delemät knew he could not stay, yet fear of his brothers reception when he returned to Giahn empty-handed gave him nightmares. This was why he needed to locate the Went - the one thing Huldar would give his life - or possibly even the lives of the mothers and children, to save.

The lives of his Ashik - those few who remained, of the Uri'madu, and of the Host were forfeit anyway. His brother's orders had been quite clear. Only Kandät Enna and his crew were exempt - and who knew how long they would survive once they'd returned to the Imperial City? He certainly had no illusions about how long he'd last if he didn't have any of the information his brother had required him to gather.

He sniggered. Huldar! Always singing the same, tired song about the Went's right to citizenship. Maybe the Lethian was correct. He who was Sacred to Leth. Maybe the creatures were citizens. But they could not communicate with any except their own kind, and if they died, no one beyond this planet would mourn their loss.

Again, he sent his vision around the continent until the same scenes, landmarks, glades and customary gathering sites made his mind glaze over. Why could he not see them? He paused at the place where the trail encountered the isthmus, a treacherous stretch of channels and shallows, where tall monoliths projected like jagged teeth. Surely the clumsy lumps could not cross it - at least not until the freeze began and water-levels dropped. But at some stage, cross it they did. The path continued on, although it narrowed markedly on the other side.

His head hurt. There seemed no need to search beyond it - until a peculiar movement caught his attention. They *had* crossed it! He focused in on the slow-moving hairy backs. There seemed to be far fewer of them. Ahead was a series of canyons and short climbs, and right beside the path, an easily accessible portal. His face relaxed. Thank you, Huldar, he said cynically to himself, and a smile formed in his mind. Victory seemed possible at last.

Back in the encampment Kandät Enna was involved in deep discussion about the final positioning of the heavier cargo. Perfect. There was no time to waste. Wherever the Uri'madu were hidden, he was certain Huldar still watched his pet creatures.

To me! he summoned his remaining troops. He'd spent days refining his trap, and now, finally, the bait had presented itself.

As he marched from his pavilion, the ground gave an ominous roar. Violent tremors split the ground and tumbled tents, but what did it matter? Soon, there would be no one left to live in them. He balanced himself and strode on. Six Ashik were left him. They formed up, brave and unquestioning behind him. The score with Huldar must be settled.

Wait!

He stifled his irritation as he sensed Farushael of Cantori's hurried efforts to catch up. "Where are you going?" Farushael asked breathlessly. "Shamkarun Kandät Enna will be ready to leave by nightfall!"

Delemät did not answer, did not pause. His plan would be executed. Kandät would have to wait. He sang his troops through the gate, and left the clamor of the camp behind.

Farushael stood in disbelief as Delemät and his remaining Ashik stepped through the portal, then an even more violent shaking dropped him to his knees. The subsequent explosion left his ears ringing. A huge column of ash and flame boiled from a nearby mountain-top. He looked up as the skies darkened under the billowing cloud. Put his hands over his ears and tried to focus. In the encampment below, tents pitched and swayed and piles of cargo lay scattered around the Djan'rū.

Farushael! Kandät Enna's voice was powerful in his mind. *We must leave now!*

Delemät has gone, he replied. *I don't know where he is.*

Bastard! Did he say how long he'd be?

No, and he took his Ashik with him.

Kandät's presence cut off, but his anger seemed to linger.

He tried to run back down the hill, but aftershocks made his gait more of an on-going stumble.

Already, spinners had begun to maneuver flotillas of cargo towards the East gate. They fought to keep their heavy loads stable while they, themselves were not. He hurried around the ridge-line to intercept.

"What's happening?" he asked.

"Moving!" one replied. "Setting up a chain."

Farushael staggered on toward the Djan'rū. He wasn't sure what the spinner meant, but they were already gone.

Within the encampment, those who weren't busy with cargo stood transfixed by the spectacle of the burgeoning plume. Lightning flashed amid its upper reaches. Their disregard of imminent catastrophe seemed surreal. Then another deafening boom announced the first of the lava bombs. He dimly remembered Lady Andel's description of such an event, but the details were lost to him, as was the expertise of the Uri'madu. The refectory burst into flames. People were trapped. Others ran to help. Activity at the Djan'rū site escalated. He lurched onward to where Kandät Enna stood like a beacon of calm.

"We'll move as much as we can to the old Djan'rū," Kandät said to him. "Leave the rest here." He pointed to a series of three boxes, each as long as his arm. "Quickly! Can you take this?"

Farushael nodded.

Leave through the West gate, Kandät said firmly. An image of a location and a rough path were thrust forcibly into his mind. *Take them to the canyon there. Hide them well.*

What if I get lost, he asked. The way seemed long and convoluted, and how did Kandät Enna even know of it? *Qalān is tricky these days.*

Another detonation shook the air around them. The ground heaved and cracked. He saw everything with double vision. *Can you do it or not?* Kandät demanded.

With an effort of will, Farushael calmed his thoughts. The songs for both gates came clearly to mind. He nodded.

Come back when you've hidden them – you understand?

He looked again at the boxes. They were ornate, sturdy, expensive, and suddenly, the task he'd been entrusted with became clear. He met the navigator's gaze and nodded more definitely. Kandät Enna was making sure the Eyes of the Bel Nishani stayed where they belonged. He lifted them with a song he'd practiced far more often on this contract than he'd thought would be necessary.

Kandät gave him a small bow. "Return to me as soon as you can."

His tone was solemn, and there was a hint in his well-schooled veils that chilled Farushael's soul. But there was no time for questions. He reached the portal, firmed the song in his mind until its sequence was irrefutable, then applied it.

DEPARTURE

Andel and Huldar woke, hearts racing, at the same time. Inanna screamed inconsolably. Andel hugged her baby tight as waves of distress battered their minds.

Shh, Shh, she said, *Inanna, my love, Inanna …* but there was no reaching her.

Around them, every blessing cried in the same devastating way.

What is it? Andel turned to her husband. *What's going on?*

I don't know, Huldar replied helplessly. Then Casco's voice came to them, overloud and laced with outrage.

Huldar! It's the Went!

Huldar grabbed his pants and ran outside.

Casco hurried to meet him. *Shameera worked it out. Let me show you!*

The two gripped each other's outstretched arms. Huldar's head swam through a flood of knowledge. The emotional bombardment of the babies faded into background noise. Huldar found Casco's perceptive envelope had changed and grown in accordance with his Mark. It took precious seconds to re-calibrate their connection, but once they had, what he saw shocked him beyond thought. The Planet's presence began to reverberate through his being. Casco grew silent in awe.

When Anu ran toward them, Huldar saw him as a shining aura of light - one of such significance it was as if their very surroundings were shaped by his presence.

"What's happening?" Anu asked. The tones of his voice rang in Huldar's mind like the bell of the Planet herself.

"Huldar?"

Finally, he found himself, and coherent thought returned. *Ziquarra?*

Casco nodded.

With their arms still joined, they went to a pile of rugs and cushions where Casco could make himself comfortable. Anu followed as if he didn't know what else to do. "Casco is Ziquarra," Huldar forced himself to say. "The Went are under attack."

Although Anu must have had many questions, he had the grace to merely nod and stand by as Casco's spirit fled his body.

Huldar bowed his head and waited. Moments later, he hovered with Casco above a large clearing where a quickly erected structure held the remnants of the herd in a bewildered group. Beyond the corral, two Went hid in the shadows - one of them a mother laden with eggs, the other the little blind Went he'd watched all its life.

On the margins of the enclosure lay a mutilated body Huldar was deeply shocked to recognize as the blind one's carer - the one he'd touched. Delemät Ashik stalked toward the milling creatures like a hunting bento. One stood to show its colors. At Delemät's signal, four Ashik immobilized the creature. There was the flash of a sword, and the Went's soft nose lay limp on the crushed vegetation. Blue fluid gushed from the wound. The Went made a terrible, blubbering sound, but was held fast in the tsemkar grip of its captors and could not move until it fell and was dragged toward the other bodies.

Another sword flashed and was buried deep in a frightened Went. As it sank to the ground, another blade stabbed and another. With each thrust, the Went's agony grew louder.

Several Went dropped to their knees and began to drone.

"Keep going," Delemät laughed. "You'll kill it eventually." He looked up. Huldar sensed his farsight ranging. "Are you seeing this, Huldar?" he cried. "Lord Sacred to Leth? When this one's done, I'll start on the next. You'd better come quick, and bring those mothers and their offspring with you, or I promise you, this whole sorry lot will die!"

Casco returned to his body.

Huldar released his grip. Tears chilled his cheeks. His heart ached. Images of blood and pain filled him beyond capacity. How any sentient being could manifest such cruelty was beyond comprehension.

"What is it?" Anu asked. His expression showed open concern, and Huldar would have smiled if he could. Within a very few days, the First of Maatu had become Uri'madu.

"Delemät Ashik is slaughtering the Went, one by one," he forced himself to say. "He'll continue until all are dead unless I come to him and bring the mothers and their blessings with me."

"You can't!" Casco said.

"Of course not, but what can I do? We must stop him before more are killed."

"And that's why they're crying?" Anu said. He gazed at the cavern ceiling as if the stars beyond spoke to him. "I wish my little brother was here. No one can beat him at Ashut."

"Ashut!" Casco snapped. "You want to talk about a board game?"

Anu gave a quick bow. "My apologies, Archerra Casco. I meant to say that my brother, Asa, is a precocious genius when it comes to strategy. I am not so adept - but what I would suggest at this time is a rapid evacuation. Get everyone to the secret Djan'rū as quickly as possible - just as we discussed. Get them clear and safe, then we can deal with the Imperial thug."

There was disdain in Anu's tone, and Huldar wondered what business the navigator had had with Delemät Ashik in the past.

"You do that," he said. His own plan was suddenly clear. "Get everyone to safety. Casco, you and Daric Enna are in charge. Work with Anu. I'll go to Delemät alone. Try to reason with him."

"Reason with him?" Casco cried. "Are you mad? He'll kill you. You heard him. He hates you."

"The planet is with me," he said, and it was true. His whole being resonated with her power. "She will protect me. Casco, it's up to you and Daric now to mobilize the Uri'madu. Get them to the Djan'rū and Anu will do the rest."

"I'll need spinners," Anu said.

"Bush, Topper, Malena's crew, there's no reason any of the males can't help you." He turned for his tent. Andel wouldn't be happy with what he was about to do, but he knew he was right. This was his moment. The Planet told him so.

FARUSHAEL

Cloudless blue skies arched overhead. Critters chirped, buzzed and sang as if there was nothing wrong. Farushael squinted northward across the small clearing which surrounded the portal. The horizon was marred by what appeared to be the head of an oddly colored cloud, but only if one knew where to look. From where he stood, nearly three hundred miles from the eruption, this was the only sign of crisis and in every other way it seemed Went remained at peace with itself.

He reviewed the sketchy set of directions Kandät Enna had given him, and wished it was on paper - manifest, as a map should be. How had the navigator even known the canyons existed? He'd never stayed long enough to explore. It must have been Huldar, he concluded. A place he'd spoken to the navigator about. *Great,* he thought to himself. The map was not only vague, it was third-hand.

To the south, above the forest of strap-tree fronds, he saw the snaking line of ridge-tops that marked the beginning of canyon country. There was a very productive gold mine there, but Kandät wanted him to go to the other end of the formation. The next portal would take him closer, but he still had a long and difficult walk ahead, and limited time to accomplish it.

He looked at the boxes and thought of their contents. So much strife and damage had been caused by their matchless beauty. In his opinion, the Realm had clearly shown itself unready for such riches. Would Kandät Enna leave without him? He didn't think so … he hoped not.

With a philosophical sigh, he hoisted his precious load. The trail to the next portal was difficult to see amid the rampant growth, but it was there - which he assumed was more than could be said for what he would face on the next phase of his journey.

Ten minutes later, he stepped through the second gate. He was surrounded, as expected, by a dense growth of thick-boled strap-trees, and set off into the green gloom with only Kandät's image and an instinct for direction to guide him. Upright green fronds swayed to an un-felt breeze. Their rubbery embrace obstructed every step as if they consciously worked against him. Sweat trickled down his face. His frown deepened. Did the things have some sort of primitive consciousness? He'd not heard about it, but maybe he'd made a discovery of his own.

Giant paddle-bugs screeched their displeasure. A herd of small, emerald-green lizards flowed past his legs in hot pursuit. He ducked as a scintillation of transparent wings heralded a flock of slugs. Despite his efforts, several pelted into him and consequently stuck to his shirt as if welded to it. The boxes he carried were soon hidden by vividly striped, boneless bodies and gauzy, multi-colored wings. With a series of wet lurches, they launched into what space there was and flew off to rejoin their more agile brethren.

At last, he burst through the tangle into a broad glade. He set the boxes down, took a deep breath and looked around. Canyon cliffs towered overhead, and a broad swathe, possibly part of the Went's road, seemed to lead in exactly the direction he wanted to go.

He sang the boxes clean, then his shirt. Surely in this clearing there would be no more slugs to land on him, or if there were, at least he would see them coming. To his way of thinking, the delicate beauty of their wings was well and truly negated by the heavy unpleasantness of the liberal mucus with which he'd been imbued.

A roll of thunder made him flinch. The sound seemed loud and immediate, yet he knew it had come from far away. Fear for the Host pushed him into a run. He had to get back quickly, or there would be nothing to return to, and lovely as they were, he did not relish the thought of trying to survive with the Uri'madu for the next several years while Went reverted to a snowball.

A narrow gap between two narrow, towering stacks enticed him, and he squeezed through into a world as yet unseen by any annangi. There was a forest of tall trunks with short rosettes of leaves at their crowns. Each trunk sprouted long, wickedly sharp thorns. What seemed to be a small, pale rock leapt at him when he stepped too close. He jumped back and was nearly skewered. Ahead, in the canyon wall, he could make out a series of small caves and niches. There was little scrub or under-storey, but the ground was swampy and every sinking step released the stench of swamp gas.

More rocklets launched at him. He stumbled as one fastened to his leg with a deep and painful bite. He reefed it free and for several anxious moments searched inwardly for signs of venom, but if there was, it was slow-acting and imperceptible for now - or maybe he just didn't know what to look for.

The small cave he selected was dry inside, apparently uninhabited, and deep enough to take all three boxes. He took one last look before heading back. Satisfied the precious containers were out of sight and as safe as he could make them, he turned for home. .

The wound in his calf throbbed horribly. Sweat poured down his back and dribbled through his brows to sting his eyes. He looked up as a small movement caught his attention, and froze. Stationed beside the only exit was a towering creature. From each corner of its triangular head, bulbous, multi-faceted globes regarded him with dispassionate interest.

Long, predatory claws unfolded slightly from its upper body, as if getting ready to strike.

He closed his eyes and waited. Perhaps it would not see him if he stayed still … or perhaps he would die.

Minutes went by. Fire raged in his leg. He searched for the creature with his mind and couldn't find it. He looked again through slitted eyes. He remembered the stories of the Uri'madu, and particularly the fate of Joumelät Enna. Such predators could be cryptic indeed.

Slowly, slowly he turned his head. The light seemed over-bright. A collection of tiny creatures crawled across his feet. His heart raced. There was no sign of danger. He started forward, and a rustle behind him gave his feet wings. As the gap came within reach, a spine-edged claw snapped beside his ear. Another grazed his opposite cheek.

He threw himself at the slim opening. Spines ripped his arm. He groaned with effort and finally fell to the ground on the opposite side. AS he rolled clear, two long, hinged arms reached frantically between the rocks, but fortunately the creature itself could not follow.

Blood soaked his battered shirt.

He pulled his medical kit from Qalān. It was still shiny and unused. Inside, he found a wide bandage charmed to staunch blood-flow and a brown powder to keep a wound clean of infection. He'd thought the cost of a kit for each individual member of the Host a waste of coin. How wrong he'd been.

With arm and leg securely wrapped, He hobbled downwards, retracing his steps.

When he reached the portal with the easterly view, he was alarmed to see an orange stain above the horizon, and the last, huge explosion returned to mind. With one step, he could be back there … or perhaps it would be best to go to the Uri'madu's old campsite first and wait for Kandät there.

He stepped through into semi-darkness. Ash-flakes rained like snow and settled heavily on every surface.

"Farushael!"

He turned to Kandät Enna's voice.

"Breath be praised you've returned." Kandät quickly took in his bloody shirt and bandages. "What happened to you?"

"Wildlife." He blinked and wiped his face clear. "The cargo is safe."

Kandät clapped his shoulder, careful not to hurt. "We must go. Taras, one of my crew, has Naghari skills, and as soon as we're clear, he'll attend you, but two of my spinners were killed in the cataclysm and I can't afford the loss."

"Has Delemät returned?"

"No."

The navigator's voice seemed flat and final. He looked around. The envelope could be heard rather than seen through the ash. It was much smaller than he'd expected. There was an surprising emptiness.

"Where are the host?"

"Dead." Kandät's calm façade momentarily crumpled. His haze wavered alarmingly. "Incinerated. There was a huge cloud - boiling, inescapable. Everything in its path destroyed." He held out his arm. Farushael's eyes widened. Savage burns marred the navigator's skin. "I happened to be beside the portal. Even so, I barely escaped with my life - and my spinners ..."

"Shouldn't we wait a little longer? I made it back. Maybe he will too - or his Ashik." He peered northward through the darkness. To the north-east an ominous red glare penetrated the blanket of ash. "If we knew where he was, we could look for him. Send out a search party."

"There is no one left to search," Kandät said. "He has food and shelter if he still lives, but we cannot risk staying here. Every breath damages our lungs, and our voices."

Farushael felt himself fail inside. Was he the only survivor? What of Huldar and the Uri'madu? He shook his head. If they could stay safely hidden all this time, the volcano would most likely leave them unscathed.

The navigator put his arm out as if to shepherd him. "We will return in due course - I promise you."

Farushael closed his eyes against tears and limped toward the Djan'rū. How could everything change so quickly? Breath had blown. That was the only answer.

HULDAR

Wrath pushed on Huldar's concentration. It was only with great effort he could put it aside to sing himself through the string of portals. Each gate seemed a hindrance between him and his purpose. The distance between each step accomplished at a run. How many Went survived? How many had been horribly mutilated – tortured to death? The noseless one's uncomprehending screams tore at him. The Elder's corpse ate at his soul. Their Blessing's screams still rang in his ears. All were connected in ways he could not fathom.

At last he reached the final step. Andel's presence cut off abruptly, and he knew she and Inanna were safely off-world.

All gone? he asked Casco.

Blessed all through, his friend replied. *Just waiting for … ahh, here he is. I'll come to you now.*

No. Get them settled. Be strong. That's your job. Worry about me when the rest are secure. If I'm not back at camp, or the southern isles when that's done, look for me here.

Casco's mind snapped from his. No doubt he was angry, but it was best they were unreachable. They could not be found by anyone now. Not even him.

Delemät's farsight flickered closer. He pulled the invisible cloak over himself and waited for it to pass. The time was right while his enemy was distracted. Daric had taught him that much.

With hurried movements, he folded the garment into its bag and dropped it by a distinctive, pink granite boulder. Daric had put a minute tracer on the drawstring so they could pick it up later without trouble.

He straightened his shoulders and stepped through the gate.

A scene of carnage greeted him.

Rage filled him.

The ashik looked up from their murderous stabbing.

Delemät! he roared.

Tendrils of power leapt from his fingers and swept the ashik aside. Several broke against the makeshift railing. Another lost his head to a flailing sword. Their bodies landed in a singed and smoking heap.

Delemät! he roared again.

The God-Emperor's brother turned. His expression of triumph vanished.

Huldar's body burned with power. White-gold flames licked his arms, filtered his vision – his whole being was alive in a way he'd never imagined possible. Song coursed from his throat and wove with the power of the planet herself.

Regella, the Blessings named her …

REGELLA!

For the first time, he sounded her name in his mind … and her answer came in a blast of fury more intense than he could hold.

Part of him knew he would not survive it, but another reveled in the revenge he was about to wreak.

Delemät tried to flee, but try as he might, he could only run on the spot. Eventually, his efforts ceased. He turned. Resolve, defiance, hatred; he made no effort to hide himself anymore. Huldar saw year upon year of layered fear and spite engendered at the whim of a brother mad with the lust for power.

With sudden resolve, Delemät's Tsemkar spurted. Intense light shot from his face and hands as if every erg of hatred he'd harbored over the long millennia was spent in that last, make-or-break moment.

Time slowed. Huldar saw jumbled patterns writhe into being and snake toward him.

Regella sang to him and through him, and drew directly from the mind of Jaldan of Trianog.

Ribbons of light twisted awry as Delemät lost control of the forces he'd engendered. The burly Ashik's eyes bulged as strand by strand, the extensive Tsemkar was torn from his forehead. At last, it hovered, a fading shape of light just beyond his reach. Then it was gone.

Make it stop! Delemät howled. He clawed at his eyes. Bloody gashes opened on his cheeks. "Make it stop!" he whimpered.

Huldar sensed Casco behind him, flanked by Daric and Anu.

Their presence was integral to the pattern. They would bear witness to this outcome, all three in their own way, and the course of history would be changed.

The sacrifice, Regella said. *Beloved, you have paid enough. It is time.*

Huldar? Casco said. *Huldar, leave it now … please.*

His friend's pain filled him.

I love you, he said. *Tell Andel she was my all.* Then he let go.

NO! Casco screamed as his empty clothing crumpled to the ground.

Daric's pain split the skies. *Don't do this!*

Huldar looked back sadly, knowing they would not even have a body to mourn. Andel and Inanna were far away, beyond his reach. He could only hope Casco and Daric would care for her well though her time of crisis. But he knew she would survive, and so would their child – as Andel's mother had foretold.

NIELLI

Cries and screaming. Sadness and loss. When the presence of aliens diminished, the usual sounds of the trail were replaced by the stumbling footfalls of a lone two-leg and the high pitched ululation it made. The pain it expressed spoke for Nielli's pain. The terror the noise embodied equaled its own. Hnarse no longer answered its call. Nor did Neetha. Nielli could not understand. The most dangerous part of the trail had been negotiated - cold water and swirling currents, and they had come to Selly Farn … but they had found only death. Was that the foretelling? And now, with no one to follow, where could one go?

More time passed.

Something touched its back.

Nielli shied sideways, hair flattened with shock. Trees pressed against its side, but it could not be sure where anything was, or where to run.

Moments later, the scent to registered, and the sound of quiet breathing nearby.

Another Went! With a low cry, Nielli blundered forward until it found a warm, living mound and pressed against it.

The other bugled a soft greeting, and Nielli recognized the voice and scent of the last Mother. Odors of shock and great sadness emanated from her dense pelt. Her distended body shook as if she was cold. Did she hold Hnarse's soul now? And Neetha's? Her trunk stroked Nielli's back and face again and again with comforting pressure, leaving wet trails of inconsolable grief.

Eventually, with soft sounds of comfort, the Mother wrapped its trunk around Nielli's and tugged.

Nielli took a step.

The Mother nudged and it took another.

Eventually, Nielli understood. It rested its trunk on the Mother's back, and soon, the two moved forward with greater confidence.

But the air had a thick, unpleasant smell.

Gradually, the temperature dropped.

Snow began to fall.

Food became scarce.

The hurt of Hnarse's absence did not go away. Now, there was no one to ask if the ice in their coats and bitter winds meant the cleansing had already begun.

When they finally reached the burrows, rather than separate for the sleep of renewal, Nielli and the mother found a tunnel that suited them and curled up together to fall into the long dream, as all Went did to await the world's rebirth.

Nielli did not know its companion would die to give birth to the last eggs of their species, or that the scattering of an Ender was necessary to send the next generation on their way to the oceanic phase of their life-cycle.

No new Went would reach maturity, cocoon, and complete the cycle of life anew.

No Went would tell stories or sing their observations to the Heart of the World to ensure all would be reborn as it must be.

Nielli had no idea it was the one of the prophecy - doomed to wait alone in the dark until the circle could find its ends.

www.ingramcontent.com/pod-product-compliance
Lightning Source LLC
Chambersburg PA
CBHW020238120726
47904CB00001B/17

* 9 7 8 0 6 4 5 5 2 8 9 0 9 *